X

CATHERINE COOKSON

The Cultured Handmaiden

SIMON & SCHUSTER
New York   London   Toronto   Sydney

Simon & Schuster
Rockefeller Center
1230 Avenue of the Americas
New York, NY 10020

Originally published in 1988 in Great Britain by Guild Publishing

For information regarding special discounts for bulk purchases,
please contact Simon & Schuster Special Sales at 1-800-456-6798
or business@simonandschuster.com.

Manufactured in the United States of America

1   3   5   7   9   10   8   6   4   2

Library of Congress Cataloging-in-Publication Data
Cookson, Catherine.
The cultured handmaiden / Catherine Cookson.
p.   cm.
1. Secretaries—Fiction. I. Title.
PR6053.O525 C66 2005
823'.914—dc22   2005049003

ISBN-13: 978-0-684-80855-0
ISBN-10: 0-684-80855-2

PART ONE

1

'Listen, and listen carefully, because you'll remember what I'm saying till the day you die, and it's this: chastity is the most expensive commodity in the whole world. The longer you keep it, the more you pay for it. The expense will shrivel you up. Some women are born virgins because the male in them has tipped the scales; others, like you, who aim to become one of the Brides of Christ, whose bloody harem must be chock-a-block by now, are nothing but runaways, runaways from life. . . . The essence of it. . . . And what's the essence of it? Why, that dreadful word, sex. You're afraid of it, so you sublimate it in locking yourselves up; submitting to obedience, tyrannical obedience, and humiliating practices: spreadeagled on floors . . . face down of course . . . kissing feet. . . . God! to think of it. . . . I wonder if He does, does He turn a little sick to see what rights man has inflicted on woman, and all in His name? . . . Go. Yes, go; hurry, your spouse is waiting for you. One last word: remember He's promised there's no giving or taking in marriage on the other side. So you are going to lose out all along the line. . . . What did you say?'

'I said, I'll pray for you.'

'Go to hell.'

'I've been there; I'm going the other way.'

Jinny Brownlow's hand holding the prompting script dropped to her side, and she was about to lean for support against a piece of scenery, when its very decided inclination warned her that it would be dangerous inasmuch as her action could bring it and a number of pieces behind it tumbling about her, and that would indeed be the finale to a disastrous week.

She watched the company of eight players now taking their bows amid the dismal clapping. The curtain dropped, and there was no second lift: the clapping had ceased and there was only the sound of scuffling feet and the scraping of chairs as the last of the small audience scrambled for the exit.

She turned and joined the players now as they made their way to the so-called dressing-rooms provided by the Fellburn Social Hall, and her eyes sought out Ray Collard, but he was away ahead of the others. He hadn't looked at her as he passed her. There was something wrong. She had guessed at it for some time now, but mostly during this week while he had been playing the lead in this disastrous play. Even the notice in the *Fellburn Gazette* on Wednesday referring to the bad taste of the final speech . . . almost blasphemous, it had said . . . had failed to bring in the atheists, the agnostics, or the merely doubters. The critic had gone on to say, that if the play had been trying to prove that all good women lived in misery and that there was nothing worth having in life but sex it had failed, for the hero had wanted to marry the girl, he hadn't said. 'What about it? Let's shack up.'

Saying, 'Excuse me,' she pushed past Jess Winters who, always the comedienne, laughed as she said, 'Now why should I excuse you, Jinny, you've done nothing for me, only got me over those two bad patches the night. I'm supposed to be funny; the only light relief in that damned indigestible tirade. . . .'

The rest of her words faded away; and again Jinny excused herself as she went to pass Hal Campbell, the actor-manager, the man who kept the whole thing going and the one who usually had the final word with regard to which four plays the Fellburn Players would put on each year. But he wasn't to blame for this last one. Philip Watson, the producer, had plumped for it on the surmise that it was time the people at this end of Fellburn were made to think.

Well, apparently they had thought . . . and thought it best to stay away, after the first night.

Hal Campbell now put his hand on her arm and drew her to a momentary stop, saying, 'See what you can do with Ray. He says he's not coming to the party. Anything wrong?'

'Not that I know of.'

He pulled a face and let her go. She knew he didn't believe her. Well, what did she know, anyway? The only thing she knew, and with certainty, was that she was a fool. But then she couldn't help being her particular kind of fool.

She caught up with Ray Collard at the end of the passage. He was going for the producer. 'Well, you got your bloody way, didn't you? During the three years I've been with this dud outfit there's never been a flop like it.'

'Perhaps it wasn't the fault of the play so much as of the

4

acting: some people can put it over and some can't. . . .'

'*Ray*!' Her voice surprisingly was almost a yell.

Collard lowered his arm; then turning to her, he barked, 'Get your coat! I'm leaving now.'

He opened a door to the side of him and went in, then banged it closed behind him. And Philip Watson, looking at Jinny, said, 'Do as your boss tells you. He said, get your coat. Well, why aren't you running?'

She stared at him. She had never liked him, yet he had always been very nice to her. In a way, she supposed, he had tried to make up to her. She was about to turn from him when in a different tone of voice he said, 'If you take my advice, Jinny, you won't get your coat, you'll come to the party with the rest of us. I'm . . . I'm only speaking for your own good.'

She paused, and looked hard at him over her shoulder before moving away. Whenever there was something unpleasant to impart, people always said they were only speaking for your own good.

She made her way down the passage to the so-called ladies' dressing-room, and there, ignoring the prattle, all concerning the madness of putting on such a play in this town, she took up her coat, woolly hat, and scarf and went out without anyone having commented on her presence, for after all she wasn't considered to be an actress, so-called: she was good for prompting or accompanying a singer at the piano, but, as had been pointed out to her more than once, not in a very professional style. In fact, her lack of an accompanist's talent had often caused the performer to give anything but of his or her best.

When they did a musical show there was always a post-mortem by the leading lady and soprano Gladys Philips, the wife of the tenor, Peter Philips. It was odd, Jinny thought, that singers never blamed their voices for anything that went wrong with their performances: it was the acoustics, or the draught whizzing along the passages at each side of the stage, or they didn't feel at their best, but more often than not it was the accompanist who had put them off.

Ray Collard was in the car waiting for her, and she was hardly seated before he started it up. He gave her no explanation for the rush, nor did she ask for any. She knew what was coming and she didn't want to hear it, for in a way she was to blame. . . . No! she chided herself; she wouldn't use that word blame in connection with this matter. No, she wouldn't.

5

No word was exchanged between them as the car sped along Bog's End waterfront where the headlights picked up the name *Henderson & Garbrook, Engineers,* in huge letters along the top of a blank wall. Then they showed up the gates and another long wall dotted with windows. The third from the end of the bottom row was her window, at least the typing pool's window by which, for the past year, she had sat most days, except when called upon to fill in for a secretary on holiday, or someone who had fallen sick in one of the offices.

It crossed her mind that she wouldn't miss the pool if she left. A week ago she had put in for another post and she had the qualifications for it: she was good at shorthand, although it must have got a little rusty over the past months through lack of use, but her French wasn't at all bad. This she had kept up through radio programmes and reading, but never once in Henderson's had she been given the opportunity of using it. In fact, Miss Cadwell, the head of the pool, for some reason seemed set to retard the progress of anyone with a knowledge of French. Neither she herself nor Noreen Power, whose French was also good, had ever been given the chance to go to the top floor.

But what did French matter, what did work matter, what did anything matter but what Ray wanted to say to her?

The car had stopped in a street of tall narrow terraced houses. And now Jinny thrust open the car door, crossed the pavement, passed through a little iron gate, went down the area steps, put her key in the lock, then entered her home, the three room, kitchen-cum-bathroom flat, and she switched on the lights to reveal a comfortable looking but cold room. She lit the gas-fire; then turned towards her escort.

Collard was standing with his hands by his sides staring at her. The look on his face was aggressive. Then without any preliminary chat he barked at her, 'You've brought this on yourself. Do you hear? You've brought this on yourself.'

She didn't ask what she had brought on herself, but she waited for him to go on.

'I told you weeks ago, I was nearly round the bend and I couldn't wait. It would have been the simplest thing in the world for you to . . . to. . . .' He jerked his head to the side, then shot out his arm and, his finger pointing not a foot from her face, he added, 'All this bloody week I've been speaking the last lines of that blasted play to you. Do you hear me? I've been speaking them to you not to that silly bitch Wainwright, but to you. And

6

I'm telling you this now, you'll end up like that character. Not in a convent, no, you're not made for that, but in this stinking little basement room with a couple of cats.'

Still she didn't speak, she just continued to stare at him. Stinking little basement room, he had said. It might be a basement, but it had some better pieces of furniture in it than ever he would see in his life. What had he been offering her, anyway? Two rooms and a kitchen above his shop. And what was the shop? A single house window with the words: *Raymond Collard, Painter & Decorator.* He was a one man business. But he meant to expand. Oh yes, that was his aim he said, to expand. That was why he had joined the Players and the Fellburn Bog's End Working Men's Club. He couldn't get into anything like the Rotary, but, as he said, the more things you joined the more connections you made, and already he had got two jobs from among the amateur actors. And another thing, he had already decided what pieces of furniture she was going to sell, and what she would take to the rooms above the shop. But he was talking again.

'Emily has more sense and understanding than you'll ever have, and you've looked down your nose on her, haven't you?'

So it was Emily. Of course it was Emily. Why was she still kidding herself? She had known it all along, so why had she closed her eyes to it all?'

Just over a year ago when her mother died, she had been forced to leave the house to which her father had brought her mother on the day they were married, the house in which she herself was born and had been brought up in an atmosphere of love and gaiety. That was the word, gaiety; the feeling that emanated from both her parents had been one of pure happiness: her father managed a small antiques shop and her mother had been a music teacher. There was never an overabundance of money but that lack had never seemed to trouble them. She supposed it was the example of their married life that had set the pattern deep within her of how she wanted her own life to be formed. She was nineteen when her father died and within a year her mother had followed him. They were both comparatively young, in their late forties, but it appeared that her mother had been unable to bear to be separated from her husband, for as the doctor had said, there had been nothing physically wrong with her, she had just pined.

They hadn't owned the six-roomed house they had lived in.

The controlled rent was still only nine pounds a week, and she could have managed very nicely, but she had been harassed into leaving it: she couldn't stand up to the pressure of the landlord, and he had offered her this basement in replacement. But as this was in a good class quarter of the town, the rent was fourteen pounds a week. What was more, she had to sign a three years lease to get it. But she considered herself fortunate in almost immediately getting someone to share it, a state registered nurse called Emily Houselea, whose work was obtained mainly through an agency, and since she preferred night work the arrangements suited them both and they only saw each other for any length of time on alternate Saturdays and Sundays.

It was some weeks ago that Jinny had smelt the cigarette smoke, and as neither she nor Emily smoked she had concluded Emily must have had her boy friend in. But why hadn't she mentioned him? In the course of the time they had been living together, Emily had had a number of boy friends. They came and went and she had joked about them. But she'd never referred to this last one.

When she now purposely looked towards one of the doors leading from the sitting-room his voice came at her almost in a growl, saying, 'She's gone. She's taken her things. It was better that way. And look' – his voice softened now – 'I didn't want it this way, you know I didn't. And what's more, she's eight years older than me, and so nothing would have come of it. I would have still waited, but she's fallen. I think she's done it on purpose, but that's neither here nor there. And I'll say again, you brought it on yourself.'

What was the matter with her? What was this strange feeling inside? She had never experienced anything like it before; never had she had any occasion to feel aggressive; but she was experiencing now the greatest desire to hit him. No, not just to hit him, but to tear at him, to scratch his face, to break things on him. She didn't want to talk this out, she wanted to act it out violently.

And then he said, 'I'm sorry, Jinny. Oh, for God's sake! why don't you say something? Retaliate, woman. That's another thing about you, you're like a wooden dolly; people hit you and you come back for more. Those two Philipses always at you about your playing, why haven't you turned on them before now and told them to go to hell? Or better still, told the great Hal Campbell to pay for a proper pianist if he wasn't satisfied

8

with what you were doing. But no, you just took it. And from the rest of them an' all, running here and there at their bidding like a bloody cultured handmaiden. Yes, that's a good description of you, a cultured handmaiden. So agreeable, so polite, so damned eager to please, you let people wipe their boots on you. I'll tell you again, Jinny, you'll end up here' – he stubbed his finger towards the floor now – 'unless you learn to be hard to get.'

She would . . . she would . . . she would go for him.

She felt her head snap back on her shoulders and she heard somebody laughing, but she couldn't at the moment believe it was she herself who was making that sound, nor that she was now yelling at him, 'Well, it didn't work on you, did it? Being hard to get, it didn't work on you. Get out! Get out before I do something. Go on! Go on!'

He was at the door, his back towards her, and he stood there in silence for a moment before slowly turning and looking at her again and, his voice low now, he said, 'I'm sorry, Jinny. Honestly I am. I'd do anything to alter things at this minute, but I can't. And the irony of it is, she's not keen to marry me, just live with me. But I'll marry her when the bairn comes, because after all it's only fair to it. Goodbye, Jinny.'

As she watched the door close after him she repeated to herself, 'I'll marry her when the bairn comes, it's only fair to it.' Strange the ideas of some people, these sparks of morality that oozed through. Why couldn't he marry her before the bairn came? No; she saw his reasoning: she might have a miscarriage, the baby might be born dead; he would have tied himself up when he needn't have done and be left with no solace for having done the right thing by his child, the decent thing.

Slowly she unwound the scarf from around her neck, pulled off her woollen hat, then her coat, and went into her bedroom and hung them in the wardrobe. The room was icy cold and without their warm comfort she shivered visibly.

Back in the sitting-room she drew a pouffe up towards the fire and, crouching on it, she crossed her forearms tight against her waist and sat staring into the glowing red vertical bars. Cultured handmaiden. She supposed it was as good a description of her as any. It was a failing of hers wanting to please people. Ever since she had lost her parents and her home there had been in her this thing which was like a craving to belong, to be part of a family once again. She had been an only child but her family seemed to have encompassed the world. There were just the three of them, they had needed no one else. There had been one discordant note in their lives: Nell Dudley, her mother's cousin. Nell, she had always been given to understand, was kind of common, and being her mother's cousin, she found this strange because her mother was genteel, refined. But Cousin Nell had a nice husband who was a solicitor. Her mother often said she could never understand how Nell had got him, and she was very lucky for he had provided her with a nice terraced house and a garden on the outskirts of Shields.

On one of her duty visits to Cousin Nell's that lady had said in the voice of a prophet: 'It can't go on: you and your mam and dad are living in a fool's paradise up there. 'Tisn't natural, all sweetness and light, and wanting nobody else. There'll be a bust up one of these days. Just you mark my words, an' prepare yourself for it, girl.'

Even at her mother's funeral Cousin Nell's censoring didn't stop: she had been really too good to live, she said. And then she had turned the statement from one of approbation into a comment that almost held disdain when she finished, 'You've got to have guts to face up to people and this life,' only for her tone to change again when she said kindly, 'You know where we are if you ever need us, lass.'

But she had made up her mind on that particular day that no matter how badly off she was for company, she wouldn't seek it in Cousin Nell's house. Before long, however, she found out it was as her cousin had said, you had to have guts to face up to people and this life, and at times she felt she was a little short on them.

She thought back over the events of the past year. She had been working at Henderson's only a month when she came under the notice of Mr Pillon. One rainy night he stopped her and asked her if she would like a lift home, and she had gladly accepted it. Another time he asked her to join him for a drink before going home. The third time she had accepted his invitation he had turned the car into a quiet lane and set about what he considered to be the real business of the night and payment for his entertainment. She had almost pushed him through the car door. And when she had made to leave, he had grabbed at her and said, 'Come off it. You know what it's all about, else why did you come?'

She hadn't experienced any rage on that particular occasion

only fear and humiliation, and a cold on the Sunday as a result of having become drenched walking home in a downpour.

But on the Monday morning her humiliation had been increased a thousandfold when Betty Morris said to her, 'I saw you out with Pillon on Friday. You want to watch your step there, else you'll have his wife after you.'

She had never for a moment dreamed he was married; he hadn't acted like a married man. But what did a married man act like? She was an idiot, a fool. But she was learning.

It was through Betty Morris, too, that she had joined the Fellburn Players, and there had met Ray Collard. His acting in school plays and scout pantomimes had given him a taste for the stage, and most members of the company said he was talented.

She drooped her head until her chin lay deep on her chest. She wanted to cry. She could see the days stretching ahead, five days a week at the office: the click, click, click of the typewriters, interspersed by Miss Cadwell's grating commands; then the clatter and chatter and gossip in the canteen, the white-collar workers at one end, the floor men at the other. Mr Henderson's idea that they eat together or there was no big canteen hadn't worked: they ate under the same roof but at different ends. His idea of doing away with class distinctions had caused more trouble than enough. As someone said, they had never known a strike there, but forced fraternization had nearly brought one on.

He was a devil of a man was Mr Henderson. She hadn't glimpsed him more than half a dozen times. They said he was in the works before anybody else in the morning and he left late. Not so his partner Mr Garbrook. He showed up about once a quarter on board days.

At five o'clock, not a minute before at Henderson's, there was a rush for the gates and the car parks or the buses. Her mode of transport was the bus. Sometimes she was lucky in getting into the first one, more often it would be the second or even the third. Then back to these rooms and a scrap meal; perhaps a word with Emily if she wasn't out. Then if there was a play in preparation, two nights a week she would go to rehearsals. One night a week she kept for the pictures; on the others she stayed at home listening to the radio – she handn't a television – or she brushed up her French. Sundays were the worst days, especially so should it be wet.

But all this had been before Ray Collard had asked her out. She liked him from the beginning, primarily because he hadn't pushed her. They had been out three times before he attempted to kiss her, and although his love-making had become more intense as time went on, he had never attempted, as she put it to herself, to eat her up.

When he asked her to marry him she had gladly accepted. Oh, and so gratefully. . . . Why had she been so grateful? for he was no great shakes. In no way was he any great shakes, in looks, or position, or personality. When she got to know him better, she began to realise he was more than a bit of a know-all, he was an egotist. Yet, she had still loved him, or at least had a feeling for him. But once they were engaged, his attitude had changed. It was as if he had taken out a licence for intercourse: he seemed to expect it as his due. What were they waiting for? They were engaged. They were going to be married, weren't they? And why was she acting so old fashioned? She was twenty-one, wasn't she, and this was nineteen seventy-eight; Victoria was only remembered in the antique shops. And what was marriage anyway, only a bit of paper.

When she attempted to straighten her back, she found it a painful process. She had sat so long in the one position she'd got cramp in her neck. Slowly she turned her head from side to side, and the very action recalled the numbers of times she had done that in desperation as she had fought him off. It was during one such battle that Emily Houselea had returned unexpectedly. That must be four months ago, and it was the last time she'd had to struggle with him.

As she rose to her feet she asked herself if she had known all along what was going on. Had she asked herself, even wondered, why he had stopped plaguing her and was barely civil to her? And there had been no more talk whether they should live here until the lease ran out or live above the shop and relet this flat as furnished accomodation.

She must have known, so why hadn't she done something? 'Why?'

The answer was all around her: the quietness, the silence that could be heard, broken only by the hissing of the gas-fire. Of a sudden she ran to the door and turned the key in the lock; then still running, she went into the bedroom and, dressed as she was, she flung herself on to the bed and, burying her face into the pillow, she cried, 'Mam! Mam! I can't bear it. I won't be able to stand the loneliness. Help me not to do anything silly.' Oh, God, God help me not to do anything silly.' . . . The author had been right in the final speech in that play: chastity was the most expensive commodity in the whole world.

2

Her eyes felt stiff, her face was swollen with the bouts of crying that had gone on intermittently all yesterday. This morning she had put on extra make-up, but it didn't hide from Noreen Power the fact that there was something amiss. 'What's up?' she said tactfully. 'Heading for a cold?'

'Yes, I think so.'

'Well, don't expect any sympathy from the Cad. Look at her through there.' She made an almost imperceptible nod towards the screened off glass-fronted office at the end of the room. 'There's someone on the phone giving it to her, unless I'm mistaken.'

The office door opened and the supervisor stalked down the row of eight desks. She kept her eyes directed towards the last one and when she reached it she looked down on the typist, saying, 'Miss Power, you are to go up to Mr Henderson's office. Miss Honeysett has been taken ill and is in hospital. How is your French?'

Noreen Power opened her mouth to speak, then glanced towards Jinny before looking back at Miss Cadwell and answering, 'It's . . . it's all right I . . . I suppose, speaking it, that is. But . . . but not writing it.'

'There shouldn't be any suppose about it, you're *supposed* to be proficient in French, Miss Power, so please go up at once and give Mr Henderson the benefit of your proficiency.'

'Yes, Miss Cadwell.'

As Jane Cadwell turned about and made back towards her office, Noreen Power gathered up a clean pad from her drawer, quickly attempted to sharpen a pencil, broke the point, then started again, before glancing across at Jinny and muttering under her breath, 'She . . . she should have sent you.'

Forgetting her own particular misery for the moment, Jinny whispered back, 'You'll be all right. I hear his bark's worse than his bite.'

'I've heard otherwise.' This muttered remark came from Miss Ann Cartnell in the desk in front of Jinny, and she, turning to Noreen again, said, 'Don't worry. Take it slowly.'

'God! That's advice to give, take Old Thunderbolt slowly. Huh! You won't have time; he'll eat you.'

As Jinny continued with her work she supposed that there would be an Ann Cartnell type wherever girls worked together. Perhaps they were lucky they had only one out of eight of them here.

With regard to herself, she was well aware that Miss Cadwell had never liked her. Why, she didn't know; she only knew that the feeling was mutual. But Miss Cadwell had power, she could make things easy or otherwise, and she had certainly made it otherwise in her case.

It was quarter-past ten exactly when the telephone rang in Miss Cadwell's office and almost simultaneously the outer door opened and Noreen came hurrying back into the room, her head down and the tears streaming from her eyes.

All the typewriters stopped at once, and Jinny, rising from her seat, went towards her, saying, 'What is it? What's happened?'

'He . . . he threw . . . he threw a pad at me and . . . and swore something . . . something awful.'

They were all now looking towards Miss Cadwell's office. She had the phone held away from her face which had turned scarlet. They watched her slowly place the instrument on its stand as if it were so fragile it might break, and she stared at it for a moment before opening her door and coming into the office proper. And her eyes now fixing on Jinny, she said, 'Miss Brownlow, go upstairs at once to Mr Henderson's office and see if you can do a better job than Miss Power.'

All eyes were on Jinny, until Miss Cadwell cried, 'Why, may I ask, have you stopped working? You have before now, I suppose, seen a girl making a fool of herself. Inefficiency!' She was glaring at Noreen now and, her voice almost cracking, she ended, 'Get back to your desk and see if you can accomplish the ABC of typing there . . . in English. *English*!'

Miss Cadwell was nothing if not emphatic.

As Jinny left the room she said to herself, imitating Miss Cadwell's voice, English! English! then aloud, 'She can't even speak it.'

As she stepped out of the lift into the carpeted hall of the top floor, young Paul the lift boy pointed to a door almost opposite and in an undertone said, 'I'd put your armour on, miss, if I was you, he's in fine fettle the day, been bawlin' since early on.'

She smiled faintly at him and she had the urge to say, 'I couldn't care less.' And at this moment she couldn't, for she was at war with men, all men.

Yesterday she had sat by herself the whole day and between her bouts of crying had thought things out. And she had come to the conclusion that she hadn't met a decent man since her father had died; and that men today wanted one thing only: they had one aim in life. The approaches to it might be different, but the end product was the same in all cases, to strip you of your clothes. . . . No! not even to wait for that.

It was at this point there came to her mind a phrase of her grandmother's to fit her feelings. It was a common phrase, something that her mother wouldn't have used: it was, 'she'd had her bellyful'. But immediately she contradicted the saying because in her case it was the wrong metaphor. . . . She was becoming coarse; she must watch it. Her mother would never. . . . Oh damn! That was another thing she must watch, becoming pi.

Well, here she was going to see another of them, and if he threw a pad at her she'd throw it back at him. Yes, she would. All right, she'd lose her job, but the way she was feeling at this moment she didn't give a damn. There she was at it again. She mustn't start swearing; there was no need for it. Her father had always said that if you couldn't express what you meant without swearing it only went to prove you were mentally inadequate.

'Come in!' The shout brought her through the door and almost to the middle of the room, and she looked at the man sitting behind the desk. She had never seen him full face before; the glimpses of him she'd had, had been fleeting. He looked tall sitting there, but he must have short legs because she knew he was only of medium height. His hair at one time must have been of a nondescript sandy colour, bits of it were sticking up straight from the crown of his head, but around the sides it was a grizzly grey. His eyes were a sharp blue, his skin looked rough, and not so much wrinkled as marked with deep lines. The top of his shirt was undone and his tie, although still knotted, was hanging a good way down his chest.

'Well!' He stared at her, and she continued to stare at him. 'Well, girl, what are you here for?'

'That's what I'm waiting to find out, sir.'

16

'Oh, you are, are you?' His eyes narrowed as he glared at her in complete silence for a full minute before he said, 'What's up with you? You've got a chip on your shoulder.'

'Well, if I have it's been placed there since I came in, sir.'

Why on earth had she said that? It was as if she was with her father and they were chaffing each other. She had been very good at repartee when she was at home. Her father had once paid her a compliment: he said that she was witty, not humorous, but witty, Apparently there was a difference.

'Huh!' he pulled his chin into his chest and sat back in his chair now as he said, 'Well, miss, if your French is as sharp as your tongue we'll get along well together. I suppose you know that's why you're here?'

'Oui, monsieur.'

'Oh, that doesn't wash any clothes with me, lass. Any damn fool can say, Oui, monsieur. There, even me. The last one that was in said, Oui, monsieur, and her French wasn't as good as my English, and that's saying something, for the accent anyway. Now get your book and sit yourself down; then later, after you've taken down what I say you'll translate it.'

She sat down, thinking as she did so, He's a hog of a man. There were only hogs among men, Emily had said. . . . Oh . . . Emily. Why had she to think about her now? Get on with it.

'What have I just said?'

She raised her eyes as she replied, "You have just said, 'Dear Monsieur Fonier, With regard to your order of two thousand steel rods, which was agreed between you and my son on the 24th October, 1978, I have pleasure. . . ." That is as far as you got, sir.'

'I didn't say that, did I?'

'You said words to that effect, sir.'

'I said, "About that order."'

'I thought, "With regard to," sounded better.'

'Oh, you did, did you? Did you know Miss Honeysett?'

'No, sir; I never met her. Not to speak to, but I've seen her.'

'She would have done it like that. How old are you?'

'I was twenty-one last September.'

'Ah! You look older.'

She said nothing.

'Where did you learn your French?'

'From my parents mostly. My paternal grandmother was French; she spoke very little English. My father spoke the language well.'

'How long have you been workin' here?'

'Over a year, sir.'

'Over a year!' He screwed himself forward to the edge of his seat now, his forearm on the desk. 'Why the hell hasn't she sent you up here afore, that Cadwell woman? Have you been stuck in the pool all that time?'

'No; at times I've been directed to other offices.'

She watched him turn his head to the side as if he was thinking. Then looking at her again, he said, 'Old Aggie . . . I mean Miss Honeysett has been off for weeks at a time over this last year. Why weren't you sent up then?'

'You had Miss Bellamy, sir. She . . . she left to get married.'

'Oh, aye, yes, Miss Bellamy. Huh! Miss Bellamy. Bloody lot of good she was; she couldn't spell. . . . And don't look like that. You're goin' to hear a lot of words that aren't in the dictionary if you're goin' to work for me. Well, now, let's get on with it. Where were you up to?'

She repeated again what she had written; then continued taking down his dictation. He said nothing while she was typing the letter, but when she had finished he said immediately, 'Let's have a look at it.'

She rose and went towards his desk and handed him the sheet of paper. After staring at it for some seconds, he turned his hard blue eyes up to her and said with a grin on his face, 'You know, I can't read a blasted word of it, and I don't know if you've made any mistakes. Have you?'

That sounded like a demand, and so she said, 'Yes, I put a full stop there' – she pointed – 'it would have read better with a semicolon.'

'Huh. Semicolon. Huh! Long time since I've even heard that word. You know something, lass?' He narrowed his eyes at her. 'I think you'll do. You know why? You've still got that chip on your shoulder, and as long as it's there you'll be alert, on the qui vive, so to speak. Well now, let's get on with it. There's a pile there and I don't suppose you'll have them finished by five o'clock or half-past. Are you a stickler for time?'

'Not particularly.'

'What do you mean by that? Married?'

She drew in a long breath before she said, 'No, sir, I'm not married.'

'Well, in a way that's a pity because somebody will come along and snap you up. They do that in this place, you know.

The only one I could rely on was old Aggie. Nobody came and snatched her up.' The corner of his lip twisted into a smile, then he added, 'But she was a good old stick. She knew her job. But when she comes back I'll see that you don't return to the swimming pool.' He grinned widely now at his own joke and she was forced to give a faint smile in return and add, 'Thank you, sir.'. . .

At lunch-time the girls from the pool were waiting for her. How had she got on? Wasn't he terrible? What was the work like? Did she think she could stick it? They said he had his secretary's desk in his office and not in the adjoining office so he could see what she was up to.

She had got on very well. The work was just ordinary business letters. And yes, she could stick it. . . .

It was twenty minutes past five when she finished the last letter. He was still sitting behind the desk and when she said, 'Will that be all, sir?' he looked up at her and said, 'Yes, lass, that'll be all for the day. It'll be the same routine the morrow an' the day after that. Do you think you'll be able to stick it?'

'I don't see why not.'

'What's your first name?'

'Jinny.'

'Jinny, not Jenny?'

'No, Jinny, with an 'I'.'

'Well, I like that . . . Jinny. Got a good North Country sound. There's nothing fancy about that, not like your voice an' manner.'

She felt her face blushing.

'Do you live with your parents?'

'My parents are dead. I live alone.'

'That's a pity. Nobody should live alone, least not at your age. Now if I'd been younger I would have seen to it. . . . Oh! Oh!' He lifted his hand. 'Get that look off your face, lass. And while we're on, if we're gona work together, an' it looks like it 'cos old Aggie is going to be in that hospital for some weeks yet, we should know where we stand, eh? Now me, I'm in me fifties but I'm not past it: I can still admire a pretty face, an' I like something nice to look at from across that desk now and again when I have time to look up. But don't get any ideas into your head about the secretary an' the boss. Oh! Oh!' Again he lifted his hand, 'Pull the curtain down on that colour of yours, and I'll put me case to you. Perhaps you've heard it already, but

I'll say it plain. I'm a very happily married man with six of a family. The one you've been writing about today, Glen, he's the eldest. He's going to be married next month, and who but a bloody fool would want to be married in December and in white an' all. But that's her of course, not him.' He laughed now.

As he was speaking the phone rang and she put out her hand and picked it up and a voice said, 'Mrs Henderson speaking. Has Mr Henderson gone yet?'

The phone was grabbed from her hand and he yelled into it, 'Hello, pet. No, I haven't gone yet. I'll be another half-hour. I'm just saying goodbye to me secretary.' He turned his head and winked at her. 'She's a young 'un. Old Aggie's in for an operation on that bloody stomach of hers. I've been at her for years to see to it. Yes, I know we're having company, love, and I wish we weren't. I'm tired; I'm gettin' old.'

He listened for a moment, then pulled a face. His lips tight together, his eyes wide, he nodded up at Jinny. Then his voice dropping, he said, 'Be with you soon, dear. 'Bye.'

As he replaced the receiver, he looked again at Jinny and said, 'Wonderful woman. If you stay long enough you'll likely meet her some day, but it won't be here, 'cos she'll never come near the office. She's never been in it since the day we married. A kind of principle of hers. Wonderful woman. And a looker. Aye. Wait till you see her.' And then his voice rose. 'An' you'll likely say like the rest of the bloody dimwits, what in the name of God did she see in him!' He was digging his thumb into his chest now. 'Well, she saw somebody who was goin' places, and is still goin'. Go on, get yourself away lass; you've had enough for one day. Given you something to think about, eh?'

She had reached the door when he shouted, 'Is that chip still on your shoulder?'

She turned to him now and looked at him for a few seconds before she said, 'Yes. Yes, it's still there. But it isn't as heavy as it was this morning.' It was again as if she were chaffing with her father.

It had been a long day, an exciting day, but a tiring one. How tiring she hadn't realized until she reached home. She was about to cook herself a poached egg, and had just dropped it into the boiling water when she suddenly closed her eyes tightly and sat down. It was for a moment as if all the strength had drained out of her. She sat with her forearms on the small kitchen table, her head bent over them. It seemed a long, long time since this morning; so much had happened, yet all that had really happened was that she had been sent into another office to work. But what an office. And what a man. She had never encountered anyone like him. Would she like to continue working for him? She paused before her mind gave her the answer. Yes, she would. He was rough. She had never met anyone as rough. Coarse would be a better description of him. Yet there was an honesty about him. She couldn't imagine anyone ever getting the better of him. But having said that, she knew it would be a very tiring job working for him. There was no let-up where he was. He was either telling you something or demanding something of you. She imagined that he very rarely asked anything of anyone. She could understand how he had terrified Noreen.

Why hadn't he terrified her too? Likely because she had been in a temper when she first went in to him. If she hadn't been it was more than surmise that she would have come out as quickly as Noreen had done. No, she wouldn't; she would have stood her ground, yet without standing up to him. But feeling as she had done, she had stood up to him, and he had seemed to like it.

Well, it had certainly taken her mind off the business of Saturday night and Mr Ray Collard. Her nose twitched slightly as if at a bad smell . . . and there was a smell in the kitchen. She rose hastily and went to the stove. The water had boiled dry and the egg was sticking to the bottom of the pan.

Ah well, she wasn't hungry. She'd have a bath and an early night. . . .

An hour later she was sitting in her dressing-gown before the gas-fire munching slowly at an apple when she heard the doorbell ring. She didn't get up immediately and go towards it, but stared at it for a number of seconds. . . . She hadn't heard anyone come down the area steps; and now that Emily had gone, and Ray with her, she knew of no one who was likely to call on her.

When the bell rang again, she went towards the door and to her question, 'Who's there?' the voice answered, 'It's me . . . Hal.'

Hal? Mr Campbell? Quickly now she glanced back and around the room; then pulled her dressing-gown cord tight about her waist before she opened the door.

'Do you mind? I . . . I saw your light on as I was passing.'

'No. No, not at all. Come in.'

When she closed the door behind him she looked at his hair, and then at his shoulders, saying with some surprise, 'It's snowing!'

'Yes; it's just started, just a bit of sleet.'

'Come to the fire. I was just about to make some coffee. Would you like one?'

'Yes. Yes, thank you; I would.'

'That seat's the most comfortable.' She pointed to the wicker chair with the padded seat and back.

'Thank you. Do you mind if I take off my coat?'

She paused before she said, 'No. No, not at all.'

In the kitchen as she put some milk into a pan, then switched on the kettle, she was asking herself why he had come. As far as she knew they hadn't even thought about another play. And anyway, they only did four a year and the next rehearsals shouldn't start until February.

His voice came to her now as if he were calling from a distance: 'I told you a lie.'

She went to the kitchen door and looked across the room at him. 'You what?'

'I told a lie.'

Her face stretched in enquiry, and he smiled as he now said, 'I wasn't just passing; I made it my business to call. I was rather worried about you.'

'Oh.' She looked downwards for a moment; then, 'That was kind of you,' she said before turning and walking back to the stove.'

'I . . . I wanted to tell you some time ago' – his voice came to her – 'but I thought it was none of my business, that perhaps it was only a flash in the pan and he would see sense. . . . He's a fool.'

Not until she had made the coffee, put the two cups on a tray, and had taken it into the sitting-room did she speak, and then she asked, 'Did they all know?'

'No, I wouldn't say all of them. But some of them did. They wanted to tell you about . . . well. . . .'

As she handed him the cup of coffee she said, 'I suppose they considered me an idiot not to have guessed something was up . . . so let her find out for herself, they said; one has to live and learn. I can actually hear Gladys Philips saying it.'

He was staring at her; then his eyes narrowed and he peered at her for a moment before saying, 'Odd, but you seem different.'

'In what way different?'

He smiled gently. 'I can't put my finger on it at present,' he said.

She sipped at the coffee, then laid her cup and saucer down on the side table before she spoke again. 'Perhaps I can help you by simply repeating what Ray said to me on Saturday night. He said I was a handmaiden. He did me the honour of putting cultured before it . . . a cultured handmaiden. If he had used ordinary terms he would have said I was a bloody fool' – there she was swearing again – 'making myself cheap. Not, I may add, in the way he wanted me to, but that I was so anxious to please everybody I did all the dirty work during the rehearsals without complaining, and was too gullible to realize that I was being put upon. . . .'

'No. No.'

'Oh yes, yes. And he was right. I was so anxious to make friends that for two evenings a week I became a doormat. But you see, they were the only company I knew. And when Ray Collard took notice of me right away my gratitude can be explained by the usual phrase, it knew no bounds.'

'You surprise me.'

'In what way?'

'That you acted as you say you did while thinking as you do.'

'Oh, I can afford to be honest now because, you see, I've grown up. The Fellburn Players has provided me with a kind of Open University course, a short course admittedly, but one that has certainly paid off.'

'You sound very bitter; it isn't like you.'

Slowly now she bowed her head and looked towards the fire; and after a moment she said, 'I'm . . . I'm not really bitter; I'm angry because I've been such a fool. When people are nice to me I feel so indebted to them I can't do enough for them. It stems, I suppose, from having had loving parents.'

'Jinny.' He was leaning towards her now, his elbows on his knees. 'I'm going to tell you something. I understand every word that you've said, I mean the feeling behind it, because I've experienced the same emotion stemming·from the same needs, wanting to be liked, wanting to be loved, wanting to be one of a family. It's still with me. I suppose you've heard I've been divorced?'

She nodded at him, saying, 'Yes, yes, I've heard that.' She did not add that she'd heared he would have been divorced twice only his first wife died before the proceedings could go through.

'I've been married twice, and both times have been failures. Yet I shouldn't say that because I got what I wanted from them, and that's a family. . . . Do you want to hear about it?'

'It's a private matter. . . .'

'No, no. Most of my life is public property now. Anyway, it started like yours, having a loving mother. I can't remember my father, but my mother was everything to me. When she died, I was as empty as you described yourself. And then I met Peggy. She was twenty-four, I was twenty-five, and she had two small children, a boy and a girl; the boy was eight and the girl seven. She had been married very young, and I must say it, she was still very young, almost childish. But there was my ready-made family. We were married just over two years when—' He paused, looked to the side and said, 'when she died. It was a bit of a struggle looking after the children but I wouldn't part with them. They were all the family I had. But . . . well, in my job as an estate agent, I sometimes had to go out at night, and so I applied for a housekeeper. And I got one.' He laughed now. It was a gentle, deriding laugh. 'Her name was Dora Morton. She had a sixteen-year-old son called Michael. Well . . . two years later we were married, and then two years after that she walked out. She did ask Michael if he wanted to go with her, and surprisingly he said no. That was two . . . no, more, nearly three years ago now. And well . . . now I can say I have almost brought up a family: Michael has passed his finals in accountancy; he's a very bright fellow. And Rosie, at fifteen, is a sweet girl; and Arthur . . . oh, Arthur' – He laughed gently now – 'he still remains a bit of a problem. Chips on both shoulders.'

She was smiling now as she said, 'I know how he feels. But it was very good of you to take them all on.'

'Oh, I enjoyed it . . . well, in parts. . . . But anyway, how would you like to meet them next weekend?'

'Oh, thank you; I'd like that. Yes, I would.' She nodded at him.

'Good. So we'll leave it at that. Say Sunday for dinner? But now I must be off. . . .'

After she had seen him to the door and said goodbye she returned to the fireplace and stood looking down at the glare.

Things weren't turning out too badly, were they? But then she immediately gave herself the answer, she had a week of nights to get through. But still – she made a face at herself – there were the days, new kind of days ahead, and they certainly wouldn't be lacking in interest as long as she was on the top floor; in fact, if they were anything like her initiation today she'd be too tired to bother about what she was going to do with her evenings in the future, she'd be only too glad to get to bed and sleep.

Of a sudden there came a change in her feelings: she couldn't say she felt happy, but she felt brighter and eager for the morning; which was a change anyway, she told herself.

3

⨳

Naturally she wasn't as yet acquainted with all her boss's moods, but as soon as she entered the office the following Friday morning she knew she was about to be introduced to a new one.

'Are you goin' to be one of them clock watchers?' he greeted her, turning his head and looking at the wall clock. 'Nine o'clock on the dot. I was down on the shop floor turned eight this mornin'.'

She stared at him, lost for words. But only for a moment; and then she said, 'Well, of course; it's your business, sir; you have a special interest in it.'

'Now, look here, young lady, don't you come that with me! I'm not havin' any bloody cheek from a youngster.'

'And you won't get any, sir, if you don't bully. My bus gets in the yard at five to nine. If I get an earlier one from my district I would be here at twenty minutes past eight, and not having a vested int—'

She stopped even before he checked her. She was going too far. She didn't know how she'd had the nerve.

'That's enough!' She watched his lower jaw moving from side to side; his hard blue eyes were flashing their anger straight at her.

His hand was already gripping the coarse hair hanging over his brow and he was making to turn away as she said, 'I'm sorry.'

He stopped and looked at her again; then after a moment he said, 'I suppose you're going to add, you don't know what came over you.'

'No, I wasn't.'

'Huh!' Again he made to turn away. But then his tone slightly more moderate, he said, 'Well, it's all experience, I suppose. Get your things off and get on with it.'

She got on with it for the next half-hour. The phone had rung a number of times, and she had answered it. When it rang again she recognized the voice as that of Mr Arthur Pillon. She listened to him speaking for a moment; then covering the mouthpiece, she looked across at Mr Henderson, saying, 'It's the assistant works manager, sir. He says there's a deputation; they wish to see you.'

'Deputation? Which deputation? Where from?'

'The rod sheds, and the transport, I think.'

'Huh! Union or canteen trouble again. Well, I'm in right fettle for them. Tell him to send them up.'

She gave the message, then put the phone down, and she had started to type again when he said, 'What class do you reckon you're in?'

'What class? What do you mean, sir? Social class?'

'Aye, I mean just that, social class.'

'Well, I'm ... I'm a working girl, but I should say ... well. ...' She hesitated before ending, 'Lower middle class.'

'Oh, you would, would you?'

'Yes, I would, just because you asked; but I really haven't given it much thought, in fact, none at all.'

'Well, that's something in your favour anyway. So you reckon you're in the middle class, the bottom end like?'

'For the sake of argument, sir, we are all working class.'

'Oh! Traces of the socialist in you then. But it's my guess that's only on the surface, an' that's only for argument. With your refined twang and your manner I think you're right to place yourself in the middle lot.'

'My parents placed me where I am, I had no say in the matter.'

'Eeh, we're getting deeper now, lass, aren't we? That's what folks generally say when they're rejecting religion.'

He was in a mood. Something had evidently upset him.

Within a few minutes she knew what it was. After a knocking on the door and he having bawled, 'Come in!' there entered two workmen. Their chins were out, their necks stiff, and she recognized they were in much the same mood as he was.

His greeting was overlaid with heavy sarcasm: 'Oh, good morning, Mr Newland. And you, Mr Trowell. And what can I do for you the day? Wait. Don't tell me. You have come to tell me that you are underworked and overpaid, that you have been given better conditions of work here than anywhere else on the

Tyne, but that, being bloody fools, you don't appreciate it. And you're here now to say that you're going to turn over a new leaf. Isn't that why you've come?' He looked from one to the other, and it was the taller of the two men, Jack Newland, who said, 'We're quite used to your approach, Mr Henderson. Being sarcastic won't help. You know why we're here; it's about the canteen.'

'Oh, the canteen. The canteen.' He now turned his head and nodded towards Jinny, saying, 'Now you go to the canteen, don't you? And wouldn't you say it's a fine canteen, as good as any high-class café you'd get in Newcastle?'

She made no reply; nor apparently did he expect any, for, turning back to the men and, his tone changing, he said, 'Now look here, Jack Newland, and you Peter Trowell. I had that canteen built to supply refreshments for all, and I repeat for all the workers in this factory.'

'Aye, we know you did, Mr Henderson.' Peter Trowell's neck was no longer stiff and his head was moving from side to side as he went on, 'But you see, it's like this. We want a place of our own. It would be quite easy to put a partition up, sort of. In any case, the white-collar lot stick to one end and us at the other. You never see them sit at the same table. It was better the way it was afore.'

'Officers, sergeants, and men, like.'

'Aye, if you say so, Mr Henderson, like that.'

'And where do you two come in, being shop stewards? The sergeants' mess?'

'Well, no. It was Jack Newland speaking now. 'We . . . we . . . we mix.'

'Oh, but that isn't right.' Mr Henderson now shook his head. 'In the army, the sergeants' mess is. . . . What's the word?' He turned his head from side to side; then looking at Jinny, he said, 'Can you give me a word that'll fit this?'

After a moment's hesitation she said, 'Sacrosanct.'

'Oh aye. Yes, now, she's said it, sacrosanct. That means, if I know anything, keep out.'

'Well, it isn't like that with us.'

'Don't tell me that, Newland' – his voice had changed to a deep growl, all light sarcasm gone now – 'because you've had the makings of an upstart right from the first. Now when I started this business thirty years ago, you came in straight from school and you didn't know B from a bull's foot, but afore many years were gone you soon found out that you had pretensions, but of course you had nowt up top to carry them out. It's the sheep down on the shop floor who've put you where you are the day: follow me leader. If the other fellows who get on with their jobs and use common sense took the trouble to fill the meetings you would be out on your arse, let me tell you.'

'I object to your manner, Mr Henderson.'

'You can damn well object to anything you like. You've objected afore to it, and it won't be the last time I suppose. Who's put you up to this anyway, about dividing the canteen? Some of your red friends?'

'I object. . . .'

'Shut your mouth, and don't spout any more of your objections to me. . . . What were you going to say, Peter?' He now looked at Trowell.

The man's voice was quiet and his tone reasonable as he said, 'Well, Mr Henderson, I was just gona say I don't think the white-collar lot . . . I don't think the clerks and such want to mix. I mean, they would prefer a dinin' place on their own. In fact, some of them have said so.'

'Aye, I can believe you, Peter, that some of them would say so, but I'm astounded that you lot say it because it gives them the idea that you don't consider yourself fit company to eat alongside them. I still think of meself as a working man; I go and eat downstairs, don't I? Sometimes at one table, sometimes at another.'

'Well, you can do that, you're in that position, Mr Henderson.'

'I do it' – he now leant across the table towards the man – 'not because of my position but because I think I'm bloody well as good as anybody down there, white-collar, high topper and tails, the lot, and I haven't thought that just the day or yesterday, I thought it when I was workin' on the shop floor, and humpin' those rods from the sheds to the lorries in Carter's over in Sunderland. And there the bloody manager wouldn't give me the time of day or the smoke that went up the chimney. That's what spurred me on and got me where I am the day. And yes, I know what you all say, marrying a woman with money was a damn good help. It was an' all. I was lucky, wasn't I? But the thing is I was determined then and I'm as determined now to break down bloody narrow-minded barriers. There's only one barrier that I recognize an' that's intelligence, 'cos if I had my

29

way I would divide the intelligent lot from the numskulls. Aye, I would.' As he finished speaking he kept his eyes on Jack Newland, and this big man, red in the face, muttered, 'It's no good talkin' to you, Mr Henderson, is it? If you won't listen to our demands we could go to Mr Garbrook.'

'You can go to hell, if you like. And let me tell you, Newland' – he laughed now – 'you'll get better joy out of hell than you'll get out of me partner, because I can tell you exactly what he'll say. He'll look at you and he'll smile and he'll say, "Yes, Jack" – oh, he'll always call you by your Christian name – "Yes, yes, Jack", he'll say; "I understand you perfectly, and I'll have a talk with Bob about this." That's what you'll get from Mr Garbrook, word for word. But go on, try your welcome. And now both of you' – his voice dropped – 'get yourselves downstairs to your respective departments, and then at dinner-time, be brave, aye, be brave, go into the canteen, to the far end, and sit down next to, say, Mr Pillon, or Mr Waitland, or. . . . Oh aye, go and sit next to Mr Waitland, from along the corridor here. Then there's Mr Meane from the drawing-office. Now he's a nice fellow. They're all nice fellows. Forget you feel inferior, put yourselves to the test. That'll be all . . . gentlemen.'

The two men stared down at him for a matter of seconds before both turned away and without a word left the room.

There was silence for perhaps one whole minute; and then his fist came down on the desk so hard that the heavy paperweight slid almost to the edge of the polished wood surrounding the blotting pad, and through clenched teeth he exclaimed, 'Bloody numskulls!'

She kept on typing. He was a dreadful man, really; yet, strangely, she agreed with what he had said. 'But it was the way he said it. The only thing was that she hadn't seen him in the canteen when she herself had been there. But there must have been times when he had been, or else he wouldn't have said it. She knew that on Fridays he had a tray sent up with sandwiches and coffee.

He startled her now by yelling, 'Enjoy your first lesson in shop floor diplomacy?'

After hesitating just a moment she said quietly, 'Well, it was enlightening in its lack of the latter.'

'What! . . . What did you say?'

'I . . . I think you heard what I said, sir.'

'Aye, I did. You meant that diplomacy was the last thing it had in it?'

'Yes, sir.'

'By!' He was looking down on the papers on his pad. 'You don't only find them on the shop floor, they seep up into the bloody offices. But you're right when you say you're from the bottom of the middle. By, aye, I'd confirm that any day.'

After glaring at her for a moment longer, he attacked the papers on his desk, and she continued with her typing.

However, the atmosphere changed absolutely at eleven o'clock, when the door burst open and a young man came in. He was of medium height, dark complexion, with bright brown eyes. And he stood for a moment in the doorway, then banged the door closed behind him before coming to the desk and, leaning over it, saying, 'Well, hello there. I'm back.'

'I haven't lost me eyesight yet. Does your mother know?'

'Of course, she knows.'

'Aye, of course she would. You've been home first then?'

'Again, of course I have.'

'You should have come straight here from the plane; I want to know about things.'

'You'll get to know soon enough.'

The young man turned and looked to where Jinny was continuing to type, and he said, 'What's happened to Aggie?'

'She's in hospital, where she should have been this long while. We've got a new one here; and I can tell you straightaway she's a . . . cheeky piece. Her name's Jinny.'

Still Jinny didn't look up; but she heard the muttered reply, 'Oh yes?'

Glen Henderson now took off his coat and sat down at the side of the desk. There was no resemblance between him and his father, either in looks, manner, or speech, yet they had one strong bond, they were both very much alive. And this came over in their cross-talk. Jinny could hear only snatches of it above the rattle of the typewriter keys, but when the letter was finished she heard Mr Henderson saying, 'Good. That's good. Better than we'd ever hoped for.'

'It wasn't easy. Don't think that. Six competitors. One gets the idea out there that every country in the world is turning out steel now. You've got to realize that the profit margin on this order is thin. Well, it had to be to beat the others.'

'But it's a new contract; that's what we want, new contracts.'

'They want delivery on the date stated.'

'Well, don't we always deliver on the date stated? That's what's made us, laddie, delivery on the date stated. Hell or high water – that's the motto – we'll deliver.'

'What's this I hear about a strike?'

'They won't strike. It'll come to nothing. They're not bloody fools altogether, cutting off their noses to spite their faces. There'd be a close down like nothing that's ever happened afore in this industry if they did. A pity some of them couldn't be sent over to Japan and Germany. That would open their eyes and make them realize that we're not the only people in the world who are turning out steel; and that there's such a thing as competition, cut-throat competition; and that if we can't get the orders they can't have the work. . . . There's something happened to men, these days. Something. Something.'

Glen laughed now as he said, 'By what you've told me, pumped into me about bygone conditions, it didn't happen soon enough.'

'Aye, but there's moderation in all things. And there's such a thing as greed. The motto the day seems to be, You've got it and I want it, but I'm not bloody well going to work for it. . . . Anyway, you going back home for dinner?'

'Yes. And Mother says you are to come back with me.'

'Eeh! I can't do that, man.'

'Of course, you can. The place is not going to fall down because you've left it for an hour.'

'Now look here, me lad.'

'I am looking.'

Glen had turned to Jinny and he asked, 'What does he do at dinner-times anyway, Jennie?'

'I wouldn't know, I haven't been here long enough.'

'And that's right' – his father nodded at him now – 'she wouldn't know. And by the way, her name's Jinny not Jennie, Jinny, common like. And, as she says, she hasn't been here long enough. But the time she has been here she's given me some stick. I can tell you that.'

'I'm glad to hear it.'

Glen smiled across at Jinny, and she answered his smile.

'And you know something else?' Mr Henderson was now looking at his son. 'She's middle class; from the lower end, she says.'

'Oh, that's interesting.' Glen pursed his lips as he nodded towards Jinny now. 'It's good to know where we stand.'

'It was the position your father put me into. As I told him, I hadn't given it any thought up till then.'

32

'You see' – Bob Henderson was nodding at his son – 'she's got an answer for everything, this one. And in that polite voice of hers.'

'Well, I'm glad to know you've met your match at last, because poor Aggie had a time of it.'

'She didn't. Old Aggie could hold her own.'

'Yes, when you weren't reducing her to tears.'

'Nonsense. When Aggie cried it was because I was kind to her.'

'Speaks for itself.' Glen picked up his coat and hat and said, 'Listen. Don't forget' – he looked at his watch – 'leave here on the dot.'

'We'll see.'

'Goodbye, Jinny.'

'Goodbye, sir.'

The office to themselves again, Bob Henderson looked at Jinny and with an air of pride he said, 'What did you think of him?'

'I don't know him. And anyway. . . .'

'Oh my God! lass.' He now leaned his elbow on the desk and rested his head on his hand and closed his eyes as he continued to say slowly, 'Don't add, it isn't my place to say.'

'I had no intention of doing so.'

He lifted his head again. 'Well, what were you going to say?'

'If I had been going to say anything, sir, I would have said that I would imagine he is the exact opposite from yourself.'

'Oh, you would, would you?'

'Yes, since you ask.'

'And what makes you think that?'

'Well, for one thing he doesn't bellow; and for another. . . .' She stopped. No, she just couldn't say, he doesn't have to stress his position; that would be going too far. Rising to her feet, she said, 'These letters are ready for you to sign.'

'You finish what you were going to say.'

'I have no intention of finishing what I was going to say.'

'Because it was something nasty, something against me?'

'Perhaps.'

'Eeh! Oh, you know you are a cheeky bugger.'

She swallowed deeply. She should walk out. She should be running back to the pool crying, like Noreen had done.

He surprised her now by bursting out laughing and saying, 'Lass, I think you and me'll fit in nicely. Low middle class and lower working class, eh?'

What a strange man. He had a very endearing side to him.

The lights had been on in the office all afternoon; it had been raining heavily.

'Is it still coming down?'

She went to the darkened window, saying, 'I think it's turned to snow. It's so early, only November.'

'Aye, well it's likely working up to a white Christmas. Then it'll change its mind again. I like a white Christmas. . . . How do you get home?'

'Oh.' She paused. 'By bus.'

'Aye, that's what you said afore. You haven't got your own car yet then? Most of them have. My God, when you think of it. My dream of transport in me young days was having a bike; now they take a car for granted. They don't know they're born. Oh' – he flapped his hand at her as he went towards the wash room – 'I know that saying's got whiskers, but it's true, nothing more true. And the more they get the more they want. People are greedy. You know that?' Before closing the door he turned round and looked at her.

She stood now gazing down at her hands resting on the desk and thinking yet again he was the strangest man she had ever come across. But she liked him, and she would find working for someone else very tame after him. Most people in the building seemed to be scared of him, yet she knew that were she working in any of the other offices she wouldn't dream of answering her particular boss back. Yet she could do it with him. It was a most peculiar situation.

She was placing the cover over her typewriter when he came into the office again, saying, 'Get your coat on, I'll give you a lift home. With the weather like this they'll be rushing like Gadarene swine for the buses the night.'

The Gadarene swine. That was a quote from the Bible. He was a funny man. . . .

A few minutes later they got out of the lift and were going across the main hall together towards a porter who opened the door ready for their exit, saying as he did so, 'Good-night, sir. Nasty weather.'

Mr Henderson gave him no reply, not even a thank you. But as he settled himself in the car – she'd had to go round and let herself in the other side – he said, not without a note of glee in

34

his voice, 'That'll set the tongues waggin', 'cos nobody ever saw me come downstairs with Aggie Honeysett. You're honoured. You know that? You're honoured.'

'Well, I would think the honour is questionable if its only merit is to set tongues wagging.'

As he swung the car out of the main gate he chuckled as he said, 'You get a kick out of coming back with things like that at me, don't you? All precise and nicely parcelled up. A cross atween a schoolmistress and a news-reader.'

Really! A cross between.... Really! But she knew he was right, she did get a kick out of answering him back, and in that precise fashion as he had said, which wasn't a bit like how she thought. She was amazed at herself. If the Fellburn Players could hear her at times talking to this man they wouldn't believe it was the same person who had skittered, and that was the right word because she had skittered here and there at their bidding, tripping over herself to please them. What a fool they must have thought her, inane, characterless, and all because she wanted to be with people, please them. Well, that part of herself was finished, she'd never be like that again.

'What do you do with yourself over the weekend?' he said. And she replied truthfully: 'Read and tidy up mostly. But this Sunday I've been invited out to dinner.'

A short while later when the car stopped and he leant over her to open the door, he said, 'Don't sit mopin' alone there the night. Get yourself out to the pictures or some place. Leave your tidyin' up. Go for a drink.... Well, no, that isn't such good advice, not on your own. But it's a long time till Sunday, till you go to that dinner.'

On the pavement, she bent down before he closed the door and said quietly, 'I'll be all right. Thank you, Mr Henderson. Have a nice weekend. See you Monday.' And she banged the door closed, and saw him through the rain-splattered window jerk his head at her in farewell before driving off.

Underneath all that bombast he was a kind man, thoughtful; she felt that he was concerned for her being on her own. It was nice to feel that someone was concerned for you.

It was like stepping into an icebox when she opened the door of the flat. It seemed colder inside than out. And so she didn't take off her outdoor things until the fire had been lit for some time, and she had a tray set for her tea.

It was as she sat with her knees almost touching the glowing bar, drinking her second cup of tea, that there swept over her the most odd feeling. It seemed to erupt from deep within her. It brought her to her feet, her hand, outstretched, gripping the mantelpiece, her chest heaving as if she were gasping for breath, and when the tears spurted from her eyes she dropped her head on to her hands while asking herself, 'What's wrong with me?' Yet at the same time being aware of what was wrong: Mr Henderson's kindness and concern had highlighted this evening, and tomorrow, and stretched it into an eternity.

Hal Campbell called for her at eleven o'clock on Sunday morning. The streets were wet after the night of rain, but the sun was shining. He drove the car through town, past the park, and up Brampton Hill, and as they passed some tall iron gates that gave on to a long drive he inclined his head towards them and said, 'That's where your boss lives.'

'Really?' She leant forward, but the car was already past the gates and all she saw was a high laurel hedge.

'And his son who's getting married shortly has bought the one at the top. It's not so big, but he must have paid a pretty penny for it.'

'Your firm didn't sell it then?'

'No; worse luck.' He laughed. 'But we've got charge of three houses on the Hill. They're all in flats. I think there must be only five private ones left altogether. This used to be the swell end of Fellburn at one time. I suppose it still is even in the flats, because they cost a pretty penny.'

At the top of the Hill the road passed between agricultural fields before coming to a modern estate. When he drove through this she said, 'You live a long way out?'

'Not all that far. It's just about a mile further on. We were very lucky. We came across this, I mean my mother and I, when houses were dirt cheap, at the beginning of the sixties. The only trouble is the garden, it's too big. I have a man come in twice a week, but he doesn't seem to get through much. They don't when you're not standing over them. It's the same inside: Mrs Grayson leaves a lot to be desired where cleanliness is concerned. I spend most of my weekend cleaning up and cooking. I hope the meat isn't burnt.' He cast a quick smile at her. 'I left Rosie in charge, and with orders not to switch the television on. I doubt if I'll be obeyed.'

36

They were well past the modern estate and on a country road now, and as he swung the car into a narrow lane he lifted his hand from the wheel and pointed, saying, 'See there? That's it.'

She looked over a field to where, rising from a clump of trees, she could see the upper storey of a house. After a moment she said, 'It looks big.'

'Oh, it isn't all that big; but there's ten rooms altogether. That includes the attics. It was in a pretty rough state when we took it. I've had a lot done to it.'

'It seems right out in the country.'

'Well, we are between two farms. We're lucky, I suppose. For how long one never knows these days. Farming land was sacrosanct at one time, but now, if it's a freehold farm and hasn't any conservation tags laid down on it, it only needs a developer to come along and you have a new town.'

He turned the car now between two open white gates, and there, at the end of the short drive, stood his house. She was amazed at the sight of it; it was like a little mansion. It was built of natural stone. The front door which looked black and solid was flanked on each side by three tall windows, with replicas above them but on a smaller scale. And above these were attic windows.

He helped her out of the car. Then pushing open the front door, he held out his hand and guided her over the step and into the hall, calling as he did so, 'Where's everybody?'

As if at a signal three people appeared. The first she noted was a young girl who looked to be sixteen or seventeen. But this must be Rosie, the fifteen-year-old. She was standing in the kitchen doorway.

The stairs, she noted, led up from the side of the hall, and next to them was a half door with a head peering round. It was that of a slightly built boy. This must be the brother. His face was thin, with a pinched look. But in the doorway to the extreme left of her there stood a young man. He was tall, as tall as Hal. His hair was brown, and his face rather long. She scanned the three faces in turn; then Hal Campbell, helping her off with her coat, said, 'This is Miss Brownlow, otherwise known as Jinny, and' – he nodded – first to the girl – 'that's Rosie'; then to the boy, 'And that's Arthur'; and lastly he inclined his head towards the far door, saying, 'And Adonis there is Michael.'

Michael Morton was the first to move towards her. 'Hello,' he said. And she answered, 'Hello.'

Then the girl came, and standing some distance from her, she nodded her head slightly, and Jinny said, 'Hello.'

'Come on out of that!' It was Hal calling to the boy now; and he came from the doorway, but did not speak. He just looked at Jinny, and she at him. Then the awkward silence was broken by Michael saying to her, 'Come into the sitting-room.'

'That's right. All of you get yourselves in there, while I see to the dinner.'

The young man now led the way into the sitting-room which Jinny noticed immediately was very well furnished: a comfortable chesterfield suite, besides a sofa table, and two china cabinets each holding a colourful array of figures. There was a fire burning in an open grate set back in a stone fireplace, and the room, like the hall, was covered in a deep red carpet.

Jinny sat in one corner of the couch, and the young man in the other; the girl curled up on the rug before the fire, but the boy remained standing with one shoulder leaning against the corner of the stone fireplace. His head turned slightly, he continued to survey Jinny with a penetrating stare, of which she was conscious all the time she was answering Michael Morton's questions.

She worked at Henderson's, didn't she?

Yes.

Did she like it?

Yes, she liked it very much. Particularly lately since she had been working for the boss.

He said he had heard about old Henderson; he was a bit of a devil, wasn't he?

She wasn't finding him so.

How long had she been there?

Over a year.

Had she always lived in Fellburn?

Yes, she was born here.

He understood she was an orphan.

Before she had time to answer this the boy spoke for the first time: derisively, he said, 'Little Orphan Annie came to our house to stay, to chase the chickens from the porch and sweep the crumbs away.'

'That's enough of that, Arthur. Now watch it.' Michael Morton turned and looked at Jinny again, saying, 'I'm sorry to say that my stepbrother is uncouth and ignorant, but there is one excuse for him, he is young, so there's some hope that he may develop into a normal human being before long. At times I have my doubts though.' He smiled at her now.

'Oh, you fancy pants!' The boy now pulled himself from the support of the fireplace and went hurrying from the room, and the girl, getting to her knees and leaning forward to push a log further on to the fire, spoke for the first time, too, saying, 'Don't take any notice of him. I bet he'll be all over you the next time you come. He likes to show off.'

She turned and smiled at Jinny, and Jinny smiled back at her, thinking, Well, the boy's rudeness had broken the ice, if nothing else, and it had been very thick to begin with.

'Would you like a drink?'

'Yes, I would, please. A sherry.'

'May I have a drop, Michael?'

'All right then, but get it down you before Big Pop sees you, else I'll be for it.'

As she sipped at her sherry Jinny wondered why no one was going to the kitchen to help Hal with the dinner; then as if her thoughts had been picked up by Michael, he said to Rosie, 'Did you set the table?'

'Yes. Of course, I did. And I've done the vegetables too. I can if I like, you know.'

'Yes, I know, but you don't always like, do you?'

'Well, I don't see why I should when there's Mrs Grayson all the week and Big Pop dashing around at weekends. There's no need for me.'

'Well, I think there might be need for you now, miss. So go in the kitchen and see what you can do. Go on now!'

'You're worse than him. You know that?'

Jinny watched the girl rise slowly from her knees; then when she was standing she made a face at Michael before saying, 'Behave yourself or I'll tell Pop.'

'Get out!' he said, making a pretence of rising; only to sink back into the couch, saying, 'She'd embarrass a New York detective. Girls of her age are dreadful: no veneer, life oozing out of every pore.'

'Why a New York detective?'

'Oh.' He jerked his chin upwards now as he laughed. 'It's the television, I suppose; they seem tougher than the English ones, unflappable. . . . Have you known Hal long?'

She was slightly surprised at the question; she had somehow thought that Hal Campbell had put them all in the picture as to why she was here today, the recipient of his compassion for the lonely.

'A little over a year. Let's say the time it's taken to do four plays.'

'You've been with the Players for a year?' There was a note of surprise in his voice now.'

'Yes.'

'What do you think of them?'

'What do you mean, what do I think of them? Their individual characters, or their acting abilities?'

He now slanted his gaze at her as if he was slightly puzzled by her reply; then he said, 'A bit of both.'

'Well, there are some and some; but they all have one thing in common, they think they can act.' Now why had she said that? It sounded bitchy.

His peal of laughter brought her head round towards the door expecting any minute one or other of the family to come in to see what the joke was about. But it remained closed. And as she looked back at him again he said, 'You certainly hit the nail on the head there. How some of that lot dare get up on a stage and expose themselves, and that's the word, expose, I just don't know.'

'I don't think Mr Campbell holds that opinion, else he wouldn't have gone on with them.'

He was looking at her now, his face quite straight, and the question he put to her caused her own face to become stiff, for he said, 'How long have you been going out with him?'

Her voice reflected her expression as she said, 'I have never gone out with him. He was kind enough to ask me to dinner today because he knew I had suffered a disappointment and was on my own.'

He made no reply other than to raise his eyebrows; then looked down towards his feet, and made a number of small movements with his head as if in disbelief, before saying quietly, 'We live and learn;' then turned his head and stared at her in silence until she became embarrassed and searched for something to say.

'You're an accountant, I understand.'

'Yes, you're right; I am an accountant. Just lately fully fledged. Our offices are not far from Henderson's works. We are Ford and Branham's.'

'Oh. It's quite a way to travel each day.' Her immediate

thought was, What a stupid thing to say? What was five miles in a car? But he answered, 'Yes, I've thought so, too, for some time now, but from February next I'll be living in the town. Setting up house there.' He pursed his lips.

'Are you going to be married?'

He lowered his head for a moment while keeping his eyes on her, saying now, 'I'm not going to shock you by saying this, females are unshockable these days: no, I'm not going to be married, but we're setting up together, my girl friend and I.'

She did not say, 'Oh,' she just looked at him.

And now his head jerked upwards in what she was already recognizing to be a characteristic gesture, and he laughed softly as he said, 'You are shocked. Good Lord! You are shocked.'

She could find nothing immediately to say to this, but she asked herself why testy replies just skipped off her tongue when she was with Mr Henderson, but now in the presence of this young man she seemed to be back in the Social Hall, chary about opening her mouth in case she displeased some one. . . . But those days were past; she wasn't afraid of displeasing this fellow or anyone else, and so now she heard herself saying coolly, 'You're mistaken; I wasn't shocked; I was only thinking it was so unoriginal. Everybody is shacking up with everybody else. It's like musical chairs, and one day there'll only be one person left on the chair. The music will have stopped but there'll be no more partners on either side. He'd be the winner, but of what?'

She saw immediately that she had annoyed him, yet his voice had an airy sound as he said, 'A female philosopher as ever was: public library graduation.'

When she made to rise from the couch he sprang to his feet and, standing in front of her, he said, 'I'm sorry. It's very bad of me. I'm acting worse than Arthur. Please . . . please overlook it.' And he smiled now gently. 'Let's imagine you've just come in.'

It was at this point that the door opened and Hal entered, saying, 'Well, it's ready, if anyone feels inclined to eat. Have you had a drink? Has he been looking after you?' He came over to her and put his hand on her shoulder. It was a possessive gesture, but she didn't shrink from it, and he went on, 'Has he been entertaining you? He's a cynic, you know, out to break all the rules of society. But come on, let's eat.' And he took her elbow and led her from the room, across the hall, and through a

41

door into the dining-room. The boy and girl were already there, and the food was on the table, the vegetables in covered dishes, and at the top of the table a joint of sirloin on a side dish.

The dinner was excellent but didn't seem to be anything out of the common to them, even the wine glasses set for the young people as well. They had a glass each but were offered no more, while her glass and Michael's and Hal's were refilled.

Following the main course, they had a plum crumble. Plums out of their own garden she was informed; they had enough fruit of different kinds in deep freeze to last them all winter.

When the meal was over she asked if she could help with the washing up, and she was surprised that the offer was accepted when there were the other three who could have helped, but here she was in the kitchen drying the dishes, and liking it.

She was beginning to feel more at ease. She had learned that she needn't waste any sympathy on Hal for having to do the cooking for on his own admission he loved cooking. He had asked her if she could cook, and she'd replied she could cook a roast dinner, but then had been quick to add not of the quality that he had presented today. However, one thing she could do in the cooking line was make cakes. Her mother had been an expert cake-maker.

What kind of cakes could she make? Rosie asked.

Oh, fruit loaves, sponges, Swedish wedding-cakes.

What were Swedish wedding-cakes? The enquiry came from all quarters, and she replied, 'Oh, they are not our idea of wedding-cakes, they are simply like apple tarts, made in a deep tin, with cinnamon pastry.

What was cinnamon pastry?

Should she show them?

So she cooked a Swedish wedding-cake, and later they had it for tea; and the meal turned out to be quite merry.

Following this Hal asked her if she would play the piano, and as if she were at a Players rehearsal she consented immediately. It was when Hal, Michael, and Rosie were standing round her singing one of Jim Reeves's old favourites 'I Love You Because', which was a favourite of hers too, that Arthur, who hadn't joined in but was sitting near the fire, suddenly shouted, 'I'm going out.'

His voice had been so loud that Jinny stopped playing and the voices of the singers trailed off, but Hal Campbell didn't turn round to his stepson. What he did was to take up a piece of music from the piano, place it in front of Jinny and say, 'You're not. Not tonight.'

'I am.'

'Then you'll have to walk. You're not taking that bike out tonight; it's pouring with rain.'

'I can manage it. You know I can.'

'Not in the dark.' He still hadn't turned towards the boy.

'You can go to hell; I'm going out.'

Almost before the boy started to make for the door Hal Campbell swung round, rushed at him, caught him by the shoulders and pushed him from the room.

The door was left open and the boy's protesting cries came to them. Quickly now, Michael walked to the door and closed it. Then returning to the middle of the room, he was about to speak when Rosie, throwing herself on to the hearthrug and into her usual position, said, 'He spoils everything. He always spoils everything.'

'He doesn't.'

Jinny looked from one to the other and was surprised at the tone of Michael Morton's voice.

'You always take his part.'

'I take the part of those in the right.'

Well, well. So he thought the young, uncouth, bad-mannered youth was in the right. And Hal, the patient — and he certainly was patient — stepfather was in the wrong. But why? There was something below the surface here. Well, it was none of her business, but somehow it had spoilt the day.

There was the sound of a door banging overhead; then as if somebody was kicking against it. The next sound that came to them was definitely recognizable as somebody stamping on the floor. And at this, Rosie scrambled to her feet, gave Michael a hard stare, and then almost ran from the room. Michael sat down heavily and turned to Jinny with an apologetic shrug of his shoulders.

'I'm sorry about this, but if you are going to be a visitor here you might as well be initiated into the pattern right away: The stepfather dominating the stepson; the stepson doesn't like it. A lot to be said on both sides. But mostly on the stepfather's you think?'

She didn't answer for a moment, and he scrutinized her through lowered lids before she said, 'Yes, you're right. To the outsider, which I am, he appears like a handful.'

43

'Yes, he would do. Anyway, come and sit down, because you won't be seeing your host again for a quarter of an hour at least; he likes time to cool down before putting in an appearance;' which remark she thought suggested that the bouts were not infrequent.

She was once more seated at the other end of the couch from him, and he said, 'I'm not usually here on Saturday or Sunday evenings, or very few evenings for that matter, but my girl friend, Cath, is away for the weekend, and at the moment I am not very popular with her people, particularly her mother who has a fixation about marriage.'

He waited for her to make some reply to this, but when she didn't he said, 'Are you set on marriage?'

She gulped in her throat before she answered, 'Well, let me say I'm not set on shacking up, as the term is, with anyone.'

'Your answer doesn't surprise me.'

'Why is that?'

'Because it's the usual one. No nice girl such as you are is going to admit that she would like to follow her instincts and inclinations.'

She felt the colour sweeping over her face, and she had the urge to jump up from the couch and stalk out of the room. But then, with that action she felt she would have acknowledged him to be right. He was making her angry, even causing her to feel as she had done the night she was confronted with Ray Collard. It was as if some secret part of her was being attacked and a new force was being created in her with which to defend it, because up till lately there had never been an occasion in her life which had aroused such anger in her.

Michael leant towards her, apologizing again, saying, 'I've rattled you. Believe me, I didn't mean to. It wasn't my intention. You know' – he laughed softly – 'perhaps it's as well we are not likely to meet very often after this because we'd always be arguing. That's if you'd deign to answer me. Perhaps you'd just sit looking at me as you are now as if you were wishing me far enough. Ah' – his voice dropped – 'here's the saviour of all mankind.'

She turned her head quickly and looked towards the door to where Hal Campbell was entering the room, and she noticed immediately that his face looked strained. Yet his voice sounded ordinary as he said, 'Family dispute. Show me the family that doesn't have one and I'll say it's no real family.'

44

He sat in a chair to the side of the fireplace, and now looking at her but inclining his head towards Michael, he said, 'Has he been behaving himself? He's an agitator, you know, a natural stirrer. If he hasn't got a cause he creates one. Isn't that so, Michael?'

Jinny now looked at the two men who were exchanging glances, and she recognized the feeling of animosity between them, and this came over in Michael's reply as he said, 'Yes, you're right. I'm always for the underdog wherever I may find him.'

So much for the happy home. Yet it seemed to be Hal Campbell's one aim in life to create such an atmosphere; he seemed to go out of his way to do everything for all of them. But then, she was only thinking of the material things, such as their bodily welfare through his cooking, and providing a comfortable home; for apparently there were other things needed for harmony, and in a way, Michael was accusing him of missing out on them, whatever they were. One of them was likely his being too harsh with the boy. Yet, taking a father's place, he would have to show some authority; and, as she had already remarked, that boy was a handful. For a moment she wished she were home, home being the lonely flat. Yet, she wanted company. There was something in her that craved companionship.

That one member of the family was loyal to the head of the house was shown when Rosie re-entered the room, for, sitting down on the hearthrug, she leant her head against her step-father's knee and he, putting his hand on her hair, began to stroke it. And they sat like that while the talk wavered in a desultory manner from one topic to another.

At nine o'clock Jinny thought she had better be making her way home, for she had to prepare for work tomorrow morning. It was at this point that Michael, standing with his back to the fire, looked at Hal, saying, 'You've had two drinks tonight. You're against drinking and driving, shall I see Jinny back, because I've got no scruples along that line, feeling that I can keep my head.'

For a moment Jinny saw the dark look spread over Hal's face that she had witnessed earlier when he had run the boy from the room, but his voice did not betray his feelings as he replied, 'Oh, I think I can manage on this occasion. You don't mind if we hit a lamppost or two, do you, Jinny?'

'No, not at all.' She forced herself to smile, not because she felt any nervousness at being driven by Hal but because she wanted to convey in some small way whose company she preferred.

When a short while later she stood in the hall saying goodbye to Rosie, the girl smiled widely at her as she said, 'Will you come again?' And Jinny answered, 'Yes. Yes, I'd like to.'

She then turned to where Michael Morton was standing some little way back from them, and she inclined her head towards him, saying, 'Good-night.'

And he answered in the same vein: his head bowing a little deeper than hers, he said, 'Good-night.'. . .

They had driven some distance towards the town before Hal Campbell remarked, 'I don't think it's been a very nice day for you.'

'Oh, yes it has. I've thoroughly enjoyed it.'

He kept his eyes on the dark road as he said, 'That do with Arthur, then Michael showing his worst side, couldn't have left you with a very good impression of my family.'

'Well, let's say my initiation started at the deep end, and can now only get better.'

'Well, that's one way of looking at it.' He gave a short laugh. Then presently he said, 'I'm sorry I had to leave you to hold your own with Michael.'

'Oh, I think I managed.'

'Yes, somehow I think you would now. You know, you're a bit of a surprise, Jinny.'

'In what way?'

'Well, the Jinny I knew in the Players was . . . a sort of kindly mouse, scampering hither and thither at everybody's bidding, giving the impression you'd be frightened to say boo!'

'Yes.' Her voice held a sad note now as she replied, 'I suppose that's how I did appear. As I said the other night, I was starving for company. I suppose I still am.'

'Well, in your case that trouble shouldn't be difficult to erase. If you put your mind to it I think you could get any kind of company you chose. I . . . and the family will just be a stop gap.'

'No. . . . No. I'll never forget how kind you've been to me. If you never invited me back again I'll always be grateful for today, and for the other evening.'

'That's nice to know anyway. Are you going any place for Christmas? I mean to a relative?'

46

'No. Not that I know of yet. My only relative is a cousin who lives in Shields, and I have to be pretty desperate before I visit her.'

'Would you like to come and spend it with us? I can't promise that the Christmas spirit will prevail all the time, but there'll be breaks. Of course, it's a few weeks ahead yet, but it'll sort of give you a focal point for the holidays.'

She didn't answer for a moment; then she said, 'You know you are very kind, Hal. . . . I keep on thinking of you as Mr Campbell, but from now on I'll think of you as Hal. And yes, I would love to come and spend Christmas with you all, and feel so at home that perhaps I could join in with the domestic disputes.' They laughed together. But presently, after he had stopped the car and had got out and opened her side door for her and they were standing in the dimly lit street facing each other, she wondered for a moment what his next words would be. Likely, could he come in for a moment? Or would he take her down the area steps to the door and put his arms around her, expecting to extract payment for the holiday? Or would he just kiss her here?

He did none of these things, but, putting his hand out, he touched her cheek, saying gently, 'Good-night, Jinny. It's been nice having you. If I'm past this way one evening in the week I'll look in, but if not I'll pick you up next Sunday again. All right?'

'Yes, all right, Hal. And thank you, thank you again. Good-night.'

'Good-night, Jinny.'

He was nice. Oh, he was nice. And so different. She liked him. She liked him very much.

4

'Would you like to come to the weddin'?'

'To the wedding?'

'Aye, that's what I said: would you like to come to the weddin'?'

'But . . . but it's next week and I don't think I have suitable clothes. And what's more, Mrs Henderson. . . .'

'Don't worry about Mrs Henderson. If you had been Old Aggie you would have been asked. As for suitable clothes, if the weather keeps like this the appropriate gear'll be flannel underwear and a blanket coat. . . . Anyway, would you like to come?'

'I should love to, Mr Henderson. And thank you very much.'

'Well, be at St Matthew's around twelve next Wednesday. That's a week the day. Eeh, my! how time flies. I'll miss our Glen, you know, breezin' in an' out, although he'll only be up the road. But it won't be the same. We'll just be left with Lucy. And then as far as I can gather now from her mother she'll not be long afore she's off an' all, and not just to the top of the road from what I'm told, but New Zealand. Not if I can help it though. Things happen under me nose and I can't see them.' He nodded at Jinny, saying, 'She's been spoilt rotten.'

'And who is responsible for that?'

'Cheeky. Cheeky.' He jerked his chin towards her. 'Well, she was the last, and you always tend to make a fuss when you come to the end of the road, so to speak. Anyway, it'll be nice havin' me wife to meself, for short periods at any rate because they all keep descending on us like locusts. You know something?' He closed the folder of papers on his desk and, putting his hands on top of it, he patted it before saying, 'It's a funny thing but after the second one was born, that was Florrie, or Florence as she demands to be called, I got a bit jealous of the attention Alicia gave to the bairns. Funny that. I couldn't under-

48

stand meself being jealous of me own bairns. I could make as much fuss of them as I liked but if she gave all her time to them when I was kicking around, I used to get peeved. Can you believe it?'

'Oh yes.' She nodded at him. 'It's a known fact that men's eyes, and not only their eyes, but their hands too, are inclined to stray after the second child.'

He swung round in his swivel chair towards her desk, and now his face stretched and his eyes widened as he said mockingly, 'Now is that a fact?'

'You're laughing at me.'

'Well, what do you expect me to do? Say, eeh! aren't you clever? Did you go to university and take psychology or some such? Well, let me put you right about that one. If a man's eyes ... and hands, as you put it, start straying after his wife has a second bairn, both his eyes and his hands would have started strayin' long afore that. Tommy-rot! . . . Tommy-rot.' He swung round again, then said briskly, 'Now back to business; enough personal nattering. You know' – he cast his glance at her once more – 'I never had this with Old Aggie; she knew her place. If I had, as I did just a while ago, mentioned flannel underwear to her she would have flushed scarlet and said, "Oh, Mr Henderson!"' And he accompanied his last words by putting his hands to his chest and pushing up an imaginary bust. Then ended, 'And she would have stomped out. But she was of an age when women knew their place.'

She had to suppress her laughter. How was it, she asked herself, that she could feel so much at home with this man, that work had become a pleasure under him. She had been working in this office now a month and three days, and her whole life and outlook seemed to have changed. And she felt he was responsible for it, not Hal. Although Hal was so kind, so good, she could never be bright, even gay in his presence like she could in this man's. But during the last two days there had come on her a dread for she had heard that Miss Honeysett was out of hospital and convalescing. What would she do if she had to go back to the pool? She'd be unable to stand it. Miss Cadwell's attitude towards her had been petty before, but she could see her becoming even sadistic if she once more had to work under her control.

'Jinny.'

'Yes, sir.'

'Get me wife on the phone, will you? And ask her if she'll meet me outside around half-past four.' He poked his head towards her now, saying, 'There's a piece of jewellery in Bentley's that I would like her to see. I was talking about it to her last night. She thinks it's for the bride, but it isn't, it's for her. But don't go and tell her that. Just say what I told you: can she meet me outside?'

She picked up the phone and got through to the house.

A male voice answered and she said, 'Mr Henderson would like to speak to Mrs Henderson, please.'

'Then tell Mr Henderson that Mrs Henderson is out. Better still, put Mr Henderson on the line, Jinny.'

'Yes, Mr Henderson.'

'By the way—' The voice on the other end dropped on the next question, 'How's His Nibs?'

She stopped herself just in time from saying, 'His Nibs is as usual,' because His Nibs was looking at her. What she said was, 'Yes, the weather is stormy as usual. But the sun has peeped through once or twice today.'

When a burst of laughter came over the phone she pressed her lips together, widened her eyes, and tried not to look towards her employer. But she saw his hand going out to his phone, and now she heard his voice as if from two different levels yelling, 'You get your mother for me, smarty-pants, and pronto. And stop wasting my secretary's time. I'm not paying her in order that she may sharpen her wits on you, or anyone else. Now, where's your mother?'

As she put her extension down she heard Mr Glen Henderson say, 'She's out, Dad. Can I be of any use?'

'Where is she?'

Covertly she watched her boss looking into the mouth piece, and then he demanded, 'What's she doing up there?'

But after a moment he said, 'No, you can't. And no, I'm not telling you what I wanted her for. I'll see you later.'

He banged the phone down and sat muttering to himself for a moment before he said, 'Get me the Longman's file. And tell Mr Waitland I want him. And Bill Meane from the drawing office.'

She had picked up her phone again and had got through to Mr Waitland's office when Mr Henderson barked at her, 'Put it down!' He was standing now, pulling his waistcoat into place and straightening his tie. 'Give me me coat,' he said; 'and get your coat and hat on.'

'Me?'

'Yes, you; there's nobody else here,' he said, turning and looking round the room.

'Where am I to go?'

'Oh, you want to know where you're to go now? Well, you're going with me to a jeweller's shop. . . . I'm sorry.' He hung his head now, rubbed his hand over his chin that had been clean-shaven this morning but was now showing a slight stubble and said, 'Here I go again, apologizing to you. I've done more apologizing to you, lass, since you came on this floor than I've ever done in me life. Look, would you like to come with me to a jeweller's and pick a piece of jewellery for me wife?'

'Yes, Mr Henderson. I would enjoy that very much indeed.'

'Thank you. Thank you, Miss Brownlow. So what you waitin' for? Get our coats.'

With a feeling of bubbling excitement inside her she got their coats. Then she glanced at the clock as she left the office. It was a quarter to four. She doubted if he had ever before left his office at this time.

In the hall, the doorman looked at them in surprise, and he said, 'You want your car, Mr Henderson?'

'Well, Sam, I wasn't thinking about walkin' the day.'

'Well, if you give me your keys I'll fetch it for you to the door.'

'It's almost at the door, Sam.'

'Well, Mr Henderson, not quite the day. Mr Waitland moved it. He got the spare keys from the office because his secretary, Miss Phillips, couldn't get in and it was pouring.'

'*He what!*' The two words resounded around the mosaic floored hall, and people crossing it turned their heads, but they didn't look at all surprised.

'The bugger moved my car? Wait till I see him! Nobody . . . Nobody—' he was stubbing his index finger towards the doorman's chest, and he repeated, '*Nobody*, Sam, moves my car! You should know that by now.'

'Yes, sir. Yes, Mr Henderson, sir. But he expected to be down and away before. . . . Well, you see you're early.'

'Early be damned! If I never came downstairs for three weeks I'd still expect my car to be in the same place. It's been there for years. At least all the cars I've had have been on that spot. My godfathers! just you wait till I get me tongue round him the morrow. Come on!'

He almost pushed Jinny through the door.

His car was beyond the shelter of the awning. It was running with water and by the time they got into it they were both slightly damp. But Jinny had the great desire to let rip a loud, loud laugh. There was never a dull moment where this man was. And here she was on a working day being taken to a jeweller's shop to buy a present for his wife.

His driving was erratic, and she found this not a little frightening. He talked all the time. His conversation peppered as usual with damns, bloodies, and buggers which were as natural as God bless you to him. She had the sneaking feeling that he prided himself on not being like other factory owners. But whatever business he had been in she knew he'd have remained an individualist.

It was apparent he was known to the jeweller, and was greeted with something near to obsequiousness; also that her own presence was viewed with not a little surprise.

'It's the pendant you were interested in when you were last here, Mr Henderson?'

'Aye, yes, that's what I said. Still got it, I suppose?'

'Oh, yes, we've still got it. . . . Was the future bride pleased with her gift?'

'I don't know, she hasn't got it yet.'

'Oh.' The man turned away and went to a glass cabinet, from which he took down a velvet plaque and on which reposed a gold chain supporting a medallion in the shape of a bow rimmed with two rows of stones.

Placing it on the counter, his hand moved over it as if performing some rite as he said, 'It's a beautiful piece, isn't it?'

'Aye, and it's a beautiful price an' all.'

'One gets what one pays for.'

'Aye, an' I've heard that an' all afore the day. Well' – he turned to Jinny – 'what d'you think of it?' And she, dragging her eyes from the pendant, looked at him and smiled. 'It's beautiful; more so, it's exquisite.'

'That's the right word.' The jeweller was looking at her. 'It is made for a young neck.'

'What do you mean, made for a young neck? What you gettin' at? The bloody thing's for the wife, this is me secretary.'

The words seemed to knock the jeweller back from the counter. His face paled slightly and his hand now wavered in front of it as it had done over the pendant a few minutes earlier as he muttered, 'I'm sorry. Indeed, indeed, I'm sorry. It . . . it was a mistake.'

'I'd say it was a mistake. I'm bloody embarrassed, and for Miss Brownlow.'

'I . . . I apologize.' The poor man was looking appealingly at Jinny now; and she smiled at him, saying, 'It's perfectly all right. It's understandable. It certainly isn't your fault.' She now glanced at her employer, and she knew it was on the point of his tongue to reply, 'And whose bloody fault is it, then?'

But something in her look seemed to reveal to him the situation that he himself had created. And now his tone somewhat subdued, he said, 'My wife couldn't come; I wanted a bit of advice, female advice, because I haven't got two thousand three hundred quid to chuck about every day.'

Jinny almost gasped audibly. Two thousand three hundred pounds! Granted the thing was beautiful, but she had seen imitations somewhat similar for twenty pounds in a shop in Northumberland Street in Newcastle.

'Wrap it up.'

The jeweller wrapped it up; then took Mr Henderson's cheque with grateful thanks, and he himself ushered them to the door.

Once in the car and settled behind the wheel, he did not immediately start up the engine, but looking at her, he said with a wry grin, 'Ever been taken for a mistress afore?'

'No; that was the first time.'

He continued to stare at her, the smile widening now as he said, 'You said that as if you hoped it won't be the last.'

'There you are mistaken, because I have no desire in that direction.'

'Good for you, lass. Stick out for the ring.'

As he started the car, he said, 'I could do with a cup of tea, what about you?'

She hesitated for some seconds before saying, 'A cup of tea is always acceptable, but. . . .'

'Aye, but.' He turned into the main thoroughfare. 'Go on. What were you goin' to say?'

'Nothing.'

'That's something new. . . . Can you risk goin' in Germaine's Tea-Rooms with me? But I'd better warn you, you'll get your name up if you're seen.'

'I'll risk it.'

'Good. Then we'll go to Germaine's. A bit since I've been

there. It used to be a favourite place of Alicia's when the bairns were small. It's a bit posh, but they didn't mind bairns. And the teas'll take some beatin'. The . . . the restaurant'll take some beatin' an' all, 'cos it's under good management. He's a Frenchman. Why do Frenchmen go down better with women than us blokes? He's kept the same staff for years. One waitress has been there now on thirty years, and I'm sure it's just 'cos she fell in love with him at the beginning.' He jerked his head towards her and laughed out loud. 'Not many lasses fall for English bosses. Oh aye!' He was nodding now towards the windscreen. 'They marry them, but it's their position and money and their big houses that are the main attraction; and gettin' one over on the others in the company. Oh, I know what I'm talkin' about.' His head again jerked towards her. 'It's happened in our place. Bloody fools. Ah well, here we are. It's stopped raining, thank God. The car park's at the side, and we can go in by the side door.'

A few minutes later he pushed open the swing doors that led into the lower end of the restaurant. This end was made up mostly of glass and one could look out on to a pleasant stretch of lawn bordered by rockeries and trees. And looking towards it, he stopped dead as he exclaimed under his breath, 'My God! What a situation! I can't believe it.' He turned and looked at her; then back to the three people sitting at the corner table to the left of them and who were looking directly towards them.

Putting his hand out, he caught hold of her arm and led her towards the table, saying in the loudest of voices, 'Caught in the act. Here I am presenting the evidence.'

She found herself standing looking down on the faces of two women – his son had risen – and when he said, 'This is Jinny,' and added, 'Jinny, let me present to you the other woman in the case, me wife,' his hand went out towards an extremely smart woman who looked to be in her forties. She was plainly dressed, but with plainness that expressed exclusiveness. Her face was unlined except for some laughter lines at the corners of her eyes, which were almond shaped.

Jinny wished at this moment she could sink through the ground, at the same time thinking, She's beautiful. And so unlike him. It was like Beauty and the Beast. No, no. She couldn't liken him to a beast, he was too good, too nice. It was just his rough manner that caused her to make the comparison because he wasn't bad to look at. But still, he looked much older than her.

'How do you do? Come and sit down. We've just this minute ordered tea.'

Jinny had no need to answer for her boss was now saying, 'And this piece here is me future daughter-in-law, as if I haven't got enough females to contend with.'

'Hello.'

Still Jinny could make no reply. But she took the seat which Glen Henderson was holding out for her. There was a grin on his face that indicated it could spread into laughter at any moment.

'What you doin' here?' Bob Henderson was looking at his wife.

'Now don't you think, Mr Henderson' – her eyes were twinkling as she looked from one to the other – 'that that's the question I should be asking? Glen' – she turned to her son – 'when have you known your father leave the office before five o'clock in the evening? I'm asking you, because, as you know, I never go near the works.'

Looking solemnly back at his mother, Glen said, 'I've never known it happen before, Mother. As I've told Yvonne here' – he inclined his head towards his fiancée – 'if it wasn't that he's curious to know how we'd manage without him he'd take up his quarters there.'

'Aw! you lot. It would serve you right if I was goin' off the rails. I'm not appreciated. But mind, I can tell you this, if I was thinkin' about it it wouldn't be anybody like her' – he thumbed now towards Jinny – 'because she's too much like you.' His look now was directed towards his son as he ended, 'Has an answer to everything and can't mind her own business.'

'I don't think I'd want a better recommendation for my husband's secretary.' Mrs Henderson was now looking at Jinny, whose face was scarlet. 'Poor Miss Honeysett allowed herself to be trampled on. I tried to tell her it was the wrong way to tackle him. I once told her to either stand up to him or ignore him.' She now leaned towards Jinny, and her voice becoming lower, she added, 'She was slightly shocked. She couldn't understand my attitude.'

'Nor can many people.' Mr Henderson was looking at his wife, a deep warm glow in his eyes now. 'A lot of people are sorry for me.'

'Name one.' Glen Henderson now turned to his fiancée and said, 'Even you thought he was someone from the backwoods when you first met him.'

'I did not. I did not, Papa Bob. Believe me. What I said was you were different from the Englishmen I had met, more outstanding.'

The girl was French and, like most French people speaking English, she had an attractive accent. She wasn't very pretty to look at; a better word that could explain her was, she supposed, petite. She was small, and in a way dressed much like Mrs Henderson. Both their suits were dark, a touch of white showing at the neck. In the young lady's case it was a small frill attached to the dress of the suit. She was wearing a tiny hat to match, which was more of an accessory than a covering for her hair, which was dark, almost as dark as her fiance's. For a fleeting moment she thought that they could be brother and sister except for their height and build.

The young girl turned towards Jinny now, saying, 'You find him a nice man under the skin, do you?'

When Jinny now looked at her employer and laughed, he said, 'Well, go on an' tell her.'

And with a twinkle in her own eyes now, Jinny looked back at the girl and said, 'Unfortunately, I haven't penetrated very far into the skin as yet.'

The ensuing chorus of laughter and chattering remarks was interrupted by Bob Henderson saying, 'Your time'll be short, miss.' And at this the girl turned to Jinny again, saying, 'I shouldn't worry about that threat. You can come over to the French office. I understand your French is very good, Glen says.'

'Perhaps it's as well my accent doesn't come over in the written word; it's . . . . it's rather provincial, I'm afraid.'

'What matters that? Mine is too – You have been to France?'

'Some years ago, and then only for a short time. My grandmother was French, from the north. . . .'

'When you're finished jabbering about your ancestors I'll thank you all to give me a little of your attention. And I'll tell you why I left the office so early. And it isn't the first time, laddie' – he nodded now towards his son – 'that I've done a bunk in the afternoon, if you only knew. But if you remember rightly I phoned me home to ask if I could speak to me wife, didn't I?'

'You did, sir.' Glen nodded solemnly across the table towards him.

'And you informed me that she was out.'

'Right again, sir.'

'Well, just by the way, a kind of insertion like, I'll put a question in here, and it is, how do you manage to be along of these two now if she was out and you were in?'

'Well, sir, I had arranged to meet them, precisely here at a certain time.'

'Oh! Well, missis' – he now turned and looked at his wife – 'you'll grant that I tried to get you first afore I decided to trail her' – again his thumb was stabbing towards Jinny – 'along of me.'

'Yes, dear. I take your point.'

'Well, remember last week when we were in Bentley's spending money like water?'

'Yes, I do, dear. And we were spending money like water, just as you say. And it was such a nice experience.'

'Shut up! And listen. I saw you looking at a pendant, an' I heard you asking the price of it on the side . . . so.' He put his hand into his inner pocket and, pulling out the case, he pushed it towards her.

There was silence at the table for a moment; and then his wife said, 'Oh, Robert. Robert. Oh, my dear.'

'Well, don't waste so much time on slavering. Open it and see if it looks the same here as it did in the shop.'

Immediately she opened the case she bit tight down on her lip.

'It's outrageous,' she said. 'The price was outrageous.' Her eyes were shining bright. She once more bit her lip; then, rising quickly from her chair, she stepped behind him and put her arms around his neck and, bending her face to his, she kissed him on the lips.

'Eeh! Did you ever see anything like that! What'll the people think?' He was looking about him at the two or three tables that were occupied. But he still kept hold of her hand; and now, looking up at her, his gaze soft on her and the tone of his voice one that Jinny had not heard before, he said, 'Presents can't pay for what we've had together, lass, and we'll go on having together, eh?'

As she nodded at him he gulped audibly; then his voice returning to its normal timbre, he commanded, 'Well, go on, sit yourself down and don't make an exhibition of yourself.'

She sat down, and, taking the pendant from its case, she held it in the palm of her hand, and looking first at her future daughter-in-law and then at Jinny, she said, 'Isn't it ridiculous, getting a gift like this in a public tea-room! He should have presented it to me when I was in my negligee.'

'Don't give them mucky ideas, they know enough already. And look, me tongue's hanging out. I came in for a cup of tea. At least, we did, didn't we?' He poked his head towards Jinny.

At this moment she was overcome with a new and strange emotion, as strange as had been her first experience of raw anger, for she knew she was in the presence of an association that was rare: the love that these two had for each other encased them like a halo. If she could have followed her inclinations she would have laid her head and her arms on the table and cried.

And Glen Henderson who happened to look her way must have sensed something of what she was feeling, for now he brought the conversation around to his coming wedding by saying abruptly, while nodding towards his parents, 'If you two can forget your maudlin passion for a few minutes and pay attention to an event that has to happen next week we'd be much obliged, shouldn't we, Yvonne?'

'Yes, we should be much obliged.' The young girl seemed to have taken her cue from Glen; and she went on, 'Today I had a letter from an aunt in Bordeaux; at least it came from my mother. We had never been touched with her for a long time, my aunt I mean.' She now turned to Jinny and in an aside she said, 'My English *is* very provincial, yes?'

'Yes, I'd say, Birmingham accent, I think,' Glen said.

'Nonsense!' his mother put in now; 'it's a lovely accent. Go on, Yvonne.'

And so Yvonne went on to explain how the aunt would like to come to the wedding, and that her mother wasn't very happy about it.

'Then write back and tell her we're full up, both houses.'

'Don't be silly, Father. They can stay at an hotel.'

The conversation ranged back and forth, and eventually they all rose from the table. And in the foyer of the restaurant Mr Henderson said, 'I'm going to run Jinny home. Are you going on straight ahead?' He looked at his son. 'Or are you going to follow us?'

'We'll follow you, 'cos we don't trust you.' Glen turned his head and grinned at Jinny. And she smiled back at him.

As they made towards the exit, Mr Henderson looked from one to the other, saying, 'By the way, I've asked her to the weddin'. Jinny, I mean. She'll be no bother. And you, Yvonne, the last thing you do afore leaving is to throw your bouquet at her because it's time she was married. I don't know what the fellows are thinking about. Go on with you.' He herded them all towards the door now, and as the two men went to get the cars Mrs Henderson turned to Jinny, saying quietly, 'There's no better meaning man in the world than my husband, Miss Brownlow, but he can be the most tactless person in the whole of that same world. And he likes arranging other people's lives. At the same time he can't manage his own.' She now pulled a little face, and Jinny, warming to her, said, 'Oh, please don't worry on my account; I've never been so happy working for anyone. He does me good.'

'His manner has never frightened you then?'

'No. Never. I can honestly say that. I'm afraid I've got into the habit of answering him back.'

Mrs Henderson now looked at Yvonne and shook her head as she remarked, 'His last secretary, Old Aggie as he called her, was scared stiff of him. She liked him; in fact she was very fond of him, but she couldn't stand up to him. It's just as well she's retiring.'

There was no time for Jinny to make any comment on this, even if she had decided to, for the cars drew up at the kerb. But as she took her seat beside her employer, she thought, He's known this, yet hasn't told me, keeping me on tenterhooks. The Devil. . . .

Ten minutes later, as he leaned over to open the door for her to leave, he kept his hand on the handle for a moment while looking at her, and he said, 'Thanks for your company, lass. It's been a good day. I've enjoyed it.'

'Thank you, Mr Henderson. I, too, have enjoyed it, most of all meeting your wife.'

'Aye, well.' He pushed the door open. 'You can see there's no chance for you, can't you?'

She had the handle of the door in her hand ready to close it, but she bent down and said, 'You know something?'

'No, what is it?'

'I wouldn't have you if . . . if there was.'

She thought she heard his last words which sounded like, 'Eeh! you cheeky bitch.' Then she was standing on the pavement answering the waving hands from the other car.

Oh, they were nice. A wonderful family. And wasn't she lucky! She had fallen on her feet.

The street was ill-lit, the pavement was greasy, she was going downstairs into a cold, cheerless basement flat, yet she was feeling strangely happy. A week today she would be at a wedding. A posh wedding. But before that she'd be seeing Hal. Oh, yes, she'd be seeing Hal. And she'd be with him most of Sunday. Saturday was still a day to be filled up. She usually stretched it out by the cleaning of the flat. But on this Saturday she'd go out looking for a wedding present. It would have to be something not too expensive, but nice, good quality.

The world was suddenly a beautiful place. Had she ever felt shy? Lost and lonely? Yes, she had, but she'd never feel that way again. No, never.

> Never is forever,
> Never never ends.
> Be careful what you tack it to,
> It's a word that can sever
> Lovers and friends.

Now why should she think that? Where had she read that? Just because she had said she would never be lonely again. Yes, now she remembered. Her grandfather had been in the habit of spouting rhymes and sayings, and that was one of them. She hadn't thought of it for years. But why should she recall it to mind now? Funny, how one's thoughts had the habit of jumping out of the blue and putting a damper on you. Of late she had been inclined to be pessimistic. She'd have to get out of that way of thinking. Yes, she would, because the future promised to be bright.

5

Hal Campbell endeared himself further to Jinny on the Sunday afternoon when in the sitting-room she told him that she had been invited to Glen Henderson's wedding, and how she had walked the town all yesterday looking for a present, but had failed to find one at her price. After Michael's suggestion, 'Take a bottle of plonk; it's always acceptable,' and Rosie's derisive reply, 'Don't be silly, they swim in champagne at weddings like that,' Hal had got up and walked to one of the china cabinets, and opening the door, he had stood looking at the shelves before his hand went to a small figurine. Lifting it out, he turned towards her where she was sitting in a chair to the side of the fireplace, a seat she had chosen in preference to the couch and the close proximity of Michael, which she was finding disturbing, and he said, 'Perhaps this will fit the bill, small but good. It's a piece of Worcester.'

She rose and went to him; but she did not take the figurine from his hands, she just stared at it. It was about four inches high and depicted a lady sitting on a chair, one arm extended over the back, the other holding a red parasol. Her bonnet was yellow, the skirt of her gown white lace and arrayed in four tiers. The bodice of the gown was mauve, as were her shoes. The figure was based on a white and gold platform.

As she heard herself muttering, 'I . . . I couldn't accept that,' Michael's voice came at her, saying, 'Never look a gift horse in the mouth. Take it and gallop.'

'Could you temper your remarks to the occasion for once, Michael?' Hal's voice was cool. And Michael retorted, 'I thought I was very appropriate. You don't often go around giving your prize pieces away.'

'I've always liked her; she's dainty.' Jinny looked at Rosie who was now standing by her side; then away from her to Arthur who was saying, 'I saw one in a shop recently, not as big as her, and it was ninety-six pounds.'

It was rarely he commented on anything, but his manner of late had seemed to undergo a slight change for the better towards her. Looking at him, Hal said, 'Well, this certainly didn't cost me anything like that.'

'I . . . I couldn't take it, Hal; I mean . . . unless I bought it.'

'Well, all right, if you want to buy it, if it would make you any happier, fifteen pounds.'

'That's ridiculous.'

'Too much?' He was smiling widely at her.

'I can go to twenty-five.'

'Fifteen or nothing.'

She held out her hands and took the figure from him, and gazed at it. 'Did you mean that? It's beautiful. I won't want to give it away.'

'Well, don't.'

'Oh, yes. I must. And thank you. Thank you very much.' She looked up into his face. It was just as she had imagined it last night before going to sleep, warm, kindly . . . handsome. Her mother used to say that blue eyes could never look warm, but his did. He had brought a sort of niceness into her life. After the episode of Ray Collard, it was wonderful to meet a man who could take you out and not expect payment. Last week he had kissed her for the first time. It had been a gentle kiss, and she had closed her eyes at the feel of it. And more than once during the past week she had asked herself what type of women had they been that they could walk out on such a man as him. But the first one had died, hadn't she? How could such a nice man make the same mistake for a second time? Likely just because he was nice.

'I've got the right box for it. I'll parcel it up for you.'

As he went from the room she sat down again, and as she did so Michael rose to his feet, saying, 'Well, here's someone off to see his true love. And—' he took a step towards her and, bending down, said softly, 'don't look so damned grateful. It could be a sprat to catch a mackerel: our dear Bella, Mrs Grayson, has left, so I shouldn't be surprised if you find yourself here on a Saturday helping him to clean through.'

'Mrs Grayson's left?'

'That's what I said.'

'Oh well' – she forced herself to smile at him – 'it would be no hardship to come on a Saturday and help, except your room, and I'm sure you do that yourself. And anyway, after you've inveigled your girl friend into giving a hand during your spare evening in the week I'm sure there won't be that much left to see to at the weekend.'

He straightened up now and laughed down on her as he said, 'You know, there's more than one of you. I was wondering whom you reminded me of lately. And then I got it on the television the other night in *Butterflies*. You look like Wendy Craig. But that's only on the outside for you're not a bit like her underneath, are you?'

'Nobody could be as dippy as she is.' Once again Arthur had got their attention. 'She can't cook; and she goes out and sees another fellow every day. And her husband never finds out. There wouldn't be anybody as dumb as him, even if they tried. Week after week he comes home to meals that you wouldn't give to the dog, and nobody's let on to him about her mooning about with this other bloke, with the chauffeur trailing after them in the car while her red, white and blue banger sticks out like a sore thumb wherever she parks it.'

They were all laughing now, except Arthur, and when Jinny said to him, 'I like *Butterflies*; I think she's marvellous,' he retorted, 'Oh well, you would because you are a little bit dippy underneath. You must be to. . . .' He now shook his head. And when he didn't finish what he was about to say, she put in, 'When I fall for such programmes?'

He made no answer, nor did Michael, but he, saying, 'Be seeing you,' went out of the room.

The door had hardly closed on Michael when Rosie asked her, 'Would you really come and help on a Saturday?'

'If needed, yes. Why not?'

'But you're a secretary; you're not used to housework.'

'I do my own flat, and before my mother died I used to help with the housework.'

Rosie now looked towards the fire, saying, 'I never thought secretaries would sort of . . . well, take to jobs like that. Mary Randall at school whose mother is a nurse, she says that nurses don't like housework either. She wants to be a secretary . . . Mary does. She's good at French. . . . Would you look at my homework?'

'Yes, of course. Go and get it,' she said, nodding towards Rosie who scrambled up from the hearthrug and ran from the room. And now she was left alone with Arthur, and she found this an embarrassing situation for the boy sat staring at her for some while before, jerking himself up from his chair, he went to the fireplace and reached out to the log basket, saying as he picked up a log, 'Do you like Hal?'

She paused and smiled gently at his bowed head as she answered, 'Yes, of course I like Hal, or I wouldn't be here.'

'I . . . I don't mean just liking. Do you more than like him?'

'Now what do you expect me to say to that? What I should say is that it is an impertinent question and mind your own business.'

'But you're not going to.' He slanted his eyes towards her.

'No, I'm not going to.'

His hand went out again and he picked up another log, and as he pressed it into the grate he said, 'Michael likes you.'

Her eyes widened slightly, the smile went from her face and she said, 'I . . . I don't know exactly what you mean by that because Michael hasn't shown me a very good side of himself since I started coming here.'

'That's because he likes you.'

'Don't be silly.'

'I'm not silly.' The words were like a harsh bark. He had swung round on his knees and was within an arm's length of her, and he almost glared up into her face as he said, 'You're soft, and you'll be chewed up. Michael says you will, and you will. And he'd be a better bet for you than Hal. So there, I'm telling you.' And on this he pulled himself to his feet and stomped out.

She was shivering. The warmth had gone from the room; the pleasantness had gone from the day. She should be thinking that that boy is vicious, but her mind was telling her that his attitude was one of concern; he wasn't resenting her being here. And she knew this; in fact she had been thinking of late that they might get on quite well together once they started talking. But now he had set her mind asking why, why he should take this attitude against his step-father. Perhaps he was retaliating against restraint, the slightest discipline. And in a quiet way Hal was a disciplinarian. He was used to directing, ordering. In his ordinary life he was still manipulating players. But that boy's statement that Michael liked her and that he'd be a better bet than Hal, what exactly did it mean? Hal was a lovely person; there was no one kinder than Hal, and not only to her, but his kindness spread in all directions. Three nights a week he visited old people; that was when there was no play in preparation of

64

course. She sat now staring at the fire, and into her mind came a word which she rejected immediately. Oh no, he couldn't be a homosexual. He didn't look like that; you couldn't pin the word 'gay' on to him in any way, and as far as she knew he hadn't any special men friends. But then she saw him only at week-ends. No, he wasn't a homosexual. Then what was it? There was something. But it couldn't be anything of great importance.

Then her face stretched slightly. Perhaps that was it, perhaps Arthur was jealous: he didn't want Hal to marry again. This often happened. The boy wouldn't mind her marrying Michael, for then in a way both she and Michael would be out of his hair, so to speak, and he'd have Hal to himself. Yes, yes, this could account for his aggressiveness. It was a cover-up for his feelings for Hal; he was afraid of losing him, his second father.

She sat back in the chair and closed her eyes and smiled to herself. It's a wonder she hadn't seen it before. The source of emotions such as those shown by Arthur were not always evident. If they were they could be solved directly. She would in a way, a very, very tentative way, make him aware that she didn't want to deprive him of Hal's love.

The room was warm again; the day was pleasant; the future bright; she was going to a wedding on Wednesday, and she had a beautiful present to give to the bride. And that was thanks to Hal. So much of her happy feeling now was thanks to Hal.

6

She had never imagined a wedding like it; she had never envisaged a spread like it; and even her dreams hadn't conjured up
a house like it.

The bride and bridegroom were almost ready to go. They
were standing amidst a chattering throng in the hall. The bride
had changed from a cream brocade, white fur-trimmed wedding-
gown to a travelling suit. She was looking so happy at this
moment that there returned to Jinny's breast the small pain that
she had felt when she saw her walking up the aisle to meet her
waiting bridegroom. She thought now as she had thought then,
Such a ceremony, such a day, such evident happiness was worth
waiting for . . . worth fighting for.

She watched Glen Henderson now zig-zag his way through
the crowd, and she was somewhat surprised when she saw him
raise his hand and signal to her to move towards the corner of
the room that was temporarily clear.

When, excusing herself, she pressed past people, and met up
with him, he said immediately, 'Jinny, about the bouquet.'

'Bouquet?'

'Yes. Yvonne's wedding bouquet. You know, Father told
Yvonne to throw it to you. Well, she was a bit worried. You
see, she had already told her aunt that she would throw it to her
cousin Jeanette.' He now pulled a face, then went on, hurriedly,
'Jeanette's kicking thirty-three, and her mother's despairing.
You understand?'

'Oh, yes.' She was laughing now. 'I have thought no more of
it; I thought it was a joke.'

'Oh, Father didn't. He's set on getting you married off, thinks
you're wasting time.' He pursed his lips now and added, 'For
once I'm in agreement with him. And look, Jinny.' He leant
slightly towards her. 'Take care of him, will you? What I mean
is, try to lighten things there and get him out of the office early.

66

Mother . . . well, the house is getting more empty every day, and Mother misses him. Oh, she doesn't say so, but she does. She misses all of us, but mostly she misses him. So do your best, won't you?'

'Certainly. Yes, yes, I will.'

'Thanks, Jinny.'

As he went to turn away he added, 'He thinks a lot of you, you know. After Miss . . . after Old Aggie, you're like a breath of fresh air to him. And you can hold your own with him. By! that's something. Oh, look; they're yelling for me now. Goodbye. Goodbye, Jinny.'

'Goodbye, Mr Henderson.'

Over his shoulder he shouted now, 'Glen!'

As he disappeared into the throng she laughingly repeated to herself, 'Glen.'

Weren't they a lovely family! Wasn't she lucky to be working for them?

Everybody was surging towards the double doors; the car was drawn up just outside the porch. She couldn't see what was happening outside; she could only hear the laughter, the shouts, the goodbyes, and then the sound like that made by tin cans being dragged over the paved drive.

A few minutes later they were all back in the hall and making their way to the drawing-room, and Mr Henderson in no small voice was saying, 'It's bloody childish, sticking pans and things on the back of a wedding car.'

Jinny now saw Mrs Henderson laughing as she took her husband's arm. 'Let's all take it easy,' she called, 'at least for the next half-hour. Wander where you will until the music starts.' She turned to someone at her side and as if in answer to a request she said, 'Oh, the library's been cleared.' Then added, 'Would you like to go up and see the babies? The girls will be going up there.'

Jinny was standing on the outside of the throng when Mrs Henderson, stopping quite near her, said in an undertone to her husband, 'Don't worry. John's at the bottom of the drive; he's going to see to taking them off.'

'Oh, aye. Well, it's a good job he can do something right for once.' Then looking towards Jinny, he said, 'What you standing there for, lass, with all these men about? Why hasn't somebody got you in a corner?'

Alicia Henderson now closed her eyes whilst still continuing to smile as she said, 'It's a good job you know him, Miss Brownlow.'

'O . . . oh! Away with surnames; her name's Jinny. You never called Old Aggie Miss Honeysett.'

'And I never called her Old Aggie either. Look, I've got to go and see to things. Now behave yourself; be polite. Oh, I know. Miss . . . Jinny' – her smile broadened now – 'will you see to him? If you think he is going to make use of one of his northern phrases, press none too gently on the side of his shoe. He has a very tender corn on his right little toe.'

She went off laughing, and Mr Henderson, looking at Jinny, said, 'She meant it an' all. But if you mean to carry it out you'll have to keep on the right side of me, won't you?' He grinned at her.

'I can do that while at the same time following instructions.'

'And I wouldn't put it past you either. . . . What do you think of the wedding?'

His tone had altered, and hers did too as she answered, 'I . . . I haven't got words to express what I think about it. The ceremony, the wedding feast, and it was a feast, beautiful; and . . . and your home.' She spread out her arms. 'I never imagined it being like this.'

'Too good for me you think? Too uppish?'

'No, I don't think that.'

'No, you wouldn't. But it's no credit to me. All I did at the end of twenty-five years work was supply the money. It wasn't her money this time, it was mine. I was able to give her the kind of home she'd been used to, buy it meself. But I only bought the bricks and mortar, the taste comes from her. What do you think of her?'

They were walking now down a side corridor towards a glass door that led into one end of a long L-shaped conservatory and she didn't speak until she was standing looking out of the window into the dark garden that was partly illuminated from the lights in the house, and she said, 'I've never met anyone like her. I . . . I think she's remarkable, and' – she turned her head – 'and so right for you.'

'You think that, lass?'

'Yes, I do indeed. I'm not just saying it; I really think that. And also, you for her.'

'Eeh, now!' He rubbed his foot on the stone slab of the floor and looked down towards it as he said, 'I can't go with you

68

there. I'm a rough lot. I could have learnt, smoothed meself out a bit, but I've prided meself on havin' got where I was through being what I was. She took me like I was, so there I stayed. You know something?' He looked into her face now, 'When we first got married, prophets from all quarters said we were doomed. It wouldn't last. Chalk and cheese. Oh, chalk and cheese was a poor description. Gold dust and clarts would be more like the mixture they attributed to us. They waited day in, day out; week in, week out; some, year in, year out, for the break. And you know something?' He grinned devilishly at her. 'It almost broke some of their hearts when they found out they were wrong. Like Chris Waitland, him in there' – he inclined his head backwards – 'hanging on to Garbrook. He went to university, and as I once told him it dulled the only bright part of his intellect. And that's why he couldn't understand Alicia falling for me. And there's something else he can't understand, why with his type of education he isn't in my seat. Anyway, he's only on the board because he's Garbrook's wife's second cousin. That reminds me. Talking about him, I heard a rumour. Oh' – he nodded at her – 'I've got wires running here and there through these works. Top floor, middle floor, and bottom. Well, I heard that he'd been enquiring privately like if there was any chance of me retiring afore me time. And so I sent a message along the wire that yes, I just might, but me son was prepared to take me place. I bet that gave him sleepless nights. Oh, lass, I'm tired.' He sat down now on an ornamental iron chair. Then pulling his trousers away from his thighs, he said, 'My! won't I be glad to get out of these togs. The crutch is so bloody tight it's choking me.'

As Jinny spluttered into her hand and his laughter joined hers a young man entered the conservatory, saying, 'Oh, there you are, Father. I just wanted to say I'm going.'

'Why?' Mr Henderson now turned his head and glanced in Jinny's direction and in his usual manner, he stated, 'This is my other son, John. He's kept himself in the background else you'd have met him afore now.'

The young man who was of medium height and fair and not unlike his father except that his face had a tight, drawn look inclined his head towards her, saying, 'How do you do?'

She answered in the same vein; then looked from father to son as Mr Henderson said, 'Not going to stay for the dance, then?'

'No.' The answer was brief.

'Your mother would like it.'

'I would have liked to, too, Father, but I've left my partner outside.'

'Aw, to hell! You know what I feel about these things. I can't understand you, lad. There's nothin' to stop either of you. Why are you doing it?'

'For the simple reason that we want to.'

'You've never been shown a bad example here.'

'No; that's perfectly true. But this house isn't the only example we've got to go on. And perhaps neither of us is very sure of the other. That might be the reason. But anyway' – his voice was lowered – 'it's a private matter.'

'Oh, if you're worried about her' – Mr Henderson indicated Jinny with a motion of his thumb – 'there's nothing that she doesn't know, she's me secretary.'

The young man stared hard at his father before saying, 'I'm going now.'

'All right, you go; but when you're tired of your freedom the door's open.'

As his son marched out of the conservatory Mr Henderson got to his feet and, looking down at Jinny, said, 'Stubborn young bugger. Living with a lass, he is. Only one of my lot to go off the rails. Walked out when he was twenty-one. . . . Like I said to him, why did he wait? If he was in such a bloody hurry to get down to it he should have left when he was eighteen; the law was on his side. The bloody law's on the side of everything that's rotten these days. Pornography's as common as God Bless You now. . . . Do you go along with loose livin'? And don't go and tell me it isn't loose livin'. Oh aye, men go off the rails, I know, and it was only the rich at one time who could afford their mistresses. But at one time an' all the majority of men seemed to have respect for a woman. They've got none now. If any of them even have the common courtesy to stand up and give a woman a bus seat they expect to nip her backside in payment. And I'm tellin' you this' – he wagged his finger in her face now – 'I don't consider meself old-fashioned. I'm as advanced as the next man when we get down to rock bottom, and rock bottom is sex. But in my young time if you had a boy friend or a girl friend it meant just that, it didn't mean that a lass was lowering herself to the level of a whore. And as regards that lot, they've got to suffer the name, it's a kind of profession, but an ordinary lass in college the day can flit from one man to another like a bitch in season. Oh, one mustn't defame the animal world; they're clean compared to some of them.'

He now stood back from her, put his hand up to his cheek, held his head to one side, and as he gave a small wry smile he said, 'You know, lass, next to Alicia you're the only one I can let off steam to, for I'd have them falling around me feet in faints. Our Florrie, the one that looks like me you know, with the three youngsters, up from Devon, when she hears me at it she practically swoons. Aye, she does. You'd think she had been brought up in a convent, and she's been used to me language since the day she poured some scalding soup over our John's head. He was on two at the time, and she was coming up five. He nearly died from shock. You can see the scar round his ear yet.' He turned from her now, adding sadly, 'Wish somebody would pour something over him now and bring him to his senses. Eeh! I do that. Well, come on, lass; we'll get our name up for sitting here talkin'. . . . Do you like dancing?'

'Yes. Yes, I like it very much.'

'Well, get your fill of it. Go on with you, get your fill of it.' He pushed her from him and towards the conservatory door and almost into the arms of Mr Garbrook who, looking past her shoulder towards his partner, said, 'There you are. I've been looking for you. What you up to? Oh, your secretary. Talking business again, eh? Must put a stop to this.'

Jinny passed him, having to walk sidewards to do so. He was a big man, with broad shoulders and a protruding stomach. His face was red, and his voice was hearty. She had met him a number of times before; she hadn't liked him. He was a man who didn't improve on acquaintance. She was glad that he spent most of his time at the metal box factory.

There were several of the staff here. Mr Meane, head of the drawing-office. He was a pleasant man; always had a word for you. Not so Mr Waitland. . . . Mr Waitland, his wife and daughter had all ignored her. In a way she could see their point: why should she be invited when neither Mr Garbrook's nor his own secretary had received an invitation? Still, what did it matter; she was going to dance. . . . That's if anyone asked her.

Jinny was asked. She hardly left the floor during the next four hours, except to take refreshments. And when at last the band packed up and the guests left one by one, most of the men unsteady on their feet, she was left alone with the family, nine in all. And under Mr Henderson's insistence and that of his wife, she joined them in a room on the first floor, which was the only place in the house apparently that hadn't been invaded by the guests, and which, she learned, was Mrs Henderson's own private sitting-room.

There was a great deal of cross-talk between the daughters Florence, Nellie, and Monica and their husbands, all trying to guess the hotel at which the bridal couple would be staying in Paris. Mr and Mrs Henderson sat together on the couch, and Lucy, no care now for her peach bridesmaid's dress, sat curled up close to her mother's side.

The scene presented such a family picture that Jinny felt she was looking through a window on to it and was not part of it. And as if Alicia Henderson had caught her feeling, she said, 'It's turned two in the morning, and there's no sense in you going home now, Jinny. There are plenty of spare rooms. Lucy here will show you and get you settled.'

'Oh, but. . . .'

'Now shut up and do what you're told. Her word goes here.' Bob Henderson was shouting again. 'And I'm too bloomin' tired to argue with you. In fact we're all bloomin' tired. So, come on, let's break up. There'll be plenty of time for more talk the morrow night, and the night after that.'

'Oh, there won't, not for me. We're off tomorrow, you know, Father.'

This was Florence, the one who lived in Devon. And now Nellie's husband, a plump, fair man, put in, 'I've got a business to see to, Father-in-law. We must be off tomorrow too. We haven't secretaries to do our work, have we, Harry?' He was now looking at Monica's husband, who looked little more than a young boy and who now caused a laugh by declaring, 'For my part, I don't care if I never go back to Manchester.'

The company broke up with good-nights all round; and Jinny, about to leave the room, looked towards her benefactors and said quietly, 'Thank you for a most wonderful day . . . and night.'

Alicia Henderson said nothing, she just smiled; but in his usual manner Bob Henderson, in a pleasant growl, answered, 'Go on. Stop your soft-soaping and get to bed.'

In the bedroom Lucy waved her hand casually as she said, 'I think you'll find everything you want;' then pausing on her way to the door, she turned and, looking at Jinny with her head held slightly to the side, she asked, 'Don't you mind the way Father speaks to you?'

'No.' Jinny's smile was broad now. 'Not in the least.'

'Some people do. They think he's coarse, awful.'

Her smile slowly faded as she looked at the young girl, and she wondered if she too considered her father coarse, awful.

'I think your father's a wonderful man, exceptional.'

'Oh yes' – the fair young head was bobbing now – 'he is in a way, I suppose. There's one thing sure, he always stands alone in company.' And after a pause she added, 'Huh! You never know what he's coming out with.'

'It's mostly sense . . . common sense.'

'Oh, I can see you and Mother will get on famously together. She thinks he's related to Socrates.' She laughed now, shrugged her shoulders, then said, shortly, 'Good-night. Sleep well.'

'Good-night.'. . .

She had thought she would drop off to sleep as soon as her head touched the pillow, but for a long time she lay wide-eyed looking around this beautiful room, illuminated now only by the light of the bedside lamp. Her thoughts ranged over the whole day and the whole family until they rested on Lucy, the youngest and the one who, on her father's admission, had been spoilt silly. And she was spoilt, because she didn't appreciate what she had, not only this beautiful home, but also her male parent. But then she wasn't the only one; there was the son John, who was living with his girl friend.

It was as she was drifting into sleep the thought wavered in her mind that possessions such as the things this beautiful house held and luxuries like the bathroom going off this guest bedroom with its separate shower and bidet, and even having servants in the house in this day and age when nobody wanted to be a servant, all these things put together couldn't compete against a personal want, a personal need, such as the one which must have possessed the son John to leave his home, nor yet erase the condemnation of her father that was in Lucy. If she herself had the choice of having this house and all it possessed or Hal, not in his very comfortable home but living in the basement flat, she knew without hesitation which she would choose. And so what it all boiled down to was the need for love, the need to care and to be cared for; yes, that's all it boiled down to. She went to sleep happy.

7

'Now are you telling me the truth? You've really got some place to go over Christmas?'

'Yes, I really have. I'm spending Christmas Day and Boxing Day at Mr Campbell's house.'

'Why *Mister* Campbell? Hasn't he got a Christian name? And he's the fellow you're going with, isn't he?'

'Yes, he's got a Christian name, it's Hal.' She gave a slight shrug of her shoulders. 'And yes, I suppose you could say he's the fellow I'm going with.'

'You don't seem very certain.'

And he was right, she wasn't very certain: there wasn't a firm name she could put to the relationship that existed between her and Hal. He hadn't as yet asked her out for a meal or suggested going to the pictures or the theatre. When she had told him she was going to the theatre in Newcastle he had said, 'Good. You'll enjoy that.' But he hadn't suggested going with her. Yet he was most affectionate whenever he left her at home. But she questioned her thinking here: what did she mean by most affectionate?

'Take that look off your face, I know I poke me nose in where it isn't wanted, but it's just that Alicia said to tell you that if you're at a loose end you've got to come up. And ten days takes some filling in. Why the devil there should be a ten-day break at Christmas God alone knows. There never used to be. The time's not far ahead when they'll be working ten days a quarter; and that'll be their lot. And then they'll find something to go on strike for out of that. Aye, but I suppose I shouldn't grumble as far as strikes are concerned, we're pretty fortunate with our lot; although I don't know how long it will last for there's trouble brewing ahead in the steel business. They're shutting down plants, and that's going to cause a hell of an uproar, if I know anything. And it's no use us saying why worry 'cos we don't make it, we just transport it and turn it into odds and ends, because even an idiot knows that you can't make bricks without straw.'

'There's breeze blocks.'

'Don't you be funny, miss. Anyway, have we wound up everything as far as we can go?'

'Yes, I think so.'

'The Radley concern all tied up? Of course; I've just signed them. I must be slipping.' He leaned back in the chair now and closed his eyes; then put his thumb and first finger on his lids and pressed them as he said, 'I'm tired. It's been one hell of a year one way and another. I'll be glad of the rest. Yet, I was saying only last week to Alicia that I wasn't looking forward to Christmas and an almost empty house: no bairns running about mad, all the lasses having decided to spend Christmas in their own homes this year. Well, I suppose you can't blame them. Then no John and no Glen, just the pair of us left, because Lucy will be running hither and thither like a scalded cat. Speaking of Glen, we had a card from them this morning. They've reached Barbados. Did you know I have a house out there?'

'No, I didn't. . . . In Barbados?'

'Aye, in Barbados. It's amazing the number of relatives you've got when you've got a house in Barbados. It's never empty. It's not a big affair, mind; half a dozen rooms. Eeh! . . . I say that offhandedly, don't I, Jinny? Just half a dozen rooms. And there were eight of us in two rooms for years. And I'm the only one left. Odd that, isn't it? I've often thought what I could have done for me parents and me five brothers and sisters now: put them all on easy street. I lost me dad, two brothers and a sister in the last six months of the war. Life's funny. . . . Why do you get me talking like this?'

'It's better than talking to yourself, I suppose. And listening's part of the job.'

''Tisn't part of the job. And neither is my nattering part of the job. . . . Sure you wont' come along for Christmas?'

She paused on her way to the cloakroom and quietly she asked, 'Could I accept for New Year's Eve?'

'Aye, you could, if not afore, and be very welcome. And here.' He opened the desk and took out an envelope and held it out to her, saying, 'A Merry Christmas. And don't open it till you get home. I don't want any more arguments the night.

With some folks I know I wouldn't have any, but with you I'm not sure. Anyway, Happy Christmas, Jinny.'

'And the same to you, sir. And may I say thank you for my job.'

He raised his eyebrows, pursed his lips, then said, 'Aye, you may, because you're very lucky to be working for me.'

'That's a matter of opinion because you're known as an awful man.'

They looked at each other, and then laughed loudly, but when a minute later, in the cloakroom, she stood with her back to the door and looked down at the opened envelope in her hand disclosing five ten pound notes, she bit on her lip to suppress the moisture that was gathering in her eyes. It was as he had said, in fun or not, she was indeed lucky to be working for such a man. She had the feeling at this moment that there hadn't been a time when she hadn't worked for him, when she hadn't known him. His daughter Lucy came to mind, and she envied her her father.

8

Christmas Day itself had been wonderful: not one incident had marred the harmony; even Arthur had appeared happy. How much this was due to Hal's generosity in buying him a new motor-cycle helmet, gloves, and leather boots, Jinny questioned. Not a hundred pounds would have covered that bill. And there had been no innuendos from Michael. Again Jinny wondered if the silk shirt and matching tie might not have something to do with his pleasantness. As for Rosie, among other things the sheepskin coat and gloves had been received with whoops of joy. For herself she had been delighted with the crocodile handbag and small matching dressing-case. But his generosity made her own presents to them all appear very insignificant.

Hal had picked her up early on the Christmas Eve morning. They had gone shopping together, and in the afternoon she had helped prepare the turkey for the next day, and then busied herself generally about the house.

After the present giving on Christmas morning she had again helped Hal in the kitchen, which they had to themselves as Arthur had gone out on his bike and Michael visiting, he hadn't said where. Rosie, as usual, was curled up before the fire reading one of the books she had been given.

It was during this time in the kitchen together as Jinny stood at the sink preparing the vegetables, that Hal came behind her and put his arms about her and kissed her on the back of the neck, saying, 'You know, you are a beautiful being, Jinny. There's something about you that gets hold of one.' He now turned her towards him and, taking his fingers, drew them down her cheek, across her chin, and up the other side of her face, and his voice just a mere whisper, he said, 'It's wonderful to have you here.'

Her lids blinked rapidly as she answered as softly, 'It's wonderful to be here.'

Again his fingers moved round her face, and again his voice low, he said, 'You ... you know how I feel about a family; well, you make this part of my life complete, like ... like no one else has. And ... and I feel you understand.'

Their faces were close now and as she looked into his eyes she wanted to say 'What should I understand? Is there something I don't know?' But her mind came back at her, crying, Be content. Make haste slowly. Leave it to him. A man who has divorced two wives is going to be chary about taking a third. Make haste slowly.

When he kissed her his lips rested gently on hers; and now, her hands still red from the vegetable water, she put them round him, and in spite of herself she held him close for a moment. Whether he pressed himself gently away from her before the sound of the sitting-room door being opened came to them or just as it was actually being opened she didn't know, but he was back at the table and she had turned to the sink again when Rosie entered the room. . . .

Only one little jarring note marred the day. It was in the evening when, sitting on the couch next to Hal, he for the first time put his arm about her shoulders and drew her to his side. And it was this gesture of his that caused the concentration that had been on Arthur's face as he endeavoured to demonstrate a magic trick to change suddenly to an expression she could only name as resentment. And when the trick misfired, he threw down the cards and sat for a time in sulky silence.

On Boxing Day, all was merry and bright again because it was snowing. In the afternoon they all went out into the garden and had a snowball fight. She had Michael, Hal had Rosie and Arthur. It was as Michael stooped down to scoop up more snow that he said, in an aside. 'There's a dance on tomorrow night in the Assembly Rooms. How about it?'

She threw the snowball she already had in her hand, then stooped to gether up more snow and said, 'Has your girl friend deserted you?'

He now turned his back on a snowball that Arthur had aimed at him and as he did so he muttered, 'I suppose you could say so.'

'Is that why we've been honoured with your company?' She was forced to duck her head to evade a snowball coming at her, and this brought them facing each other, as he replied, 'Not really. I wanted to be home. And then of course, we had a guest.' He lifted his arm now and threw a snowball before he finished, 'And that doesn't happened often here.'

The last remark made her recall her observations of yesterday: there had been no visitors of any kind over the holidays; the only person who had knocked at the door was the postman. Rosie had often talked of her school friends, but she hadn't seen even one on any of her visits. As for Arthur's, his friends seemed to be of the motor-cycle fraternity who met in a café in the middle of the town, and, knowing Hal, that type certainly wouldn't have been welcome under any circumstances. And she hadn't yet met Michael's girl friend. By the sound of it she wouldn't in the future either.

Michael made her uneasy. It wasn't that she didn't like him; actually he improved on acquaintance, and he was attractive . . . and intelligent. She had found that she liked listening to him, but with a wariness because most of their conversation ended in exchanges dealing with personalities.

She said now, 'How about Hal? What would he think if I went to a dance with you?'

There was a pause while more snowballs were exchanged and shouts and cross talk. And then he answered her, saying, 'I don't suppose he'd mind as long as I brought you back here to be one of the fixtures.'

She threw the snowball with increased force, saying angrily, 'I don't suppose you consider yourself as being disloyal to him or insulting to me? Let me tell you, I don't consider myself one of the fixtures of this house. Nor do I think for a moment that he does either.'

Pressing a snowball tightly between his palms now, he said, 'You're a strange mixture. As I see you, you're one third super-secretary, business woman. That's the top end of you. In the middle, you're what's known around these parts as a nice lass, a canny lass; but the last part is most important as I see it, for it's that bit of you that'll direct you in spite of yourself because you're a product of your nice parents, and today that's a handi-cap.'

As she stood stiffly, watching him stooping, Hal's voice came to her shouting, 'Come on! You're losing; we're thirty-three to your thirty.' And Michael, after yelling, 'So you should be with one extra battalion,' said to her in a much lower tone, 'Aren't you going to ask me what name I put to the third part of you?'

She clapped her chilled hands together; then said, 'I'm not

79

interested in your trisection of my character; I know myself, and that's all that matters.'

She wasn't prepared for his turning on her now and hissing, 'Well, if you do, all I can say is you are a bloody fool; and I take back my assessment of your character as far as it has gone because you must be inane, or insane, to want nothing more from life but what is offered here.'

On this, he did not throw the snowball towards their opponents but turned about and pelted it towards his feet as he started towards the house.

The angry gesture was not lost on Hal. Leaving Arthur and Rosie, who had now begun to pelt at each other, he came towards Jinny, saying, 'What was all that about?'

'Nothing. Nothing.'

What was he saying to you?'

He turned and looked towards the house now before, looking at her again, saying, 'You mustn't take much notice of what Michael says; he's very emotional, easily upset about trifling things.'

Well, if she were assessing Michael's character she would certainly not say he was easily upset about trifling things. Nor did she think he was emotional; his conversation was too caustic to tend that way.

'What did he say?' Hal asked again.

She paused a moment. She couldn't say, 'He suggests that you only want me here to use me in some way. At least that's the impression I get. Is there any truth in it?' Instead, she said, 'He asked me if I would like to go to a dance. He said you wouldn't mind. I . . . I thought you might.'

His blue eyes were bright with the cold. Then his lids covered them for the moment as he looked downwards before raising them again to her and saying, 'In a way, he was right. If it would make you happy to go to the dance with him I . . . I wouldn't have minded, as long as you came back here.'

Her mouth was slightly agape; her eyes were wide: he had, almost word for word, repeated Michael's statement. And he had not changed it at the important point which would have changed here to me; he had not said, 'As long as you come back to me;' it was, as Michael had said, to here . . . his house.

The gaiety of Christmas faded away. She felt cold all through, perplexed and strangely sad.

9

It had been snowing for days and the roads beyond the town were almost impassable. Last night, Hal had brought her home. She had wanted to leave on the day after Boxing Day; but, except for Michael, they had all pressed her to stay; even Arthur had joined his voice to those of Hal and Rosie, which was somewhat suprising. And so she had stayed until yesterday.

The flat was dark and cold, and smelt musty, and looked dismal after the large airy rooms in Hal's house. He had remarked on it immediately, saying, 'This is awful. You'll freeze here. And the bed will be damp. Come on back. I'll get you in tomorrow in time to meet Mr Henderson.' But she had assured him that the bed would be all right, that she had an electric blanket on it, and once the fire had got going and the curtains were drawn and the lights put on, it would take on a different atmosphere altogether.

The fact that he was leaving her with evident reluctance brought her some little comfort, and when he took her in his arms and kissed her, she hugged him, and he stroked her hair as he said, 'My place is not going to be the same without you. It isn't often, you know, Jinny, that one meets someone like you, warm and understanding, making no demands. Women as a rule are very demanding, at least that's how I've found them, but you, you're so different.' He lifted her face up to his and, his voice thick with feeling now, he said, 'You're so wonderful, Jinny. You know that? I'm amazed that you've bothered with someone like me; a man who has had two wives is always suspect, especially when he's been divorced. Most women want to know why you were divorced, what happened, who was to blame, and, you know, there's never the one person to blame in such a case, it's usually fifty-fifty. Granted, sometimes sixty-forty.'

Even as he talked her mind was teeming with questions that could not be asked. One of the main things now was where she stood with him. True, she had only really known him for two months, but their association had seemed to have made no progress since the first time he had kissed her. . . . Well, what did she expect? What did she mean by progress? The end that Ray Collard envisaged? Did she expect that? No, no. Then what was she grumbling about? What was niggling at her? She didn't know.

She was ready and waiting when Mr Henderson called on the Sunday morning at eleven o'clock; and when she opened the door to him and he stepped into the room, now unsoftened by the glow of the fire, he stood looking about him for a moment.

'Lass, you must freeze down here,' he said.

'Oh,' she replied lightly, 'when the fire's on it gets very warm.'

'But it's so bloody dark, lass.' He looked towards the window that was shadowed by the outer basement wall.

'Well, it's a basement flat, and I was lucky to get it.'

'Eeh, my!' He walked across the room now and pushed open the kitchen door; then turning to her, he said, 'You deserve something better than this, I'll say.'

'What do you propose? Setting me up in a flat?' She laughed as she made the statement at the same time thinking, Fancy daring to say such a thing like that to him.

Coming towards her now, he said flatly, 'No, I don't. You know me better than that. But I think you should put yourself into a better one. At least somewhere on ground level.'

'For the time I'm in it, it serves its purpose.'

'Haven't you any ambition?'

'Oh, yes, yes.' She picked up her woollen gloves and weekend bag now as she said, 'I've got my eyes set on a millionaire.'

'Aye, well, and why not? Most models seem to aim for them. That's what you should have been, you know. With no bust and no backside you'd have made a good model.'

'Thank you. Shall we go?'

'Aye, we'd better. Be warmer outside.'. . .

They had hardly entered the house before he was describing her flat to Alicia. 'Like a bloody mausoleum, it is. You want to go and see it.'

'Do you think, dear, there'll ever be a time when you'll learn to mind your own business? Come along, Jinny. Sit down.

Lucy's out; we've got the place to ourselves. It's going to be a very quiet time, you know; there'll be one or two dropping in for the first-footing, but that's all. I hope you won't find it dull.'

'Oh, Mrs Henderson.' Jinny laughed quietly before adding; 'Dull? Apart from everything else, I don't know who could be dull when your husband is about.' She inclined her head now to where Bob Henderson was going into the hall calling, 'Dorry! Dorry! What about that coffee?'

Alicia Henderson pouted her lips slightly as she said, 'You've got something there. But he can be a trial at times.' The smile slipping from her face now, she said, quietly, 'People respond to him in two ways: either they love him or they hate him.'

'Oh, I couldn't imagine anyone really hating him.'

'You'd be surprised, my dear. Oh, you'd be surprised. A self-made man is a target for enemies. And strangely, the majority come from his own people; not his relations in this case because he's lost them, but from so-called friends. As he is apt to say, you would expect an enemy to shoot at you and you could survive, but when the bullet comes from a friend no operation can ever get it out. Anyway, that's enough of that. Come, tell me about yourself. We've never had a talk together.'

And so Jinny told her all there was to tell, until she came up to the Fellburn Players. Then her telling became rather stilted, and when Alicia prompted, saying, 'Have you got a boy friend?' she answered, rather hesitantly, 'I . . . I have a friend, but boy friend has a very wide connotation these days, and he's not a boy friend in that sense, if you know what I mean.'

'Oh, yes, I know what you mean, dear.'

'I met him through the Players and he has three adopted children. Well, they're his stepchildren from his previous wives.'

As she watched Alicia's eyebrows give the slightest movement upwards, she said, 'His first wife died and he divorced his second. His first wife had been married before, and she had two children; his second wife also had been married' – she gave an embarrassed laugh now – 'she had a teenage son. He is now . . . well, about twenty-three. The other two are still teenagers. They were the friends I stayed with over Christmas, just a mile or two on from here.'

Following a silence between them, Alicia asked quietly, 'Are you thinking of getting married?'

What answer could she gave to that? Yes, she was thinking of getting married; but it took two people to think of marriage. And so she answered, half in truth, 'I think about it. But that's as far as it goes.'

Mr Henderson re-entered the room at this moment, followed by a middle-aged woman carrying a tray. She was wearing a light blue woollen dress. When she placed the tray bearing the coffee jug, and cups and saucers, on a table to Alicia's hand, she asked in a broad north-country voice, 'D'you want the brandy, ma'am?'

But before Alicia could speak Bob Henderson put in, 'Aye, we do. But I'll get it meself, 'cos you'd have half the bottle empty afore it reached her.'

'Eeh! Mr Henderson, you get worse.'

'That's impossible, Dorry,' said Alicia, shaking her head; and Dorry answered, with a broad smile on her homely face, 'Yes, ma'am, I think it is. . . .'

Jinny had never before had brandy in her coffee; she found she liked it. She liked the lunch, too, that followed; she liked the dinner that night; in fact she liked everything about this house and the people in it. Mr Henderson had cornered her during the afternoon and taken her into his office, which was bigger than the one on the top floor at the works, and as well equipped, which surprised her, as did the fact that he'd had it set up like this four years ago after a heart attack, when for a time he worked from the house.

Sitting in the big leather chair behind the desk, he said to her, 'Eeh! I'll be glad to get back to work, won't you?'

And when she replied immediately, 'Not me,' he said, 'So much for enterprise.'

She then asked him why he didn't work more from the house, as it would be easier for him, cut out the travelling, most of it, and he answered, 'What! And let that lot have the run of the place? I know what happened afore when I was off. Chris Waitland likes me as much as I like poison. He'd not only jump into me boots, but pull me socks off as well. You see, I was against his being on the board in the first place. But, as I've told you afore, he's a relation of Dick Garbrook. I think the word is nepotism isn't it, Jinny?

'Yes, the word is nepotism,' she said.

'I've always tried to keep the company on an even keel; but I'm not so sure I can do that much longer, 'cos the whole country's gone mad; strikes everywhere. And now if the bloody transport drivers come out we'll be in a pickle because half our business is transport. It's no good making things, and even gettin' orders for them, if you can't deliver them, is it? I wish our Glen was back. He can sniff out things . . . Glen. I never thought he'd take to this business like he's done. Now, John. . . . Oh aye, I thought our John was made for it, seeing he looks like me.' He grinned at her. Then his expression and his tone tinged with sadness, he added, 'Cuts me to the bone the way our John carries on. He was at university an' all you know when he packed things up. That's where he met this hot head of a lass. And what's he doing now? Helping with backward bairns. Eeh, my God! to think of it. And with his brains. Because he was smarter than Glen; smarter than any of them. Although our Florrie's got quite a bit up top, but Nellie and Monica are just two lasses. And our Lucy. Oh, our Lucy. As I said afore, she's spoilt rotten. I've got to admit that all Lucy thinks about is Lucy.'

He paused for a while; then looking hard at her he said, 'You know, behind that soft look of yours you've got a head on your shoulders. You could have been one of mine, you know. I thought that the first day you came into the office. And after a week or so I knew I was right, 'cos you've got the hang of the business; you know how to deal with people, like you dealt with that French representative. I'd have been all at sea.'

He got up from the desk and, more briskly now, said, 'Well, there'll be some afternoon tea goin' on somewhere; let's go and find it. And by the way, I'm doubling your wages, from the morrow.'

'Oh no.'

'Good God! Somebody doesn't want a raise. Look, it isn't my idea, and it's not goin' on the books either, else there'll be hell to pay; it's Alicia's idea, 'cos she knows you're right and in the right place, and you should get the right money. But as things stand, were I to put you up by threepence a week I'd have a deputation on the doorstep. You know that yourself. As Alicia says, there's nothing to stop me doing a private deal. And you'll get it in order to get yourself out of that dungeon you live in. Go on, and shut your mouth; you look like a fish.'

Later that evening, when she had tried to express her thanks to the elegant woman, Alicia Henderson had said, 'It is nothing, my dear. You are good for him, and you have lightened his work. And not only are you good for him business-wise but also because you are a match for him verbally, although it amazes me that you are able to do this, because you have that delicate, refined appearance. . . .'

At this point Jinny had laughed aloud, saying, 'Oh, Mrs Henderson, delicate, I certainly am not. I never ail anything. As for being refined, oh dear, the only claim I can lay to that is . . . well, I don't go along with the modern thinkers. I suppose it's because of the way I was brought up. But I think there's a lack of morality in all ways today, so much so that what was wrong once is accepted as right now, and if you can't see it that way you are . . . well, out.'

As Alicia Henderson stared at her in silence she closed her eyes and lowered her head for she remembered that this woman's son, perhaps her favourite son, was one of those people who accepted the morality of today, not only accepted it but had acted upon it to the extent that he had broken away from her and his father.

Lifting her head again, she said, 'I'm sorry. I shouldn't have expressed myself like that.'

'I understand perfectly, my dear, and I admire you for it.'

'Oh, there's nothing to admire, really; I sometimes feel a fool and an idiot to take the stand. You see, I was engaged to be married, and it was broken off because I couldn't see eye to eye that way.'

'Yes, yes, I see. I'm sorry. But you have your present boy friend?'

'Yes. Yes, I have.'

She took the conversation no further for she had the idea that whereas she herself didn't hold with . . . shacking up, Mrs Henderson was not very enthusiastic about men who had twice been divorced. . . .

They had numerous friends in, and during the evening she was introduced to so many people that she couldn't remember their names. And then the phone was constantly ringing, and Alicia, answering it, would look across the room and cry to her husband, 'Oh this is Florence and the children', or 'Nellie', or 'Monica', and he would go across and take the phone from her and shout into it nearly always the same thing: 'Happy New Year. But you should be here, you know.'

Then when Glen phoned there was great excitement. And his father yelled at him, 'It's about time you were back. Three weeks is enough for anybody.' Then, 'Yvonne! you get him back here; I'm sick of lookin' after your house. It's freezing here an' the pipes have burst; it's runnin' with water.' And Alicia would pull the phone from her husband and cry into it, 'Don't take any notice, Yvonne. Everything's all right. Beautiful. It's waiting for your coming. . . .'

Yet, there were only three of them standing together when the New Year was brought in on the television.

'A Happy New Year, me love.'

'And to you, my dear.'

Watching them embrace and their tenderness towards each other brought a lump to Jinny's throat. That was how her mother and father used to act, holding each other, looking into each other's eyes in silent seconds that spoke of an eternity of loving.

And then Mr Henderson put his arms about her and kissed her with a smacking kiss on the lips. Then Alicia kissed her, saying, 'A Happy New Year, Jinny. A very Happy New Year.'

'Aye, and that goes for me an' all. A very Happy New Year, lass. Oh' – he turned – 'and here's Dorry. Happy New Year, Dorry. Come in. Come in, love. . . . And Cissie and Eddie.' The man and woman behind Dorry came into the room, saying, 'A Happy New Year, sir. Happy New Year, ma'am.'

As exchanges were being made Bob Henderson said, 'I thought you had the family over in the cottage.'

'We have, sir, but we've never missed calling in on a New Year in the last twenty years and we don't want to break it. Just wanted to wish you again a very happy new year, and may they go on.'

Cissie Gallon was the cook and Eddie the gardener, and Dorry, she understood, had been with them for twenty-five years. And who wouldn't want to stay with people like these.

After the three had gone the phone began to ring. Then from half-past twelve onwards there were various people kicking the snow from their shoes before coming in and calling, 'Happy New Year, Bob! Happy New Year, Alicia!'

It had all been wonderful. She couldn't remember ever spending a New Year like it. At half-past two when the last caller had just gone and Alicia, looking at her husband, said, 'It's bed. You've had more than enough of everything for one night, including food and drink,' there came another ring on the bell.

87

'Oh, God above! This can go on till dawn. I wonder who it is this time. I thought we'd seen the lot. No! sit where you are, I'll go. . . . I tell, you, I'll go!' He pushed his wife back into her chair and went out of the drawing room, across the hall and to the front door. When he opened it his eyes narrowed at the sight of the figure standing there silhouetted against the snow; and then in a whisper he said, 'John.'

'Yes, Father. Happy New Year.'

'Come in. Come in, lad. Happy New Year.' His voice was still low. And now he caught his son's hand in both of his and shook it vigorously before turning to close the door. His hand going out again, he put it gently on his son's arm, saying, 'By! She'll be glad to see you. Aye, she will that. A Happy New Year indeed! Come on. Come on.' And as if his son were a stranger to the house he led him towards the drawing-room door; then thrusting this open and his voice assuming its usual loud timbre, he called, 'Look who's here!'

Alicia Henderson was already standing in the middle of the room as if awaiting a guest, and she didn't move towards her son; it was he who walked towards her, saying, 'Happy New Year, Mother.'

'Oh, John!' For a moment they were enfolded in each other's arms; but only for a moment for, gripping his hands, she said, 'You're frozen. Come and sit down. Here, give me your coat. Oh, you are cold. Where have you been? Did you walk?'

'No, no. But you can't keep the heat on in a stationary car.'

'Stationary car? You mean you have been sitting out there?'

'Well, it was like Newcastle Central; I thought I'd wait until the last train left.'

'Silly bugger.'

Jinny watched Alicia close her eyes, but there was a smile on her face as she did so.

'Have you had anything to eat?'

John Henderson looked at his mother, and then at his father, and he said, 'Not since half-past ten last night. Candidly, I'm starving.'

When his parents exchanged glances, Jinny thought it was as if they had both been given a gift, and under the circumstances perhaps they looked upon the fact that their son wanted to eat with them was a gift indeed.

'I'll go and get you something.'

'Has Dorry gone to bed?'

'Oh, ages ago.'

'Well, don't bother.'

'Don't be silly.' As Alicia went to leave them, Bob Henderson said, 'I'll come and give you a hand with the tray.' It was as if at this moment, at least, he was finding it an embarrassment to be with his son unless his wife was there too. But before he made to follow her, he turned and said, whilst pointing to Jinny, 'She's not a figment of your imagination; you've never wished her a Happy New Year.'

John Henderson had been standing with his back to the fire, and he now came forward to where Jinny was seated in a wing chair. Bending towards her, he said, formally, 'A Happy New Year.'

'And to you.'

Then going back to the fire, he took up his position again with his back to it. Looking round the room, he said, 'The first time in my life I've seen this place so empty on a New Year's morning. Of course, I didn't see it at all last year, but I knew that they were all here.'

He brought his gaze to rest on her, and he looked at her without speaking for a moment; then he said, 'It was good of you to have stayed with them.'

'Oh; it was very good of them to ask me. It's been wonderful.'

'Wonderful? They're an elderly couple. Well' – he shrugged his shoulders now – 'Mother isn't. Mother never acts her age. Let's say they're settled middle-aged. Wouldn't you rather be at one of the mad New Year's do's?'

'No, not at all. And I'm surprised that you think they are old, even, as you say, settled middle-aged. Neither of them appears like that to me.'

'Well, that's nice for them.' He shifted his stance now and rested his elbow against the high mantelshelf as he said, 'I suppose Lucy's out gallivanting?'

'She's at a dance.'

'Yes, she would be.'

He sounded disgruntled, and somewhat sad. She didn't find his remarks detrimental to his people; she felt sorry for him. Why, she didn't really know. He had chosen to lead his own life, yet, here he was, drawn back to his people. He was of a different temperament altogether from Glen, more thoughtful, more introspective, she imagined.

89

His next question surprised her because it came sharp and more in the form of a demand: 'How old are you?' he said.

'I'm twenty-one.'

'You sound older, but you look younger.'

'Compliments come in all shapes and sizes; I'll have to have time to work that one out.'

'It was merely a statement.'

'Yes, I should imagine it would be, but statements usually have to be looked into.'

'He now turned fully towards her for the first time and smiled as he said, 'I can see how you get along with Father; you're quick on the draw. He admires anyone who can stand up to him verbally.'

'Couldn't you?'

'Yes. Yes, I could, but there can only be one winner in a verbal battle, and I should imagine your success with him lies in the fact that you realized that from the beginning: he's got to be right. Still' – again he shrugged – 'it's New Year's Day, forgive and forget. If only one could. Oh, here!' – he turned – 'let me take that,' he said, hurrying down the room to where his father was carrying a laden tray. And his very action conveyed to Jinny what he had said earlier: he looked upon his father as an elderly man. And she found that strange because there was one thing certain, no matter what Mr Henderson's age was he acted young, vigorously, and he certainly talked in the same way. Oh yes, indeed.

About ten minutes later she made her excuses and, after bidding them all good-night, she left them alone together. And she was to remember long after this that her last waking thought before dropping into luxurious slumber was that she hoped something would happen to bring Mr Henderson and his John together again. And it did; but at what a price.

PART TWO

1

❦

The weather had been and still was the worst most people could remember. There seemed to be no let up. This, coupled with the state of the country, made Bob Henderson's language more colourful as the days went on. But on this particular Friday in February he sat with his fists doubled on the desk, and in between them lay a sheaf of letters ready for his signature. Glaring at Jinny, he said, 'What's the bloody good of signing them? If they won't bury their own dead now they're not going to move our stuff. Eeh! That I've lived to see the day when the dead are lying stinking in the mortuaries, and north-country fellows who pride themselves as honest to God men letting them lie there. It's unbelievable. And if they get what they're asking for what'll happen. The bloody prices'll go up, and they'll be no better off. Silly buggers can't see it. And all the school bairns roaming the streets 'cos the schools are closed; and the car workers out again. And now 'tis unbelievable, but even the civil servants are at it. I've always scorned that bloody lot, sitting on their backsides all day. No wonder the fellows on the floor get edgy. I've got a representative lot downstairs, haven't I, on both counts. It'll be all out next' – he nodded at her – 'you'll see, once the steel blokes get the smell in their noses they'll be like hound dogs. We're a private firm: it can't happen to us, we say. But nothing's private, nobody's private, everybody depends on somebody else. Why can't the silly buggers understand this?'

Jinny watched him take up his pen and jab his signature at the bottom of the letters. Then when he had finished she gathered them up and said quietly, 'Don't forget you've got to be downstairs by quarter-past five. Mr Glen's picking you up. And then you're to go on and meet Mrs. . . . '

'Aye, I know, Jinny. I'm not in me dotage yet. And don't say that surprises you, because I'm not in the mood either for backchat.' He paused as he looked at her now, and then said quietly, 'I'm worried. It's bad enough the strikes and us not being able to deliver things on time, but I'm not happy about Garbrook an' the container company. No, I'm not. Not enough attention paid to work there. If the waistband gets slack, then the skirt drops off. That's what me mother used to say. And it's right you know; there's got to be a firm hold in the middle to keep the rest in place so to speak. And if that lot goes broke we'll have to carry the can.'

'Are you not empowered to alter the management there?'

'No, I can't go over Dick's head. He's a managing director like meself. *No.* What am I sayin'? He's not like meself. I don't take a month's holiday three times a year.'

'Perhaps it's a pity you don't.'

'Now don't start talkin' bloody rot, girl. I thought you had more sense than to come out with palaver like that. You know the state of affairs on the floor as well as I do now, and when the cat's away the mice'll play. It's just human nature. By! there's a lot of truth in these old sayings.'

'Yes, there is.' Her voice too was loud now. 'My father used very often to quote one. And it went like this: Everybody can be done without, and if they don't realize this death will come as a shock to them.'

'Did he now? Did your father say that?'

'Yes, he did.'

'Oh aye? And you're not putting a tooth in it in telling me that I could be done without.'

'If you die tomorrow you'd have to be done without.'

'Thank you for telling me.'

'I'm sure I'm not telling you anything that Mrs Henderson hasn't told you a thousand times before.'

'Now what I should answer to that, Jinny, is, aye, and I'll take it from her but I don't see why I should take it from you. But there, I know you mean well. But, lass, you've got a long way to go yet. And being a woman, you'll never understand that being loved by a marvellouse woman isn't enough in a man's life: it's the threads that hold it together, but it isn't the whole of it; it's work in the long run that matters to a man. Aye, work. Have you ever wondered why I had that verse framed up there? I'm no man for poetry, never was. I leave that to those who think they know better than others, numskulls half of them, never done a day's work in their lives. But when I came across that bit it spoke my thoughts, and I had it framed. I don't know who wrote it. But look, take it down and bring it here.'

Jinny crossed the room to where, above a filing cabinet in a small frame and under glass, was a sheet of quarto paper and on it a verse headed *The Workers*. She had read it a number of times, and wondered why it was the only form of picture in the office. Taking it down, she returned with it to the desk and handed it to him. And he stared at it for some time before handing it back to her, and saying, 'Read it to me. Go on, read it to me. I've never heard anybody read it aloud; I've only heard it in me own head. Go on.'

She paused for a moment, then began to read:

> 'Without work the days are long
> And the nights are longer
> And the weeks stand still in frustrating ease
> Which slide into months of boredom,
> And the year is gone without appease.
>
> And in the days that are long
> And the nights that are longer
> Respect shrinks to a wizened core,
> For work is the oil of man's existence,
> The only resistance against the endless death
> Of enforced ease.'

'What does it say to you?'

'It simply speaks your thoughts.'

'Aye, well, that's one way of putting it. And that last line: the only resistance against the endless death of enforced ease. You know, I think hell must be a place where there's nothing to do, nothing to come to grips with.'

'You could be right.'

'I could be?' He stretched his face at her. 'I know I am.'

She looked down on him now and, a slow smile spreading over her face, she said, 'It would be funny, wouldn't it, if you were made to endure the endless death of enforced ease for your sins? That would be poetic justice, don't you think?'

It was only to be a matter of days before she was asking herself, why in the name of God had she come out with a remark like that? Why did one say such things? Did some creator of destinies pick up your thoughts and, using them as a blueprint, build them into life?

He was saying, 'You cheeky bitch, you! Put it back on the wall. You know' – he turned his head now and looked at her where she was hanging the framed poem above the cabinet again, and he went on, 'They made a mistake when they were giving out faces in your case because underneath that ladylike exterior of yours you're a hard nut. The fellow who gets you is going to have my sympathy. If he doesn't hold his own he'll be a doormat.'

'Definitely.'

'Aw! away with you. Get those letters off and let's get downstairs.'

'No; I won't be coming yet, there are one or two things I want to clear up.'

'But how are you going to get home in this? There are hardly any buses running.'

'I'm being met.'

'Oh. Then why didn't you say so? Who is it? Still the same bloke? You're mad, you know. If a man can't make a success of two goes he's going to have a hard job on the third try. You're worth something more than that. My God, if you belonged to me I'd send him off with a flea in his ear.'

Tolerantly now, she said, 'No doubt. No doubt,' as she made her way to the cloakroom. She returned with his outdoor things. Having helped him into his coat, she handed him his scarf and his gloves, and as she did so she had the almost irresistible desire to lean forward and kiss him, just on the cheek. The thought brought the colour flushing to her face, and he, noticing it and thinking it to have been caused by his last remark, said, 'Don't take it as an affront, the things I say. It's because I'm concerned for you. And Alicia is an' all. I'll tell you something now.' He leant towards her, his rough red face close to hers. 'She's planned to take you out to Barbados with us in the autumn.'

'Oh.' She shook her head. Then on a whisper, she said, 'Oh, Mr Henderson.' Her eyelids blinked, she swallowed deep in her throat; and he, now tucking his scarf inside his coat, said, 'Oh, don't start slobbering; you haven't got there yet. And who knows, you might go and marry that fellow.' He stepped back from her and, as he pulled on his gloves, he surveyed her through his narrowed eyes and, his voice low, he said, 'I'm getting out of range.' Then he added, 'Are you living with him?'

Before answering, she drew in a deep breath, 'No, I'm not

96

living with him,' she said. 'And I have no intention of doing so.'

'I'm . . . I'm—' His head was bobbing now, and he said again, 'I'm—' before pursing his lips and finishing, 'glad to hear it. Very glad to hear it. Well, good-night, lass. And stop lookin' daggers at me. Good-night.'

He had reached the door before she said, 'Good-night, Mr Henderson.'

She rested an elbow on her desk and, gripping her chin within the palm of her hand, she muttered aloud, 'And I have no intention of doing so.'

Then what was going to be the end of it between her and Hal, for he certainly hadn't mentioned marriage, not even an engagement? And his love-making was mild in the extreme, even, she had to admit to herself, creating in her a feeling of frustration. Although she had denied that she would ever live with Hal, nevertheless she wondered what her answer would be if the proposition were put to her. If it meant that or losing him, what would she do? After all, what was marriage but a man muttering a few words over you, and afterwards being supplied with a piece of paper to prove you had gone through some sort of ceremony and that everything from then on would be all right: you could go to bed as many times as you liked with the man because you were what was called married; you had entered another state, a smug state.

She lifted her head from her hand. Yes, she supposed it could be called smug; nevertheless, that was the state she wanted to be in. But she also wanted to be loved. Oh, how she wanted to be loved. Well, it was up to her; she was a free agent.

But was it up to her where Hal was concerned? Love after marriage or love before, neither the one way nor the other had come into their conversation. And not once by the extra pressure of his lips or his arms had he suggested that he had need of her.

And so what was she going to do, feeling as she did about him? But how did she feel about him? Did she love him? Yes. Yes, she loved him. But how did she know it was really love? Whom had she loved before? Ray Collard? She had thought she loved him. The calf feelings she had experienced at school, the love she'd had for her father and mother, all these feelings came under the heading of love. Was the feeling she had for Hal so different?

Oh, yes, yes, it was, because more frequently now she had

imagined what it would be like if he actually made love to her. . . . Of course after they were married.

Damn! She had sprung up from the desk, and, her hands now gripping the edge of it, she was on the point of adding, Blast it! Blast everything! when the nice refined girl that was still dominant in her make-up chastised her, saying, 'Stop it. This is what comes of working with Mr Henderson.'

And now she was attacked by another section of her mind. Don't start finding fault with Mr Henderson, it said; you'll never find another boss like him as long as you live, nor a kinder person. Get the business finished and get out. . . .

It was nearly a half-hour later when Sam opened the door for her, saying, 'I think we must have entered the ice age, miss. In all my sixty years I've never experienced anything like it, not to go on day after day like this. Go careful now; it's like glass.'

She went carefully across the now almost empty car park, and there at the gate a car was waiting. But it wasn't Hal's. Before she reached it, Michael had got out and, holding the door open for her, he said immediately, 'Don't ask questions, just get in. I'm frozen.'

Once seated inside, she said, 'What's the matter?' and to this he answered, 'Nothing serious. Only his car got stuck in a drift. It's likely to be there for days. He took the side road. He must have been mad. Do you want to go home first or straight there?'

'I would like to call in at the flat, if you have the time.'

'All the time in the evening.'

She glanced at him. He was bent over the wheel, peering ahead as he said, 'I'm at your service from now on, I'm a bachelor again. She walked out on me, left a note last Monday. Our trial trip was short and sweet. . . . Then, on reflection, not so sweet. She's taken up with a dustman.'

He nodded a number of times before enlarging on this: 'I'm not joking; she actually has. A tough guy. Muscles like a rhino's.' His head was still nodding, his eyes narrowed. 'I should hate all dustmen from now on, shouldn't I, but I don't. I knew it wasn't going to work out.'

'Careful!' She put out her hand towards the windscreen. Didn't you see that car?'

'Yes, I saw that car, but he didn't seem to see me. Don't worry, I'm a very careful driver. I love my skin and don't want it damaged. Here we are!' He looked out of the side window. 'Nobody's bothered to clean these pavements. Good lord! it's nearly up to the railings.'

'Well, I think nearly everybody in the street goes to work.'

After she had unlocked the door and switched on the light, he followed her into the room. But he didn't speak for some time, he just stood looking around him. Then, unlike Mr Henderson's, his remarks were complimentary. 'Could be quite comfortable,' he said. 'Better than the one we had. I've got to get rid of it now. I'd signed the lease for a year. Some hopes I had, hadn't I? But Hal will see to that.'

'I won't light the fire,' she said; 'I only want to pick up my case and a few things.'

'I wish you would.'

'What?' She turned to him from the bedroom door.

'Light the fire, and we could sit here and talk.'

'Don't be silly.'

'I'm not being silly, Jinny.' His bantering tone had changed. 'I'm serious, and . . . and I want to talk to you.'

'Well, we can talk in the car on our way.'

'No, we couldn't talk in the car. There are things I've got to say to you, things I must say to you.'

'What if I don't want to hear them?'

'You're not silly.'

'Perhaps I am.'

She went into the bedroom now, and a few minutes later she returned with her case, saying briskly, 'Let's go.'

As he came towards her she watched his face darken, and when he said, 'You may be sorry you didn't listen. In any case, what I intended to say was not what you expected me to say, namely, that I have fallen for you . . . because that's what's in your mind, isn't it?'

For the second time in less than an hour her face became scarlet, because that was exactly what she had thought he had been about to say. And she was unprepared to be disgusted at his disloyalty to Hal. But now she could not bring herself to ask, 'What is it then you want to say to me?' And so she walked past him and towards the door. But here she paused, and to save her own face, she turned and confronted him, saying now, 'You have an opinion of yourself, haven't you, while your opinion of my intelligence is almost nil.'

His expression was almost as angry as her own as he replied, 'You're quite right there, perfectly right: you're dim, stupid, you haven't got the sense you were born with.'

He marched past her and up the area steps, and as she locked the door she found herself gasping as if she had been ploughing through a heavy snowdrift.

The journey seemed interminable because they never exchanged a word. When they reached the house, Hal was waiting for them at the opened door. After taking her hands in his he kissed her, then looked to where Michael was making straight for the stairs, and in a low voice said, 'What's the matter with him?'

Hers equally low, she answered, 'We . . . We've had a slight argument.'

'Oh. There's nothing like a family for providing grounds for slight arguments. Come on, get your things off; the tea's all set. I've got some muffins, all hot and buttery. I had all the groceries in the car when I went into that drift. What a job it was to lug them back here.'

It was Hal who talked during most of the meal; Michael's quietness could have been put down to his broken romance, yet Jinny knew that Hal was aware of something beyond this. But it only seemed to make him talk the more. His questions to Arthur about school received laconic answers. Only with Rosie had he any cross-talk.

It was after the meal was finished and the washing up done that he called from the kitchen doorway to Michael who was making his way into the sitting-room: 'I've got to slip out for a while. May I take your car again? One of my old people isn't too good. Ths weather's getting a lot of them down.'

Michael turned and looked back at Hal, but did not immediately answer; but when he did his voice was bright and high, over high, as he replied, 'Of course, Hal, take the car. I can understand your need to see to the old people. Most commendable of you.'

When Hal returned to the kitchen again Jinny could see that all his teatime joviality had gone from him. The expression on his face was one she hadn't seen before: it recalled to her the day he had run Arthur from the room. Yet his look now did not wholly indicate anger, but had in it a kind of surprised wariness.

For a moment he didn't speak; then looking at her, he said, 'I've got to go. You understand?'

'Yes, yes.' She nodded at him. 'But it's an awful night and, the roads the way they are, would they be expecting you?'

'*What*?' It was as if his thinking had been far away. Then he said slowly, 'Yes, they'll be expecting me. People get very lonely. Well, you know all about that, don't you, Jinny?'

Yes, she knew all about that. Yet, that niggling part of her mind was telling her there was something here that she didn't know all about. And Michael could and would perhaps have explained it if she had only listened to him. But she didn't listen to him, and she didn't wholly believe him when he had said he hadn't intended to tell her that he had fallen for her. If the attitude he adopted with her was the same as that he used with all women then he must have raised quite a few high hopes. Even she had asked herself: if she hadn't felt the way she did about Hal would she have responded to Michael? But she had given herself no answer; life was complicated enough without creating further obstacles.

Hal's kiss of goodbye at the front door was a perfunctory one, similar to one he might have bestowed on Rosie, and as he pulled up his collar in the act of turning away from her, he muttered, 'Don't wait up, I . . . I might be late, or get stuck. You never know. Anyway, don't wait up.'

After she had closed the door on him and was crossing the hall towards the stairs, intending to go to her room, Michael appeared at the sitting-room door.

He didn't speak, but he raised his eyebrows and pursed his lips, and his expression appeared like one large question mark that was saying, 'Well?'

Just for a moment, she half turned as if to go towards him and demand an explanation of the innuendoes he was always dropping. But what would she find out? Not that Hal was a homosexual. No, she couldn't believe that. Not that he had another woman. Hadn't he told her how afraid he was of marriage? But with this thought her mind hit her like a blow, astonishing her by bringing with it Mr Henderson's favourite word, bloody. Don't be a bloody fool, it said. Is a man going to keep away from women because he's expressed an opinion against a third marriage?

She mounted the stairs. No, no. There was no other woman. She was sure of that. He wasn't like that. If he wanted a woman that way, his love-making would have been different; by now he would have shown himself in a different light altogether. You couldn't hide those kind of feelings of passion for long. . . . Then what was it?

In her room, she sat on the foot of the bed. The room was warm, as was the whole house. Everything here was made for comfort; perhaps not in the grand style of Mr Henderson's house, but nevertheless, everything that one needed was here. She had thought more than once that Hal's mother must have been an ideal home-maker. Since that night in the flat when he had talked about the loss of his mother he had never mentioned her. There were four photographs of her in his room: in one she was cradling him in her arms when he was a baby; the other three were of her alone, one full lengtn, the other two head and shoulders. She had looked a big woman, rather handsome, but her features were bony; her eyes were large, like Hal's, but more heavily lidded.

Her whole attitude now was denying the warmth of the room, for she sat with her hands under her oxters, her arms crossed, and she rocked herself gently as a child rocks itself in a cot when in need of comfort. And that's what she needed at this moment, comfort. She wanted someone she could talk to, explain her feelings to. She thought of Alicia Henderson. Yes, she could talk to Mrs Henderson. She could even talk to Mr Henderson. Yes, that was strange. If either of them had been here at this moment she would have said to them, 'I feel like walking out but I'm frightened. I'm frightened of being on my own again. No place to go at the week-ends. I should have it out with him but what could I say?' And they would have said, 'You must come to us.'

Could she have then gone on to say to them, 'I want more than companionship from him, I want love, real love, like you two have, married love'? Could she have said that to them? Perhaps. Yes, perhaps she could; they were special people.

She rose from the bed and, going to her case, she took out a woollen cardigan, and as she put it on her chin jerked upwards as she came to a resolution: she wasn't going to be made a fool of for a second time. At the first opportunity she would ask him point blank if there was any one else.

2

The opportunity didn't arise over the weekend for her to bring things into the open, for Hal had caught a cold, and on the Saturday and Sunday he remained in bed. When approached even to ask how he was feeling he showed yet another new side. However, his particular peevishness she put down to the fact that most men thought they were going to die when they caught a cold; at least, she had been given to understand that. Even her mother had said it.

On the Monday morning she left for work on foot for the drifts were so high that now Michael couldn't get his car out and on to the side road. But the buses were running and although the main road was not half a mile away, it took Michael and her almost half an hour to reach it. And during the journey they even laughed together, when she had to pull him out of a drift and, the snow having gone down the top of his Wellington boots, he did a kind of St Vitus dance in an effort to get it out.

They were lucky enough to get a bus and before he got off, some way before her stop, he was smiling broadly as he said, 'You know, Jinny, I've enjoyed this journey better than any I've made for a long time.'

She had turned towards him, while she smiled too, saying now, 'Well, I hope you enjoy it going back tonight.'

'I might turn up at your place looking for shelter.'

'You'll find a closed door.'

'Never.'

He waved to her from the pavement, and she lifted her hand in reply.

It was five-past nine when she walked through the cleared path in the car park. Only about a third of the usual cars were scattered here and there, and Mr Henderson's wasn't parked under the awning.

As she approached the glass door Sam opened it for her, and

she said to him, 'It doesn't get any better, does it? There'll be a few empty seats here today, I've no doubt.'

The doorman stared at her; and as she went to move away from him and across the hall his voice stopped her. 'Miss!'

'Yes, Sam?'

'Where are you going?'

'Where am I going?' She moved back to him and looked into his face. 'I'm going to work.' And she gave a small laugh. Then when he didn't speak she said, 'What's the matter? What is it?'

'Don't you know, miss?' His voice was a mere whisper.

It was some seconds before she managed to say, 'Know what?' And when he still didn't answer, she repeated, 'Know what?'

'About the accident on Friday night.'

'Accident to . . . to Mr Henderson? *Oh no! No!*' She put her hands tightly across her mouth. 'What . . . what happened? Is he . . .?'

'Have you been away for the weekend? Didn't you hear it on the wireless?'

'Hear what? Yes, yes, I've been away. . . . But hear what?'

'Well, it's going to be a shock, lass. It has been to everybody. A lorry ran right through them. The two women, the two wives . . . went instantly, so it's said. They were in the back seat. But Mr Henderson and Glen . . . they were smashed up badly, so I hear. Very little chance.'

'*Oh my God!*'

'Sit down, miss. Sit down.' He led her towards a chair which stood near a rubber plant, and when she was seated he said, 'Stay there; I'll get you a drink of water.'

She sat staring before her, unable to take it in, yet already devastated by the news, part of her mind screaming at her: 'Not those two. Not those two! Not Mrs Henderson and that nice girl. No. No. God wouldn't do things like that.' You read about it in the papers. It happened to other people, people you didn't know, people who hadn't been kind to you, people about whom you could say, Isn't it awful? but without feeling this terrible sense of loss which was creating in her a pain the like of which she had never before experienced. She had been so distressed when her father died, and had never thought to experience again the sense of aloneness she'd had after she buried her mother. But those feelings now appeared like rippling waves compared to the deluge of compassion and sense of loss that was enveloping her now.

'Here. Drink this.'

She sipped at the water; then looking at Sam she said, 'Where ... where's Mr Henderson?'

'As far as I know, miss, they're both in the Royal Victoria over in Newcastle.'

There seemed to be a long pause before she said, 'Are there any taxis running, Sam?'

'I could try for you, miss.'

'Please.'

She sat still on the chair, oblivious of the door opening and shutting and of people crossing the hall towards the lift. Some looked in her direction, but no one came up to her, until Sam returned, saying, 'There'll be one here in five minutes, miss.'

When she rose to go towards the door, he took her arm, and as he did so he said, 'By! if anything happens to Mr Henderson this place'll know it. I'm telling you.'

If anything happened to Mr Henderson ... if anything happened to Mr Henderson. Not only this place, but she would know it. Her life would be changed completely. That man had come to mean so much to her. She hadn't realized before just how she looked forward to coming in to work. His brusque, very often rude remarks seemed to stimulate her; nothing he said ever offended her. Yet it would have done coming from another man. She felt she understood him, perhaps in a way that Mrs Henderson hadn't done. Oh! that sounded awful. Like the prattle of the "other woman". But she wasn't meaning it in that way; she was meaning the business side of him, how he treated people, and why so roughly, as at times he did. There was nothing mean or small about him.

And now he was near death by the sound of it. But people exaggerated. Yet would he want to live now that his wife had gone, because he had adored her? Oh yes, if any man had adored a woman he had. And she in turn had reciprocated his feelings, and looked up to him. Yes, that was the strange part about it, a well-bred woman had looked up to him, because likely there were qualities in him that only a wife would know of.

A few minutes later Sam took her arm and led her to the taxi, saying, 'You'll be coming back, won't you, miss? I'll be glad to hear the latest news.'

The taxi was held up three times during the journey, and it was slow going all the way. It was almost a half-hour later when she entered the hospital.

From the desk she was directed towards the ward. There she was met by a staff nurse who said, 'I'm afraid you'll not be able to see them.'

'Are . . . are they very bad?'

In answer the nurse said, 'Are you a relative?'

'No, I am Mr . . . Henderson senior's secretary.'

'Oh. I am afraid only the family are being allowed in so far. The young Mr Henderson is in a coma, and Mr Henderson himself is not aware of very much.' She paused now as Jinny turned her head quickly and looked along the corridor to see John Henderson coming towards them.

At first he did not notice her, but, speaking to the nurse, he said, 'What time will the doctor be in?'

'About ten, I should say, if not before.'

'Thank you.' He turned to Jinny, and when he looked at her but did not speak, she said, 'I've . . . I've just found out. I've been away for the weekend. I . . . I can't believe it.'

When he walked away she went with him, and, her voice almost a low gabble, she said, 'I don't know what to say. It's so dreadful. I . . . I just can't believe it . . . that . . . that your mother is . . . is really. . . .' She stopped.

They had entered the waiting-room and when he sank into a chair she took one opposite him; and she watched him lean forward, then drop his forearms on to his knees, and clasp his hands tightly together. His head was bent towards them as he said, 'Yes, she is really dead. That's what we've got to face, that she and Yvonne are really dead.' His head was moving in time with his words, giving each one emphasis. Then casting his glance towards her, he said, 'How he's going to take it if he comes round God alone knows. I hope he doesn't come round.'

'Oh, don't say that.'

He sat up straight now, his back tight against the chair, and staring at her, his eyes and face hard, he said, 'Why not? What is there left for him? He cared for her like no man should allow himself to care for a woman. It was of such deep intensity that it hurt one to watch it in action. I've witnessed it since I was a child. The both of them cared for us as the family, in a way I suppose you could say they loved us, but they adored each other; it was painful . . .'

Under other circumstances she would have replied to this, 'How selfish can you get? You should have been glad that they loved each other so much.' But she realized that this son, the only one of the family, as Mr Henderson had said, that had gone wrong, was suffering intensely, likely feeling guilt for walking out on them. Yet perhaps he had been drawn by a love as strong as theirs. She didn't know, she was only guessing. But there was one thing sure, this haggard young man was not the same person she had met on New Year's morning. That one had had a large chip on his shoulder – she could recognize chips – but this one who seemed to have aged ten years in the past few weeks was wide open, rent apart by pain as it were.

'Is there anything I can do?' she said softly. 'I . . . I mean business-wise.'

'I wouldn't really know; but Mr Waitland would likely tell you, he's taken charge for the time being.'

'Are . . . are all the family here?'

'Yes. And Yvonne's too.' He closed his eyes now as he said, 'That was terrible, having to tell them. Their only daughter. I hope Glen dies too. Why should he be asked to suffer that loss because he and Yvonne were going to be like Father and Mother. Glen patterned himself on Father. He always denied it, but he did. And he saw his marriage being like theirs. He once said they were the most ideal couple in the world.'

'I think they were too.'

He looked at her now as he said quietly, 'Everything in life has got to be paid for; you should never let yourself care like that. From such heights, there's only one road, and that's down; you can't stay on top of the mountain forever.'

Again at another time his cynicism would have evoked a tart reply from her, but now she could only look at him and think that whoever he had been living with certainly hadn't made him happy, and she doubted if he had made the girl happy either. His life must have been a battleground governed by his thinking.

She now asked softly, 'What . . . what is the extent of the injuries?'

'With Glen it's his head. They are going to operate on him later today.' She watched him swallow twice before going on, when he said, 'Father's back's broken; at least that's as far as they know. And he hasn't regained full consciousness yet. There's. . . .'

He was about to go when he looked towards the entrance to the waiting-room, and she followed his glance and saw the eldest daughter Florence coming towards them.

They both rose and Florence gave her a perfunctory nod before looking at her brother and saying, 'I have to go now; my train leaves at half-past ten. I'll be back on Wednesday. Ronnie'll come with me then. Granny Brook will stay on and see to the children. I . . . I don't want to go' – she shook her head – 'but there's nothing one can do at the moment. You'll phone me if there's the slightest change, won't you?'

'Yes, yes, I'll do that.'

As John took his sister's arm to escort her away, Florence said stiffly, 'Goodbye, Miss Brownlow,' and Jinny inclined her head as she answered, 'Goodbye, Mrs Brook.'

Of the three daughters, she liked Florence the least. Florence had her father's colouring but none of his disposition; nor yet did she possess any of her mother's charm, as far as she could see. If there was a snob in the family then it was Mrs Brook.

Alone in the waiting-room, she knew she was about to cry, and she put her hand tightly across her mouth, telling herself she must get outside or she would break down.

As she made her way along the corridor she saw John Henderson coming back towards her, but now he was accompanied by Mr Garbrook. When they were almost abreast of her he inclined his head towards her but said nothing, and they went on.

A few minutes later she was standing in the street like someone dazed, looking first one way, then the other. It was no use hoping she could get a taxi back; she would have to catch a bus.

After some searching she caught a bus that would take her as far as Gateshead. From there it was comparatively easy to get transport to Fellburn. . . .

When Sam once again opened the door for her she was feeling on the point of exhaustion, and she gasped as she answered his question: 'How did you find them?'

When she told him he said, 'God help them,' then added, 'No one here can believe it. The place is in a hubbub.'

He opened the lift door for her, and when she stepped out on to the top floor she found the impression of hubbub was for the first time made evident. There were six doors on this landing, and four of them were open. There was a coming and going from one room to another. She went towards what she termed her office, and as she stood in the doorway her mouth opened into a gape. Her typewriter and the table were gone; but not very far. She could see it at an angle in the adjoining room.

There was another filing cabinet next to hers. Mr Waitland was standing behind the desk; his secretary, Miss Phillips, was standing in front of it, and she had a number of files in her arms.

Becoming aware of her presence they both turned and looked at her.

She moved into the room, but didn't speak, she merely looked about her, until Mr Waitland, his voice seeming to demand the reason for her presence there, said, 'Well?'

'What is happening?'

The coolness of her own question surprised her.

'What do you think is happening, miss? You are aware, I suppose, that Mr Henderson is in hospital, but what you are not apparently aware of, because' – he now looked at his watch – 'you happen to be just a couple of hours late, is that I am taking his place until . . . well, such time as he will return.'

'I . . . I know Mr Henderson's business, I could. . . .'

'I, too, know Mr Henderson's business, miss.' The miss was stretched somewhat. 'I think I have been familiar with this business a little longer than you, ten years longer, I should say, as has my secretary.' He nodded towards the tall woman who was surveying Jinny with a look that could only be described as triumphant; it was as if she had won a long and hard battle.

The animosity of both the man and the woman hit her as if with physical blows; yet in a way she knew these weren't directed at her, but at Mr Henderson. Mr Henderson had never trusted this man, and, being himself, he must have made it evident.

Miss Phillips now said, 'You are expected in the pool.'

My God! the typing pool. Oh no, no, not that again.

She only just managed to prevent herself from protesting as she said now as calmly as she could, 'I will collect my things.'

'They are on the table there.' The secretary was pointing to a small table to the side of the room, above which had hung Mr Henderson's parable as he called the poem. But now it was no longer hanging there.

Swiftly she turned about and, pointing to the wall, said, 'The poem. Where is it?'

Mr Waitland looked at his secretary and she looked at him. 'It's been put away,' she said.

'Then you had better get it out from where you've put it; I've just come from the hospital and seen him, he would like it.'

Again Mr Waitland and his secretary looked at each other – her tone had more than surprised them – but after a moment he inclined his head towards her and she went in into what was now presumably her office, and after a moment returned holding the offending 'picture' between finger and thumb, as if she were about to drop it into a waste-paper basket.

Jinny took it from her, and as she did so she held the woman's eye for some seconds, her look conveying her thoughts. Turning away, she gathered up her notebooks and pencils from the desk; then paused and looked from one side to the other before saying, 'There were two French books; I would like them please.'

Miss Phillips nipped at her lower lip, as she muttered, 'I . . . I must have overlooked them. They are likely in the cupboard.'

When she returned with the books, she did not hand them to Jinny, but threw them down on to the desk, and as Jinny picked them up she glanced sideways at the woman, saying, 'There are quite good French night classes at the Technical College. Of course, it's much easier if your English is good.'

She walked out with the satisfaction of seeing the woman's face turn scarlet.

In the lift once more, she thought, I'm going to be sick. Oh, I am going to be sick.

When she entered the typing pool it was as if everybody had been awaiting her arrival. There they were, all the old faces: Noreen Power, Ann Cartnell, Betty Morris, Nancy Wells, Flo Blake . . . and Miss Cadwell. Miss Cadwell was in her little glass office at the end of the room. She had been seated, but had now risen. And Jinny watched her move slowly towards the door and pause a moment before entering the office proper.

There was an empty desk behind Nancy Wells, and she dropped her books and papers, also her handbag, on to it. She was pulling off her woolly hat as Miss Cadwell came to her side.

Miss Cadwell was smiling. Jinny had never really seen her smile before, and had she witnessed it when she had first come into the office it would have filled her with apprehension, to say the least. But now if left her cold because she was no longer afraid of Miss Cadwell. At this moment she was afraid of nobody. The deep sorrow she was experiencing was almost overshadowed by anger, anger at the evident pleasure, almost joy, that was emanating from Mr Henderson's office. Talk about jumping into dead men's shoes. Mr Waitland wasn't even waiting for that.

'So we have the pleasure of your company again, Miss Brownlow.'

'I'm glad you see it like that, Miss Cadwell. That being so, doubtless we can work amicably together for the time being.'

The tone of her voice and the audacity of the words seemed to stun the occupants of the room, and Jane Cadwell too. But in her case only for a moment, for, rearing, she almost yelled, 'Don't you dare take that attitude with me, miss! Who do you think you are anyway?'

'I am Mr Henderson's secretary. Mr Henderson is not here at the moment, but he is likely to return, at which time I shall again move up to the top floor.'

'You think . . . you hope. Oh, the nerve of you!' Miss Cadwell now looked about her, turning her head from side to side to take in the staring faces; and she repeated, 'The nerve of her!' Then her eyes sending out shafts of venom, she said, 'You . . . you should be ashamed to show your face. But now that his wife's dead you hope to make it legal, I suppose. Your type will do anything for money and position. And with a man like that, old enough to be your grandfather, and coarse-mouthed into the bargain. Nobody would stay up there, only you, because you knew what you wanted, jewellery. Supposed to be buying it for his wife. You've been the talk of the works. And now you dare come in here . . .'

'Shut up! Shut up, this minute!'

Miss Cadwell not only shut up, but she took two paces backwards up the aisle between the desks, and Jinny, stepping towards her, her body leaning forward, her face aflame, cried, 'You dirty-minded old bitch, you! There was never anything like you suggest. And Mr Henderson's a gentleman. You filthy, frustrated hag!' And with the last word, her hand came out with such force across Jane Cadwell's face that the woman cried out and staggered back. But when she was hit on the other side she fell sideways over the desk.

And now there was pandemonium. Jinny was only aware that Betty Morris was tugging at her arm, pulling her backwards, and that the other girls were helping to support Miss Cadwell. And now Miss Cadwell, the tears streaming down her face, which she was holding between both hands, screamed, 'This'll be the end of you. I'll have you in court for this.'

Jinny, after grabbing her things from her desk, turned and, pushing Betty Morris aside, took three steps up the aisle again towards the woman; and she answered her, but she did not scream or yell, for her voice was now deep and each word carried weight as she said, 'You do that. I'll be waiting for you doing it. And you'll have to take all the money you've scraped up for years to meet my slander charge, and that against Mr Henderson. There are five witnesses here; they heard every word you said, and I didn't hit you before you said them, I hit you after. Think of it, Miss Cadwell. Put your charge in as soon as ever you like, you dirty old woman, you. And that goes for the rest of you who thought along her lines.' And on this she turned and marched from the room.

Once more in the front hall and sinking on to a seat, she was approached by Sam. 'What's up, lass?' he said. 'You look like death.'

The tears oozing from her eyes now, she answered, 'They've already taken over Mr Henderson's office . . . Mr Waitland and his secretary . . . and I went down to the typing pool, Sam, and—' She squeezed her eyes tightly and swallowed before she said, 'They are saying . . . Miss Cadwell said that I've been having an affair with Mr Henderson, and that he bought me jewellery. And Sam, it isn't true, not a word of it.'

'No. No, lass. I never believed it either.'

Her eyes widened now. 'So they have been saying *that*?' The last word ended on a high note, and he nodded and said, 'Aye. Yes. Somebody that works in . . . the jeweller's has a cousin in the offices up here. Mr Henderson was supposed to be buying you a necklace and pretending it was for his wife when his wife walks in and there was a bit of a polite shindy.'

'It wasn't like that at all. Mrs Henderson was never near the jeweller's that day. Oh, Sam; believe me. We're all friends. Mrs Henderson was so woderful to me. And he's been like a father besides a friend. Oh, Sam.' Her voice broke, and she ended, 'People are awful. People are awful.'

'Aye. Aye, lass, they are. As you go on in life you'll find people are awful. But there's good 'uns an' all, and Mr Henderson was a good 'un. And I pray God that things aren't as bad as they say they are with him and that he'll come back, because between you and me, Garbrook isn't much good. As for Waitland, well, he'll be as welcome on the shop floor as a dose of poison. Look, can I get you another taxi?'

'Yes. Yes, please, Sam.'

When she was alone she asked herself where she would go in

the taxi? Back to the flat? No, no; she couldn't be alone. And it was so cold there. She wanted warmth, because she was cold to the very, very core of her. She wanted the warmth of a kindly voice, of tender arms. She would go to Hal's office. And he would take her home, and she could stay with them for a time, for she would go mad if she were left on her own. . . .

When Sam came back, he said, 'You're lucky again, lass; there's one coming. He's dropping off somebody just along the road and he should be here in a few minutes. He bent towards her now, adding, 'I'll miss you an' all, because you won't be coming back.'

'No, I won't be coming back Sam, not . . . not unless Mr Henderson comes back.' She now looked up at him, her eyes blinking the moisture away, and her lips tried to move into a smile as she said, 'You know what I did up there, Sam?'

'No, miss. What did you do?' He spoke to her as if she were a young child, softly, coaxingly.

'I hit Miss Cadwell. I slapped her face. Not once, but twice. Both sides. . . . Huh. Huh!'

'You what, miss? *You* . . . you hit Miss Cadwell? Never!'

'I did, Sam. I lashed out at her when she said that about me and Mr Henderson.'

She watched his shoulders shaking; she watched him nip on his prim grey moustache; she watched him close his eyes and rub his hand across them; then in a voice that wasn't steady he said, 'I can't believe it. You're so ladylike, gentle looking. You don't look as if you'd say boo to a goose.'

'I'm not ladylike, and I can say more than boo to a goose. I . . . I'm so shocked, no, outraged is a better word, that I would have gone on pummelling her if they hadn't pulled me off.'

'You know something, miss?'

'No, Sam?'

'That's the best bit of cheery news I've heard in a long while, for I've been on that door, you know' – he thumbed towards the end of the hall – 'these ten years or more, and that woman hasn't bidden me good-morning once, not a word. You can open the door for her when she comes in, you can open the door for her when she goes out, the only sign of recognition that you're there at all is she turns her eyes on you. . . . Come on.' He chuckled as he took her arm. 'The car should be here any minute now.'

As he opened the door for her he looked at her and said,

'You know, you haven't been here all that long, but you've been the subject of more talk than anybody I know of. And this latest . . . why, wait till that reaches the shop floor. I bet some of the lads'll be after you, seeing that you've struck a blow against the white collar lot. It won't matter to them in what cause it was, just that you've done it. Here you are, lass. Here's your car. One last word. I pray to God that you'll be back some day along of Mr Henderson.'

'Thank you, Sam. Thank you very much.' She took his hand and shook it; then got into the taxi and was driven away. . . .

Hal was surprised to see her, and she was surprised to see his office. She had seen it from the outside, but had never been in it. There were two girls in the outer office, both young, under twenty, she would say. The place was well-furnished, well-carpeted, and the walls held sporting prints. It had the same overall well-kept feeling as his house.

When she asked one of the girls if she could see Mr Campbell, she was in turn asked what her business was.

And to this she said, 'Just tell Mr Campbell that Miss Brownlow would like to see him.'

Within a minute Hal was out of his office and taking her into his room. He wasn't all that surprised to see her, for apparently he had already heard the news of the Henderson accident. And yes, yes, of course, he said, she must go home to his place. And stay there as long as she liked. She knew she could, didn't she? She hadn't any need to ask. Give him five minutes and he'd take her there.

During the five minutes that turned into fifteen she listened to him phoning, making arrangements with clients. And lastly he spoke to a Mrs Taylor, saying it was difficult to get out to the house at the moment but if she came at ten o'clock the following morning they would discuss the situation.

Having put the phone down he looked at her and said, 'I advertised for a housekeeper; we just can't go on the way we are. It's all right at the weekends when you and I are there. But Rosie comes back from school and has to let herself in, and it's rather lonely out there, and I get a bit worried at times. Then there's the meal to get ready at nights. And so I thought it the best thing to do.'

The bus took them as far as the side road again, and from

there they had to plough their way to the house as she'd had to plough her way away from it just a few hours earlier.

Once inside, she again almost collapsed on to the settee. Solicitous as always, he took off her boots and brought an electric fire on to the rug to warm her feet; then he chafed her hands, after which he gave her a not too small glass of brandy.

It was when she had recovered herself somewhat that she told him in detail the happenings of the morning, and like Sam he gaped at her about the incidents with Miss Cadwell. But he didn't laugh as Sam had done, nor did he even seem amused. She couldn't quite make out his reaction, except, as she put it to herself, he seemed very surprised that she was capable of doing such a thing, for he said, 'Oh, Jinny. You actually hit her?'

'I told you. Yes, I hit her. Well, after what she said.'

'Well, you should have expected people to talk.'

'Why? Mr Henderson's in his fifties, he's a grandfather.'

'Don't be so naive about such things, Jinny. Men of that age go for young girls, they prefer them, as some young men prefer older women. It's nothing to be ashamed of.'

'But Mr Henderson was not like that. You've never met him or even heard him. He swore practically every third word. And he was so in love with his wife that, as his son said just this morning, it was somehow painful to witness.'

'Painful to witness?'

'Yes. He was trying to explain the intensity of the love between his mother and father. Well, I think it must have aroused a kind of jealousy in him; they must have been so taken up with each other. And she was a lovely woman, and a beautiful woman, really beautiful. I felt dowdy beside her, the way she dressed, the way she looked, the way she talked. And . . . and he was just the opposite. Well, it proved to me that opposites attract.'

'Yes, I suppose so. But knowing there was no truth in the rumour, why did you let it disturb you to the point of hitting the woman? There'll be trouble about it, I suppose.'

'Oh, I fully expect so. But just let her take any action and I'll have her up for slander.'

He sat back on his hunkers and slanted his eyes towards her as he said, 'This isn't the Jinny I know. 'Tisn't like you a bit.'

'Perhaps you don't know me at all, Hal. I'm unfortunate in having an exterior that, as Arthur says, looks like Wendy Craig, a bit up in the air. But I'm not like that inside. Oh, I know I made myself cheap sith the Players, acting dogsbody to everybody, because I suppose there is a part of me that wants to please and will put up with most things rather than that I should be alone. I'm still a bit like that, but beyond that there is another me, and somehow it's developed in the companionship of Mr Henderson; I've sort of come into my own being. . . . Oh I don't know how to express it. And anyway, I'm feeling too upset to talk about myself now; I just can't get over the tragedy. I'm devastated. You know, they were all so nice to me, it was like another family. I . . . I felt I had two families, yours and theirs.'

'Well, you've still got this family, and for as long as ever you want it. You know that, don't you, dear?' He was holding both her hands now. 'I . . . I love to have you here. And the others do too. . . . Now I'll have to get back. Will you be all right on your own?'

'Oh yes.'

'I'll give Michael a ring. If he's got free time, he'll likely come home.'

'Oh no! No, I'd rather be on my own. I've got to think. I'll have a lot of thinking to do because I shall have to get a new job. And it's just struck me that I'd need a reference, and I'd certainly not get it from Mr Waitland, or Mr Garbrook, not after this business. I'm going to be in a bit of a quandary.'

'Well, don't worry, something will turn up. With your experience you won't have much trouble. I know that. And there are other things to do besides office work. Be a courier, you could. You could be anything. Anyway, in the meantime take it easy and rest.'

'Thank you, Hal. You are so kind.'

'Who could help but be kind to you?' He bent and kissed her. 'You're a very special person, you know, Jinny. If only. . . . Oh' – he shook his head – 'I've got to go; we'll talk tonight. Bye-bye.' He smiled now and patted her cheek, then went out.

She sat where he had left her for almost an hour. She wanted to cry again, but found she couldn't. She had the impression that part of her life had been cut off, as if she had lost a limb. She felt she would never be the same again, she would never see the world again from the same viewpoint as she had done yesterday. The loss she was experiencing now far exceeded any in her life before: the loss of her parents, though not trivial, seemed a minor affair. She admitted without even a touch of guilt that her feelings for them must have been on a different plane, their loss having engendered only an apprenticeship to grief, because now she was really experiencing grief. But nowhere in her grief was she mourning for the loss of her job. No, it was for the loss of people, for Alicia Henderson and for Yvonne. She hadn't met Yvonne often but when she had they were, as Yvonne had once said, *sympathique*. Perhaps her understanding of the language had gone a long way towards this feeling; but not all the way because it was also as two young girls they had responded to each other.

And there was Glen. Glen of the sharp wits, the sharp tongue which, unlike that of his father, was not punctuated with swear words, and so in a way lost a little of its colour. It was odd how she had become used to swear words. Her parents had never sworn. Nor had she liked to hear people swearing. But Mr Robert Henderson was a special man . . . had been a very special man. What would he be now with a broken spine? Oh dear God. If only she could see him. Do something: hold his hand and say 'Broken spine or no broken spine – do you hear? – you're coming through, you're coming through.' For that's what he would have said to her had she been in a like situation. 'Bugger it!' he would have said. 'What's a broken back? You've still got your tongue, your eyes, your hearing.' And he would have counted all the faculties she had left.

Oh, Mr Henderson . . . Oh, Mr Henderson. . . . Oh, Bob Henderson. Oh, Bob Henderson. Get better. Please, please get better.

She was crying now and gasping for air. She stood up and began to walk around the room, her hands to her head, and all the while muttering like a nun saying her novena, 'Bob Henderson. Bob Henderson, get better. Do you hear?' until, stopping abruptly, she cried at herself, 'Give over. Stop it! You're becoming hysterical.'

Yes, she was, she was becoming hysterical. She would go to the kitchen. She would do something. Work. That was it. Use her hands. Bake. Make a meal for them coming in. Yes, yes. Anything. Anything to take her mind off this tragedy. . . . But her mind would never be off. . . . 'Go on, get yourself into the kitchen. No, no, don't sit down. No, go on into the kitchen.' She was talking aloud and she obeyed her last command and went into the kitchen.

The tears still raining down her face, she began to prepare a meal.

*

They were all very grateful for the meal, hot shepherd's pie with apple tart to follow; and they were all nice to her.

It was Michael who towards the middle of the evening looked at Hal and remarked, 'You said you were interviewing a woman for housekeeper tomorrow, didn't you?' And Hal said, 'Yes; yes, I did.'

'Well, why bother, at least for a time? Jinny's not, as she just said, going to fall into a job straightaway without a reference. She'll have to wait and see if Mr Henderson recovers. She could get one from the son, but she can't ask for anything like that yet awhile. And so, in the meantime, her remedy is to keep busy, isn't it?' He looked at Jinny; and after a moment she said, 'Yes, I suppose so.'

'Well, then. We've got a housekeeper.'

'Would you like that?' Hal was looking at her.

'Yes. Yes, I would, for a time, and be grateful for it.'

'And you wouldn't have to go out in the mornings.' Rosie grinned at her, and she smiled weakly back at her, saying, 'You're right there. That would be an advantage I'd have over all of you.'

'And if you give me the key I'll drop into your flat and see that it's all right. I've got to pass that way.'

She was sure Michael meant this as a kind offer; yet she would be reluctant to give him her key. But she said, 'Thank you. I'll be grateful.'

And she was grateful to all of them, for they all seemed to be pleased that she was staying; even Arthur. Yes, even Arthur.

And so she became a housekeeper.

It was Michael who drove her to the crematorium on the Thursday. In the chapel, a number of chairs had been left empty for the family, the rest were already full, and there was a crowd standing outside. She joined this, and later watched two hearses arrive, followed by a line of cars. She watched the families file into the chapel; she listened to the muted tones of the organ; she watched women here and there wiping their eyes; she watched men, their heads bowed deeply, stand in reverence; and she wondered why she alone among all these mourners wasn't feeling any emotion whatever. It was as if this wasn't the funeral, that Alicia and Yvonne weren't in boxes in there soon to be reduced to ashes; she wanted to say to someone, 'They can't be dead. That's not them in there.' You couldn't kill a woman with a lovely spirit like that, a woman whose life was made up of love, and such love that it joyfully enslaved people. You couldn't kill someone like that. She was bound to be somewhere.

Was there such a place as heaven? No. That was ridiculous. But spiritualists claimed to be in touch with people on the other side, and spiritual healers healed through doctors who had died and chose people whom they could work through, so she understood. And they did heal. They had a neighbour once who had been cured of something by a spiritual healer in the town. Perhaps, Alicia and Yvonne were with them. . . .

What was the matter with her? For days now she had at times felt that she was becoming odd, or sickening for something, for her mind would jump from one thing to another and present her with the most weird thoughts, as it was doing now.

She started somewhat when Michael came to her side, saying, 'Must you wait?' He had only a short while before refused to come into the crematorium, saying he couldn't stand funerals; he had made a joke about it, saying he hated standing up when the principals in the play were lying down. But here he was, and she caught hold of his arm, saying, 'Stay with me, will you, Michael? Stay with me.'

'Yes, of course. Of course.' He took her hand and pulled it through his arm, and held it close to his side. And his voice low, he said, 'You shouldn't have come. They are the most depressing things at the best of times. And there's no best of times about a funeral. To my mind they should be strictly private, just the family, no more. . . . You're shivering. Come on. Come on home.'

'No. No, Wait until they come out.'

'But why?'

'I . . . I just want to see them again . . . well, all together.'

Some time later she saw them; but not all together. They were dispersed among a large number of people, all offering condolences. The three girls passed close to her without seeing her. But John saw her, and cast a glance in her direction, but didn't speak.

She had been to the hospital twice this week to make enquiries. Each time she was told that there wasn't any improvement in either Mr Henderson or his son. And also that only the family were allowed to visit.

'Let's go,' she muttered, and as they turned away her mind said, 'It's over.' It was as if she had said goodbye to Mr Henderson, and to Glen too. She felt that a phase of her life had ended, and with it had gone forever the subservient self, the cultured handmaiden as Ray Collard had dubbed her, because never again would she meet people like the Hendersons; and the world as she viewed it now would be full of Mr Waitlands and Miss Cadwells.

She didn't ask herself at this moment in what category she placed Hal and his family, because deep down in her she knew there was something here she had to straighten out, for she had no intention of ever being any man's dogsbody or handmaiden. However she felt that with Hal she was on the border of it, and so the sooner there was some plain speaking the better.

3

After the fourth visit to the hospital she had the impression that someone in the family had left orders that she wasn't to be admitted to Mr Henderson's room.

'Nobody but the family are allowed in,' the nurse said. 'It's doctor's orders. They are both still in a very bad way. Young Mr Henderson hasn't come out of the coma yet, and they're to operate on him again.'

As the nurse continued to stare at her she wanted to ask, 'Did Mrs Brook leave orders that I wasn't to be admitted?' but she refrained, for whichever answer she got wouldn't make any difference, she wouldn't be allowed in.

After that visit she did not go back to the hospital again, but phoned the house. Generally it was Dorry who answered the phone, and the report was always, 'Very little change.'

Once, Florence's voice came over the wire, saying, 'Father and Glen are being sent to other hospitals. Glen is to have further treatment. That's as much as I can tell you, Miss Brownlow.'

She felt she was being dismissed, and she couldn't understand why, unless the gossip had reached the family and they thought there was something in it. Yet they knowing their parents, how could they imagine such a thing. But people also being what they were, they could. Oh yes, they could. . . .

After the third week acting as housekeeper she was finding life boring. She was alone most of the day. The only consolation was that she hadn't to go out into the atrocious weather because there seemed to be no end to it.

She had seen one advantage in taking on the post: she had imagined she would have more time with Hal and that they would come to some understanding. But Hal had taken not only to visiting his old people during three weekday evenings, but the last fortnight he had gone out on Sunday too. And on the second occasion they'd had what she could call their first quarrel, although the anger had been mostly on her side.

She had offered to accompany him, and to this he had said, 'It's bad enough one of us having to brave the weather.' But she had immediately come back at him, 'I've never been out for almost a week; I feel housebound. And I've had to brave worse storms than this to get to work.'

His response had been to turn and walk from her, and she had put out her hand and grabbed his arm, saying, 'Look, Hal. What am I supposed to be?'

'What do you mean?'

'You know what I mean. I think we should do some talking around that particular question, what I am supposed to be.'

At this his face had assumed the stiff mask which he adopted when anything didn't please him, and he said, 'Don't become intense, Jinny. It doesn't suit you. And remember, we are both free agents.'

As she had watched him walk away there had arisen in her such bewildering feelings of rage that she had wanted to yell at him, only restraining herself by recalling his words: 'We are both free agents.'

She supposed she was acting like a nagging wife. No, she wasn't, she came back at herself; she just wanted this thing talked out, that's all. There was something going on and she couldn't get to the bottom of it.

It was later in the day she decided that she must get out, if it was only for a walk down the lane.

She made her way through the kitchen into the utility room and was about to open the door that led into the garage where the wellingtons were kept when she heard Arthur's voice coming from behind the door, saying, 'I thought when he brought her here and let her stay he . . . he'd marry her. He's a twister, and I'm going to tell her.'

'You'll do no such thing. Let her find out for herself.'

'She'll never find out. She'll just go on and on being a cat's-paw. I didn't like her at first, but she's all right, and it's a bloody shame.'

'Now look here, Arthur, you keep your mouth shut, at least for the present. She's in need of company at the moment. She'll have to find out sooner or later that he has no intention of marrying her. He's got the best of both worlds, and he thinks it can go on. Being so crafty, you can't imagine him being such a fool.'

'You like her, why don't you tell her?'

'She wouldn't take it from me. She's got to find out for herself.'

'But how can she? I only spotted it by chance. Who would have thought about him going there? Daisy's Parlour: Hair Stylist.'

'You've been following him then?'

'Aye. Yes. The old people was a cover-up; they always have been.'

'Not entirely. He's always done that work. Apparently he and his mother. . . .'

'Oh, his mother.'

'Yes, you can say that again, Oh, his mother. But anyway, you promise me you won't let on.'

'But she'll go on thinking. . . .'

'She won't go on thinking. I tell you she won't. I can see a storm rising. She's asking questions herself all the time; in fact, she's been asking him questions. But naturally, he's evaded them. So it won't go on. But don't you do anything about it, because you've got to live here, at least for another year or two. And you were talking of going to university, weren't you? Well, you get on the wrong side of him and you'll be out on your neck. And you'll end up one end of a conveyor belt on a factory floor.'

'I won't though.'

'You will if you have to go out now and fend for yourself.'

'You've still got your flat, you haven't let it. I could go there.'

'Oh, no, you couldn't. I have other ideas for my flat, so get that out of your head. Now come on, and just think before you open your moth. Play him at his own game. Act as if everything was normal.'

'Normal? Did you say normal?'

Jinny sprang back from the door, ran quietly through the kitchen, across the hall and up the stairs into her room. Standing in the middle of it, her fists doubled against her lips, she bit on the flesh of her first finger. What could it mean, Daisy's Parlour, Hair Stylist?

Don't be stupid.

She had never heard of Daisy's Parlour. There were four hairdressers in the centre of the town, but none of that name. . . . Bog's End? Yes, there was likely such a hairdresser down there.

One thing at last was clear now. There was a woman in it somewhere. . . .

Why a woman?

No. She shook her head as she again answered the thought, No; I . . . I can't see him as a homosexual. He wouldn't have married twice in that case. Once, yes, but not twice. No, it's a woman. But what kind of a woman?

Wasn't she herself a woman?

Yes, but had he ever treated her as a woman? Had he ever become passionate? Had his hands ever attempted to stray? Had there been a look in his eyes that told her he wanted more than kisses? The answer was no.

Well, her sojourn here was going to end abruptly. She knew that. But before she went she would get the answer to why she held no appeal for him. Marriage apart, he hadn't even wanted to seduce her. At least Ray Collard's attentions had proved to her that she was female and desirable; he hadn't left her feeling as if she was a neuter. . . .

The weather on the Monday was really atrocious. The radio gave out that the whole North was cut off, with even twenty foot drifts in some parts. Earlier on Hal had phoned to say that both Rosie's and Arthur's schools were closed for the day. Both he and Michael had made their way out together hoping to get transport on the main road if the gritting machines had got this far.

She had ascertained in the phone book that there was a hairdresser trading under the name 'Daisy's Parlour', and that it was in Bog's End. Bog's End ran along by the waterfront. At one time there had been a thriving shipyard there, but it had been closed down these five years or more. Nobody who was of any account in Fellburn had lived in Bog's End. Now a small West Indian quarter had grown up, as also had a Pakistani quarter, and it was said that the lower white quarter caused more trouble than either of these two factions.

She was full of unrest all morning, and after giving Rosie and Arthur a light lunch, she dressed herself for the weather and, going to the sitting-room door, she said, 'I don't know what time I'll be back. Be good.'

They were both surprised and Rosie, who had been sitting on the rug reading, called, 'Where are you going?' And to this she replied, 'Into the town.'

But Arthur, leaving his spread of homework on the table, got up quickly, saying as he moved towards her, 'What are you going out for?'

She looked at him closely for a moment; then turned without speaking and went towards the front door. And when he followed her and asked again, anxiously now, 'What are you going out for, Jinny? You'll never get down the road,' she answered, 'I'll get down the road, Arthur. I'm . . . I'm going to have my hair done.'

She watched his mouth fall into a slight gape, and a feeling of tenderness coming over her, she put out her hand and touched his cheek, saying, 'Stick it out. Work at your A levels. It'll pay off in the end.'

She was half-way down the path when his voice came to her, calling, 'Jinny! Jinny!' And when she turned he called, 'Don't go. Please don't go.'

'I've got to, Arthur. You know I have, I've got to. As Michael said, I've got to find out for myself. But don't worry. Be a good lad.'

She thought the last admonition sounded faintly like one from Mr Henderson. If only things were as they had once been, she could walk out of here now and go straight to the Hendersons' house. And if that had been possible she might not have bothered to probe. But things would never be as they were. Her world was rocking, not only backwards and forwards, but from side to side. It was like being in one of those tubs at the fair-ground: they knocked you all over the place before they ran down a slope and dived into the water. Well she had been shaken about these last weeks. And she was on top of the slope now. In a very short time she would be in the water.

When she mounted the bus, she asked the driver, 'Do you go as far as Bog's End?'

'To the very end, miss,' he said.

'Anywhere near Chambers' Row?'

'Oh yes. We pass the end of it. You're in luck,' he said.

Twenty minutes later as she went to step off the bus he pointed across the road, saying, 'There it is, Chambers' Row. Sort of cul-de-sac. Couple of shops and a warehouse. Old part of the town. Oldest part of the town, that is. All right?'

'Yes, thank you.' She crossed the road and entered the narrow street. The first shop was a second-hand clothes shop; then followed two narrow houses, and these were separated from the hairdresser's shop by an alleyway.

She stood for a moment looking in the window. It wasn't at all prepossessing. In the front stood one or two cardboard adverts showing hair styles; then half-way up the window, in a recess, was a rod from which hung lace curtains. The shop, strangely enough, was single-storeyed. And next to it was what appeared to be two garages. These formed the end of the street, and running at right angles to them and down the other side were warehouses. There was no sign of a habitable house attached to the shop as far as she could see. But then she hadn't been up the alleyway.

Slowly now she turned and went up the alleyway. She passed a window through which she could just see into the hairdressing salon; then she saw the house. It was set back but attached to the end of the shop. It was in the style of a bungalow, and looked to have been recently pointed. The yard was open to the alleyway, and on each side of the gateway and along the wall facing the side of the house were flower-tubs. She looked at these. She felt she had seen them before. They were painted green, and although the tops were snow-covered she could see that they held plants of some form. They were the same as Hal had arranged as borders to the patio of his house. She felt the urge to knock on the door, but resisted. What would or could she say? Did she look like somebody selling things? She had only a small handbag with her.

She went back to the street. And now she stood staring at the price list hanging to the side of the window. The next minute she had pushed open the door and had entered the square room with a counter just large enough to hold a till. There were four wash-basins along one side of the room and four standing driers interspersed with chairs along the other side. At the far end of the room a passage led off somewhere.

There were two customers sitting in front of wash-basins: one was obviously in the middle stage of having a perm, the other was having her hair washed. The assistant attending to the perm looked towards Jinny; then kept her gaze on her for some seconds before leaving her customer and coming to the small desk, enquiring, 'Yes?'

'I . . . I haven't made a. . . . What I mean to say is, do you think I could have a trim?'

The girl looked her up and down; then looked towards her companion who made a small movement of her head, and the girl said, 'Well, I suppose so. But you should book, you know.'

The voice was thick with the north-country twang, and when Jinny said, 'I'm . . . I'm sorry, but . . . but I was just passing, and it's getting a bit long. I don't want much off.'

'Well, sit down there.' The girl pointed to a chair further along the room. It was opposite a basin with a mirror above it, and to the side was the window she had noticed from the alleyway.

She took off her hat and woolly scarf and sat down. And the girl looked at her through the mirror as she approached, saying, 'I might have to leave you in the middle of it, 'cos I've got a perm goin'. See?'

'That's all right.'

'What d'you want doin'?'

She wondered what would take the longest: the trim would be over in minutes and she would have no time to ask questions, and so she said, 'I don't mind if it's just a trim, but if you have time and could layer it a bit.'

'Well, if you've got a mind to have it done in bits.'

'I . . . I have plenty of time.'

As the girl started clipping she said, 'You've got nice hair. You're not from round here, are you?'

'No, I'm just passing through. Terrible weather.'

'Aye, it's awful.'

'I said I'm just passing through, but I've been in Fellburn before; yet I never knew there was a hairdresser here. Is it your establishment?'

'Mine? Oh no. It's Mrs Smith's. She's the owner.'

Jinny now turned her head and looked towards the other girl, and the indication wasn't lost on the assistant because she laughed as she said, 'Oh no, she's not Mrs Smith.'

A minute of so later, when the older assistant left her customer and came down the room and took a bottle from a shelf, the girl who was doing Jinny's hair left her for a moment and went towards the shelf as if she was going to pick up something, and the whispered words came to Jinny on a laugh: 'She wanted to know if you were Mrs Smith.'

'Oh aye?' There followed a joined laugh; then the words: 'They're on their way. I saw them comin' across the road. He's changed his time, hasn't he? Couldn't wait.'

They parted now, and as the girl began to snip again at Jinny's hair, the window to the side darkened and there, as plain as if she was looking at him in the sitting-room at the house, was

Hal, and to his side she caught the fleeting glimpse of a woman, a big woman. But an old woman.

She caught the assistant looking at her through the mirror and when she asked 'Did I hurt you?' she said, 'No. Only I've got a very tender sc . . . scalp.' And she stammered on the word scalp.

When a few minutes later the girl said, 'I won't be a tick' and left her to attend to her perm customer, Jinny looked to the side to where she could see the passage and a small board that stuck out from the wall and on which was plainly painted the word *Ladies*.

What was the meaning of it? If that was the woman he came to see it could be for no bad motive. How old would she be? She'd had only a fleeting glimpse of her, and the impression that she'd got was that she was big and fat. But that was likely the fur coat she was wearing. No, her face had been fat . . . and old. What did she mean by old? When you were in your teens everyone in their thirties appeared old, so what did she mean by old? Mrs Henderson had been forty-seven. Had she considered her old? No. No. Well, how old did she consider *that* woman was? In her late fifties? Oh, she didn't know. . . . But what was it? Why all the secrecy if he was only visiting an old woman? But this was no ordinary old woman; she had a business. And the way she had walked past the window hadn't indicated age. Nor had her laugh. Yes, she had laughed. And Hal had laughed.

When her hair was finished she'd go round and knock at the door. And what would she say? I've been spying on you. Could she say that? But there must be something to find out, or else Michael wouldn't have gone for Arthur like he did yesterday.

First of all she must go to the lavatory; her stomach was turning over so much she felt she could be sick.

When she paid her bill and tipped the girl well, she said, 'There's a toilet there?'

'Yes. Just where it says.' The girl pointed.

And on this Jinny went down the short corridor. But she paused outside the lavatory door, for there, at the end of the corridor, was another notice across the top of the door, and this said: *Private*.

She was shaking from head to foot as she stood in the lavatory, telling herself that if she went and knocked on the door he would have time to come up with some excuse, but if she barged in. . . . But dare she? Yes, she dared, because wasn't he supposed to be in Durham today? That's what he had told her before he left. But again, she must also remind herself that he'd said they were free agents.

Free agents be damned! He had used her. For months now he had used her. And he had pretended to be in love with her. Even though his love-making left a lot to be desired, he had pretended to be in love with her, and told her countless times how he needed her and how he loved to come back to the house, knowing that she'd be there. And at first she had loved him all the more for what she had imagined to be his consideration.

Quietly she returned to the corridor. The two girls were busy with their customers. It took three steps for her to reach the door marked *Private* and to open it. And then she was through and standing in a kitchen.

It was surprisingly modern, with all the latest gadgets. She put out a hand and supported herself against the formica topped table and drew in two long shuddering breaths before she quietly opened the further door and found herself standing in a small hall, from which the front door and three other doors led off. The door to her right was half open and showed what she took to be a sitting-room. There was no sound coming from there. But from the far door she heard the murmur of voices and the distinctive sound of a giggle. This was followed by a laugh. It was Hal's laugh. Sometimes for no reason whatsoever, he would laugh like that, when he was in the kitchen baking or when he was sitting on the couch, one arm around Rosie, the other around her. Perhaps they would be looking at the television, when he would suddenly laugh, and there would have been nothing on the screen to have evoked laughter; and she would look at him and smile, and he would squeeze her tightly to him.

Slowly she moved towards the far door. Before opening it she knew it would be a bedroom, and she knew in a way what she would witness. Yet when, with a sudden jerk, she pushed the door open she stood, her eyes stretched wide, her mouth agape and her whole body stiff, and the two figures on the bed looking back at her with similar expressions.

She saw that the woman who looked like a mountain of wobbling flesh had bright metallic red hair, her breasts and stomach were enormous, and her thighs like those she had seen bursting out of bloomers on coarse seaside postcards; her whole body seemed to spread over the bed. And there was Hal, the gentle, thoughtful, charming Hal, naked as the day he was born.

She saw his mouth frame her name. She saw him reach to the foot of the bed and grab at a bedcover lying there; she saw the great mountain of flesh sit up and yell in a voice as coarse as her body, 'What the hell you doin' here?' before the rage in her burst.

To the side of her was a dressing-table, and the first thing her hand caught up was an open box of talcum powder. She threw it, and as it spread over both of them they choked and jumped from the bed. The next thing she gripped was a scent spray. When she saw it make contact with the top of his head she wanted to shout. She watched him, one hand held against his bleeding brow, endeavouring to restrain the woman from advancing towards her, her flesh billowing like waves, as she yelled, 'Who is she? The bugger's mad.'

'Get out, Jinny! Get out. Stop it, for God's sake!'

But she couldn't stop it, she wanted more things to throw, and there was nothing left on the dressing-table. Suddenly, however, she was caught by the arms and turned about and dragged sideways, one of the assistants pulling, the other pushing her back into the shop and towards the door. And there it was the elder one who gasped, 'Are you his wife then?'

She stared back at the girl but couldn't speak. And then as if he had dropped out of the heavens there was Michael running down the street towards her.

The shop assistant kept hold of her arms until he came up to them, and when he said, 'Come on. Come on, Jinny,' she said to him, 'Who is she anyway? She's gone berserk.'

'And not before time,' he answered. Then he led Jinny along the street to where a taxi was standing. She hadn't spoken, nor did she wonder how he had come to be there at that precise moment. But she sat in the back of the cab staring in front of her.

When the taxi stopped outside her flat Michael paid the driver; then taking her handbag, which luckily was still in the crook of her arm, he took out the key. And they went down the area steps.

Once in the flat, Jinny sat down. She did not take off her things, but she watched him light the gas fire; she heard him put the kettle on and do all the things that are supposed to bring one comfort, such as make tea. And when eventually he handed her the cup, and she didn't raise her hand to take it, he said, 'Come on. Come on. Snap out of it! It isn't the end of the world. Remember, I tried to tell you ages ago, but you wouldn't listen. And it isn't his fault; he just likes older women. That's why his two marriages went astray. He should have married his mother. She was the trouble. Some men should never leave the breast. It isn't their fault; it's the women, the mothers. Don't blame him too much. But it's a pity he had to pick such types. He's in conflict all the time: he wants youth, he wants a family, but he can't help himself the other way. Come on now. Drink this tea.'

She had to force her hand to take the cup from him. It was as if she was dragging her limbs up out of a bottomless sea of misery. Her body had certainly hit the water. But having done so, it had sunk and, just as in a nightmare, she seemed to be swimming for her life, but in a well. Water wa supposed to be cleansing, but she told herself she would never feel clean again in her lifetime. Worse still, she was back to where she had been, lonely, ineffectual.

As if Michael was reading her thoughts, he said, 'You're looking upon this as the end of the world, seeing yourself all messed up as if you were to blame. You feel you're dirty and you'll never scrape it off, for the simple reason that you've let him near you, touch you. You wouldn't be feeling so bad if he had wanted more. But no, he didn't. He used you as he used my mother, and Arthur's and Rosie's. It was my mother who told me about his peccadilloes. He did try with her though, because she wasn't all that young. But she was still not old enough to be a cuddly mother.'

'Shut up!'

She hadn't intended to speak; she had wanted to remain in the well, walled in by silence; but if you had hearing there was no such thing as silence.

But he came back at her now, saying, 'You're sorry for yourself. How do you think I felt when my mother walked out? At that time when I was eighteen I couldn't really see why it mattered. Let him have his entertainment on the side, I thought. But then I wasn't a woman. But Arthur's and Rosie's mother had it worse; she was going to divorce him on the conjugal rights bit.'

'Michael.'

'Yes, Jinny?'

'Will you stop talking about it, please?'

'If you say so, but it's much better to get it off your chest. Do you want to see him?'

'No! Never again!' She was on her feet now. 'And he won't want to see me. I've split his head open; at least I hope I have.'

'Jinny! *You what?*' He looked amazed.

'The scent bottle caught him on the brow. I hope it went deep.'

'You threw things?'

'Yes, I threw things. Everything that was on the dressing-table: talcum powder, the lot; I smothered them.'

She now began to walk up and down the room, and he shook his head as he watched her; then said slowly, 'You know, Jinny, you're a bit of an enigma. This is the second attack in the matter of weeks. No one would believe it.'

She stopped and, putting her arms around her waist, she hugged herself as she thought, He's naming my retaliation as attacks, and a voice inside her head almost in a whimper now said, I . . . I wouldn't attack anybody. But you did. There was Miss Cadwell; and now today. But she came back at the whimper, crying, It was justified. In both cases it was justified.

Of a sudden she felt weak and faint. She sat down on the couch again, and now she looked up at him and said quietly, 'Would you bring my things, Michael? I've packed my case.'

'You intended to leave then before you went there?'

'Yes. Yes, I did. I . . . I heard you and Arthur talking yesterday.'

'Oh, I had guessed that already from what Arthur told me. He phoned me just after you left. That's why I was on hand. He's a good kid, Arthur, underneath; and he's very fond of you, you know. He'll miss you. So will Rosie. And so shall I. . . . Do you want your things tonight?'

'Would it be too much to ask to get them now?'

'No, no. I've nothing else to do. It's a good job I'm in charge of my own little department. If I can get a bus along there now, I should be back around teatime. Will you be all right?'

'Yes, I'll be all right. And . . . Michael. Thank you. Thank you for being so kind.'

'That's what I want to be; I had hoped to be kind to you all this time. But what did I achieve? Nothing, except make you hate my guts at times.'

She didn't smile at him, for what he had said was true.

It was almost eight o'clock when he returned. When she opened the door to him and he dropped her case at her feet she thought that he too was about to fall beside it, and she put out her arms to steady him, saying, 'You shouldn't have come tonight. Not . . . not so late. I . . . I could have waited.'

He was gasping as he replied, 'It was the last part of the journey. The bus got no further than the market square. I'd had a taxi, but he dropped me with my things off at my flat, and I thought the bus would make it along here, but it didn't.'

Looking at her large case, she said, 'How on earth did you manage your things, too, down the road?'

Arthur helped me. 'Have you got a drink? Anything stronger than coffee?'

'No, I'm sorry.'

'A black coffee'll do then.' He sank into a chair before the fire and, closing his eyes, said, 'What a night! Storm outside and storm in.' He turned his head towards the kitchen now, saying, 'We nearly came to blows. He blames me for the exposure. And by jingo! You must have thrown that scent bottle with some force. You know, he's had to have his brow stitched. He said his lady friend, or his mother friend, whatever you like to call her, was for putting the police on to you. I said he should have let her; it would have made a good story for the *News Of The World*. You know, this afternoon I was defending him to you; but that was this afternoon. His whining explanation sickened me. I couldn't believe he would find so many ways of excusing his actions. He wanted to put it over as simply a by-product, that his real life was at home with us all.'

He paused for a while; and then he said, 'Jinny!'

And after a moment when she appeared at the sitting-room door, he turned his head towards her, saying, 'He was emphatic that he'd explained everything to you right from the beginning of the whole situation.'

'*What!*' Her head was poked forward as she came towards him. 'He said what?'

'He said the first time he came here' – he now thumbed towards the floor – 'he was sorry for you over the broken affair you'd had with one of the Players. He said he explained things to you that night.'

'Oh, the liar! Do you for a moment think that I would have gone to that house, that I would have . . .? Oh!' She thrust her head back on her shoulders and rocked it from side to side. Then looking at him again, she said, 'The only thing he told me that night was that he missed his mother and how he loved young people about him, loved the family, and that you were his family. You didn't believe him, did you?'

'No, I didn't, and I told him so, and in no polite language either. Anyway, that's the end. And—' He looked at her, then he finished, 'The beginning I hope.'

She turned quickly away from him now, and went back into the kitchen where she made the coffee. And when she brought it into the room and handed him the cup, he said, 'Thanks, Jinny;' then tapping the sofa, he said, 'Come and sit down here. Not over there, come and sit here.'

She sat on the couch, but not close to him, and for the space of a full minute there was silence between them. Then, his voice low, he said, 'You know how I feel about you, Jinny, have done from the very first I may tell you now, but we sparked off each other like a match against brimstone. On my part, it was because I was so mad at you for I thought you were being purposely blind. Then I realized you were too nice to think anything bad of him. . . . Well, anyway, now we are both adrift, and. . . .'

'Michael, please don't.'

'All right. I won't go any further tonight. Only I'll say this, we could make a go of it, we two, and I can assure you you would be fulfilled because . . . because I'm in love with you.'

Oh my God! You would be fulfilled. Why didn't he say, Come and kip in with me. And there wasn't any doubt but that she would be fulfilled.

'I'm sorry, Jinny; I shouldn't have started it. I'll go now.' He drained his coffee cup; then getting to his feet, he put on his coat without speaking further. But now, bending, he took her hands and pulled her up from the couch and, looking into her face, he said, 'I can make you happy, Jinny. I can. I know I can.'

'Are you asking me to be your girl-friend, Michael?'

She watched his teeth drag at his lower lip for a moment; then his right shoulder moving upwards in the characteristic gesture, he said, 'Putting it boldly like that, yes, I suppose that's what I'm saying. But I'm also saying that I love you, and I can make you happy. And I can make you love me. You don't dislike me, do you?'

'No, I don't dislike you, Michael.'

'Then that's a start. Liking's always a good start.'

She wanted to say, 'You've found that this has proved a good basis on other occasions?' But no; all she wanted now was to get him out of the flat, and never to set eyes on him again; or, for that matter, anyone connected with Hal Campbell.

'Good-night, Jinny. I'll look in tomorrow dinner time. All right?'

'All right.'

As he leant forward to kiss her she drew back, and he smiled wryly as he said, 'That was a silly move; I'll improve. Make haste slowly, as the saying goes. Good-night, dear.'

'Good-night, Michael.'

After closing the door on him she stood with her back to it, her hand covering her eyes, and she whispered to herself, 'Goodbye, Michael.'

She now walked over to the fire, her mind racing. She had to get away from here. She'd go to the agent tomorrow morning and see if he would sublet the flat on a monthly basis, for there was over a year of the lease still to run. But would she be able to get another flat? It would have to be a furnished one, and they charged the earth. She had £250 in the bank; but that wouldn't last her very long these days. She'd have to get a job. But in the meantime where could she stay?

Her cousin Nell? Oh, she had always said she'd be the last person she'd go to. But there was nobody else she could think of. Anyway, it would only be for a few days, until she knew what she was going to do. Perhaps she could get work in Shields on Peter's recommendation. And then she wouldn't need a reference. Well, she could only ask them. It was her last resort. There was a phone in the hall upstairs; she would do it now. . . .

When she heard Nell's voice on the phone, she said, 'It's me, Nell, Jinny.'

'Who?'

'Jinny. Jinny Brownlow.'

'Jinny? . . . Oh, Jinny. Well, fancy hearing from you. Where are you?'

'I am still in Fellburn.'

'Are you all right?'

'Yes, and . . . and no. I was wondering if I could impose upon you for a few days.'

This request was greeted by silence; then Nell's voice, the tone of which had changed now, said, 'Are you in trouble, Jinny?'

'No, Nell; not the kind of trouble that you mean.'

'Oh.' The voice was much lighter now.

'I will explain if I could come just for a couple of days.'

'Well, you're welcome. We've never seen you for ages, but again I say you're welcome. When are you coming?'

'Tomorrow. Tomorrow morning.'

'All right, lass; yes. Will you be able to get through the snow?'

'Yes, I'll manage. And thank you, thank you very much, Nell. . . . How is Peter?'

'Oh, still being Peter, still bullying poor thieves in the court. You know Peter.'

Jinny smiled and nodded towards the phone as much as to say, 'Yes, I know Peter.' Her poor father used to call him The Lord Chancellor. He was a small dark man who appeared quiet, until he got into court; and there, her father used to say, he was a holy terror and one of these days he'd make a mistake and find the judge guilty.

She thanked Nell again, said goodbye, and put down the phone. Then going back to the flat, she packed another suitcase, wrapped up a few good ornaments and the silver that she had collected, and placed them in another case and some cardboard boxes, and labelled them ready for storage.

It was close on midnight when she finished the packing. Then she went to bed. But it was some time before she fell asleep. And her last conscious thought was, Wouldn't it after all be easier to go along with Michael's offer, because he was a nice enough fellow, and sooner or later, nature being what it was, she would find herself succumbing to its demands, because marriage had gone out of fashion and shacking up was in. . . .

When the alarm went, she couldn't believe she had been asleep. It was half-past six, and the bed was warm, and she had no desire to get up; she felt heavy and miserable, and whereas last night she'd felt too angry to cry, now she felt she wanted to howl.

As she stepped out of bed and into the ice-cold room, she asked herself, Why not just stay put and fight Michael off? Then there returned to her the thoughts that had drifted with her into sleep, and these seemed to add a spur to her movements.

Getting into her dressing-gown, she hurried into the sitting-room, lit the fire, then filled the kettle and while she waited for it to boil she went through the cupboards, sorting out the crockery. Her mother's best dinner service and tea service, together with some good glass, she put away in a cupboard that had a lock on it.

By half-past eight she was all ready to go. When she phoned for a taxi and asked if it could be there by nine o'clock, they said they would do their best. It didn't arrive until a quarter to ten. But then the taxi driver was very helpfuil. He carried up the labelled boxes; then ran her to a Pickford's depository where she left them in store. When they returned to the flat she looked down on her three cases. She wondered how she was going to manage them on the train, and she realized she wouldn't be able to on her own for the large one was as much as a man could lift. The taxi driver was proving it as he went out of the door. And she halted him for a moment, saying; 'I know I said I wanted to go to the station, but do you think it would be possible for you to run me right into Shields?'

'I don't see why not, miss,' he said. 'Which part?'

'The top of Sunderland Road, The Heath.'

'Oh, I know Shields well. I used to deliver papers round that quarter when I was a nipper. The only thing that will stop us getting there is the road.' He laughed now; then added, 'But it's a good one; straight through. An' the gritters will have been busy. . . . Nothing easier.'

Before closing the flat door she looked back into the room. She had never been happy here, and she would never live here again. Once the lease was up she'd collect her furniture, if not before, because she might be lucky and get a flat in Shields. Which reminded her: she would get the taxi driver to stop at the agent's so she could make arrangements with regard to the business of subletting.

As she reached the top of the area steps the sun suddenly burst through the clouds, and the taxi driver, gazing skywards, exclaimed, 'Well! just look at that. Happy days are here again.'

As he took his seat behind the wheel he leant his head back and said, 'I think you can put up with most things if the sun's shinin'; puts a sort of different complexion on life. Don't you think, miss?'

'Yes; yes,' she answered; 'I suppose that's one way of looking at it,' while thinking it would take more than the sun to put a different complexion on her life. And as the taxi stopped and started its way through Fellburn, she thought, Not only will I never go back to the flat, but I'll never come back to this place. Nothing good has ever happened to me here.

Her father had died here; her mother had died; her first real romance had died; then Alicia Henderson and Yvonne Henderson had died; and Mr Henderson could be dead now for all she knew, and his son with him; and lastly all the romantic feeling she had garnered and stored over the years with regard to love and men had certainly died yesterday. No; never again would she come back here; this part of her life was finished. In fact, when she got herself straight she would leave the North altogether; there was bound to be better places in which to live. There could hardly be any place worse, what with the fact that you daren't go out into the streets by yourself at night, and the old people being murdered by youngsters, and these hooligans rampaging through the city. And this didn't take into account the strikes and the moonlighters and the work dodgers. Then there were so many bitches among women, such as Miss Cadwell, and Mr Waitland's secretary, and some of the girls in the pool; not counting those middle-aged women in the Players who were fighting off age with their claws out.

Why hadn't she noticed all this before? One thing was certain: there wasn't one person in the world for whom she had a kind word at this moment. And certainly not the taxi driver, who, again putting his head back in his shoulders, regaled her with; 'I hope it clears up afore next Saturday, me daughter's getting married. The eldest of six. One off and five to go. It's gona be a church do, an' I said to her this mornin' afore I came out, "You pray to God that He doesn't bring the parson out on strike, else that'll put the kibosh on it."'

A church do. Likely the only time the girl would have been in church since she was christened; and more likely she was five months pregnant. . . .

Oh my God! How she wished she could stop thinking like this. And oh no, she mustn't cry, she mustn't, not in front of this man.

There was silence in the taxi for a few minutes, and then the driver who had been watching her through the mirror said, 'You all right, miss?' And when she didn't answer but put her hand to her throat, he said, 'Anything I've said upset you? I . . . I keep chattering like this, you see. Betty used to say that I was like a gramophone, I kept on an' on. But I'm apt to do it when I'm worried. You see, miss, as I said, me daughter's gettin' married, but' – he paused – 'but her mother's in hospital and . . . and I don't think she'll come out again. Talking, chattering, yammering seems to be the only way to keep me mind off it.'

She blinked her eyes, swallowed deeply, and said, 'Oh, I'm sorry; very sorry. And no, no, it's nothing you've said. And please go on telling me about your wife and your daughter. Please.'

But after this the man didn't have much to say, his talking becoming at best spasmodic, and when he finally carried her luggage into the hall of the tall terraced house, she thanked him warmly and hoped that his wife would get well. But once the door was closed she immediately fell into her cousin's outheld arms and cried unashamedly. And after some moments when Nell Dudley said, 'Come and sit down, lass, and tell me what it is. What's happened?' all she could say was, 'A nice man, the taxi driver. His daughter's going to be married on Saturday, and his wife is dying of cancer in hospital.'

4

For almost six weeks now she had been living with Nell and
Peter Dudley. She knew that they were pleased to have her, and
she was equally pleased to be with them, except for one thing,
one snag: they seemed determined to get her married off. They
had the man. He was Peter's partner, name of George Mayborough, and he had a very nice house, almost twice as big as
this one, and this one was no small terraced house, but had ten
rooms if you included the attics, and a forty foot long back
garden that sported a fountain. But George Mayborough's house
was near Sunderland, in an acre of land, and with a view of the
sea. His wife had been dead for two years, but he was prepared
to let someone take her place, so long as, or so it seemed, this
person was prepared to live with the furniture his late wife had
chosen and arranged, and with the décor.

Jinny was cynically amused by George Mayborough. Twice
she had been to dinner at his home, and on the second occasion
he had given her a personally conducted tour around every
room, with a running commentary on when he'd had that particular wardrobe put in, and when he'd had the en-suite attached
to the second guest room. Moreover, he gave her the price of
everything that he had bought for years past, all the time
comparing his distant purchases with what they would cost
today.

George Mayborough was forty-three years old. He was tall
and stolidly built, and the stolidness had penetrated his character:
he was referred to by Peter Dudley as, 'Good old George, a
most reliable type, none better. They don't make them like that
today. The kind of man you'd be lucky to have in a tight corner.
And a man most women would give their eye-teeth to call
husband.'

Her relationship with both Nell and Peter Dudley was such
that now she could laugh at their friend George, and as a re-

joinder to the last recommendation she had said, 'Peter, I want my eye-teeth,' causing Nell, in her hearty way, to slap her on the back and say 'That's what I mean. I said to Peter last night you'd be good for him; you've always got an answer. He's everything that Peter says he is, but he wants stirring up.'

'Oh Nell,' Jinny had said; 'do you want rid of me so much?' And Nell had come back at her, not in a jocular way, but in a serious voice: 'We want you to be happy, lass, to see you settled, after what you've told us you've gone through.'

Jinny had indeed been able to tell them from the start all that had happened to her since her mother had died, leading right up to the reason why she was staying with them now. And Nell had voiced Jinny's own thoughts when she said, 'Life being what it is there'll come a time when you mightn't have any strength left to hold out against the licensed rapers.' And then she had laughed at herself, ending, 'That's a good description of them isn't it? Licensed rapers. I'll take a copyright out on it.'

More and more, Jinny was finding that Nell was nice; she was a comfort. And she was made to wonder why she hadn't taken up their acquaintance before now. But then she recalled what her mother had thought, that Nell was just a wee bit common, and very lucky to have married a solicitor; while Nell herself had confessed she had not only stood in awe of her mother but was more than a little jealous because she had a daughter, whereas she herself was unable to have children.

Apart from being very comfortably housed, well fed, and enjoying the good company of Nell during the day, Jinny was becoming a little bored, and was looking forward to the week after next when she would enter Peter's firm as secretary to the third partner. The present girl was emigrating to Australia with her family and, as Peter said, she couldn't have been doing it at a better time. It all fitted in.

But on this Friday evening in early April, the romance that was being manoeuvred by Nell and Peter Dudley with the sole purpose of Jinny's welfare at heart was not only nipped in the bud but the whole branch wrenched from the tree. And this incident was followed the very next morning by a letter that was to alter the course of Jinny's life, yet again, for good or ill, whichever way you looked at it.

Being Friday night, Peter went as usual to his bridge club, and Nell, which had at first surprised her, had three friends in to make up a foursome at home. Jinny didn't like bridge.

Canasta yes; chess, yes; but not bridge. So, during past Friday evenings, she had looked on, made the coffee, and whenever the rubbers finished early, she had, as Nell put it, knocked out a few tunes on the piano for them, making a nice finish to the evening. Tonight Nell was a little taken aback when Peter returned before her friends had left. Most Friday evenings he didn't get back till elevenish, and here he was just turned ten. She knew immediately that something had displeased him, and the door had hardly closed on her friends before she heard what it was: 'George,' he said.

'What's wrong with George?'

'Everything to my mind at this minute.' He now looked towards Jinny and added, 'You were right not to lay much stock on him. I wouldn't have believed it.'

'Believe what? Come clean,' said Nell. 'State your case' – she laughed – 'present your witness.' And glancing at Jinny, she ended, 'And I can assure you, milord, that anything old George has done won't be enough to send him down.'

'I don't know so much.'

The expression on Nell's face changed; her humorous approach disappeared as she said, 'That so?'

'Yes.'

'What's he done?'

'Made us look damn fools, that's what he's done. And led her up the garden path.'

'Oh no!' – Jinny was looking towards Peter, and shaking her head – 'no, whatever he's done, Peter, it isn't concerned with leading me up the garden path. He's never done that. As Nell might say' – she glanced towards Nell – 'he never got any further than the gate.'

'Out with it. What's happened? I've never seen you like this, not concerning George, anyway.'

'It just shows you; you never know anybody. In this business you think you've learned to know human nature inside out. You've come up through a school that deals with nothing else but emotions, emotions expressed on the face: the tightening of the jaw muscles; the flicker of the eyelid; how a man's mouth is set; what a woman does with her hands when she's talking. It's all there in the book. And I thought I could read George Mayborough from the title page to the end. But there's one thing I forgot. . . . Yes, there was one thing I forgot, there's always a cover to a book: paper or hard back, there's a cover

142

and by God, his is a hard back. Do you know what he told me tonight?'

'No; I'm waiting patiently. And stop smoking; that's the fourth one you've lit since you came in. Your pension won't be all that big.'

'Well—' Peter stubbed out his cigarette. Then looking towards Jinny, he said, 'He got me to the side and started talking about Lola, his late wife, you know, and how he missed her. And I said, of course, yes he would. I went along with him all the way. Even when he prattled about the wonderful woman she was. . . .'

'She was no wonderful woman, she was a bitch.'

'I know that, you know that, and he knows that, and because of that I thought he would be out to marry some one different.' He cast his glance towards Jinny. 'But he turned the tables, saying that he didn't think he could ever put any woman in her place, Lola's place. Eeh! when you think of it. So he had vowed he would never marry again. But—' and now he wagged his finger at his wife as he went on, 'wait for it. He decided instead to take a girl friend. Aha! Our George, our placid, God-fearing, church-on-Sunday George decided to take a girl friend. He's got her ensconced in a house in Sunderland, conveniently near yet not too near. He even described her. She's in her twenties. Like Jinny here.' He nodded at Jinny now, saying, 'Like you.'

'The dirty old bugger.'

It was too much. The sound of the exclamation, so much like Mr Henderson, and the outraged look on Nell's face caused Jinny to turn her head into the corner of the couch and laugh until the tears rolled down her face. Strangely, she was finding she could laugh these days, and she'd put it down to Nell's lively company.

Almost immediately Nell's laughter joined hers, but not Peter's. He, going to the sideboard, poured himself out a stiff whisky and, throwing it off almost at one gulp, he turned on them, saying now, 'It's all right, you can laugh, but he's been our lifelong friend and I've got to work with him. He's made a fool of us; he must have known what we were after. Of course he did, else he wouldn't have spilled the beans tonight. But why didn't he spill them before? Well, that's me and him finished.'

'Oh, Peter.' Jinny wiped her eyes. 'Don't blame him, because it would never have come off, not . . . not on my part. I couldn't imagine living day in day out with a man like Ge . . . orge.' She drew the name out. 'I should have become fossilized, or gone mad looking at Lola's décor. And I knew he had no intention of changing it because it had cost. . . . What had it cost?' She glanced laughingly towards Nell, but she was looking away from both of them, her head bobbing slightly and she exclaimed, 'Sunderland! I'll find out who it is, and when I do I'll play him up. I'll frighten the wits out of dear George, the nasty old swine.'

Jinny bit on her lip as she thought as a man might think, for her mind said one word, 'Women!' The kind, loving Nell would in her own way blackmail George for not falling in with her plans. . . .

Half an hour later, as she lay in bed staring into the darkness, she repeated Peter's words: 'She's in her twenties, like you.' Had that girl succumbed suddenly, or had she started earlier, perhaps before she left school? She turned restlessly. Was she a fool?

The letter came with the eight o'clock post. It was from the agents in Fellburn. Inside was a single sheet of paper and another envelope, stamped and addressed to the flat. She read the single sheet first and was half-way through it when she exclaimed, 'Oh no! No!'

'What is it?' Nell turned from handing the dirty breakfast dishes to Mrs Bailey her daily help, adding, 'Something wrong?'

'I'll say. I . . . I can't believe it. Peter.' She handed the letter to Peter, but looking at Nell, she said, 'They've cleared the flat, everything. The agent says that couple must have done it shortly after they went in. They hadn't paid the second month's rent in advance, and when for the second time he had gone there and found the curtains still drawn, he forced the back door open. And' – she pointed to the letter – 'he says the place is utterly stripped. They only left the curtains. They even took. . . . They've broken into the cupboard where the china was too. Everything.'

'Dear God! What will they do next? And your mother had some nice pieces.'

Peter looked up from the letter and in a businesslike way he said, 'Well, it's happening all the time. I've got a case on now. The people came back from their holidays and found even the chandeliers and the wall lights gone. Are you insured?'

'Well, I have a small insurance that I've kept up on the furniture. It's a continuation of what Mother used to pay. She took it out mostly to cover the bureau. It's got Verni Martin paintings on it. And there's a matching cabinet. They're the only antiques. But there was so much.' She shook her head. 'I simply can't believe it.'

'Oh, there are frightful people about.' Nell nodded at her. 'Some of them would take your eyes out and come back for the sockets. I once left a sweeping brush outside the back door. I couldn't have been gone for a couple of minutes, but me broom was gone. And there wasn't a soul to be seen.'

'Leave it to me. I'll contact the agents and the insurance company. Did you keep an inventory of your furniture?'

'No.' She shook her head. 'But I could name practically everything that was in the flat.' She now turned her attention to the envelope that had accompanied the letter, and the gasp she gave as she read it could be described as one of delight and, turning to Nell and Peter, she waved the letter at them, saying, 'It's . . . it's from Mr Henderson, the son John. He's got his father home, and he, Mr Henderson senior, he wants to see me . . . He's asked to see me. So . . . so he mustn't be too bad. Oh my!' She was looking at the letter again. 'It must have been lying there for nearly a fortnight, it was written last month. Oh, I'll have to go.' She was looking from one to the other. 'It will be wonderful to see him again . . . alive. I never thought I would.'

'How old is he?'

'Who?'

'Mr Henderson, the one that was your boss.'

'Oh, in his fifties.'

'And the son?'

Jinny just prevented herself from biting on her lip and lowered her head as she made herself answer flatly, 'In his twenties—' adding, 'He lives away from home in a flat and has a girl friend.' And on this she turned from them, saying, 'I'll look up the times of trains.'

'You needn't bother about trains, we'll take you up.'

'Oh, I can't put you to that. . . .'

'Don't be silly!' Nell waved her hand. 'I feel like a run out. It's April anyway, and spring's in me blood. And I'd like to see how the other half live, the top half, in this grand house you've described.'

'You'll be disappointed,' she said; 'they don't live as well as you do. And I'm warning you' – she looked at Peter – 'you'll likely be shocked at his language.'

Peter Dudley didn't swear. The nearest to a swear word she had heard him use was damn, and then he apologized. But he didn't seem to object to his wife using colourful language, and it was Nell who now said, 'Sounds someone after me own heart. Well, let's get ready. It could be an interesting day.'

As Jinny ran up the stairs she called back, 'And the happiest day I've known in a long time, for he must be better if he's asked to see me.'

PART THREE

1

'Woman! If you straighten that quilt just once more I swear I'll get onto me legs and kick your backside out of that door.'

'Now, now, Mr Henderson.'

'And don't now, now, me, miss. I'm not a bairn at the breast.'

'Really! In all my. . . .'

'Yes, I know. In all your long service you've never come across anybody like me. So you should think yourself privileged, damned lucky I'd say.'

The nurse drew in a deep breath, and so expanded her already full bust still further as she looked down upon her charge, her prostrate charge, with an expression that was utterly devoid of any sympathetic feeling. And she told herself she couldn't stand much more of this man, this thankless, rude, ignorant type who had such a high opinion of himself that he could not be made to understand that he was not the only one in the world who had had an accident which had left him almost powerless. And not for the first time during the past fortnight she had been looking after him did she wish that his paralysis had affected his speech also. She was being paid good money, but all the money in the world couldn't make up for this type of abuse. She would speak to Dr Turner about him when next he came.

She was about to leave the room when the door was opened and Florence entered, and the look on the face of the nurse told Florence that her father was at it again, as she called it.

Approaching the bed, she smiled down at her father, saying lightly, 'And how are we this morning?'

'We are not feelin' very well this mornin', Florence. And we are not in the mood to take kindly to bein' turned over, powdered, and having our backside smacked. And while we are on it, I haven't reached royal rank yet and so we'll drop the "we" and return to "Father", shall we?'

As the nurse had done, so Florence drew in a long breath, then let it out slowly as she said, 'She's only trying to do her best for you; she's carrying out her duty.'

'Aye; she might be, but she's a stranger to me and I have three married daughters, women who know all there is to know about a man's body, and I would have thought they could have arranged it atween them to take a turn to see to me now and again. I don't expect it of Lucy, she's still a lass.'

'Father . . . we've been through all this. I have three children to see to. But even so, if you would be reasonable and see it our way, then I could see it your way, and yes, yes, I could, attend to you.'

'And the payment, Florence, is that I've got to take Ronnie into the business, is it?'

'He's very good, Father.'

'Shut up, girl! Your Ronnie's very good at nothing. He wouldn't be able to keep down the little job he has now if it wasn't for his own old man. Greengrocery's his line. And what in the name of God could he do in a factory like ours? You imagine him sitting in an office all day dictating little notes to a typist. No, Florence, never! You tell him that from me. If it was a business man you wanted you should not have married him, one of four brothers all in the fruit game. I know what's in your mind, our Florrie. Oh aye, I do.' He moved his head on the pillow, and he lifted his right arm slowly from the eiderdown towards his neck, and when his hand fell on to it he lay gasping for a moment before he could go on, 'When his old man goes the split won't be all that big; but if he was ensconced here and expecting me not to be long for the top he'd. . . .'

'Oh, how dare you say such things to me!'

'I can because I know they're true, lass, and because everything's changed, everything. I'm bein' treated as if I was an idiot. I may have lost the use of me body, but not of me mind And there's another thing: nobody has spoken a word about your mother since it happened. She need never have existed.'

'That's because nobody wants to hurt you. And I'm telling you too, you'll get no one to stay with you in the end: Lucy's scared stiff of you; and by the look of Nurse Lasting, she's already packing her bags. Something else while I'm on, because if you're strong enough to give it you're strong enough to take it: you won't hold our John for long. You think he's back here for good, don't you? But I know John, and at the first opportunity he'll be off. I'm surprised that he's stuck it this long.

You never got on, and you never will. And I'm . . . I'm going now, and I'll say this, Father: there might come a time when you'll be glad of Ronnie's services, because there's no hope of your getting Nellie and Bill from Jersey. As for our Monica, she can't look after her own children; she has to have a nursemaid for them, and two helps in the house. So I can see her attending to you. By! yes, I can. Well, I'm going; and if you want me there's always the phone.'

When the door was shut none too gently behind his daughter, Bob Henderson closed his eyes and, the words coming slow and deep, he muttered aloud, 'Oh my God. My God.' He looked up towards the panelled ceiling. 'Why has it to come to this? Why? Tell me, why?'

What had he done in his life that this should have happened to him? Aye, he had been rough of tongue, but that was all. He had put out a helping hand where it was needed most, unknownst to many; he had slaved sixteen hours a day for years to build up a business: at first Garbrook had provided the money and he had done the work, but their positions had levelled out when Alicia's father had died and left her a tidy sum, the whole of which she put into the business. But now the world had fallen about his ears. Nobody would tell him anything: he didn't know what was happenong, except what he heard on the television, and what he heard was happening to steel was anything but good news because trouble in steel works meant trouble for people like them, manufacturing engineers. You couldn't manufacture if you hadn't got the basic materials. And even then you couldn't distribute if you didn't get the market. And there was no one in that firm now who could get markets like their Glen. Oh, Glen. Glen. If only he could change places with him. If Glen's body had been crippled and his mind left he would have managed. But Glen's body was whole, his brain wasn't. He wondered what news John would bring back today.

His head moved on the pillow, and he looked about the room. It had always seemed a beautiful room, because Alicia had made it so, but now it was like a cage.

His breathing became rapid. If only somebody would come in, just to say a word to him, stop this racing inside his chest. Why could he feel he was alive inside yet couldn't move his limbs? Why? Why? Oh God, he'd go mad. If he could only get his hands on those damned tablets, he'd put an end to it. He would. Yes, he would.

The nurse came back into the room. He wanted to say to her, 'I'm sorry if I upset you,' but he couldn't because he wasn't really sorry he had upset her; he didn't like the woman. But anyway, she was somebody who was moving about, and he watched her make several trips into the bathroom. When she finally came to the bed, she looked down at him unsmiling as she asked, 'Would you like tea or coffee?' and he answered, 'Coffee please, and black.'

She had hardly been left the room a moment when the door was opened again and Dorry entered.

Going swiftly to the bed, she said, 'You've got some visitors . . . I mean one, one visitor.'

'Aye? Aye well, who is it?'

Dorry's smile widened. 'It's the one you were asking for, your secretary, Miss Brownlow.'

'No! No! Oh! Where is she? Fetch her up. Oh Dorry, fetch her up.'

His head was raised from the pillow when she entered the room, and she went straight towards him and, taking the hand that was raised from the eiderdown, she gripped it tightly as she looked down on him; and her throat was so full she found it impossible to speak for a moment.

It was he who spoke first. 'Oh, lass,' he said; 'am I glad to see you! Where've you been? Why didn't you come afore? I sent for you to the flat. And got John to write. Where've you been?'

'Oh, it's a long story. I'll . . . I'll tell you later. I only got the letter this morning.'

'Just this mornin'?' He swallowed deeply and wetted his lips; then said, 'Aw, sit down, lass. Get a chair and come and sit down.'

She loosed her hand from his and brought a chair to the bed, and when she sat down she took hold of his hand again as she said, 'Oh, it's good to see you, so good.'

'Lass. Lass. I'm nearly bubblin'.' His throat was full, and he blinked his eyelids but could not prevent the moisture from seeping down on to his cheeks. And his voice was husky as he said, 'Did you ever know anything like it? Whole lives, two of them, blown like the wind into eternity. Laughing their heads off one minute, mangled the next. We never knew what hit us. Oh, lass, lass. I'm sorry.' He turned his head away from her, and she, taking a handkerchief from her pocket, reached over and wiped his face. And when he looked at her again she could

152

scarcely see him for tears streaming down her own cheeks. After a moment she said, 'How . . . how is Glen?'

It was some seconds before he answered, 'In a bad way, lass. He got it in the back of the head. He's in a special unit in Newcastle. He went through another operation on Thursday. John's down now seeing how things have gone. But he should be home soon. Tell me, what are you doing now? You're not back there? I soon found that out. So what are you doing?'

'Nothing at present. I'm due to start a new job on Monday week. I'm . . . I'm staying with my cousin, and have been for some weeks. That's why I didn't get your letter, and didn't know you wanted to see me. I tried often at the hospital. . . . But you were too ill then.'

'You say you're not yet in a job? . . . Jinny' – there was a light pressure on her fingers – 'would you come back? I mean, there's lots of things you could do. I want to know what's goin' on, and oh, Jinny, I need somebody to talk to. Nobody mentions . . . Alicia, and that bloody nurse gets on my wick. And I've had a row with our Florrie. Nothing's gone right. Huh!' He moved his head again as he looked at her, saying, 'That's putting it mildly. The house has exploded; the world has exploded; the only thing of any worth that has happened is that our John's come home. And the payment's been very high, lass: two dead, a mind taken away from a brilliant young fellow, and a man left useless.'

'What do you mean, useless? you've still got your tongue. And that' – she smiled faintly at him – 'from what I remember of you, and from what I've just picked up from a conversation in the hall, is still at its top worst. Lots of men have been paralysed and continued to make their mark. History tells me that the President of the United States, Roosevelt, helped to run a war . . . and women, from a wheelchair.'

'Aye, you've said it, lass, from a wheelchair. But let's face it, I'm gone from the neck down, Jinny.'

She stared at him in silence now; then moved her lips one over the other before she said, 'You can move this hand.'

'Just.'

'Have you tried to move the other one?'

'Oh, lass' – he closed his eyes – 'they progged an' pulled an' probed an' pushed every single pore of me. That's how much they've tried. Anyway, what about it, Jinny? Will you?'

She put her head on one side and her smile was wide as she

said, 'Come back and be bullied to death by you? Have to put up with your swearing, your cursing, your never saying thank you? Not—' She leant towards him now, her face almost touching his as she ended, 'In the words of Eliza Doolittle, not bloody likely.' But then, her mouth wide, she said, 'My pay cheque starts from now, and it's double for weekend work. Don't forget that.'

'Aw Jinny. Jinny. Aw, lass.' His eyelashes were wet. 'You don't know how good it is to . . . to see you again. . . . Aw.'

'And you. And you. Mr Henderson.' Her voice was cracking and she swallowed and added crisply, 'But now I'll have to go downstairs: my cousin and her husband are there; they brought me from Shields. They've been very good to me. I can tell you something, they won't like it, me letting them down. Peter, that's my cousin's husband, has got me this job in his office. He's a solicitor. The pay would have been good, the hours short. I must be daft, taking you on.' She smiled softly at him now. 'Could I bring them up to see you?'

'Aye. Do that, lass. I'll explain to them my need is greater than theirs. Go on; bring them up.'

Less than a half-hour later when Jinny stood on the drive saying goodbye to Peter and Nell, it was Nell who shook her head as she said, 'I don't know, Jinny. I don't know. He's helpless. That kind of man can sap you. Between bullying and coaxing, your life isn't going to be your own. I'm . . . I'm sorry for him as much as you are, but, the situation he's in, he'll hang on to you like an anchor. And it'll take more than pity and sympathy to put up with it; you'll want the stamina of a horse.'

'Be quiet, Nell. Be quiet.' Peter pushed her gently in the arm. 'The man's got a nurse; he's got a son and daughter at home. That so, Jinny?'

'Yes, Peter. And look, don't worry.' She turned to Nell. 'I'm going to be all right. In fact, I'm going to enjoy looking after him. We got on so well together. And what's more, Nell, I'm . . . well, to put it plainly, I'm going to be needed.'

'Well, we need you, lass. We'll miss you. Won't we, Peter? We'll miss her.'

'That's nice of you, nice of both of you. And I can't thank you enough for what you've done for me. And what you're going to do' – she put her hand out towards Peter – 'about the flat and the insurance and that. And bringing my things over here ... it's very good of you. And on a Saturday too, and I know you like your golf.'

'Well, that's one good thing you've done.' Nell was nodding towards her now. 'I won't be a golf widow this afternoon. But did you see his face when you said you'd have to go back for the things? It dropped a mile. I could see him thinking that once you left the house you wouldn't come back. An' I'm telling you, Jinny, if you take my advice you'll put your foot down and have stated hours. And another thing, and this is diplomacy, you make friends with the kitchen lot, else they can lead you. . . .'

'Nell' – Peter had his court voice on now – 'will you kindly get into the car; but before you do will you please shut up.'

'I know what I'm talking about, Peter Dudley. I don't have to study law to know people. I tell you again she's going to have her work cut out. . . .'

'Get in.'

After he had got his wife seated, Peter turned to Jinny, saying, 'Take no notice. Do what you have to do for as long as you like. But always remember, when you want to come back home, the door's open.'

'Thank you, Peter. Thank you. I'll remember.'

Nell, winding down the window, now had the last word. As the car was about to move off, she said, 'And to think this time yesterday I was hearing your wedding bells.'

After waving to them, Jinny turned slowly about and went towards the front door of the house. . . . 'I was hearing your wedding bells.' Well, as far as she could see ahead, there'd be no wedding bells for her, for already she had made up her mind that as long as the man lying helpless up there wanted her she'd stay with him; good or bad times, she'd stay with him. . . .

It was as she closed the door behind her and saw Dorry disappearing with the tray into a passage to the right of her that she recalled Nell's advice with regard to the staff. And she knew that a household such as this would be run very like an office, and she'd had experience of the tensions in an office, hadn't she just, and so she followed Dorry into what was for her a new quarter of the house. She went along the passage, and passed a door opening into the dining-room. There was no one in there that she could see. And she went on to a further door, and guessing that the kitchen lay beyond, she knocked on it. It was a moment or so before it was opened, and Dorry, looking at her, said enquiringly, 'Yes, miss? You're wanting something?'

'Just . . . just a word. But is Mrs Gallon in?'

'Oh yes. Aye, Cook's here. Come in.'

Jinny went into the room, a very modern kitchen, she could see at once. It held a double Aga, besides electric wall ovens. The cook was at the table, and she turned and awaited her coming.

Jinny began hesitantly, 'I . . . I thought I'd better come and tell you, I'm taking up my duties with Mr Henderson again. I say' – she shrugged her shoulders – 'my duties. I don't know really what they'll consist of as yet. But he has asked me to stay, and as Miss Lucy is not in I . . . I wonder if you could tell me where I'm likely to be put.' She smiled from one to the other. And they both smiled back at her; but it was the cook who answered. 'Oh well,' she said, 'Dorry here'll show you a room. And if I may say so, I think it's a good thing he's takin' an interest in something because, between you and me, miss, if he didn't have a change soon I think he'd go off his head. He's had Miss Lucy scared at times. And its taken Mr John all his time to manage him. As for Nurse Lasting –' Cook now turned and looked at Dorry, and they pulled faces at each other. And it was Dorry who went on, 'Between you and me, miss, I don't think she's gona stick it out. An' mind, to be honest, I can't blame her, 'cos he does get rough at times. We understand him, see, and I suppose you do an' all, workin' along of him in the office, but strangers, well . . . they consider it a bit thick what he comes out with.' Again the two elderly women laughed, and Jinny now said, 'Perhaps he'd be better with a male nurse.'

'Eeh! now. Isn't that odd?' Dorry stuck her thumb into cook's arm, saying, 'Didn't I say that only last night, now didn't I? I said, what the boss wants is a man up there, and a hefty one at that. Mr John does his best, but he's got him practically worn out. Now isn't that funny? I said the very same thing.' She was now nodding at Jinny, and she added, 'If this one leaves, Nurse Lasting I mean, you want to put it to the boss, you do.'

'It's a thought.'

'Aye, it is a thought.' Cook bobbed her head now. And they all smiled at each other. They were conspirators.

It was a good start. Nell had been right, on this point anyway.

'Come on, miss, and I'll get you settled. Are your things here?'

'No. My cousin and her husband have gone to fetch them.'

'Oh well, in the meantime I'll show you your room.' And Dorry turned to the cook, saying, 'The one opposite, eh?'

'Well, I don't know.' Cook put her head on one side and looked at Jinny. 'It all depends, because you see, that's the one, isn't it, with the intercom telephone in? And you don't want him to get you up in the middle of the night, do you, 'cos you know, he's very demanding. And if you've been on your feet all day you want your rest. We all know that.'

'Oh, that'll be all right. I won't mind.'

'Well, come on, miss, we'll see.' And they went out, Dorry still talking. 'Miss Lucy had that room for a time, but she changed it and went into the one that you were in over Christmas. And then when Mr John came home permanently we had to do a move round, 'cos the girls have always had their rooms kept ready for them, and after the accident and when three of them were here together and all the children, oh my! And the French families. We had ten bedrooms going with Mr Glen's house up the road. Eeh! I just can't believe what's happened him.'

They were going up the stairs now. 'The changes this place has seen.' She turned her head and looked down at Jinny as she whispered, 'It used to be a happy house, gay like. Always somebody laughin' or jokin', or him ... the boss, callin' out. ... Well, you had a taste, didn't you, at New Year? But of course, it was quiet then. Yet it was nice. Wasn't it nice?'

'Yes, it was very nice, 'Jinny said softly; 'very nice indeed. In fact, it was the best New Year I can remember for a long time.'

They crossed the broad landing and went down another corridor where, Dorry's voice now dropping to a mutter, she said, 'They were very fond of you, miss, very fond. I know that.'

Jinny said nothing but followed her into the bedroom. It wasn't unlike the room she had slept in before, only much larger, and with a double bed.

'Will this do, miss?'

'Beautifully. Beautifully.'

'I can't say I'll unpack for you, can I?' Dorry poked her head forward, then giggled. Then going quickly to the window she put her head close to a pane and after a moment said, 'It's Miss Lucy. She's back. Will I tell her you're here?'

'If you please, Dorry.'

Left alone, she sat in the chair by the side of the bed, thinking: I should have gone down. But it was only a matter of minutes later when there came a tap on the door and it was pushed open and Lucy entered.

Jinny had risen and was already standing in the middle of the room but the sight of the girl checked the greeting she was about to make. This wasn't the Lucy she remembered from Glen's wedding: she had lost her plumpness, and the slightly petulant look had gone from her face and was replaced by a wide-eyed, worried expression. Altogether she looked older.

She spoke immediately, her words almost tumbling over each other. 'Hello,' she said. 'Dorry's just told me. You've come to stay. Oh, I am glad. If he could get his mind on some work it might help. Oh, I am glad. Have you brought your things?'

'No. My cousin has gone back home for them; I've been staying with them in Shields.'

'Oh, that must be why he didn't hear from you. You're the only one that seems to know about the business. Mr Waitland's called, and Mr Garbrook too, but he got so upset after. Oh, it's been awful.' She now dropped down on to the side of the bed, and began to loosen the buttons of the smart suit she was wearing, and when she had undone them she let out a long slow breath as if the coat had been tight, which it wasn't. And now Jinny watched the girl's lips tremble and the eyelids blink rapidly before tears began to run down her cheeks.

Quickly Jinny sat down beside her and put her arm around her shoulder, and immediately Lucy turned and buried her face in Jinny's neck while muttering through choking gasps, 'It's been awful. It doesn't seem to get better. I miss Mummy. Oh, I miss Mummy. And I've had to do everything in the house. I mean bills and things. And he barks at me, Father, he barks at me every time I go in. I can do nothing to please him.' She lifted her head and began to dry her eyes, saying, 'You would have thought with me losing Mummy that he would have understood and been kind, wouldn't you, wouldn't you now?'

Here was the spoilt child talking. The tragedy had aged her outwardly but apparently hadn't affected her character, for she wasn't giving much thought to the loss her father had sustained, nor yet her brother. And now she went on, 'I . . . I was going to be married. I was. Yes, I was.' Her head was bobbing. 'Father wouldn't have it because it meant my going to New Zealand. Reg has been offered this post, and if he doesn't go by

November he'll lose it. I could have got round Father. I feel sure I would have, and then this had to happen. And now I . . . I feel tied for life because none of the girls will come back. Florence wanted to; but then Father wouldn't take Ronnie into the firm. He can't stand Ronnie. But she's the only one who could come and take over. And so, there I was, left with everything to do. Oh—' She now caught hold of Jinny's hands and, shaking them, she said, 'Oh, I am glad you're going to stay.'

Jinny smiled quietly. The girl was glad she was going to stay, not because of any personal liking but because she saw her as a means to an end. She would have said there wasn't a selfish bone in Alicia Henderson's body, nor yet in her husband's, but from someone along the line their youngest daughter had picked up the threads of selfishness. Perhaps they themselves were to blame for spoiling her: the youngest of the family was often treated like an only child. Yet, she herself had been an only child; and she didn't consider her parents had spoiled her. They had been loving, very loving, but, as she remembered, firm, especially about morals. Oh, yes, especially about morals. Perhaps too firm in that way for the present day. One's character and actions should be moulded to the times in which one lived, and if she hadn't been brought up as she was. . . .

Oh, here she was, doing it again. Well, from now on she'd have something to think about other than what she was missing because she was being silly enough to adhere to certain standards that every day the television, wireless and newspapers informed her were out of date.

'Everything will work out all right, you'll see.' They were standing now.

'You think so?'

It was like an appeal from a child, and Jinny paused before answering, 'Yes, I'm sure, for you it will be anyway. As for your father, well, we'll have to see. And . . . and what about Glen?'

'Oh, he's in a dreadful state. John should be back anytime. He goes in almost every day to see him. It's his brain.' The tears once more coming into her eyes, she turned away, muttering, 'You can't believe it, can you? You just can't believe it.' Then at the door she turned and said, 'We have a midday dinner. It's easier for Cissie Gallon. I used to come up and sit with Father while Nurse had hers, but now perhaps . . . well. . . .'

'Yes, I'll see to him. Don't worry, I'll see to him.'

'Thank you. I'm . . . I'm glad you're here.'

'I'm very pleased to be here. I hope I'll be of some use.'

'Oh' – Lucy now jerked her chin upwards – 'if you can talk work you will. You can be sure of that.' Then as she made to go out she screwed up her eyes tightly and bent her head down as her father's voice came bawling from the room opposite, 'When I'm ready for it, not afore!'

Jinny saw through the open door the nurse coming out from the bedroom opposite. The woman's face was scarlet, and she addressed Lucy now as if speaking to the mistress of the house, saying, 'That's it! I give notice. I'm leaving. I don't have to put up with such talk.' She now reached behind her and closed the door with a bang. Then looking at Lucy again, she went on, 'You must get a replacement because he must be seen to. I'll stay till Monday, not a minute longer. Understand?' And at this she turned and marched down the corridor, leaving Jinny and Lucy looking at each other.

And Jinny, seeing that the girl's face was about to crumple again, put out her hand and said, 'Don't worry. We'll manage somehow. Go on downstairs; I'll see to him.'

Lucy almost scampered away, like a child who had evaded a spanking, and Jinny was left looking at the door opposite. She did not immediately go across to it, for she was thinking again of Nell and what she had prophesied, and she knew now that whatever it was she had thought she was taking on she hadn't included nursing in it. But then she told herself, that wouldn't come about for there was John; he would see to that side of it until they got a nurse . . . a male nurse. Yes, that's what was wanted, a male nurse. But would he stand for it? Well, they would have to see.

She now approached the door, opened it and went in; and she saw immediately that he was still seething about whatever had upset him, and before she could approach the bed his voice came at her: 'Thought you had changed your mind. You've been some time coming back. And that woman's a bloody fool. If you tell somebody you don't want to be treated like a child and they're not deaf, dumb or daft, then they should take note, shouldn't they? We had a session about it first thing this morning. You would think she would have learnt. But oh no, not her. In she comes, forgiveness written all over her, and starts again. "Oops-a-daisy!" she says. "Shall we do the back now;

160

eh? Eh?" And the tone of her voice like that you'd use to a bairn in nappies. Jinny' – his voice suddenly dropped and he screwed up his eyes – 'I'm nearly at the end of me tether. It's true, lass, I'm nearly at the end of me tether.'

'Well, we'll have to see what we can do about it, won't we?'

She sat down on the edge of the bed and took the limp hand in hers. 'But I'll tell you one thing: it's no good wasting what energy you've got left bawling at people. If you ever want to get back into the swim again, I mean work, you've got to conserve what strength you've got left.'

'What do you mean, get back into the swim again, work? How the hell can I get back into the swim again?'

'Oh' – she drew her chin in – 'you don't mean you have no intention of talking or getting back to it? If that's the case, then you've got me here on false pretences. What am I here for? Because, let me tell you I'm no nurse, I'm merely a secretary. I'm not going to start rubbing your back for you or carrying out other—' she swallowed before she forced herself to bring out, 'disagreeable duties. I'm here to get you back to work. Nothing more, nothing less.'

His eyes were staring up at her now, and he said quietly, 'You're a cheeky bitch. You know that? You always were.' Then his head moving slowly on the pillow, he said, 'Oh, Jinny; I'm glad you're back.'

'Well, I'm back, but only on conditions. And let's get them straight.' She was nodding at him now. 'First, you have a nurse. Whether male or female, you have a nurse. And I think a male nurse would be preferable.'

After a moment of glaring at her, he growled, 'Aye, well, perhaps you're right there.'

'Then secondly, we'll all have our hours on duty: John, Lucy, me, and the nurse.'

'Oh God in heaven!'

'No, not Him, just the four of us.'

It was a facetious statement, but that, she knew, was the way he liked things, at least when there was no big work issue at stake. And his answer was in his usual vein: 'Now stop trying to be so bloody clever. You're so sharp you'll cut yourself on your tongue one of these days. An' look, lass, let me put things straight to you. I'm at home, in me own house. I don't want a hospital routine; I played hell until I got out of hospital.' He paused and turned his head away from her and looked to the other side of the room as he went on, 'I had the idea that once I got home things would be different. I thought they'd all rally round me. And it's funny, the only one who's stood by me is our John, and he's the one I've taken it out of most all his life, 'cos we never got on, you know.' He was looking at her again. 'Funny that, isn't it? We couldn't hit it off. Our ideas were like chalk and cheese. He was supposed to despise money: far left, so to speak, he was for a time. They all go like that, these fellows who get the chance of a better education. They bite the hand that's worked to put them there. They despise the means that's keeping them there. Share and share alike is their motto. Wealth should be shared, they say. And when you ask them who is going to pay the bills, they come out with some high-falutin jargon. Yet they're not above saying they can't live on their grants. Oh, that used to madden me, the times they said that. If anybody got to university in my day he got there on his brains; and not by sittin' on his backside or goin' on holiday during what they call the vac, you worked. And I know what I'm talking about. There's Meane in the drawing-office; he came up that way. Navvied during the holidays, he did. He told me.'

As she listened to him talking she thought, he could soon get back into his stride. If only he had the use of his hands.

His chattering suddenly stopped and he returned to her demands. 'Now, you have a point there, Jinny, about a male nurse. There was a fellow in the hospital, Mason his name was, everybody called him Willie, Willie Mason. He was as strong as a bull. And kind with it. I said to him in fun one day, "I'll set you on." And he laughed back at me and said, "All right, but for time and a half." I wonder now. I wonder. I'd give him time and a half, Jinny. If I remember rightly an' all, he's single. Now, I think you've got something there' – he nodded at her – 'because it won't only be me that needs some attention; our Glen, as far as I can understand, is in a pretty bad state. And we'll be having him home soon. John promised me that he would see to it and ask about it the day. He's had three operations. . . . Poor lad. I'm longing to see him.' He pressed his lips tight together and moved his head slightly. 'He was a wonderful son, one to be proud of, an' he was going places. He was already well-known abroad, and highly respected. Why, Jinny? Why?'

The look on his face caused her to put out her hand and smooth his hair back from his brow as she said softly, 'I can't tell you. There's no answer to it. I've asked the same question again and again, even about the petty things that have happened in my own life. But when this happened to you all . . . well I was stunned by it, because, you see, to me you were all so wonderful. Alicia, Glen, Yvonne, and . . .' she nodded her head slowly now – 'and you. I . . . I was away that weekend with' – she pursed her lips – 'my one-time friend.'

Taking no notice of his raised eyebrows, she went on, 'I went to the hospital, but I couldn't see you. Then I returned to the office.' She hesitated, wondering if she should tell him what had transpired, and decided to do so. It would stir his interest, and perhaps give him a laugh. And so she went on, 'As you have since gathered. I suppose you know that Mr Waitland has taken over your . . . our office? Well, he politely, or impolitely, sent me packing down to the typing pool.'

'He did?'

'Yes, he did.'

'I heard a different version. But go on.'

'Well, you can imagine how I felt returning there, and to be met by Miss Cadwell, who was in her element as she told me in no small voice what was in store for me. Well, that was all right as far as it went, until she attacked my character and accused me of—' Her head moved from one side to the other before she ended, 'having an illicit affair.'

'You having an illicit affair? Who with, in the name of God?'

'You, of course.'

'*Me?*' His face stretched. 'My God! *me?* Well, I haven't heard this afore. Is that why you slapped her?'

'That is why I slapped her, and on both sides of the face.'

'Good for you. And so we had an illicit affair?'

'Yes, we had. And you bought me expensive jewellery, and your wife caught you at it, came to the jeweller's shop and caught you . . . us at it.'

'Never!' His voice was low now. 'Eeh!' He shook his head. 'If only Alicia had been here to listen to this. Lass' – his fingers moved slowly over hers – 'as much as I like you, if you had the royal insignia on you, or if you had been a multi-millionaire and as beautiful and young as you are, you couldn't have moved Alicia one jot in my affections.'

'I know that.'

'Eeh, the minds of people. They must have been thinking that all along.'

'Yes. Yes.'

'My God! It's a good job I didn't know. But then, if I had I'd have played them up, and Alicia would have gone along with me. Aye, she would. Oh, Jinny . . . Jinny, I miss her. The days are empty. At times I think I am goin' to go mad because life's like eternity stretching away with just me head to see it. Can you understand that, just me head to experience eternity?' He swallowed deeply. Then his voice rising, he said, 'I had to fight that bloody nurse to have her picture left there. She said it wasn't good for me when she found me talking to it one day.'

His voice dropping again, he said, 'She's very close to me you know, Jinny; she doesn't seem really to be gone. It's a strange thing: I can talk to you now about this, but I couldn't to anybody else. Night-time, I can see her standing as clear as if she was alive; but you know, it's as if she were asking me to let her go. Can you understand that, Jinny? It's just as if she were saying, "Leave go, Bob. Leave go."'

When she didn't answer, he said, 'No, you wouldn't understand; I cannot understand it meself. But it helps just to talk about it.'

Jinny looked across the bed to the large photograph of Alicia standing on a side table and felt a little cold shiver pass through her, and the thought came to her that perhaps the nurse was right, he was living with the dead. And the dead were, in some way, telling him that they were where no one could really reach them or hold them, and that if they didn't of their own accord release them, time would. But the interval could be painful.

She wished she could have expressed her feelings, in words that would not have been painful to him, for he was in need of comfort at the moment, and was finding it only in the mirage his brain conjured up in the night.

Changing the subject abruptly now, he said, 'Have they got you settled in?'

'Yes. I'm just across the corridor.'

'Oh, good. Good. Well, go on now downstairs and have something to eat. It's near dinner-time. One last word about our arrangements.' He stressed the last word. 'Call me Bob, will you?'

'Oh.' She stood up. 'I'm going to find that difficult.'

'Why?'

'Just because I'd rather call you Mr Henderson.'

'Look. We're at home now, not in the office. Bob it is. That's an order.'

'Right, Mr Henderson.' She turned on her heel, and walked

164

from the room, closing the door quietly behind her. She heard his voice muttering something, but she couldn't catch the words.

Before going down the stairs, she went into her room and stood with her back to the door as she muttered aloud, 'Poor soul. Poor soul. How's he going to stick it, being made as he is? How's he going to stick it?'

The rest of the day passed somewhat uneventfully; only one thing became more certain, Nurse Lasting, becoming aware that Jinny was to be a permanent member of the household, emphasized her decision that she was leaving, replacement or no replacement.

It was now ten o'clock at night. Bob was asleep, but only after a fight over the taking of his pill for he had wanted to keep awake until after John should return with news of Glen. His mind would be at rest for the next four hours or so: he hardly ever slept, he said, after two in the morning. The nurse had retired to her room; Dorry and Cissie had gone off duty; and Lucy, after saying good-night to her father at nine o'clock, had slipped out of the house, saying she wouldn't be long. She hadn't said where she was going, she really had no need. The man, Reg Talbot, Jinny had learned from Bob, was twelve years Lucy's senior, and, being divorced, was no suitable partner for his daughter. Jinny could have put in cynically from her own experience, that nine-tenths of men seemed to be either divorced or living on the side with someone, and so a young girl's chance of meeting up with an unattached man these days was on a par with a man meeting a girl who hadn't had it off with someone. Even while thinking this way she chastised herself for the crudeness of her approach to the situation; but then told herself it was the present-day approach, so what? And although she still might be a cultured handmaiden, and her new position seemed to merit that very title, she was no longer a gullible cultured handmaiden, nor yet would she ever again break her neck to please people in order to retain their company.

Anyway, Lucy had definitely gone to meet this man, and she was just asking herself if she should wait for her coming in when she heard the sound of a car on the gravel drive.

She rose from the chair by the fire as the door opened; then her face stretched slightly as she saw it wasn't Lucy who had entered but John. And for a moment he looked as surprised as she did. Then coming forward, he said, 'Well! Well! So you got here after all?'

'Yes, about a fortnight late after all. I didn't get your letter until this morning.'

'This morning?' He raised his eyebrows; then ran his finger round the inside of his collar before adding, 'And you're here, all set to stay?'

'Yes, that seems to be the position.'

'Well! Well!' he said again; then went towards the fire, adding now, 'Sit down. Sit down.' Then dropping into a chair himself, he closed his eyes as he said, 'Lord I'm tired.'

'Your . . . your father expected you earlier. Can I get you anything? Dorry and Cook have gone to bed. But I know where things are. At least I could find them. I could make you a coffee.'

'That would be nice. Thank you.'

She hurried from the room and into the kitchen, and quickly found what was needed; and while she stood waiting for the water to boil she said to herself, How does it happen that he's so unlike his father in temperament, manner, and everything. But at this point she checked herself: How did she know what he was really like? Except for that meeting on New Year's morning she knew nothing about him, only what his father had told her. And from that she gathered that he was a stubborn individual, if not an egotistical one. . . . Had he been pleased to see her just now? He had looked surprised. Yet it was he who had written to her. Well, she would have to see how they got on.

A few minutes later she was handing him a cup of coffee; then sat down opposite him again and waited for him to speak.

He had drunk half the coffee before he said, 'Is Lucy in bed?'

She did not immediately answer. But then, her voice expressionless, she said, 'She went out for a short while.'

'What time?'

'Well, it was. . . .' Again she paused. 'I think it was just before nine.'

He finished the coffee and set the cup down on the table before speaking again. 'I needn't ask you where she's gone because you wouldn't know,' he said; 'but you'd be doing her a favour if you don't mention to Father her leaving the house at that time.'

'Well, it won't be necessary for me to mention her at all.'

'Oh, if you intend to stay here you'll be expected to answer all kinds of questions about everything and everyone. Particularly about the works. Has he started on that yet?'

'We talked a little about it this afternoon.'

She watched him close his eyes again, then run his fingers through his hair. It was sandy hair, of a wiry texture, the kind that wouldn't take kindly to grooming. It was shortish yet for the most part covered his ears. She thought his eyes could be hazel, with a fleck in them. When he opened them wide and stretched his face as if to relax his muscles, she saw that they were grey.

'He's bent on my going into the business. He seems to forget that's what our disagreement was about in the first place . . . among other things, I suppose. But I've never felt cut out for that kind of business. Glen was his man. Glen was always his man, in all ways. . . . Glen. Glen.'

When he shook his head slowly, she said, 'How did you find your brother?'

'It's hard to describe. It's hard to imagine someone as vital as him who seemed to be all brain, alert, on the spot – as Father used to say, on the spot all the time, that's Glen – and now like a child . . . well, a boy, a young boy.'

'Oh no!'

He nodded at her. 'Yes. Yes. They operated on him again on Wednesday, and they hope that this time it will quell the aggressiveness in him: they didn't call it the last vestige of real life. It's terrible to see him. He clung onto me just like a child. . . . That's why I'm late.' He rose now and walked towards the fire, and leaning his forearm on the mantelpiece, he looked down into the fire as he said, 'I think they should have left him as he was.' He turned his head towards her. 'You see, neither can he remember anything of the accident, nor, if this operation should be what they call successful, will he ever recall Yvonne. After the first do he went berserk when some undamaged fragment of his mind touched on her. It was just as if he was experiencing the split second before the end, because he was screaming for her. I sometimes think it would have been better if his body had been paralysed and his mind had been left like Father's; he would eventually have been able to cope.' He turned his face towards the fire again, and his voice was low as he ended, 'Between them, I think I'll go round the bend myself before long.'

She broke the ensuing long silence by saying, 'Will . . . will he ever be able to come home?'

He sighed and turned his back to the fire, and looking down on her he nodded his head as he said, 'If Father got his way he'd be here tomorrow. I've tried to tell him that there's no Glen left. But he won't be convinced. He imagines time will bring him round to what he was, or a semblance of it. I sometimes feel like bawling at him, "What Glen was has been mashed to pulp. There's no Glen left." Oh—' Again he stretched his face; then for the first time a slight smile came to his lips as he said, 'You've had it all day, and now you're getting it far into the night. Does it give you a picture of what you've let yourself in for?'

She smiled back at him as she answered quietly, 'Just about.' Then getting to her feet, she said, 'I'm here to help. And with regard to the work, I . . . I really think that if he could join in some way, be in touch with them at the works, it would help, take his mind off other things. The pity of it is, he's so handicapped: if he could only move his hands. . . .'

'He could if he liked.'

Her face actually screwed up as she peered at him, and she repeated, 'He could if he liked? What do you mean?'

'Just what I say.'

'But he's totally paralysed, except for his head and the feeble use he has of his left arm.'

They were standing looking eye to eye now; they were, she noticed, of the same height, and his voice came flat and slow as he said, 'He's only really paralysed from the legs down. He'll never move those again. But he could have the use of the whole top part of his body, if he put his mind to it. He has what they call a lumbar fracture. This has caused paraplegia, true paraplegia. The rest of him is affected by hysterical paraplegia.'

'Hysterical paraplegia?' She mouthed the two words, and he nodded at her.

'When he was told this was the case he nearly gave himself a heart attack. His mind wasn't affected, he said; him to imagine he was paralysed when he wasn't. Well' – he nodded at her now – 'as long as he tells himself that he'll remain as he is. I've had two tries at getting through to him, but not again.'

She just checked herself from saying, 'He must be mad not to try and move.' Yet for a man like that to be told that he was suffering from anything appertaining to hysteria would clamp down on any attempt at trying to move; should he succeed it would go to prove there was a weakness in him, a mental weakness. And she felt she understood him enough to know that he couldn't face up to that. His was an outsize ego; he was a big man in his own eyes; a car crash wasn't going to deprive him of that conception, not right away, at any rate.

'Dr Turner is bringing a specialist to see him next week. We'll have to take it from there. By the way—' His voice softened a note as he now added, 'You look as tired as I feel. I'm sorry I've kept you up. Where have they put you?'

'In the room opposite.'

'Oh.' He pursed his lips and jerked his chin upwards as he said, 'That wasn't a good move. You'll be getting calls in the night; there's an intercom there. He's awake now in the early hours. I moved from there; I just had to. He's got to learn some kind of discipline and recognize that people can't be up all day on their feet and all night too.'

As she looked into the face before her she saw the lines of deep strain on it. He had, she surmised, been pressured almost beyond his strength these last months. Doubtless, his private life had been disrupted too; his present way of living wouldn't leave much time for his girl friend.

She wondered what type of girl he had chosen. She must have been sufficiently attractive to make him leave home, leave this house and what had, under his mother's control, been a life of easy going luxury. He wasn't an unattractive man, and in happier moments and his face without strain, she could imagine that he would appear quite good-looking in an austere kind of way. She said, 'Will you be waiting up for Lucy?'

'I certainly shall,' he answered.

'Good-night.'

'Good-night,' he said. No names were exchanged.

Before entering her own room she quietly opened the opposite door and through the dull pink glow from the bedside lamp she could see the head turned on the pillow; the eyes were closed, and from the look of him he could have been dead, all dead. Yet he was alive. Down to his thighs he was alive. She wouldn't have believed it.

Minutes later as she was undressing for bed, she visualized what he would be able to do with the use of his body: he could get about in a wheelchair; he could get into a car; he could go back to the office.

He could go back to the office.

2

'If he's able to walk about the hospital floor he's able to walk about this house.'

'John thinks. . . .'

'Never mind what John thinks; I'm sick of listening to what John thinks. Jinny' – Bob lifted his hand slowly towards her – 'I want to see my lad. It's been months. They've had three goes at him. The way I see it, if he's not any better now he's never going to be any better. As John reports, he can walk and he can talk. . . .'

'Yes, but it's how he can talk.' She was nodding towards him now. 'John's only trying to . . . well, to prevent you from being further hurt because. . . .'

'Aye, go on.'

'Well, you'd better have it.' Her voice was cold. 'Only the truth will get through to you and it's this: you'll never see Glen again as he was. His mind has reverted . . . back, gone back. . . .'

They stared at each other now for a while; then he said, 'Reverted to what? Gone back to what?'

'Well, from what I can gather, he's gone back to his childhood; he doesn't remember anything about the accident. Well, he did the once, and then he became aggressive.'

'Aggressive, you say? And now reverted to a lad?'

When he closed his eyes she said, softly, 'He's had no aggressive turns since the last operation, and they don't think they will recur.'

He was looking at her again. 'All right,' he said quietly, 'he's a lad once more; what's to stop him acting like a lad in his own home? And if he needs any looking after, there's Willie. Willie has a job to fill up his time with me. An' there's you: you have a job to fill your time with me; yet, if you would do what I ask you might be doing something towards earning your keep.'

'Oh, really!' For the first time since coming into the house she lost her temper with him; and she almost barked at him now, 'Let me tell you that just being with you is paying dearly for my keep, and I consider myself vastly underpaid. But I can alter that tomorrow. No, today, this very morning. There's another vacancy in Peter's office. Nell is begging me to go back there. She was only on about it on Friday when she was here. . . .'

'Oh, to hell with Nell! And all the bloody lot of you, you especially. If you don't know what I mean now when I open me mouth and let me frustration out you never will. Go on, get out!'

She turned from him and went quickly from the room, and she almost ran into John. Closing the door behind her, she stood looking at him in silence as she gnawed on her lip; and he, jerking his head towards the door, said quietly, 'He's hit you where it hurts at last, has he? You've amazed me you've stood it so long without retaliating.'

'I'm amazed myself.' Her voice certainly wasn't quiet as she went on, 'I think I'm mad. Yes, I am mad, because I seem to spend my life putting up with thankless people. Well I'm not too old to change that.' She almost thrust him aside, then marched across the landing and down the stairs. And John stood looking after her for a moment before opening the bedroom door and going in.

When he reached the side of the bed he stared at his father: 'You've done it this time, you know,' he said. 'The mood's she's in she could up and go.'

'Let her.'

'Let her, you say?' John's eyebrows moved upwards. 'You would know it if she did. Who do you think's been running the place? Not Lucy; I can tell you that. And Dorry and Cissie do what they're told. They always have done. As good as they are there's no initiative there. What was it all about anyway?'

'If you want to know, it was about you baulking me with regard to Glen.'

'Oh.' John turned from the bed, saying now, 'Well, I'll go tomorrow, and if the doctors say it's all right I'll bring him back with me.'

'You will?' Bob's voice was quiet now, and John, turning to him again, said tersely, 'Yes, I will. But I want you to prepare yourself, because your Glen is no more.' Leaning towards his father now and his voice dropping low, he said, 'He was your pride and joy, wasn't he . . . Glen? Wasn't he . . . Glen? There was nobody like Glen. He had it all up top, and in the right places. But now, Father, you've got to face the fact that Glen has nothing left up top, except memories of a young boy, about twelve I'd say. And why he's reverted to that age nobody can tell. But he talks of school and passing exams, and he writes poetry, little rhymes. Do you remember? Do you remember that stage? No, I don't suppose you do, because you would have thought it silly, so he wouldn't have told you that he went through the arty stage, as I did, only mine lasted much longer and it got your back up. He knew that, so that's why he didn't let you into that part of his life. But now, he'll present you with it from the minute he shambles in the door and you look on him.'

'There's a cruel streak in you, you know, John.'

'Well, I know where I get it from. It didn't come from my mother. Now I'll have to take meself and my cruel streak downstairs and see what I can do with Jinny, because, frankly, I've never seen her look like she did a minute ago. There's more to her than meets the eye, you know, Father.'

'You can't tell me anything about Jinny.'

'No?'

'No. She came on to my horizon with a chip on her shoulder as big as a plank, and she's spoken to me as nobody else has dared do. You can't tell me there's another side to Jinny.'

'Well, that being so, the other side is very much in evidence at the present time. The only thing I'm surprised about is she's lasted so long without rebelling.'

'You make me out to be a bloody tyrant. You always have done.'

'Well, to use an old phrase of yours, I speak as I find.' And on this he turned and walked from the room.

On the landing he stood looking down towards the carpet. How unfair life could be where love was concerned. For as long as he could remember he had longed for the love of that irascible man lying in that room. He could recall waiting for him to come home at nights just to see if for once he would look at him like he did at Glen. But he never did. If he put his hand on his shoulder he could rest assured that his other arm would be hugging Glen to him. And he himself had loved Glen too; and Glen had been understanding of the situation. There were times when they had talked, when his elder brother had tried to persuade him that their father was as fond of the one as of the other. Glen could see his need, his father never.

He found Jinny in the office. She was sitting behind the desk, sorting out some bills, and she didn't lift her head when he entered the room.

Pulling up a chair on the opposite side of the desk, he sat down, then said quietly, 'I'm the representative from the firm of Meek, Meek, & Meek, ma'am; I'm their conciliatory agent. My client in question is in a poor state at the moment. Such is his unusual state of mind that he cursed only twice during a five minutes conversation.'

'Oh, shut up!' Jinny's lips moved one over the other in an effort not to smile. She clipped a number of bills together, pulled open a drawer in the desk, threw the bills in before pulling another small pile towards her.

'Jinny.' John's voice was without jest now. 'He's in a bit of a state, so I told him I'd bring Glen back tomorrow, that's if they'll allow it.'

She lifted her eyes to his as she asked, 'Does he know what to expect?'

'I've told him bluntly, but I didn't tell him that what he's feeling now will be nothing to what he'll go through after a couple of days of Glen. I've been with him for only a few hours at a time, and it's wearing. He chatters, never stops. It's so pitiable. You want to cry, and at the same time land out and box his ears as you would do a boy that kept rattling on senselessly. Yet, I shouldn't say senselessly because what he talks about makes sense to him and would have to any young boy in the late sixties. But then of course, he's not going to be the only one that's to be affected. There's you. It'll be Willie's job to look after him, and he's used to all kinds of cases, but you'll be in contact with him too for most of the day.'

He stopped speaking and looked at her, and she returned his glance but paused before saying, 'Well, as I said a little while ago, I can walk out, that's my position, but you, you can't, not any more. And if. . . . Well, Glen has already got on your nerves after a couple of hours of him, what's going to happen when he's here twenty-four hours of the day?' She now leant her elbows on the desk and, joining her hands, lowered her chin on them as she now added, 'I was thinking the other day, there's no reason why with Willie and me being here, and Lucy, that you can't have a little private life, like you used to.'

His expression didn't alter. He rarely smiled, which she thought was a pity because he looked most attractive when he smiled. He was a sad person, was John, which his caustic tongue, very like his father's but without the colouring words, did not hide. Over the past months she had come to know him fairly well, and she knew that the more she saw of him the more she liked him, because in a way she recognized something in him that she identified with. It was a sense of loneliness. Undoubtedly, the reasons for such a feeling were difficult for each of them, but it was there.

Her own expression altered to one of mild surprise as he, as if imitating her stance, put his elbows on the table and rested his head on his hands and drooped it slightly to the side before saying, 'Are you suggesting that I should be happier if I spent my nights in sin?'

She let out a long breath, pursed her lips, then said, 'Yes, I suppose I am. Yes, I suppose that is just what I am advocating that you should do. You have a flat, and you have a girl friend. . . .'

'What makes you think I have a flat and girl friend?'

'Well, haven't you? You had. You left home to pursue this course, so I understand.'

'That was not the sole reason I left home, there were many, and the main one is lying upstairs. But to return to the girl friend and the flat. What makes you assume that I have a girl friend at the flat?'

She shook her elbows from the table and rested her hand on the blotter, and her lips parted, then closed and parted again before she said, 'Well, I just . . . assumed, as you say, that . . . that when you went out. . . . Oh, what does it matter?'

She tossed her head.

'It matters. *It matters* to me, *Miss Brownlow*, what you think, for, in a way, I have to live with you. Just in a way, of course.' His face stretched now, and he nipped at his lower lip, his expression indicating laughter. But she didn't respond, she didn't feel like laughing. There was still some annoyance left in her, and she was tired. For the first time she had admitted to herself, what Nell had for some time been stressing on her weekly Sunday visits, she was tired, deeply tired, and it was showing.

As if he was picking up her thoughts, he said, 'I'm sorry. It's the wrong time for the funnies. You are tired, and no wonder. And thank you for your concern. I mean, for me and my . . . private life. But I can tell you now that I haven't a flat, and I haven't a girl friend. And what is more, I hadn't had a flat and I hadn't had a girl friend for a long time before my New Year visit.'

As her eyes widened he nodded at her and said, 'I was in digs with a Mrs Burrows in Bog's End; in fact that's where my flat was; I couldn't afford this end of the town.' A small grin spread over his face; then he went on, 'I must tell you this, Jinny, and please don't be annoyed, but Mrs Burrows had a daughter who was a hairdresser.' As he watched the colour flood over her face he said, quickly, 'Now I asked you not to be annoyed. Betty, that's the daughter, came back one night and told us what had happened. Her employer, Mrs Smith, apparently knew all about you, even if you didn't know about her. She knew you had worked at Henderson and Garbrook. Your dear friend, Mr Campbell, had put her in the picture, just to allay her jealousy I suppose. Well, whatever it was, I put two and two together. And as you might have gathered, I don't laugh much – well, there's nothing much to laugh at in this life – but I laughed until I cried. What with you having a bash at Miss Cadwell, then going for that swine of a pervert and his trollop, well, I thought: Never believe your eyes, John; there goes a fighter.'

'Oh, be quiet!' She got up and walked towards the window, one cheek of her face cupped in the palm of her hand. And now on the verge of tears, she said, 'I'm no fighter. I . . . I never want to fight, or argue, or. . . . But well, I'd had so much of it, I could stand no more. And the circumstances were such. . . .'

'Jinny—' His arm was around her shoulders, and he turned her about to face him, saying, 'Don't apologize for being a fighter. Be glad you are. You should offer up a prayer that there's some part of you that resists. If I could only do that, stike out physically. But what did I do? I turned and ran; like a hotheaded teenager I ran away from home. And what did I do next? Being spiteful, I did what I knew would hurt him most, I shacked up with a girl instead of in the first place standing up to him and telling him what I thought, what I felt. And now here I am, still without the courage to tell him what I feel, because now it's too late. He would think it pity or at best compassion; he would never take it as love.'

175

She had the urge to let the tears flow, not for herself now but for him; she had the urge to put out her arms and hold him, as she sometimes held his father, yet differently. Oh, yes, differently. She drew back from him. 'It's never too late to tell someone of that kind of love,' she said.

'Just that kind of love?'

She was walking from him now towards the desk, and she turned and said, 'Yes, just that kind of love. The other kind just asks for trouble.'

'You seem to have made up your mind firmly on that score.'

'I have. Oh yes, I have.' She was now seated behind the desk, and he stood looking down on her bent head for some seconds before he said, quietly, 'Well, I'd better be off now. I'm to go to the factory once again and get a report from Waitland. It'll be the same as before, and Father knows it. They're telling him nothing.'

'I can tell you one thing. Those reports are faked; they make no mention of the order we were negotiating in January. . . . Perhaps they've lost it. I shouldn't be a bit surprised. Then there was the business in Hamburg. No mention of that either. It did mention a new contract in Belgium, but that's all; just a contract with a firm. And he's worried about the looks of things in the steel industry. There could be trouble there. They're closing down right, left and centre.'

'Well, there's nothing we can do about that; I feel just like an errand boy.'

'There *is* something that could be done.'

'What?' He had turned from the desk but was looking at her once more, and she answered, 'Well, you could get information on how things are really going from someone in the offices, or from a worker on the floor. You could walk round and have a word with them, and ask them to come up and see your father.'

He shook his head slowly as he said, 'Espionage.'

'Yes, if you like to call it that.' Her voice was flat. 'There's Mr Meane. He's in the drawing-office. And also the head clerk, Mr Bury. They're friends, Mr Meane and him. They would know how the land lay, at least contract-wise, I should think. Then there's the shop floor.' She smiled now. 'Jack Newland and Peter Trowell; and there's a Jimmy Moford. They are the spokesmen down there. Always looking for trouble, but any one of them would know the temper of the floor and what's going on. You could have a natter with them and say your father would like to see them. Yes, that's an idea. Any one of them. Oh, particularly Jack Newland would feel he was getting somewhere if he came here. And you'd get more out of them than you'll ever get out of Mr Waitland or Mr Garbrook, or Pillon. . . . Arthur Pillon, who dubs himself assistant works manager.' She grinned now. 'He runs with the hare and hunts with the hounds, and he'll likely tag on to you if he sees you around the shops. Get rid of him if you can.'

He was looking at her now and was actually smiling broadly as he said, 'There's more than even two sides to you, Jinny, I think. You should be in the diplomatic service. I can understand that it wasn't only your backchat that made you a necessity to Father.'

'Your father would never be so stupid as to pay anyone for backchat. He just had to go down to the floor to get plenty of that. I was his secretary, and an efficient one.'

'Huh! You should add, although I say it myself.'

'I have no need to; I know my own value, what there is of it.'

'Well, as a secretary, you're rotting away here, aren't you?'

She sighed now as she said, 'It looks like it. But things never stay still for long. Who knows but I'll be back in harness some day soon.'

The smile left his face. 'Don't say that,' he said flatly; 'you're needed here, not only by him.' And he held her gaze for a moment before turning abruptly and marching from the room.

She stared for some time towards the door before rising and going to the window; and there she stood looking out on to the side garden where the roses were blooming in profusion. Then like a shot ringing down from the mountain top, there passed through her head the words, 'No! No! Not again.'

If she was to be a handmaiden she would be paid for it as she was in this house. But then she'd be handmaiden again to no man, unless . . . unless? What was she thinking about? Now don't let her start kidding herself; there would be no wedding bells connected with John Henderson, for in conversations they'd had over the past months he had firmly expressed his antipathy to marriage. He had made no bones about it, which was why she had thought he still had his flat and was seeing his girl friend occasionally.

He had said she was needed by more than one. Well, his need was going to bring him cold comfort for she had played ministering angel for the last time. By God! yes, she had.

She too now marched from the room, and as if she were closing the door on an opponent she banged it behind her.

3

It was around two o'clock in the morning when the intercom bell dragged her from deep sleep. And groping, she put her hand out and said, 'Yes?'

'Jinny.'

'Yes?' She hitched herself up in the bed, then endeavoured to rub the sleep from her eyes.

'I'm . . . I'm sorry to disturb you, I just wanted a word. Don't bother getting up. I'm . . . I'm just . . . well, het up a bit. It's because of the morrow. You see, I've been thinking of what our John said, and I wonder if I'm doing right. Yet I've got to see him. I've got an awful feeling on me that if I don't see him soon I won't see him at all. Oh, I'm sorry if I woke you, Jinny.'

She had thrown the bedclothes back and was sitting on the side of the bed now and she bent over and called into the phone, 'I'll be with you in a minute.'

'Oh no, I don't want you. . . .' She put the receiver down, then pressed her eyeballs with her fingers and thumbs, and let out a long slow breath before getting up and taking her dressing-gown from the back of the chair.

When she opened his door she saw his head raised from the pillow, and he said in a whisper, 'I . . . I didn't want to disturb you. You shouldn't have come. I just wanted a word.'

'It's all right. It's all right.' She pulled a chair towards the bed and, reaching out, she took his hand, and as she did so he muttered, 'Oh, Jinny. Jinny. And there's another thing: I want to say I'm sorry for yesterday. I wouldn't have blamed you if you had walked out; but God, I don't know what I would have done without you.'

'Now don't try to soft soap me, not at this hour in the morning. I'm liable to melt and succumb to your advances.'

'Oh, Jinny.' There was a wavering laugh in his voice; and as he bit on his lip, whether to stem his laughter or tears she didn't know, she added, 'And as Nell would say, that'll get you into the *Gazette*.

'The *Gazette*?'

It was a question and she said, 'Yes, you know the *Gazette*, the *Shields Daily Gazette*.'

'Oh aye, the newspaper. I must be going dim. . . . No, no, I'm not. You know that's something, Jinny' – he turned his head towards her now – 'the times I've wished it was me head that had got it, and Glen his body, because I've lived most of my life but his was only beginning, and if he had his mind it wouldn't have mattered so much about his body, not now he's lost Yvonne.'

'Well, it didn't turn out like that, and so you have to accept things as they are. But I must say this, I feel as John does, if you were to make an effort. . . .'

'No, lass, no. What's the point? Don't start on that tack again, not the night, or the morning, whatever time it is. By!' – he smiled at her now – 'you look bonny in this light.'

'Thank you very much.' She had assumed a hurt tone. 'That means to say that the pink shade is very kind to me. What a pity it's got to be daylight.'

'Eeh, by! your tongue. I've never known another like it. Oh yes, I have.' He moved his head slowly. 'Alicia could come back like lightning an' all, but in a different way. She wasn't a Geordie, you see.'

'I'm not a Geordie either.'

'Oh yes, you are.'

'Oh no, I'm not. I don't talk the twang; I speak as I write, plain English.'

'Eeh my! Proud of it, aren't you? Well, don't let any Geordie hear you bragging like that else your number'll be up.'

A silence ensued until he said, 'I'm all right now, lass. I think I might get off.'

'Well, go on then.'

'You go on back to bed. And thanks.'

'I'll stay here for a while. I can put my feet up on this other chair. And here's a rug. I'll stay until you do go off, so be quick about it.'

As she settled herself he turned his face towards her, saying softly now, 'I've wondered lately if you get any satisfaction out of playing the ministering angel, you certainly can't get any pleasure.'

She did not look at him, but pulled the rug up under her chin as she said, 'I'm no ministering angel; I'm what you call a cultured handmaiden.'

'A what?'

'You heard, a cultured handmaiden.'

'Where did you get that from? Who called you that?'

'Oh, it's a long story. I'll tell you some day, or some night when you can't get to sleep. But not tonight. Go on, I'm tired. Good-night.'

'Good-night, Jinny. And . . . God bless you.' The words were faint but audible to her.

She closed her eyes thinking of the form in which God's blessing fell on cultured handmaidens. Down the ages they had been given different names: dutiful daughters, mother's help, lady companions, all cultured handmaidens.

She woke with a crick in her neck and Willie bending over her, saying, 'Here, drink this.'

Slowly, she pulled herself up in the chair and, blinking, she took the cup from him; and she watched him turn and look towards the bed where Bob was still sleeping soundly. And when he put his head down to her and said, 'You're a fool, you know; he'll keep you at this,' she asked, 'What time is it?'

'Just seven o'clock. Get yourself up and go to bed for a few hours. And I'm telling you' – his voice was lower still – 'he'll play on you. I've had experience. Even the best of them, like him, they suck you dry. You haven't got to let it happen. Come on, get yourself up.'

His large thick hands came out now and hoisted her to her feet as she muttered, 'Look! You'll spill the tea.'

'Better if you don't drink it. Go on. Get some kip.'

She liked Willie. He was a practical man, down to earth, and he was kind and attentive to his patient, yet although she was aware that he was talking sense she knew that if Bob wanted her company in the middle of the night she'd be hard put not to answer his call. . . .

She went to bed and slept till nine o'clock. Then after having a bath she picked up the morning routine. It was broken about eleven o'clock by a phone call from Mrs Florence Brook, and as usual, when it was Jinny's voice which came over to her, Florence's reply was a very telling 'Oh,' which could be interpreted as, 'You're still there then?'

'How's Father?'

'He is about the same.'

'I would like to speak to John.'

'I'm afraid he's in . . . at the hospital. He's bringing Glen home today.'

'*What!*'

'I said he was bringing Glen home.'

'And who's idea was that?'

'Apparently your father's. He wants to see him.'

'My God! Do you know what our Glen is like now?'

'No, I'm afraid I don't.'

'John said he would never allow him to come back.'

There was a pause before Jinny replied, 'Your father is still head of the house.'

'I'm well aware of that, madam! . . . miss.'

'I was only meaning to infer. . . .'

'I know what you were meaning to infer. Has he got the male nurse still there?'

'Yes, Willie is still here.'

'Then may I ask what your duties are?'

'My duties, Mrs Brook, are exactly what yours would be if you were running this household.'

There was a telling silence on the phone now; then Florence's voice came, the words stubbing over the wires, 'You've taken too much on yourself. Do you know that? You were a secretary, and there's no secretarial work to be done now. As for running the house, Dorry can see to that. She and Cissie have done so for years. . . . And you're forgetting that Lucy's there; she's quite capable of running the house.'

'I don't think your mother would have agreed with you.'

'*My.* . . .'

At this point the phone went dead, and Jinny, putting it back on its rest, stood for a moment with her head bent and her teeth nipping at her lower lip. It was certainly a good job that Mr Henderson had no room for his son-in-law in any capacity or her own life here would have been made impossible. As for Lucy being able to run the house, Lucy was hardly ever in it, but when she was she made a point of spending most of the time with her father. It was a diplomatic cover, for then he rarely asked questions about what she did with the rest of her time.

A short while later, standing by Bob's bed, she said, 'Mrs Brook phoned.'

'Aye. And what had she to say?'

'She wanted to know how you were and to speak to John.'

'And you told her where John was?'

'Yes.'

'And what he was doing?'

'Yes.'

'And what was her reaction?'

'Not favourable.'

'Well, that's nothing new. I've never known our Florrie to be in favour of anything except what pleased herself. She was the odd man out to me, always was, our Florrie. I don't know who she took after. Certainly not Alicia. And I can't see anything of her in me. . . . Can you?'

She paused a moment before nodding her head and saying, 'A little: if she can't get her own way she plays up.'

'Well, I'll be damned. You know, at times you're no comfort at all. Anyway, did she play up this morning?'

'A little.'

'What about?'

'She thought my presence here was unnecessary.'

'Begod! she did. And of course, you took that meekly.'

'No, I didn't.'

'No, I thought you wouldn't. I should like to have heard you. . . . What time is it now?' He turned his head towards the clock.

'Gone twelve.'

'They should be here soon.'

'Yes, they should.'

'Jinny.'

'Yes?'

'I'm all het up inside.'

'Well, all I can say is you asked for it.' But as she spoke she lifted his hand and squeezed it gently as she went on, 'Just remember you're not going to see the old Glen, so you'll have to brace yourself.'

'Aye. Aye, but I'm always havin' to brace meself. Just to go on breathing I'm havin' to brace meself.'

She could find no words with which to answer him for a moment; then she said. 'We all seem to be looking on the black side. Let's wait until we see him. And then we might be agreeably surprised, eh?'

'The answer to that, lass, is we can't do anything else. But as for being agreeably surprised. . . . Oh dear! Oh dear!' He moved his head slowly on the pillow, and she let his hand drop and went out of the room.

It was a quarter to one when John and Glen arrived. When Jinny looked at the man standing just inside the front door she wanted to put her hand over her mouth and press an agonized sound back into her being because this was Glen, his body, his face, everything about him was Glen Henderson, everything, that is, except the eyes. And it was the eyes that made the difference to the man. They were bright, yet vacant; and their glance was darting here and there as if in search of something while his head remained still. And when they came to rest on her, he opened his mouth and spoke. And what he said was, 'I'll not sit again; I didn't pass.'

'Do you remember Jinny?' John spoke quietly.

'Yes; of course I remember Jinny. What's the matter with you? Of course I remember Jinny.' There was laughter in the tone. 'I'm hungry. I want my tea. . . . What about the bike?'

'We'll see about that later.'

'But he's had it for about a week now. Anyway, I should have a new one.' His eyes stopped flickering; and his gaze coming to rest steadily now on Jinny, and his tone changing, he said quietly, 'Could I have a drink, nurse?'

She swallowed deeply before saying, 'Yes, yes, of course. Come along.' And she put out her hand and touched his arm, and as she guided him into the drawing-room she said, 'What would you like, a cold drink or tea?'

'Orange squash.'

She turned and looked at John now, and he, beckoning to Dorry who was standing a little way from them, repeated, 'Orange squash.'

In the drawing-room the man now stood looking about him. His eyelids blinked and at one point they screwed up so tightly that there seemed to be nothing left but the sockets, and when he opened them again he turned his head slowly as if he were trying to recall something. Quietly he sat down on the couch, his hands resting on his knees, very like a young boy who was visiting and on his best behaviour.

When Dorry brought him a glass of orange juice, she bent towards him and said, 'Hello, Mr Glen.'

'Hello,' he replied politely.

'You remember Dorry?' John's voice was quiet and persuasive. But his brother turned on him almost angrily, saying, 'Of course, I remember Dorry. What d'you keep on for?' Then looking at Jinny, he said, 'And Nurse Jinny. And Nurse Pratt. And Piggy Eyes.'

'Piggy Eyes?'

John bent his head towards him, and Glen nodded at him, saying, 'She's on duty at night. We call her Piggy Eyes because she screws up her face when she looks at us.' He now smiled widely and spread his gaze from one to the other. And Jinny again wanted to press the pain down but this time to stop the moan that could have preceded a bout of weeping.

John was right. This boy . . . this man should never have been brought home. If he'd had a mother to see him, then that might have been different. But he had only a father lying upstairs who was expecting to see his son, different but not so different. Oh no, not this different. Well, there was one thing sure, this house would never be the same again. Here was a handful, and it was going to take, not only John's and Willie's whole time, but also her own in a way, for already he had selected her as a nurse.

It was fifteen minutes later when they took him upstairs. John went in first, his hand behind him drawing Glen forward, and she followed. She had not wanted to be present at this meeting, but Glen had insisted, saying, 'Nurse always comes with me.'

Willie was standing by the head of the bed, and he moved aside, and Bob looked on his elder son. And his elder son looked on him. And neither of them spoke. It was John whose voice came out as a croak, saying, 'We had a good journey, Father. Glen . . . Glen enjoyed it.'

'You got a cold?'

Jinny was gripping the front of her dress as she looked at Bob and waited for the answer to his son's question. The pain seemed to be rising like sweat from his face. It was red. His lips were tight together, while his eyes were wide. The question gave no clue to whether Glen recognized the man lying there as his father, and it was John again who spoke to him, saying, 'Your . . . your father hasn't been well.'

Now Glen did turn a mildly enquiring look on John. It was as if the word had penetrated through some thick mist in his mind. But he didn't repeat it or ask for an explanation, he just turned his gaze once more on Bob. Then for the second time since coming into the house he said, 'I'm hungry.'

'In that case we shall have to find you something to eat, won't we?' With practised ease Willie had taken the situation in hand; and coming to Glen's side, he said, 'Come on downstairs and tell me what you like best. Come on.'

Glen turned immediately from the bed, saying, 'Not fish and chips. And not sausages; I like meat.'

'Steak or roast meat?'

'Oh either.' He laughed now, and the sound was more strange because it was a man's laugh; the only thing that was recognisable about him to his father and his brother was his laugh.

Like bosom friends they went from the room, Willie with his arm around Glen's shoulder. And when the door closed on them Bob's mouth went into a large gasp. His limp hand fluttered over the eiderdown, and John, looking down on him, muttered, 'I warned you.'

'God damn you, yes, you warned me. All right. All right. But he's your brother, and this is his home.'

'Well, Father, you reminding me that he is my brother, let me remind you that he is your son. But you won't have the job of looking after him. He's got to be watched; he wanders. I might as well tell you they weren't for letting him come home. And it's only for a trial period.'

'Trial period, be damned! You'd have him put away, locked up some place?'

'It isn't like that, he's not locked up in some place. It's a hospital, where he's given excellent care. And strangely, he was happy there. Don't you understand? He's lost years; he's back in his boyhood. And not only that: it isn't the boyhood that you and I remember; apparently it's only a boyhood which he alone was cognizant of, a kind of subconscious place. We all have it. From what the doctor says he goes in and out of this place. And it's just as well that he doesn't now remember exactly what happened. Like he did after the first operation. Willie's going to have more than his hands full.'

'Then we'll get somebody to help him.'

'But what about Jinny here?' John now threw out his arm towards where she was standing silently at the foot of the bed. 'He's taken her for a nurse. There were two nurses on the ward at times, and he used to follow them about.'

'Well, she's got nothing else to do but to see to him.'

When Bob turned his eyes on her and waited for her reply, she answered, 'Yes, I could see to the boy in him, but not to the man. And what would happen if his mind should leave the boy and return to the man?'

'My God! What am I surrounded with? Bloody psychiatrists? If only I could use my. . . .'

'If only you could use your common sense, which you would have us believe you've still got plenty of, you could, even at this point, possibly solve the problem.'

As she marched from the room, leaving John and his father staring at her, she paused for a moment outside her own door before going in. Once inside, she stood and pushed her hand up through her hair. What had made her say that? Only seconds before she was hoping that John would go gently with him, yet she knew what she had said was right. That man who had been Glen, the jolly go-ahead Glen, and who had now turned into an overgrown, great outsized boy, filled her with a dread that touched on real fear, at the same time arousing her deepest pity.

Going to the window, she sat down on the chair, and for the first time she thought, I wish I was far away from here. Somehow things had become complicated.

She could pack up this minute and go to Nell's. There was nothing to stop her. . . . Nothing to stop her? Only him lying across there, with his tongue so alive it could whip pieces out of you, while at the same time his eyes were telling you he was so lost that if you left go of his hand he would sink.

'Huh!' she said to herself as her mind touched on Nell again. Nell had never been happy about her being here, but on the sight of Glen, without even hearing him speak, she would likely say, 'Come on, get yourself out of here, lass, afore something happens. Paralysed men are one thing, but mad 'uns are another.' And that was the name she would put to Glen. That was the name anybody would put to Glen.

4

❧❧

'I'm hungry.'

'But you've just had your lunch, Glen.'

'No; my tea.'

'No; your lunch. Tea won't be ready for . . . well, three hours.'

'I'm hungry.'

'There are some sweets in your room; go and get them.'

'Will you play cards?'

'I can't just now; I'm busy writing letters. See. . . . I'm at my typewriter.'

'I can write letters; I write poetry.'

'Do you?'

'Yes, I do.'

'You'll have to show me some.'

'No, I won't do that. I never show anybody.'

She looked up at the man standing to the side of her and she told herself yet again, as she had done over the past two weeks, not to feel repulsed by him; he couldn't help his state, he was still Glen. Yet he wasn't Glen, he was a weird . . . man-cum-boy, and it wasn't only she who found she couldn't bear his presence for long. The pity of it was, the very sight of him agonized his father. Bob knew that he had made a mistake in bringing his son home, but being the man he was he wouldn't own up to the mistake.

'I'm going out on my bike.'

'Very well.' She nodded at him. He was always going out on his bike. But strangely he never made any attempt to go out through the front door, not even into the garden unless someone was with him. And what was more strange, yet on thinking back to the source of his troubles perhaps not so strange, he was showing evidence of being afraid of the car. When John offered yesterday to take him for a ride he had turned from him,

187

and in a kind of shambling run had made for the kitchen. And when John followed him he stood by the kitchen table and picked up a wooden spoon and started to beat a tattoo on the side of an earthenware bowl which Cissie had just half filled with flour. And then he had smacked the wooden spoon into the middle of the flour, sending a spray over the table and partly over himself and John. At this, John had become angry and said, 'Enough of that now!' and had led him protesting from the room.

She often thought that were Glen to become aggressive John would have little chance against him, because he was at least three stones heavier and inches taller.

John and Willie had worked out a system whereby they relieved each other in looking after Glen, and although the strain wasn't as yet showing on Willie, it certainly was on John, and he had said to her only last night, 'I don't know how much longer I can stick this. He shouldn't be here; he should be back in hospital.'

John had told her at the beginning that he didn't want her involved with Glen in any way. But he hadn't taken Glen into account. Glen had seen to it that she was involved because whenever possible he followed her about, and over the last three days had formed a new pattern. Whenever he could he would now take hold of her arm and say 'You coming for a walk, Jin?' or 'I'm hungry,' or 'Play cards, nurse.'

At the present moment, she didn't want to rise from the chair because she knew he would again take hold of her arm; but nevertheless, she wanted him out of the room.

She was about to reach for the intercom button that would put her through to John's room, even though she knew he was off duty so to speak, when Glen spoke. And for a moment there was no trace of the boy in his voice. 'You ringing for Willie?' he said.

'No. No.'

'You are.'

'No, I wasn't. Not for Willie.'

'Oh.'

Her finger was wavering over the button when the door opened and Willie himself appeared; and he said, 'Oh, there you are, then,' Glen looked down on Jinny and said angrily now, 'Knew you were ringing for Willie. Knew you were.'

'I didn't ring, Glen. Look, I haven't pressed the button. I didn't ring for you, Willie, did I?'

'No, no; I just happened to pop in. You coming for a walk?'

'No.'

'Aw, come on. I'm dying for a breath of fresh air, man. And I've got a couple of Mars bars in me pocket.'

The expression on Glen's face altered, and without further ado he walked towards the door, and Willie nodded towards Jinny and raised his eyebrows before closing the door behind him.

She sat back in the chair and let out a long slow breath. It was no use; she'd just have to speak to Bob. She gathered up the letters from the desk, and then went upstairs to Bob's room.

When she had first seen Bob lying in his bed she had thought that he could never look worse except if he were to die. But over the past weeks she had seen that he could look worse and still live. His features were drawn, his cheeks hollow and there was no longer any disgruntled remark from him; he seemed to have given up the battle.

She stood by the bed, saying now, 'I've done these letters, a personal one to Bill Meane and another to Mr Bury. I've just said you would like to see them. Shall I read them?'

'There's no point.'

She made no comment, but said, 'John of course told you he'd had a few words with Jack Newland and Peter Trowell from the shop floor, and indicated that you'd be pleased to see them to have a natter sometime.'

'A lot of damn good that'll do, won't it?'

'Well, we'll only have to wait and see, won't we?'

He turned his head and looked at her; but he did not speak. And she said, 'I've got to bring this up, whether you are vexed or pleased. It's Glen.'

'What about him?'

'I'm . . . well, to tell you the truth, I'm slightly afraid of him.'

'What have you got to be afraid of? He's turned into a lad, the man's gone, so what have you got to be afraid of?'

'I don't really know, but the only thing I do know is that I am afraid. His manner is changing; he follows me around.'

'Is that so terrible?'

'Yes, it is to me.' Her voice had risen. 'And I've got to tell you, I . . . I can't stand it. This is the third week, and it's getting on my nerves. John and Willie do their best.'

'That's what they're paid for, both of them.'

'You can never pay John for what he's doing, so don't say a thing like that.'

'Oh, you're on his side now. I didn't think you two hit it off.'

'It isn't a case of hitting it off, it's a case of giving credit where it's due. And if you want to know anything, I think he's had about as much as he can stand too.'

'So what's the answer.'

'It's . . . it's up to you; Glen should go back to hospital.'

'Be damned if he will! This is his home; I'm his father; if I don't have him who will? You're telling me he should end his days in a loony house. Well now, miss, if you can't put up with him there's always a way out.'

She stared down at him, and he returned her stare while his lips moved one over the other as if he was sucking something from them.

Slowly she said, 'Yes, there's always a way out, and I shall take it tomorrow.' And on this she turned from him. And his voice didn't stop her as it once would have done when it came to her, saying, 'Jinny! Jinny.'

The tears almost spurted from her eyes as she closed the door behind her, and when through the mist she saw John approaching from the end of the corridor, she ran the few steps across the landing and into her own room. But she had no sooner closed the door than it was opened again, and John, going to her and taking her by the shoulders, looked down on her bent head as he asked, 'What is it? What's happened?'

She was unable to speak because her throat was blocked, and he said urgently, 'Jinny! Jinny! What is it? Tell me. What has he said to you?'

She was going to choke; she let out a long shuddering sob, and when he put his arms about her and held her close her body shook them both with the force of her weeping.

It was a good minute later when she pulled herself from his embrace and searched blindly around for something on which to dry her face. When he brought his handkerchief out and wiped her cheeks with it, she took it from him and, turning away, went and sat down in a chair by the side of the bed. And he followed her. Sitting on the edge of the bed, he leaned towards her, saying, 'What happened? Tell me. Was it about Glen?'

She nodded. Then between gasps, she said, 'I'm . . . I'm afraid of him. He's . . . he's always wanting to—' She could hardly bring herself to say the words, 'touch me. And I said to your father that I can't stand it any longer and that he should be sent back to hospital. And' – she gulped deep in her throat – 'he told me, if I couldn't put up with it the door was open. And so . . . and so, I told him I'm going tomorrow.'

'By God! you're not.'

She lifted her head and her eyes blinked rapidly and her mouth opened and shut a number of times before she was able to say, 'Yes, I . . . I am. I . . . I couldn't stand it. I . . . I feel . . . I fear something could happen. I don't know what, but, John, I can't help it, I'm afraid of him. And Lucy is too. She told me so. That's why she's gone to stay with Monica.'

'He'll go back to hospital; I'll see to that.'

'Please! No!' She put her hand out and laid it on his. 'No. Your father wants him here. As he said, he couldn't bear to think of him in . . . well, in a sort of asylum.'

'That's where he'll have to go in the end; and Father's got to face up to it. It's terrible, I know. Not for Glen. Oh no, not for Glen, because he's gone back to a place in his mind where nothing can touch him, only his physical needs, such as food. He's put on nearly a stone since he came home. I've told Dorry and Cissie not to give him anything to eat between meals, but as they say, what can they do when he just goes to the fridge and takes it. Look, Jinny.'

He now put one hand on her shoulder and the other under her chin and lifted her face up as he said softly, 'Let me try with Father. Give it a day or two, and I'll see that Glen doesn't come near you; I'll tell Willie not to let him out of his sight. But you must know this: you must know it in your own mind that whatever Father says he's going to miss you like mad if you go; in fact, I don't know what he'll do without you. You know' – he smiled at her now, one of his rare smiles – 'it's odd, if I hadn't known he was so devoted to Mother I would have imagined he was having an affair with you. Oh . . . oh, don't look like that. It would have been the most natural thing in the world . . . if you had been willing. And now I don't know how he looks upon you; not as a daughter, he's got four of them, and they do nothing for him mentally; in fact, Florence irritates him to the point of fury at times; and one couldn't classify you in the role of mother figure, could one?'

She didn't give him an answer to this, but what she said was, 'Some one once said of me that I acted like a cultured hand-maiden, and, looking back over the last eighteen months, I . . . I can see that I have fitted that role, with emphasis on the handmaiden.'

'Cultured handmaiden? Who on earth said that to you? That's the last category I'd put you in, because a handmaiden implies submissiveness, and no one could say that Miss Jinny Brownlow was of the submissive type. Now could they?'

'It's all how the other person views you. As for how your father sees me; I was a good secretary; I can't lay claim to any other ability; and why he liked me around was because I wasn't afraid of his caustic tongue and rough manner. I think he still views me as part of the fitments of the office and his last contact with the works. I can still talk business with him, at least I could up to . . . well, up to Glen's arrival. But since then he seems to have lost interest. I'm sorry' – she shook her head – 'but even if you can control Glen's movements, which I'm afraid you're going to find difficult because if he decides to use force I don't think even Willie could handle him. Anyway, the way things are . . . have turned out, it's better that I go, because. . . .'

'Jinny. Jinny' – he hitched himself closer to her – 'I . . . I find it difficult to ask favours of anyone, but I'm going to ask this of you now: hang on till the end of the week. If you still feel the same then, all right, leave on Saturday with your cousin. But give me a few days. And it isn't only because . . . well—' He turned his head to the side and brought his teeth together before adding, 'We . . . we didn't hit it off at first, did we? But that was my fault. I . . . I might as well tell you, I too would miss you if you left.' Again he turned his head away from her as he said, 'A house isn't a house without a woman in it.'

'Oh, if that's all that a house needs, then you can bring Lucy back.'

'Oh, I didn't mean it like that. Why do you always take me up wrong? As for Lucy, I'm afraid Lucy's not coming back. I was on to Monica last night and by what she says Reg Talbot's been over there and it wouldn't surprise me if they get married on the quiet and she goes off with him. In fact, she's so besotted with him, Monica says she wouldn't be surprised if she side-stepped the ceremony. But that wouldn't make anyone faint, not these days, would it?' There was a slight upward twist to the corner of his mouth now.

And she answered stiffly, 'No; it wouldn't. Yet, I suppose there are still a few that would like a ceremony to authorize the union.'

'Oh, good Lord!' He hitched himself away from her now, and, his chin dropping almost to his chest, laughed as he said,

'You're amazing. You know that, Jinny? You're amazing. That sounded like a piece out of a Victorian novel.' Now his head was lifted, and the smile had gone from his face as he asked her, 'Do you think that a piece of paper and a few words said over you by a man makes all that difference to the act? That it solemnizes it, blesses it, whether you enjoy it or not? And if you don't enjoy it, because of that piece of paper you've got to stick it out for life, submit for life, as women had to do at one time. But now they're doing without the paper, and if they don't like it, or if he doesn't, one or other can get up and leave. Isn't that a cleaner way?'

She was on her feet now looking down at him; her face was set and her lips scarcely moved as she said, 'Your purpose in following me in here was to find out why I was upset. Well, now you know; but I cannot see the connection between that purpose and the topic you have just raised. And I don't wish to carry on with the discussion.'

He rose from the bed and his face was as stiff as hers and his voice was almost a growl as he said, 'You know what you're made of, Miss Brownlow? You're made of the material from which they used to cut out spinsters. It's written on your face, it's in the way you walk, it's in your defensive repartee; all of it real material of a frustrated woman.'

He had reached the door before she turned and cried after him, 'Well, this spinster is leaving in the morning; or perhaps tonight.'

The handle of the open door still in his hand, he turned and said, 'Good. Good,' then banged the door closed.

She had got her suitcases from the store room and packed her belongings before she took up the phone to contact Nell. When there was no reply to her ring, she stood nipping on her thumb nail before replacing the receiver. It was Tuesday, and Tuesday was the ritual tea with Mrs Collins . . . Mamie, Nell's lifelong friend. And on a Tuesday Peter usually stayed late at the office; that's if he hadn't a meeting of the Rotarians or the Masons, or some such. If she'd had a key to the house she would have ordered a taxi here and now. They had given her one before the end of the first week there, but when she came here she naturally left it behind, thinking she would never need it again.

Odd that. . . . Odd. Why should she have imagined she was here for life? And what kind of a life had it represented to her other than doing a few letters and keeping a paralysed man amused by answering him back in his own vein, a vein that very often had irritated her because you could get too much of anything, good, bad, or indifferent? And familiarity, although it did not breed contempt in this case, had often bred weariness.

It had been different when they were in the office together: backchat often stemmed from a focal point, maybe comments upon letters, reactions to visits from the shop floor, irritations stemming from his partner's ideas, or the power fight that went on in the three offices along the top corridor, but in the main from Mr Waitland's office.

She would have to stay until tomorrow morning, but she was determined not to leave this room till then. It wouldn't hurt her to go without a meal for the next few hours; as for a drink, she always kept some bottles of orange juice in the bathroom cupboard. That would suffice.

She went to the window and stood looking out on the sprawling town down below, with Bog's End and the Mill Bank standing out clearly in the afternoon sunshine. . . . The bus had gone along the Mill Bank that day she had. . . .

Her mind shrank from the scene she had witnessed in the room behind the hairdresser's shop, yet it followed the road leading out of the town and to Hal's house.

Her thoughts now scampered away, and she started when a knock came on the door, but she did not call, 'Come in,' but asked, 'Who is it?'

'It's me, Dorry, miss.'

She went and opened the door, and Dorry said, 'There's a gentleman downstairs asking for you.'

'A gentleman, asking for me? Who . . . who is it? Did he give his name?'

'No. I suppose I should have asked, but he just said could he see Miss Brownlow. And he looked all right, not common or anything. So I asked him in. He's waiting in the hall.'

Jinny continued to look at Dorry. It wouldn't be Peter; Dorry knew Peter. . . . Was it? No, no; Hal wouldn't dare come here, he wouldn't dare. Yet she had just been thinking about him.

'Is he old . . . I mean middle-aged, or . . . or?'

'No, he's young, miss.'

'Young?' Her mind was blank. She couldn't think who it could be. She said, 'I'll be down in a minute.'

It wasn't until she was descending the stairs that she thought, Michael. Of course, Michael. It could only be Michael. Why hadn't she thought of him straightaway?

He was standing near the tall window looking on to the drive and he hadn't heard her descend the thickly carpeted stairs.

'Hello, Michael.' There was a welcome in her voice.

He swung round but didn't move towards her and it was some seconds before he replied, 'Hello, Jinny. Long time no see.'

She was about to say, 'Will you come into the drawing-room?' when John appeared from the passage to the left of the stairs, and he stood staring from one to the other.

Looking at him straight faced, Jinny said, 'Will it be all right to take Mr Morton into the drawing-room?' and he looked for a moment a replica of his father and, also like his father, as if he was about to come out with a mouthful of abuse. But he said in stilted theatrical tones, 'Yes, you are at liberty to take . . . Mr Morton into the drawing-room.'

In the room and the door closed behind them, Michael, turning to her, said, 'Who's he?'

'He's Mr Henderson's son John.'

'Pleasant individual.'

'I'm not excusing him but I can say he's not himself today.'

When she indicated he should take a seat on the couch he nodded and, impulsively putting out his hand, he drew her down beside him; and still holding on to her hand, he said, 'So this is where you've been hiding?'

'I haven't been hiding.'

His face straight now, he asked, 'Why did you do it, go off like that?'

'I should think that was obvious, I couldn't stand any more. . . .'

'Any more what?'

'Oh, don't be silly, Michael.'

'All right, I won't be silly, but I'll tell you, I've spent almost a month looking for you. That damned house agent was as close as a clam. Then I had to go to London. I suppose you could say it was promotion: I was drafted there to do a job. I've been back three weeks and . . . well' – he pursed his lips – 'I thought I'd got rid of you from under my skin, but when I returned I found I hadn't, so I started again, blindly. Then just by chance an oldish fellow came into the office only yesterday with his son who wanted advice about tax. We got on talking. The father was a nice old fellow. It came out he worked at Hendersons. The doorman, he said. And yes, he knew a Miss Jinny Brownlow. Oh, yes, he did; he remembered her very well.' Michael nodded his head at Jinny now as he went on, 'Had he any idea where she was now? Oh, yes, she was looking after the boss – and he would always think of Mr Henderson as the boss – in his house on Brampton Hill.' Michael now spread his free hand wide as he ended, 'So here I am.'

'It's nice to see you, Michael.'

'Do you mean that?'

'Yes, yes, I do.' And she did. She had always liked Michael, and she knew she had been rather attracted to him from the first and, if he had put in an appearance when she was living with Nell, who knew but things might have grown between them. As it was now, well that was impossible. How many times could your affections be assailed by this thing called love. But then she hadn't loved Michael. Had she loved Hal Campbell? No, she hadn't loved Hal Campbell. Had she loved Ray Collard? No, she hadn't loved Ray Collard. Had she loved George Mayborough? Somewhere inside of her a laugh rippled. No, she certainly hadn't loved George Mayborough. Did she love . . .? A door banged shut, and a voice, sounding raucous to her ears, said, 'Enough of that. No more humiliations.' Then a question came, sharp, piercing: What about the man upstairs? She loved him, didn't she? Oh yes, she could own up to that love, she loved him; or she had loved him, but it was a love without desire, a passionless love; yet nevertheless a love. But no more, no more of love of any kind. . . . 'What did you say?'

'I said, you weren't listening to what I was saying.'

'What were you saying?'

'I was saying I am a changed man with regard to views on matrimony. Please, please,' he said, gripping her hand tightly when she went to pull it away from him; 'I'm in earnest, Jinny, very much in earnest. This is the first time this kind of thing has ever hit me. I swore it wouldn't, I might as well tell you. I'd seen so much of marriages going wrong. Well you know all about that, don't you? But there are marriages that can go right; and Jinny, I'd make ours go right. Believe me, I would. Will you?' He lifted her hand to his breast and with his other hand on her shoulder was drawing her towards him when they both stiffened at the sound of the door being thrust open and their heads both turned to look down the room to where John was standing in the doorway, his face looking blank, his eyes mere slits as if he was peering at them over a distance; but his voice sounded quite calm as he said, 'I . . . I wondered if you would like some tea?'

'No, thank you.' Jinny had disengaged from Michael's hold and had risen to her feet.

'It's . . . it's all ready. Dorry's got a tray set.'

'No thank you. We won't bother. Mr Morton is just going.'

John let his eyes rest on Michael for some seconds before he said, 'Very well,' then turned away, closing the door quietly after him.

Looking back at Jinny and sighing, he said, 'May I continue where I left off?'

'No, Michael, please.'

'You don't dislike me?'

'Oh, no, no. I never have.' She smiled gently at him.

'Well then, that could be a beginning.'

'No, because it would stay there. I'm . . . I'm not in love with you.'

'There's a difference between being in love and loving. They say if you like somebody, that's the best beginning.'

'Well, I like you, Michael, but I know the other is impossible.'

'Why?' His face was straight now. 'Somebody else on the horizon, or let's say closer inland?'

'No . . . no one.'

'What about him?' He nodded towards the closed door. 'If ever I've seen jealousy, there it was.'

'That wasn't jealousy, that was—' She swallowed deeply before adding, 'temper.'

'You're sure?'

Her pausing before answering caused him to say, 'You're not sure, are you?'

'I'm so sure that I'm leaving here tomorrow.'

'You are?' His face stretched. 'Why?'

'A difference of opinion on various matters.'

'Where are you going?'

There was no reason why she shouldn't tell him, because she considered it would be silly if he started another search for her.

And anyway, should he call here they would tell him where she was. So she said, 'I have a cousin in Shields.'

'And you say you're going there tomorrow? Can ... can I run you in?'

Yes, yes, he could. That would save the bother of getting a taxi or of Peter coming to fetch her, for when she phoned Nell and Peter later tonight Peter would be sure to insist. And so she said, 'That would be kind of you.'

'What time?'

'What time would suit you?'

'Any time, I'm my own boss.' He pulled a face at her. 'Promotion since London. So, say ten o'clock?'

'That'll be fine. Thank you.' She now moved from him towards the door, but before she reached it he had caught her arm and, looking into her face, said, 'I'm making a habit of rescuing you, so I'm going to take it as a good sign.'

She shook her head slowly now, saying, 'Please, Michael, don't. I ... I must be honest with you, there ... there is someone else.'

'Oh!' He rubbed his fingers across his chin. 'Well, where is he now, when you need him?'

'He doesn't know I need him.'

'It's like that, is it? Married?'

'No, he's not married.'

'Then there's something funny somewhere. Oh' – his head nodded now – 'he's not the marrying kind, and you don't go for that lark, do you? Well' – he smiled faintly at her now – 'I've offered to make an honest woman of you and I wouldn't mind playing second fiddle because there's always the chance that something will happen to the leader of the orchestra.'

'Oh, Michael.' She found herself laughing and she put her hand out and laid it on his as she said, 'You are nice.' Then swiftly and before he could take hold of her arms as he was about to do, she pulled open the door and led the way into the hall. And when they were on the outside step and he looked upwards as he said, 'It's a fine house this. Will you be sorry to leave it?' she answered simply, 'Yes.'

'Well, till tomorrow at ten.'

'Thank you, I'll be ready. Goodbye.'

'Goodbye, Jinny.'

As she closed the door on him a shiver ran through her entire body: she didn't know whether it was the cold wind or the fact that through Michael's unexpected visit she had surprised herself into admitting something she had refused to recognize for weeks now. As she made for the stairs she saw John descending and, about to follow him, Glen, accompanied by Willie.

'Nurse! Nurse! I want. . . .' Glen's request was drowned by Willie saying, 'Now, now; nurse is busy. Steady on, Steady on.'

And as if to protect her, John ran down towards her and, taking her by the arm, led her back into the drawing-room. But Glen's protests came to them. His voice hardly that of a boy, he was yelling, 'Why can't I? Why can't I? Nurse likes playing cards. Leave me alone.'

At the sound of a scuffle, Jinny put her hand, fingers spread wide, on the top of her head and brought it forward as if in doing so she would shut out all sound; and she didn't raise it until John's voice, coming at her quietly, said, 'You were right. One of you would have to go.' Then his tone changed slightly as he added, 'It seemed fortunate that your friend should arrive at an opportune time. Is . . . is he an old friend?'

'You could say that.'

'I suppose he's pleased you're leaving?'

'Yes, you could say that too.'

'He's a good-looking fellow.'

'I think so.'

'Why hasn't he called on you before?'

She turned away from him and put her hand on the door handle as she said, 'He didn't know where I was, he's been looking for me.'

'And now he's found you, what happens next?'

She seemed to detect a slight note of amusement in his voice, even though his expression belied his tone, and her whole body stretched until she appeared to be looking down at him before she said, 'What happens next will likely be a wedding.' And on this she pulled the door open, but had to push past him because he did not move out of her way, and as she mounted the stairs she was aware that he was watching her from where he still stood within the doorway.

She stood in the middle of her room, her eyes closed, her arms around her waist as if hugging herself against the cold, and she muttered aloud, 'Oh dear God.' And it wasn't because of anything he had said, but because at the moment she'd imagined she detected amusement in his voice she'd had a great urge to take her hand and slap his face. It was a similar feeling to that which had welled up in her when she had hit Miss Cadwell, and again when she had witnessed Hal Campbell in bed with that elderly blowzy woman. What was the matter with her? She never used to be like this. She could look back on herself right until she had lost her parents as being a gentle naive creature, she could even put the term genteel to herself, but since she had begun to mix with people and to search for companionship – she skipped the word love – there was being revealed in her character a facet that she imagined to be the antithesis of her real self. Aggressiveness, she would have said, was not in her nature; but, given the circumstances, there it was. Yet why should she wish to strike at John of all people? Granted he had a caustic tongue, but that wasn't why she was mad at him. No.

She went towards the bed, sat down on the foot of it and, putting her arms on the rails, she rested her head on them. Let her face it, she knew why she wanted to hit him. Come clean. Come clean. She knew he was in love with her, but she also knew that he would never ask her to marry him. Live with him, oh yes. He had need of her, she knew this, as much as his father had, but the need wasn't strong enough to force him to take on the responsibility of a wife. Michael had thought along those lines too at one time, but Michael had changed, he was offering her security ... and respectability. That was the word, respectability.

She straightened up and muttered the word aloud, 'Respectability.' It was so damned old-fashioned, people laughed at it. Why couldn't she do the same? What was really wrong with her? Was there part of her that had been bred for a convent? No, no. Her urges were such that they could not be sublimated. Then why was she sticking out for a wedding ring? a piece of paper?

Oh, God, she didn't know; all she knew was that chastity was the most expensive commodity, and that there must come a time when your nerves refused to pay the high price demanded of it, and the terrifying truth was that she knew she was nearing that time.

It was about seven when she finally got through to an 'I told you so' Nell to explain what had happened and that Michael would be bringing her over to Shields in the morning. And she had hardly put down the phone when Dorry brought a meal up on a tray and, after placing it on the table, she turned and looked at Jinny for a moment before she said, 'I'm sorry, an' Cissie is the same. We've just said, we don't know what himself will do, 'cos you seemed to be the only one that could raise his spirits. But I understand how you feel about Mr Glen. He gets on our nerves. We've had to move half the food to the big freezer in the stable. He took a whole two pound veal and ham pie yesterday. Cissie tried to take it off him, but he's as strong as a horse, and, as she said herself, she was frightened.' Her voice dropped now. 'It's as we said to Willie, we don't think he's really well enough for the house. And Willie says, Mr John's very much of the same opinion, but himself says he stays, and so he stays. I don't know what the end of it's going to be. Come on and eat this meal, miss. Oh, we are going to miss you. As Cissie says, you fitted in like an old glove. And you're young at that. But as Cissie says, you've got common sense and your head's older than your age.'

If she could have laughed, she would have laughed: her head was older than her age. Oh, if only that were true. She said quietly, 'I'll be sorry to go, Dorry, and I'll miss you both. It's . . . it's been like home, especially in the kitchen.'

'Did you have a good home, miss? I know you've had a good upbringing, being educated like, but it isn't them that could educate their children that give them the happiest homes. Oh, no, not by a long chalk.'

'I had a very happy home, Dorry. I was very fortunate. I know that now. You don't appreciate it at the time though, do you? As for education, it was pretty ordinary. School till sixteen, then on to a secretarial course.'

'Oh.' Dorry's face stretched. 'You've never been then to a university? Not like Miss Florence and Miss Nellie? Miss Monica never went, nor Lucy.'

'No; no university.'

'Now that surprises me. And Cissie'll be surprised an' all, because you have that kind of air, you know like people who have been to university, sort of sure of themselves.'

Now Jinny did smile. They were funny these two, Dorry and Cissie: they were still in the Thirties when, her father had said, one paid homage to anyone who had been to a college or university, because it meant something in those days.

Changing the subject now, Dorry said, 'Mr John's in a tear. He's like a bear with a sore skull. Him and Willie have been talking but they can't come up with any solution. Well, they can't, can they? Oh dear me, nothing'll ever be the same again in this house. Anyway, dear, get your supper. Your soup will be clay cold by now although it's covered up.'

'Thanks, Dorry, and thank Cissie. But I'll see you both in the morning. Good-night.'

'Good-night, miss. Good-night.'

She drank the soup and ate a little of the cold meat and salad; and afterwards, she tried to settle down and read, but when she found she couldn't concentrate, she wrote a letter. It was to Bob, simply thanking him for his kindness to her and wishing things could have turned out differently. The letter was in place of visiting him, because she knew she couldn't bear to see his face and the accusation in his eyes. His look would suggest not only that she was leaving the sinking ship but also that she, who was a good swimmer, was refusing to put her hand out to a drowning man.

At half-past nine she took a bath; and the last thing she did before getting into bed was to take three aspirins. She had never as yet taken a sleeping pill, but she had told herself that if she had had onc handy she would have taken it. But the aspirins might ease her rising headache and steady her nerves.

As she lay wide-eyed, she heard John come along the corridor and go into his father's room. She knew it was him by his cough which was more in the nature of a clearing of his throat. It had become a habit of late.

She had heard Willie leave sometime earlier after he had finally settled Bob for the night. She'd heard nothing of Glen, not even his voice from the distance. Often he talked so loudly he could be heard all over the house, but twice during the past week he'd had a quiet period when he hadn't spoken for hours. One evening as he sat playing cards he had made no comment on the game, which was very unusual, but Willie had explained this. It was part of a pattern, he'd said, and the aftermath could mean Glen would be more volatile than before; or there might even be a glimpse of his real self; or lastly, and he hoped this wouldn't happen, he could become very aggressive. And he had repeated that he hoped the latter wouldn't happen because Glen, at the weight he'd be now, would be a tough guy to handle.

After some time she heard John's cough again; he had come out of his father's room. A silence followed. The house had settled down for the night, her last night in it. How long she lay awake she didn't know. The last she remembered was telling herself that it was going to be a long, long night. And then she was dreaming. Strangely, she always knew when she was dreaming. If there was any happening in her dream that was frightening she would say to herself, 'Wake up, it's only a dream.' In this particular dream someone had switched on the bedside lamp, and this had frightened her, but she had said to herself, 'Don't be afraid, it's only a dream. Wake up.' She was deep in the dream but a voice was pulling her upwards, calling her name. She recognized the name yet it wasn't hers. When at last she forced her eyes open, her mouth sprang open too and all sleep left her as she stared up into the face staring down at her. It was smiling and it had a soft light in its eyes, and it was the soft light that prevented her from screaming. But she hitched herself up on her elbows and, her voice a grating whisper, she said, 'Go . . . go back to bed, Glen. That's a good fellow.'

His response to this was not to give her an answer but to put his hand on to her cheek and stroke it.

'Now, now, Glen, you . . . you shouldn't be here, you should be a. . . .' She was about to say asleep, but the word caught in her throat when his other hand with just one sweep threw the bedclothes aside. Now she did cry out: 'Go away! Stop i . . .!' The 'it' was strangled by his hand across her mouth.

Staring up into his face, she saw that his expression had changed: his eyeballs were moving from side to side and his lids were flicking up and down over them. Using both her hands now, she went to push them against his face to press him away, but he caught her wrists in a grip that was like a vice, then with a heave he was lying beside her and muttering a name over and over, 'Yvonne. Yvonne. Yvonne.'

Because he was on his side now his hold was more awkward and when his hand momentarily eased from her mouth she let out a strangled cry before bringing her teeth sharply down onto the flesh of his second finger.

His hand jerked from her mouth and brought a resounding blow onto the side of her face, and now she screamed both from pain and from terror. The next minute he was crying, 'Sorry. Sorry. Sorry. Yvonne. Sorry. It's me. It's me. Glen your Glen. Yvonne. Yvonne, your Glen.'

She was about to scream again when with a twist of his body he rolled on top of her, and in doing so he freed her hands and when they tore at his hair he seemed to go really berserk, for his hands, now clawing at her body, rent the night-dress from her.

As she struggled to escape his grasping fingers and the weight of his body she knew she was going to pass out, and she was no longer aware that she was screaming, calling on the three men in the house: 'Bob! John! Willie! Then when his hands tore at her breasts, his nails penetrating the flesh, she let out one great agonized scream that smothered Willie's name.

It was at that instant Willie and John burst into the room almost simultaneously, and when the weight was dragged from her she lay heaving, gasping and sobbing, and unconscious that she was naked or that there were thin streaks of blood running down from her breasts onto her forearms. She took no notice whatever of the scuffling going on to the side of the bed or of Willie yelling, 'I can hold him. It's in a box in the medicine cabinet in my bedroom, a brown box. It's on the front of the shelf. Be quick! Be quick!'

John scattered from the room. Within a minute he was back with a hypodermic syringe, and not until Willie had shot the needle into Glen's hip did they both become aware of the voice yelling across the corridor. But neither of them took any notice. Rising now, they went to the bed, and it was John who quickly pulled the bedclothes up over her, then gently placed his hands on each side of her face and turned it towards him. But he said no word, nor did she. She had stopped crying, only now and again a small moan escaped her.

'I'll phone the hospital right away,' Willie said. 'We'll have to leave him here though until they come; we could never manage him downstairs, he's a dead weight.'

As he went towards the door Bob's voice could be heard clearly now coming from the bedroom, yelling, 'Here! Here! Come here!'

Willie turned and looked at John and asked simply, 'What about it?'

And John answered, 'It's out of his hands; he'll have realized that by now.'

'I'll phone from his room; and for the doctor too. That'll make it final.' And with that Willie hurried across the corridor, opened the bedroom door, then stopped dead. His mouth open, his eyes wide, he stared at his patient; then jerking his head to the side, he shouted, 'John! John! Come here. Come here.'

John went at a run, to see his father sitting upright in the bed, his body well to the edge of it as if he had been attempting to get out.

'My God!'

He moved slowly towards the bed, and his father, his voice trembling, said, 'What's he done to her?'

'Tried to rape her I should say and battered her in the process. But after all, what does it matter? It's got you sitting up. Something which common sense could have done before,' he said, then turned about and hurried back to Jinny's room.

Bob now looked at Willie, saying, 'Is she badly hurt?'

'I . . . I don't really know, except there was blood on her breasts and she looks as if she's collapsed. John saw to her. One thing I do know, boss, is that with his strength and the urge that was on him, he could have done her in quite easily, because there's nothing of her.'

'Where's he now?'

'On the floor.' Willie jerked his head back. 'I've put him out.'

'Have you . . . have you phoned the hospital?'

'I'm going to do that now. I thought I'd do it from here.'

'You're blaming me, aren't you?'

'No, no, I'm not blaming you. He's your son; I've got an idea how you feel about him. There's nobody to blame really, it's just one great pity. But these things happen and I think what you've got to face up to is, unless they come up with a miracle in brain surgery he's going to remain pretty much as he is.'

'Help me straighten up.'

When Bob was lying back in his pillows, he said, 'I'm going to ask you now, where were you? She had been yelling for some time. I heard her from the beginning.'

'We were both downstairs wondering what we could do to prevent her going. Funny, but I'd been waiting all day for something to happen; Mr Glen had been too quiet. I'd given him a double dose of tablets, but like many such cases they become wily, they put the tablets in their mouth, swallow the water, then when your back's turned they spit them out from under their tongue. He has done that once or twice before, but tonight I stood and watched him take them, *tonight*, at least I thought so, but you can never be up to them when their minds are like that. He had known what he was going to do; he also knew a sleeping tablet would prevent him from doing it. He had taken a fancy to her from the beginning you see; she must in some way have reminded him of his wife, because he's still a man. . . .'

Across the landing John was thinking the same thing: his brother was still a man, but with the beast added.

He was bathing her face with a cold sponge. Her eye was beginning to swell and her cheek was already puffed out. As yet not one word had passed between them. Her eyes were closed and her breath was coming in shuddering gasps. It wasn't until the sound of a snort came from the far side of the bed that she showed any sign of life, for her body shuddered and her eyes opened and she gasped at the air; and for the first time he spoke. Softly he said, 'It's all right, Jinny. It's all right.'

She looked at him now and her lips moved as if mouthing words, but no sound came, and again he said, 'It's all right. It's all right, my dear. He's going. They're coming for him. It's all over. It should never have happened, but it's all over now.'

When she closed her eyes again and the tears pressed through her lashes, he put his arm under her head and, his voice low, he said, 'Oh, Jinny. Jinny. Oh, my dear, don't. I . . . I blame myself for it happening. And so will Willie. But we were downstairs trying to work out ways and means to keep you. We had decided to contact the doctor the first thing in the moring and Willie was going to tell him of the change that he was detecting in Glen and that he thought he was in need of qualified attention, but it was how we could stop you leaving before anything further could be done about him, because I couldn't bear the thought of you leaving. Oh, Jinny. Jinny. All right, don't get agitated. Look, I'll get Willie to go and wake Dorry. She must sleep like a log. And you could have your cousin here tomorrow; she'll see to you. Everything's going to be all right.' He knew he was gabbling on but he couldn't stop.

When he made to move away she suddenly caught at his hand as at the same time another snort came from the other side of the bed, and he said gently, 'He's under sedation. He won't wake up for some long time. They . . . they are coming to fetch him.' Then raising his voice, he called to Willie, and when Willie appeared at the doorway he said, 'Go and fetch Dorry, will you? . . . Have you got in contact with the hospital?'

'They'll be here within half an hour.'

'And the doctor?'

'As soon as he can.' . . .

It was almost an hour later when Glen was lifted on to a stretcher and taken downstairs, and it was a half-hour later still when the doctor came. He'd been out on an urgent call and only just got the message.

John was waiting for him in the hall when he came downstairs. He hadn't spent more than ten minutes in Jinny's room, and when John asked the question with one word, 'Well?' the doctor replied, 'She wouldn't permit me to examine her. She's in a highly nervous state, which is only natural. I've given her a sedative.'

'So you don't know if . . .?'

'No, I don't know if; only she can answer that question. The only thing that I can say at this stage is I should imagine if there's any result of his action, it wouldn't be welcome, because the process must have been more than painful. He has ripped the skin from her breasts in four places. In an ordinary way you could call them scratches, but these are more like gores. And tomorrow her eye will be black and blue and the rest of her face a bruised yellow. No, I don't think the result, if there should be any, of tonight's affair would be welcome. Let's pray your intervention was in time. And also that your father will admit he can be wrong at times, greatly wrong. I was against Glen's return from the first. I have seen his type of case before and you never know from one day to the next how they are going to react. Well, we know how this one reacted, but it remains to be seen how she reacts to it. Yes, it remains to be seen.'

5

'Oh, my God, lass, what did he do to you?' Nell bent over her and with gentle fingers she touched Jinny's cheek where the black and blue of her bruised eye faded into puffed yellowness. 'He should be brought up, he should be. Or more so, those responsible for bringing him into the house should be. Now you're getting out of here as quick as we can carry you. Just look at her, Peter. Did you ever see anything like it?'

'Leave her alone, Nell; she's distressed and you're not making it any better.'

'What are you talking about, man? She's getting out of here.'

'All right, all right.' Peter's voice was low. 'She'll come if she wants to. Leave it to her.' He was thinking of a short conversation he'd had with the son of the house just before he came downstairs. The young fellow had taken him aside and, his voice urgent, he had said, 'Please do something for me . . . for us. Don't persuade her to leave. Everything's all right now. My . . . my brother shall never come back and my father needs her. We will see to her. We will look after her.'

His answer had been much as it was a moment ago, 'Well, that'll be her decision. I don't think we'll have much say in it. If she wants to come, we'll only be too glad to have her, and she knows that.'

'Nell' − Jinny found it painful to open her lips, her mouth seemed to have slipped to one side − 'I'm . . . I'm all right. I just want to . . . rest. I'll . . . I'll come down later and . . . and stay for a time, Don't . . . don't worry, I'm all right.'

'You're not all right. And it's like men's point of view to look on the bright side, like that Willie saying if it hadn't happened his boss would likely have lain there till he died. He didn't look upon it that you could have been battered to death in order that his boss could be shocked into sitting up.'

'Wh . . . what?'

'Be quiet, Nell, will you?' Peter was bending over Jinny now, saying, 'We'll be going, dear; you . . . you need to rest. We'll look in again this afternoon.'

'Peter.'

'Yes, my dear?'

'What . . . what about Bob?'

Peter glanced towards his wife and made a small impatient movement with his head at her before looking at Jinny again, saying, 'Well, it appears that Mr Henderson heard you calling and . . . well, he made an effort and apparently it broke the paralysis, which wasn't real paralysis, that's in the upper part of his body, and now he's . . . well, all right except for his legs.'

Jinny closed her eyes. Dear God. Dear God. Was it possible? Yes, yes, it was possible. The doctors had said it was hysteria, but no one and seemingly nothing could get that through into his head. But her cries of help and his immediate recognition of their meaning had got through to him, overcoming his hysteria. Now he must face the irrevocable fact that his son's mind was damaged to such an extent that in part he was mad.

The sedative the doctor had given her last night had worn thin and she was still screaming in her mind and his weight was still on her body and his bare flesh still searing her. There was no part of her that his hands hadn't clutched at, and she was still seeing his face, but strangely, not as it appeared last night, wild, distorted, the eyes blazing as they flickered like flashing lights, but she was seeing him as he had looked on his wedding day and at those times when he had bounced into the office, bursting with confidence and satisfaction after completing another order. Yet even so his face looked different: she was seeing it without the smile on it, without the happiness Yvonne had been bringing to him, and as she had never really seen it, sad, unsmiling, the eyes seeming to beg something of her. There was penetrating her still fear-filled thoughts the idea that he was here in the room: some part of him was here begging her forgiveness, telling her that that which was perpetrated last night was not him, asking for her understanding.

She heard Peter's voice as if coming from a distance saying, 'She's gone to sleep,' and Nell answering, 'They've got her sedated now, but just wait until she really comes to herself; she'll not stay here, you'll see.'

It was some moments before she became fully aware that they had left the room.

When she opened her eyes, Dorry was sitting by her bedside and after a moment she said to her, 'Would . . . would you tell John I . . . I would like to see him, please?'

'Aye, miss. Yes, I'll tell him. He's . . . he's just across the passage.'

She closed her eyes again and it seemed only the next minute she heard his voice saying, 'What is it, Jinny?'

'Oh, John.'

'Yes my dear, what is it?'

'Don't . . . don't ask Nell to stay; I'll be all right. I just want to sleep, but don't ask her to stay.'

'If that's what you wish.' He didn't say that Nell and her husband had already left and although he had said he would ask her to stay, he hadn't done so because from the moment she had entered the house he had realized her excitable nature wouldn't do Jinny any good and, too, that her main intention was to remove Jinny as quickly as possible. He left inordinately pleased that Jinny should make this request of him. It seemed to prove to him that she was to stay where she was.

He had sat by her bedside all last night, and although she had been heavily sedated she had moaned and called out a number of times.

He put his hand out now and gently stroked her hair back from her forehead. She was beautiful. A black eye, a swollen discoloured cheek, she was still beautiful. What was he going to do about her? She'd never understand him. She would understand his father, she seemed on the same wavelength with him, but with himself the wires always got crossed. Perhaps it was his fault; he was always on his guard, afraid to show his feelings. He had shown them once and what had happened? He had been made a monkey of. By God, yes. What would have happened if he had married her, the beguiling Janice, the great free-thinker? Eighteen months they had lived together; then of a sudden she had talked of marriage, not only talked but asked, what about it? And he'd decided he was less for it than ever; he was discovering facets of her character that annoyed him. Yet, he told himself, this was bound to happen, for after all it was like a marriage. But then she had brought up the idea of a special licence. It was the rush that made him pause; and he spoke to Nick Hobson about it. Nick had been married for the past year to the girl he had previously lived with. It was the fear of illegitimacy on the coming child that had made her press for marriage. Anyway, it was Nick who had said, 'Don't do it, boy, not in this case, she's just using you. You've been hoodwinked long enough. The reason for her haste is that she's going to be named by the wife of one of the professors who's suing for a divorce. He was on her horizon long before you appeared, and has been there ever since more or less. She's got four years start on you. And there's been at least three other members of the staff before.

He could recall the white rage that burned him up as he waited for her coming home when she would follow the same procedure: breeze in, throw off her coat, switch on the record player, then flop into the couch, and he'd bring her a drink; then, depending on her mood, she would lay back and recite a few lines from Shakespeare, some modern jingle, or, as she did on that last night, the rhyme that she always resorted to when she was uncertain of his mood:

'Pussy-cat, pussy-cat, where have you been?
I've been to London to see the Queen.
Pussy-cat, pussy-cat, what did you there?
I spied John Henderson under a chair.
Pussy-cat, Pussy-cat, did he mew?
No, the last I saw of him he up and flew.

'Well, out with it, Johnny boy,' she had said. 'Why greet a hard-working girl with a look like that?'

He remembered he'd had the strongest urge to get her by the neck and choke her, in fact, to react almost as Glen had done last night on poor Jinny here. But the more sane part of him at that moment must have recognized how easy it would be to kill someone and he had warned himself to get out. And so he'd answered her: 'I'm adopting the last line and flying.'

A barrage of terse questions and answers followed, and at the end she had stood screaming at him as he went towards the door after having said, 'I removed my belongings this after-noon.'

'You are what you always were, a weak-kneed milksop. Now run back to your mammy and your daddy and ask them to show you how to keep a woman, because you haven't even reached the kindergarten stage in that school . . . boy.'

He had stayed with Nick that night and found a place the next day, and for almost a week afterwards he had been sick every night, actually sick, bringing up the food he had forced down himself during the day, and as his stomach emptied he saw himself shrinking until he felt there was nothing left of his manhood.

Looking back, it was hard to believe that he had loved Janice, but the truth was he had. She was bright, intelligent, and four years his senior. She was at first everything he needed in a woman. But then he had known very little about women and so his knowledge of them stemmed mostly from her. The period of living alone had only increased the devastating feeling against his parents for having thrown him off; and this he now knew to be ridiculous. And yet the fact wasn't ridiculous that his father had always preferred Glen. That his mother's affection was weighed in his direction didn't seem to make up for the indifference towards him shown by his father: too arty-crafty was the term he used about him, and later made it obvious that he would never be any good in business, not like Glen would be.

But all that seemed to be in another world for the tables had turned completely. He might be still arty-crafty, but he knew that his father needed him now more than he had ever needed Glen, and he knew that he himself needed this girl here more than he ever imagined he could need anyone in his life again. The thought of her leaving the house had been agony to him, even the fact that they hardly ever seemed to say a civil word to each other and that she didn't really like him, hadn't prevented him from willing her to stay.

But after she got over the shock, what if she still decided to leave. She could have left today, though, with her cousin and she had refused, hadn't she? Yet that might have been because she was feeling too ill to make the move. . . . Oh, why in the name of God couldn't he think positively for once. That was his trouble. Outwardly he gave off the impression of assertiveness, while inwardly he courted defeat even before the battle had begun.

Propped up on his pillows, Bob looked at Willie and said, 'How long would it take to get one of those wheelchairs?'

'Oh, not so long, a few weeks. You'd have to have it specially adjusted.'

'Hell! man, I wasn't talking about weeks; I was talking about hours. Isn't it possible to borrow one from the hospital? The corridors seemed lined with the blasted things when I was there.'

'I could try, but I can't promise anything.'

'Well, try. Get on the phone.'

Willie smiled at Bob now before he said, 'Where do you intend to go in it? Back to work?'

'Aye, yes, that's an idea.'

At this moment the bedroom door opened and when John entered his father cried at him, 'This big lout here has just given me an idea. I've asked him to get me a wheelchair.'

'A wheelchair? But. . . .'

'Never mind any buts. That's what I want, a wheelchair, and I want it today or tomorrow at the latest.'

'So, you want a wheelchair.' John came and stood by the side of the bed. 'And you want it today or tomorrow at the latest.' Then turning to Willie, he said, 'Well, what about it, Willie, is that possible?'

'Well, you know what they say, John, anything is possible to them that have faith.' And they laughed at each other.

'Not so much of the light banter,' Bob barked; 'I haven't finished what I'd started to say. He's just suggested' – he jerked his head in Willie's direction – 'that if I get a wheelchair I can take up work again, and by God, that's what I'll do. Aye, that's what I'll do. But I want that wheelchair first.' And in a lowered voice, he said, 'I want to get into it and go across the passage. And when she sees me, it might . . . well, take some of the sting out of it. What do you think?'

'You could be right.' John nodded at him; then looking at Willie, he said, 'Leave it to me. I'll see what I can do.'

And he turned about and went out again.

Bob seemed to have to drag his gaze from the door before turning to Willie and saying, 'There's a changed lad if ever I saw one. Well, he's no longer a lad, he's a man. And it certainly wasn't brought about by his going off on his own, the big "I am" setting up house with a woman. No, he was still the lad then. It didn't happen until the accident. That seemed to change him; well, changed us all, didn't it? And it must be still changing us, because two days gone I was asking meself what's the use of going on. And I can tell you something, Willie, if those pills had been handy I wouldn't be here to tell the tale now. Oh, you can open your eyes, but that's honest to God truth. I was as low as that. And then having to face up to the fact that you were all right about Glen. Oh God! Glen. Glen. I daren't think about him. . . . But in spite of all that, here I am grabbing at life with half a new body. And, you know, it's a wonderful feeling. Do you know that, Willie? It's a wonderful feeling.'

'Yes, I know it's a wonderful feeling, and it'll continue to be a wonderful feeling if you go steady. You know what doctor said: no high jinks; take it slowly at first, your body's got to adjust. So come on, more exercises. Come on now, up with those arms.'

Bob had jerked his head now, saying, 'Oh well, everything's got to be paid for. Do you know, I say that again and again, every day of me life, everything's got to be paid for.'

Taking hold of Bob's wrist in one hand and his elbow in the other, Willie said, 'And there's another saying that's a companion to it: You only get what you pay for; bargains are mostly second-hand.'

She was sitting up in bed. Her head was clear. She had asked the doctor not to give her any more sedatives because for the past three days she felt she had been in a kind of limbo where she knew yet didn't know what was going on around her, where the faces were familiar yet distorted, where at times she imagined she heard a man's voice talking to her and fingers stroking her hair. And once she had felt she was being kissed, right on the lips. It has been a soft kiss and she'd told herself to open her eyes to see who it was. But she had been too tired – she only knew she liked the kiss and wished it would go on.

But now the mist had cleared from her mind: it was daylight both inside her brain and out; she could now recall everything that had happened, but she no longer shuddered at it; and the voice had stopped yelling in her head. She knew that Bob had regained the use of his upper body, but she didn't know how she was going to face him because through her he had lost his son, his elder son, his beloved son, for good and all; at least that was what the doctor had said, for good and all.

But now, in her clear-thinking state, she was finding no room for pity for the man who, if he hadn't been caught in time, could have killed her. The compassion she had felt earlier had dissolved in the drugged mist, for the fact was there had been murder in his eyes: his pent-up passion against fate that had robbed him of his wife and his senses had broken through and had to be recompensed.

But the question was, what was she going to do now? Was

she going to stay here? Or was she going to Nell's? Somehow she didn't want to go to Nell's, any more than she had done yesterday, or the day before, or the day before that, because Nell's conversation for weeks ahead would be a reiteration of the whole situation, and although she knew it wasn't possible ever to forget it, the thought of hearing it over and over again would, she knew, become unbearable and would, in the end, cause her to leave the pleasant homely house and the caring couple. And that would hurt them both more than if she were to say to them she had decided to stay on here.

But did she now want to stay on here? Because the future would not be even anything like it was before Glen came on the scene. Bob, restored to partial mobility, wouldn't be as easy to handle as the paralysed man. That was sure. And then there was John.

If they could have been good companions it would have helped matters, but they acted like fighting cocks towards each other. Why, after all, she asked herself now, should this too have happened to her? Hadn't she been through enough without having to fight another sex battle?

No, she didn't want to stay. But how was she going to leave? What excuse would she give? And where would she go?

Yes, where would she go? If not to Nell's, where?

She was fully dressed and sitting by the window. Occasionally she turned her gaze towards the door hoping that someone would come in, denying that her wish centred upon John because she felt that through another abrasive exchange she would be forced to come to a decision.

Her head jerked round as she heard a slight commotion in the corridor outside. There was the sound of voices and she thought she must be mistaken when she recognised Bob's. Then unceremoniously her door was thrust open, and there he was half-way across the threshold in a wheelchair.

She was on her feet now staring at him. He looked different, almost like he used to do. His wiry hair was licked back, his face was clean-shaven, but what was most astounding, he was fully dressed in a grey suit, blue shirt and matching tie.

'It's a case of that Mohammed not coming to the mountain and the mountain having to get up and push itself to the stubborn stiff-necked Mohammed, eh?'

215

He was pushing at the wheels now while John pressed him forward from behind, and when he reached the side of the window he stopped.

'Well, what do you think?'

Her neck muscles were tight, her throat for a moment was so blocked she couldn't get words past it. She looked from him to John who was staring at her, his expression enigmatic as usual, then from him to where Willie was standing in the doorway smiling. And Willie nodded at her, pursed his lips, then closed the door.

'Well, if you've got nothing to say to me, sit down.'

She sat down; and now he went on, 'I thought you'd be over the moon to see this new man that I've become. I'm back where I was, or soon will be. Heigh-ho for Henderson and Garbrook's. Wait till we get on that top floor and go into that office. Can you imagine Waitland's face? I've had Jack Newland here and Peter Trowell and also Bill Meane and Bury, and from what I can gather the quicker we get back there, lass, the better. And here's news for you. His nibs there' – he nodded towards John – 'is going to come in. What do you think of that? That's an achievement, isn't it? Bury's going to coach him regarding the basics. You know, getting orders like.'

For the first time since coming into the room his quick fire talk halted, but only for a second. Then he went on, 'He's got a head on his shoulders, although I say it meself.' He glanced again at his son. 'And there's charm somewhere there, though it might take a pick and shovel to get at it. But he'll have to use it when he gets abroad, and the quicker he does that the better, because there's trouble brewing in the steel business if I know owt from what I hear. They talk of nothin' else on the bloody television these days. Oh' – he drew in a long breath – 'I can't wait, lass. I can't wait.'

Of a sudden there was silence in the room, with Bob, his fingers now working against each other, staring at her while John looked towards his feet; that was until his father said, 'Would . . . would you get me a hanky, lad? I've . . . I've forgotten one.'

Without hesitation John left the room; and they were alone together.

Putting his hands on the wheels of the chair, he brought it close to her side and with not the space of a forearm between their faces he stared at her. Then his hand went out and gently touched her cheek and in a voice unrecognizable from what it was a minute earlier he said, 'Lass, I'll never forgive meself, never as long as I live. When I think of it I could . . . aye, I'll say it, I could cut me own throat, because what happened was all my fault. I knew from the moment I saw him he wasn't right and never would be. I'm not going to say, Do you understand that I felt he was mine and this was his home, because that would be to ask you to understand that I was as mad as him. It was just sheer bloody cussedness on my part. I wanted to prove everybody wrong, particularly John, because somehow John had taken his place in me mind, and I didn't want that. I'd always put Glen first, 'cos Glen was like me inside, he was a go-getter, a pusher. He knew what he wanted and he went after it. Lass' – he now caught hold of her hand in his – 'can you ever forgive me? I've gone through hell. Even though you were the means of giving me back me body I know I'd rather have stayed like that for the rest of me life than have it bought at the price of what you went through. And all that talk just gone about the factory and one thing and another, 'twas all palaver. At least, it will be if you can't find it in your heart to forgive me, because, you know, somehow I couldn't take it on again without you. Doesn't that seem strange? No, I don't suppose it does to you. But you see I did take it on, I did run that place, I did do everything without Alicia's help. I had her love, but that was here in this house sort of. Now I know for a certainty I couldn't go back into that place and work as I did if you weren't there to support me. You've come to mean a lot to me, Jinny, and at times I've treated you rough. But I did think you understood that part of me. About the other though . . . well, there's no excuse. I never thought I would say I wanted to kill me own son for what he had done to you, but I think if I could have got at him that night I would have. Aw, lass, lass, please don't cry.' He put his hand and cupped her cheek, and when her chin dropped onto her chest he asked in a whisper, 'One thing more, I'm . . . I'm terrified to ask it but it's got to come, are you all right? You know what I mean.'

It was some seconds before she could raise her head, and now she nodded as she wiped her face slowly with a handkerchief.

'You're sure?'

For the first time she spoke, 'Yes, I'm sure.'

'Thanks be to God.' It was the most fervent prayer he had ever said in his life, and it seemed to leave him almost exhausted.

His hands lay limp on his lifeless thighs, his shoulders hunched and his head fell forward, and the sight touched her as nothing else would have; and now it was she who put her hand out and touched his, and when he raised his eyes to hers she said softly, 'When do we start work?'

It was some seconds before he spoke. The lines at the corners of his eyes crinkled into folds, his lips quivered for a moment, and then he said brokenly, 'You will? You're game?'

'I'm game.'

'Aw, lass.' He let out a long slow breath. 'It'll be a new life for me. You can't imagine. And' – his eyebrows moved upwards now and his eyes widened – 'for our John an' all. What do you think of that, him consenting to come in? Well, when I'm making me confession I might as well add that I misjudged that lad. And that's another thing.' He poked his head towards her now. 'He hates to be called a lad. We must be careful, mustn't we? By the way, another question. Do you like him?'

Again her throat was tight, but she forced her tone to be nonchalant as she replied, 'There's nothing to dislike about him.'

'Well, that's a neither here nor there answer. Anyway' – he turned his head – 'where's he got with that damned hanky. John!' he bawled and within seconds the door was opened and John entered; and the handkerchief he held out his father put straight into his pocket where the corner of another one was in evidence. Then looking up at John, he said, 'We're away, son: Henderson and son and private secretary are invading those works as soon as that damned doctor gives me the go-ahead. And that, if I know anything, will be next week.'

Standing now behind his father's wheelchair, John looked at Jinny, and she at him, and they smiled tolerantly at each other.

6

It was some weeks later before the doctor gave his permission for Bob to make his assault on the factory.

Following Bob's strict orders, neither Mr Christopher Waitland nor anyone at the works, apart from those he'd seen at the house, had been informed of the extent of his recovery. So it was on a biting cold day towards the end of October that his wheelchair was pushed up the ramp of the estate car and he, with Jinny, was driven by John to the works.

John had previously compared the width of the chair with that of the lift, and he knew that the lift would take the chair with a foot to spare.

It was half-past ten in the morning when they arrived. As Bob had said, he wanted to be sure that Chris Waitland would be at his desk for, being able to play lord and master, he would likely be choosing his own time to arrive, and so, following Garbrook's pattern, it could be ten or thereabouts.

When Sam opened the glass door for the man in the wheelchair and his two companions, he stood gaping. Then, his voice like a small squeak coming out of a large balloon, he said, 'Mr Henderson?'

'In the flesh, Sam, in the flesh.'

'Eeh God!'

'No, no, not God, Sam, just me, as ever was.'

'I can't believe it. Eeh! I can't believe it. Oh, man, I'm pleased to see you, Mr Henderson. But I thought. . . .'

'Aye, so did a lot of other people, Sam, so did a lot of other people. Still, don't you go near that telephone and ring upstairs now. Do you hear me?'

'No, not if you don't want me to, Mr Henderson.'

'I don't want you to, Sam. Give me ten minutes to get up to the top floor and into me office and then you can pass it round.'

'I'll do that, Mr Henderson, I'll do that. Eeh, I am glad to see you. You an' all, miss. Eeh! it's like new life comin' back into the place.'

'And this is me son, one of your new bosses.' Bob jerked his head back towards John, and Sam said, 'Well, if he's a chip off the old block, he'll do me, Mr Henderson. But . . . but we've met afore, haven't we, sir?'

'Yes, we have, Sam.'

Sam now led the way across the hall to the lift, exclaiming as he did so, 'Eeh! by lad. Eeh! by lad.'

When the lift opened two men and a young girl emerged, and all three paused and looked at the man in the wheelchair before walking on; and then, as if of one mind, they stopped dead and turned and looked towards the lift doors which were now closing. 'Good as a play, isn't it?' Bob said. His voice was low, and John replied, 'Yes. First act coming up. I only hope all the company are in their places. What do you say?' He turned and looked at Jinny, and she said, 'You know what I'm waiting for?'

Both men looked at her now. 'To get on that phone and speak to Miss Cadwell.' Her voice now assumed a superior air as she said, 'This is Miss Brownlow speaking from Mr Henderson's office. Would you please send up a secretary? One who has good knowledge of French. I would like this attended to immediately.' They were still chuckling when the lift stopped at the top floor, and when John pushed his father's chair onto the thick pile carpet, Bob held up his hand for a moment, and he sat looking about him at this place he had built. He had given special attention to how this floor should be laid out, and the size of each office.

He now took in a long slow breath, straightened his tie, slicked back his hair; then nodding his head, they went forward. According to the plan, Jinny tapped on the main office door, then opened it, went in and stood aside, and John pushed the chair over the threshold into the room and almost caused the collapse of the two people in it.

Christopher Waitland was sitting behind his desk. There had been a smile on his face as if he had been exchanging a joke with his secretary who was standing to the side of the desk, her body leaning over it and towards him. Now, as if one, they became transfixed, every feature of their faces appeared stretched to twice its capacity, and they didn't move until Bob said, 'Well, aren't you pleased to see me?'

Christopher Waitland slowly rose from his chair; then he put

220

his hand out as if to push his secretary away and she stepped aside, allowing him to pass her and come to the front of the desk, and when at last he spoke his words sounded like a challenge. 'What's this?' he said.

'What does it look like, Chris? I'm back.'

'You . . . you can't be. I mean, you can't do this, not like this, all of a sudden.'

'All of a sudden? What are you talking about? I've been gone eight months. You should have known I'd turn up sometime.'

'I . . . I understood . . . I thought.'

'I know what you understood and what you thought. You thought I was flat on me back for life, didn't you? and you were settled here. Well, I'm sorry to tell you, Chris, you're not. I've got me harness on again, and so would you mind removing yourself into your old office? And I'd be obliged if you would do it as quickly as I understood you left it to come in here.'

'This is not right. It . . . I mean, I should have had notice. What I mean is. . . .'

'I know what you mean.' Bob's voice was flat now. 'You mean you should have had good notice to try to straighten things out afore I appeared on the scene. Well, by all accounts, and I've had accounts—' He nodded at the purple-faced man now and went on, 'Oh, yes, I've been kept informed: you've made a pretty poor go of being my replacement.'

'Now look here, I've done all I could . . . well, you only have to read the papers and you'll know the predicament steel is in.'

'You're talking about the Steel Corporation. We are not the Steel Corporation, Chris, we are a private engineering firm, we just make the stuff up and push it around and as far as I can gather you haven't been pushing it very hard, have you?'

'That isn't fair; things are in a bad way. I've got two men out.'

'Yes, I know you've got two men out. And one of them is your nephew, Broadway, who was in the clerks' office. Got a quick promotion. Nepotism it's called, isn't it? Nepotism. Well, as far as I can gather, up to now he's lost the Belgian orders and he's even lost Swinburne's. Now Swinburne's are on the doorstep, so to speak, only two hundred miles away, and they've dealt with us for fifteen years. Aw, bloody hell! don't you tell me what you've done and what you haven't done. Get yourself out of here.'

'You can't do this. I'll see Mr Garbrook, he it was who put me here.'

'Well, he might have, but Garbrook is not running this factory. And let me tell you something in case you don't know, I own seventy-five per cent of the shares here and fifty-one per cent at the container concern. Now you work that out and tell me who's in charge and who can say you go here or you stay. Now, an ultimatum: I give you half an hour to get your gear out and back to where you were, or you might find yourself joining your nephew in the dole queue. Oh, I forgot, they don't have any queues these days, they have their cheques sent to them. Well, that should be nice for both of you.'

Chris Waitland now came and stood in front of the chair and, staring down at Bob, he said, 'You forget that I'm on the board and, big shareholder or not, it will cost you dear to get rid of me.'

'Aye, I'd thought of that and not just today or yesterday, Chris. Well, get going, and we'll see about it.'

All this while John had stood with his eyes cast towards the carpet. That he was deeply embarrassed by the scene in which a man was being made to look small Jinny could see. Yet it didn't affect her that way. No, for she was remembering the morning this man had turfed her out of the office, and because of it, as she told herself now, this bit of retaliation was sweet. All right, she was holding a grudge, being spiteful if you like, but what was good to give shouldn't be bad to take.

She turned now and looked at the secretary Miss Phillips. Miss Phillips looked almost to be on the point of fainting. She had both hands to her throat and her flat breast was doing its best to heave. When her boss spoke to her, saying, 'Go and inform Rodgers and Carter,' she repeated in an almost childlike voice, 'Inform Rodgers and . . .?'

But her last words were cut off by Chris Waitland yelling, 'Yes! Tell them to come and move the things, woman.' Then looking at Bob as if for a moment he was having to restrain himself from striking him, he brought his teeth together and ground them audibly before marching from the room, followed by his bewildered secretary.

Bob and Jinny smiled at each other, but John turned away and went towards the window, and as he stood looking out his father said to him, 'You didn't enjoy that, did you, lad?'

'No, I didn't.' John swung round. 'I know he's too big for

his boots and that he wanted taking down a peg, but I think your hand was too heavy, and although I was for you doing it like this, I didn't realize what it was going to mean.'

'Oh, John' – Bob sighed now – 'you're new to this game. That fellow just gone is a toady. I've put up with him for years because of his connection with Garbrook, but he's a mean man in all ways. He's got a small mind. I'm not a bit disturbed at what I've done. Neither are you, Jinny, are you?' He looked up at Jinny, and she, looking at John, held his eyes for a moment before she said, 'No, I'm not. You see, you weren't here the morning they sent me scudding like the merest schoolgirl down to the pool where I wiped the floor with Miss Cadwell. I didn't mind that, but when she accused me of having an affair with my boss' – she now cast a smiling glance down at Bob – 'well, that was just too much, that was the moment when I hit her. But now I'm only waiting to get on that phone and hit her in a different way. All right, I'm spiteful, but I've never enjoyed anything so much for a long, long time. And as your father says, Mr Waitland is a mean man.'

'She's right, John, so save your pity.' Then looking back at Jinny, he said, 'I wonder what they'll say now about us, scandal-wise, eh? We'd better give them something to think about, lass, eh? Put it about that we've shacked up, eh? That's the term, isn't it, shacked up? What about it then, eh?'

She was going towards the inner room and she turned her head and looked in his direction as she said, 'I've never been in favour of shacking up and I'm not going to start now.'

'Oh, it's marriage you're after, is it? Well, we'll have to see about it, won't we?'

He was laughing, until he looked at his son, and then the laughter slid slowly from his face as he saw that his bit of fun had touched a sore spot. Well! Well! . . . Well! Well!

The door opened now to admit Miss Phillips who had evidently regained her composure, which was proclaimed by the stiffness of her body and face as, none too quietly, she cleared the desk drawers.

And all the while John stood at the broad window looking down into the side yard where men were loading lorries with steel plates and rods; but his mind wasn't on the business, it was on what had been said a few minutes ago. Although he knew his father was joking, it had nevertheless startled him.

He turned now to see his father heaving himself from the

wheelchair onto the revolving leather chair behind his desk. And there he sat with his hands on it, looking straight ahead into the room. And John watched his face become suffused with an expression of infinite sadness which his voice expressed as he said, 'The last time I sat here, John, I was pulsing with life, almost as much as our Glen. But look at us now, him with no reason left and me with no legs. And Alicia and Yvonne, where are they now? I'd have the answer if I could believe in either heaven or hell.'

As Bob's head began to sink on to his chest, John said, 'It's over. You're here, you're back. Look upon it as a challenge, as I've got to do.'

'Aye.' His father lifted his head to the side now and glanced up at him and repeated, 'Aye, but you are whole, lad.'

'I've never been whole.' The words held a deep ring of bitterness that surprised both Bob and Jinny. But then, in his mercurial way, John turned to Jinny, his voice light now, saying, 'Well, have you forgotten your purpose in life?'

'My purpose in, . . .?' She screwed up her eyes for a moment, then smiled as she said, 'Oh. Miss Cadwell?'

'Yes, Miss Cadwell. I'm dying to hear the exchange.'

'I'll do it from the other room.'

'No, you won't.' Bob put his hand out and pushed the phone along the desk. 'You'll do it from here. I wouldn't miss this for anything.'

Now that she was on the point of getting her own back, Jinny hesitated, for in a fleeting picture she saw herself as Miss Cadwell when she should reach her late forties, when her only pleasure in life might be in showing her authority over others. But then the image was thrust aside by the thought that she would never grow to be like that. Miss Cadwell must have been born bitchy. Moreover, she'd had it in for her since she had first entered the firm and without reason. That was the crucial point, without reason.

She picked up the phone, and when the voice at the other end spoke, she said, 'Typing pool, please.'

It was some seconds before the voice said, 'Yes? Miss Cadwell speaking.'

Jinny let a few seconds more elapse; then the voice came again, higher now: 'Miss Cadwell here.'

'Oh. Miss Cadwell, this is Miss Brownlow speaking from Mr Henderson's office.' Did she hear a gasp? 'We are in residence again.' Yes, she did hear a gasp; there was no mistaking it this time. 'Please send up a typist. I would prefer Miss Power. Is she available?'

When there was no response whatever to this question she said, 'I asked you, Miss Cadwell, if Miss Power is still available.' There was a choking sound at the other end of the phone; then the voice, like a hoarse whisper, said, 'Miss Power is with Mr Brignall.'

'Then put someone in her place and send Miss Power up at once.'

'I don't think I . . . I can do. . . .'

'Oh, what a pity! The work is important. Perhaps you wouldn't mind filling in yourself.'

When the phone was banged down Jinny drew her head back, then slowly put down her receiver.

Bob was smiling widely at her, but not John. He was looking at her in a scrutinizing way which caught her attention, and when he said, 'Feel better?' she said slowly, 'No. I should do, but I . . . I feel. . . .' She could not add the word, cheap, yet this feeling was for the moment overlaid by a wave of resentment brought about by the look on his face which was distinctly conveying her own impression of herself, and before she could check her tongue she cried at him, 'Oh, don't look so smug! I know it was taking advantage, and you wanted me to do it, just to test me, didn't you? Well now, you have your answer; I can be as bitchy as the rest, and more so.'

'Here, here. What's this?' She did not answer Bob but, turning quickly, she went into the outer office and closed the door.

Leaning back in his chair, Bob looked at his son, who was taking his overcoat from the stand in the corner of the room, and said, 'Why is it, lad, you get people on the raw? Now, she would have been less than human if she didn't get back on that dried old stick. And don't forget why she did it. That woman had taken her character away, coupled her name with mine, set her up as a loose piece and' – his voice dropped almost to a whisper as he ended – 'I guess she's been fighting a battle for years against such a title. Why the hell she hasn't been picked up – no; that's the wrong word in this case, married is the word – before now beats me. There must be a lot of blind buggers kicking around. Yet that Michael bloke isn't blind and he's a presentable sort too, but too young for her, although he could give her a couple of years. But it's someone older, steadier, somebody who's going to make her use that mind of hers, 'cos, let me tell you, she's got it up top where business acumen is concerned.' There was a short silence before he ended, 'It makes you think. Aye, it does, it makes you think.'

He watched his son turn and look towards him. There again was that odd look in his eye. 'You off now?' he said flatly. 'I thought we'd have a bite together at dinner-time.'

'I don't feel like lunch. I'm going down to the floor.'

'Aye; well, yes, you'll need all the information you can pick up within the next week or so. Anyway, don't worry about seeing me back, I'll get in touch with Willie and tell him to come down around three because by that time I think I'll have had enough for one day. Excitement has its price an' all.'

'Yes. Yes it has, so don't overdo it. I'll see you this evening if not before. Take care.'

'Aye. Aye, I will. The boss'll see to that.' He motioned towards the closed door, and John looked towards it, before going out. The Boss he had called her: no, no. He was letting his imagination and, yes, his jealousy run wild.

As he made for the lift, its doors opened and Noreen Power came out. She stopped, uncertainly, and when she stammered, 'M . . . Miss Brownlow sent for me,' his only reply was to point to the door next to the main office, and she said, 'Oh yes, there. Thank you.'

After tapping on the door of the outer office and being told to enter, Noreen was confronted by a smiling Jinny, and immediately she cried, 'Eeh! I'm glad to see you back, Jinny. Eeh! I am. And you wouldn't believe what's going on downstairs. It's like you had dropped a bomb down there. She couldn't believe it . . . Miss Cadwell. We thought she was going to pass out; she has the jitters, she really has. What do you want me to do? I'm not too good at French; you know I'm not.'

'There's nothing very much as yet, Noreen,' Jinny said quietly now. 'I just want you to sort out these letters, you know like you do downstairs, filing the firms together in their date order and transferring the salient points of each on to the index cards. Then when you're finished they can all be sent into Mr Waitland's office. They're mostly bills and orders and such, covering the last six months.'

'Yes, I'll do that, Jinny. I'd . . . I'd like to work up here. He's still a terror though, isn't he?' She jerked her head backwards. Then pulling a small face, she smiled, adding, 'I shouldn't say that, should I? Not to you, anyway, because then you've always been able to manage him. Do you mind if I ask if it's right what they're saying?'

There was a pause before Jinny said stiffly, 'And what are they saying?'

'Oh, just that you're going to marry him.'

7

'We're back, Dorry.'

Jinny had entered the hall, and as Dorry came hurrying towards her she added with an attempt at lightness, 'I hope Cissie
is preparing a dinner fit for a conquering hero.'

But Dorry made no reply; she looked past Jinny to the
drawing-room. And when Jinny followed her gaze she saw
Florence standing in the doorway, and even over the distance
the hostility was evident.

'Why wasn't I informed that my father had recovered?'
Florence demanded as she moved towards Jinny.

It was almost in the same vein that Jinny replied, 'You had
better ask him that, Mrs Brook.' And turning now, she waited
as Willie pushed the chair up the ramp and over the threshold
and into the hall.

As soon as Bob saw his daughter he greeted her: 'Well, hello
there, stranger. What brings you to Fellburn in this weather? I
thought you and your lot were still away on that pricey-sounding
world cruise or whatever.'

'We flew back from Venice yesterday and stayed at one of the
Heathrow hotels overnight, but as we were right by the airport
I thought I'd take a quick flight up here to surprise you and
find out what was going on. Why wasn't I . . . I informed of . . .
of your recovery?'

'Well now, Florence, you've hardly been all that accessible of
late, have you? Anyway, it's a long story and at the moment I'm
rather tired and I think I'll have me bite to eat upstairs. By the
way, Willie—' He turned his head and looked back and up into
Willie's face, saying, 'It was a good idea of John's, don't you
think, about a lift in that corner?'

'Yes, boss, a very good idea.'

'I'll get some estimates and we'll get to work on it. Make a
note of that, Jinny, estimates for lift . . . pronto.' Then looking

at his daughter again, he said in an off-hand manner, 'You come alone?'

'Yes, I came alone. Ronnie went straight home with the children.'

'How long do you mean to stay?'

'Would you like me to go on to Devonshire tonight?' Her tone was icy.

'Now, now, Florence, I was just thinking that . . . well, you'd be here on your own during the day because I'm a working man once again. And you must be wanting to see how things are down there after being away so long.'

He watched her suck at her lips before she asked, 'Where is John?'

'When I last saw him he was learning the business on the shop floor, finding out how to lift a three hundredweight steel rod without breaking his fingernails.' As he gave a small laugh at his own weak joke and indicated by a movement of his head that he wanted Willie to lift him from the chair, Florence said, 'And our Glen?'

'Get me upstairs, Willie,' Bob said quietly. And when the big fellow lifted him up and laid him partly over his shoulder as he would have done a child, before mounting the stairs, Jinny turned away because that was a sight she couldn't bear to watch; such dependence deprived the man not only of his bombast but also, in a way, of all dignity.

It was a full minute before Jinny turned towards the stairs again, and as she did so Florence almost thrust herself in front of her, saying, 'As you seem to have taken on yourself the running of the house, will you tell me what has happened to Glen?'

Jinny drew in her chin and pressed her head back as if to remove herself further from the face that was confronting her before she said, 'He's back in hospital under strict surveillance.'

'What! What do you mean? Who's doing was this?'

'The authorities.'

'The authorities? What are you talking about?'

'Your brother, Mrs Brook, attacked me. He wasn't account-able for his actions, but nevertheless he attacked me.'

'Glen? Glen attacked you? Glen wouldn't hurt a fly.'

'The Glen you knew mightn't have hurt a fly, but the Glen he has become would; he would even have gone as far as to kill me if he hadn't been stopped in time.'

They stared at each other in hostility for almost a full minute; then Florence, her full lips pressing one against the other, almost spat out the words, 'I suppose you'll tell me now that it was a bedroom scene.'

'Yes, it was just that.'

'Then all I can say, miss, is that you encouraged him. Deranged or otherwise, you must have encouraged him. You're that type. You've worked on my father; it's evident to us all. It wouldn't surprise me what you get up to next, but I'll put a spoke in your wheel, I'll get the family together.'

Jinny put out her hand and slowly pressed the woman aside as she said, 'Do that, Mrs Brook, do that;' then with shaking legs she mounted the stairs and when she entered her room she dropped down on to the bed fully dressed as she was and lay as one exhausted. It had certainly been a day, a day and a half. She had been shocked by Noreen Power's remark, and then this, going to get the family together to prevent her . . . from doing what? Marrying their father.

Slowly she sat up on the bed and, staring ahead, she nodded as if at the reflection of herself as she said, 'Well then, why not give credence to the lie; nobody else wanted her. Oh yes, there was Michael. He was persistent, but she had no real feeling for Michael, and the one for whom she had any real feeling only wanted her on the cheap. But Bob. What feelings had she for her boss? Oh, she liked him; her feelings for him were deep. Was it love? Well, she had learned of late there were all kinds of love, and in spite of his disability Bob Henderson was still a man. Oh, yes, very much so. She had been handmaiden to him for some time now and he would always need a handmaiden. Well, let her be practical. Oh God, yes, let her be practical for once. If she was she could become mistress of this house, and what was more she would be a rich woman with her finger deep in the pie of Henderson and Garbrook.

The decision almost made, she rose from the bed, but it was as she unbuttoned her coat a voice said, 'And you'll have a stepson and you'll have to work with him, and there will be times when you'll see him day after day. What price then the compensation for being the handmaiden?

It was early evening when Bob said, 'I think I'll go to bed, Willie. It's been a day and a half.'

'It has that, sir, and you've done splendidly. My! you set that place alight this morning. I went into the canteen; you should have heard them. You'd think there'd been a revolution and the president was back.'

'Really?'

'Oh, yes, yes, sir. I'm afraid Mr Waitland wasn't very popular in himself. As for the new systems he was devising, well I think a strike would have been the end result. Apparently, he wasn't approachable. As I heard one fellow put it, one mouthful from you solved more problems than all the typewritten notices coming down from the top floor.'

'Well, that's nice to know. It's always nice to know you're wanted, Willie. And by the way, you'll still be wanted. I've been thinking about it, this business of you and me, how you're going to fill your time in when I'm at the office, so I thought that after you'd got me dusted and powdered and to the office in the mornings, what about you running a first-aid room at the works? They run off to the infirmary with scratches. There's a first-aid box with bits and pieces. But seriously, some of those fellows get nasty gashes in their hands from the rods, so how about you working out a few hours a day there, either morning or afternoon or spread around, taking your free time in between, then every other night seeing me home. John'll take over when you're off duty like, that's if he's not abroad. Which means the sooner we get that lift installed the better, and Jinny on to driving lessons. Anyway, how does the idea strike you?'

'Strikes me very well, sir. Just leave it to me and Mr John; we'll fix it up between us.'

'Aw, well, that's settled. Now get these bloody pants off me.' He laughed as he added now, 'I've been so used to a bare pelt for months that I feel all trussed up in. . . .'

The door being thrust open cut off his words as Florence entered, and now her father bawled at her, 'What the hell do you mean coming in like that! Can't you see I'm practically naked? Here, give me that cover.' He grabbed at the quilt that was lying over the foot of the bed and put it over his bare limp legs; then he glared at Florence where she stood in the middle of the room glaring back at him, and now he bawled, 'Answer me! What do you bloody well mean, stalking in like that? Even when your mother was alive you never did anything like. . . .'

'When my mother was alive things were different.'

He paused before he nodded, and, his voice quieter now, he said, 'Aye. Yes, of course when your mother was alive things were different.'

'But her place has been taken downstairs; in fact, all over the house, as far as I can gather.'

'What are you getting at?'

'That one, your so-called secretary, she was sitting in Mother's place at the dining table.'

Bob lowered his head, closed his eyes, drew his lower lip tight between his teeth, then muttered, 'Girl, your mother is dead. I've had to batter that into my brain for months now, she won't come back. Things have altered. As for Jinny taking her seat downstairs, she wasn't to know where your mother always sat.'

'She knew all right. She's taken command.'

'Aye, well, let me tell you, if that's the case I'm glad of it, because there's been nobody else come forward, rushed like to look after me or the house.'

'I offered . . . we offered.'

'Aye, on your own terms, that I promote that lump of a husband of yours from a fruit shop into my factory. Not on the bottom floor. Oh no, but the top one. Well, I wasn't having it, not for any price. So I've been damned glad of Jinny, and always will be. She's got more brains in her little finger, let me tell you, than you or your three sisters put together can acount for, although I say it as shouldn't. . . .'

'Oh yes, yes, I'm sure she has. Oh, yes, I know that. We four are dim. We haven't got enough sense to be wily, crafty, cunning. . . .'

Bob's arm was extended to its length, its index finger stabbing out towards her, when the door opened again and John entered. His face looking almost as angry as his sister's and ignoring his father, he addressed her straightaway, saying, 'One of these days somebody's going to belt you right across the mouth.'

'Well, it certainly won't be you . . . or her.'

'Don't you be too sure. If I'd been her I'd have knocked you on your back.'

'What's this? What's this now?'

John turned and, looking at his father, he said, 'She went for Jinny as if she was some low slut you had brought in from the streets; in fact, she almost said as much.'

'I did nothing of the kind. I merely told her to get out of my mother's chair, that she wasn't mistress of this house . . . not yet anyway.' She now glanced at her father, and the room became still for a moment, no one speaking, for his head was wagging slowly now, and, his words keeping in time with his nodding, he said, 'So you said she wasn't yet mistress of the house?'

This elicited no response from Florence, and he went on, 'Well, now, Florence, you've opened up a question that's been in me mind for some time. I've always believed in paying people the right wage for the right labour, and Jinny's laboured well for me for months now, and at times she's kept me from losing me reason, and I've wondered how I could repay her. This morning when I was in the office, it came to me that I could put her on the board. Aye, I thought, that's what I'll do, eventually I'll put her on the board. But I knew that wasn't enough, I knew I wanted to do something more, not only in the way of repaying her but of satisfying meself, some want in me.'

'You wouldn't! You wouldn't!' The words were spurted from Florence's lips in a spray of saliva. 'You . . . you wouldn't dare put her in mother's place.'

'Don't you say to me, lass, what I would dare to or what I wouldn't dare to. I've always gone on me own bloody way and I'll do it in this. Only one thing you're right about: I wouldn't put her in your mother's place; nobody can fill your mother's place. I know that, and Jinny knows that; but, as I said, I've to realize the dead are dead, an' if I've got to go on living I've got to have some kind of companionship. I'm made that way. Man or woman.' He now flashed an angry glance at John; and he held the look as he saw that his son's face looked distorted, it was as if he had witnessed something utterly abhorrent; his eyes were mere slits, seemingly lost in their sockets; his lips had squared away from his teeth; and his cheeks that the winter climate always reddened were now devoid of colour. His face looked grey and, of a sudden, old. He was about to say, 'And what's the matter with you? Don't you approve?' but he told himself that would be hitting below the belt. Of course he wouldn't approve. What he wanted to say in this moment was, 'Don't look at me like that, lad. Please don't look at me like that. You don't understand me. I doubt if you ever will.' But his thoughts were interrupted by Florence's crying, 'I'm going home and I'll never enter these doors again as long as she's here.'

'Well, that's entirely up to you, lass,' he called after her as she hurried towards the door, 'but I'd better warn you: if it lies with me, she's going to be here for a long, long time. An' tell that to your Ronnie. But I don't suppose it will make any difference to him, because he would bow his knee to a trollop if he thought he could get his foot in here.'

When the door banged he hunched his shoulders against the shudder for a moment and, looking at Willie who had been standing well back in the room, he said, 'Leave us for a minute, will you, Willie?'

When the door had closed on Willie, Bob did not immediately speak, nor did he look at John, but, his hands making nervous movements, he smoothed the quilt that was covering his legs before he said, 'Now it's your turn to spit it out, else you'll burst. You look like thunder. You don't hold with the idea, do you?'

'*You can't do it.*'

Strangely enough Bob did not bawl his reply to this: his voice was slow and level as he said, 'I can, lad, I can. It's up to her.' He watched John's adam's apple bouncing in his throat before he could bring out, 'She'll take you out of pity.'

'Oh, aye. Well, that could be, but there's worse things than pity. They say it's akin to love, an' she's very easy to love. And apparently I'm not the only one who thinks that way.' He paused a moment before he added, 'There's a big handsome Romeo. I hear from Willie he called again the other day. She happened to be out. He's tenacious. I'll have to look slippy, won't I? But lad, come and sit down, I want to have a talk with you.'

'The hell you do. You've said enough.'

As Bob watched his son stalk out of the room he bowed his head to his chest and gritted his teeth; then he rubbed his hand firmly round his face and pressed his fingers against his eyeballs before straightening his shoulders and reaching out and pressing the bell to the side of him.

When Willie opened the door, he was stayed from entering by Bob saying, 'Tell Jinny I'd like a word with her, will you?'

'Now? You wouldn't like me to help you to bed first?'

'No. I'd like to see her now.'

It was almost five minutes later when she entered the room. Her face looked white and drawn. She held herself stiffly. Another time he would have greeted her with, 'Hello, what's up with you? On your high horse?' But tonight he simply beckoned her forward with a lift of his hand, then said quietly, 'Pull up a chair.'

She did as he bade her, and when she placed the chair opposite to him he said, 'Bring it round the side here, I want to hold your hand.' These words were accompanied with a little wry smile, but they did not affect her expression, and when she sat down by his side and he had taken her hand in both of his, he said, 'No beating about the bush. I know the gist of what happened downstairs. Now I'm going to put a question to you, it's one of these 'if' questions, without . . . well, how can I put it, real meaning, sort of pushed in between something else, if you follow. Is parenthesis the right word? Or is it hypothetical. I don't know. But you see' – he squeezed her hand – 'I know some big words an' all. That surprises you, doesn't it?' Still she didn't respond to his mood, and so he went on, 'Well, the question I want to push in, which isn't really a question mind, is this. If . . . if I was to ask you to marry me, would you do it? Mind, I'm not asking you, I'm just putting it to you, like, you understand? If I was to ask you to marry me, would you do it?'

'Stop playing games.'

'Aw, now look . . . look Jinny, I'm . . . I'm not playing games. All right, all right, I put it that way, and I repeat, I'm not really asking you, I'm just saying if.'

She swallowed deeply then said, 'The "if" has come about because of your daughter?'

'No, no, not really. It's been in me mind some time now. Well, not exactly that, but. . . . Aw, how can I put it? Look, just for me own satisfaction, answer me straight, if I asked you, or if I was to ask you, what would your answer be?'

She looked into the round eyes, that in this moment were looking so much like John's had a short while ago when Mrs Brook had slated her in such a fashion and so unexpectedly that she had found no words with which to combat her accusations. No rage had risen in her to help her defend herself; on the contrary, the effect of the woman's slating remarks had left her feeling weak as if she had been physically attacked. And then John had put his arms about her. He hadn't uttered a word but had pressed her close to him and brought her face to rest against his. The embrace had lasted perhaps for a minute, and then he had released her and hurried from the room.

She heard herself say, 'I couldn't give you an answer straightaway. I would have to say, I would like to think about it.'

'Do you like me?'

'Yes, I like you. You know I do.'

'Do you more than like me?'

'I like you very much.'

She watched him wet his lips before he said, 'I'm still a man, Jinny. You made me into one again. I could love you a damned sight better than any younger fellow would, I know that; and cause you less heartache, too. Yet, I don't know about that, because where there's any kind of love between a man and a woman there's bound to be jealousy. It makes me sick when I hear partners saying, oh, I'm not jealous of my husband . . . or wife, I trust him. Well, my answer to that is, to put it boldly as is my wont, they're bloody liars, or, on the other hand, they don't know what love is. So I don't suppose I'd be any better than the young 'uns in that way, especially with a lass like you. And then there would be the fear. There's always the fear of losing the loved one, that's if you really love. You get jealous if he or she pays a little attention to somebody else, or as a couple of silly bitches of my acquaintance are always doing, praise up other fellows to their men. Do you know something, Jinny? You're a sensible lass but I don't think you've reached the stage where you understand men, because, you know, we never grow out of our childhood. To put it crudely, we're at the breast so to speak all our lives, for we need comfort, we need reassurance, and when we go looking for a wife, we've got the potential mother in our eye all the time. Alicia knew this. Oh yes, Alicia knew this. That's why we had such a happy life together. I'll never stop loving Alicia, Jinny. There's part of me cut off like a deep freeze, and she's in there, and always will be, but there's another part of me that's got to go on living, as I just said to that numskull of a daughter of mine, and I want companionship. But . . . but don't pull your hand away. Listen. I'm not asking you to be any old man's darling; in fact, let me come clean, I'm not asking you to marry me at all. I don't want to marry you. . . . Aw, bugger me eyes! that's a lie.' He jerked his head to one side; then turning to her again, a small grin on his face now, he said, 'A man wouldn't be in his right senses if he didn't want you. But Jinny, there's something I want more than a wife. You might think this strange, but I want a son. I had two sons and I've lost one.' His voice broke slightly now. 'So I've got one son left. And I'm telling you something that I wouldn't tell him. I love him, I love him dearly, and I always have, but I haven't been able to convince him of that. He always thought it was Glen and nobody else. And in a way perhaps he was right, because Alicia seemed to favour him and I didn't like Alicia favouring anybody else but me. There it is again, you see, it's the jealousy of your own son. He's a pigheaded, stubborn, obstinate. . . . Aw, God above! I could go on, but this much I know, Jinny.' He now patted her hand and leant towards her, and his voice dropped to a mere whisper as he said, 'If I was to have you, I'd lose him for good an' all, I'd lose him, because he wants you. And I know that he wants you more than anything else he's ever wanted in his life. That episode he had. . . .'

'Wait. Wait, Bob.' She tugged her hand from his. 'Yes, yes, I know he wants me, but only for bed, and I'm putting that plainly too.'

'Aw, no, lass, no.' He pulled back from her, his voice rising now. 'You've got him all wrong.'

'Oh, no, I haven't. He said as much.'

'He has?'

'Well, when we've talked, it's nearly always ended up in heated words because his covert opinion implied he was against marriage and what went with it, except. . . .' She paused and jerked her head to the side, refusing to add, 'the bed.'

There was silence between them for a moment, and then, his voice low once more, he said, 'You're wrong, Jinny. He was as near doing murder, an' he might have done if I hadn't been his father, not ten minutes gone, because I indicated that I was going to marry you. If I ever wanted proof that he had fallen, and it was hurting, I had it then. Do you like him?'

'I don't know.'

'Well, do you love him?'

She stared straight into his face as she answered quietly now, 'I think perhaps I do, yet I'm not sure. Someone said, to love without liking foreshadows the divorce before the wedding.'

'Oh, there's always somebody saying something, lass, and coining clever phrases, an' they are generally bitter disillusioned individuals. Look, Jinny.' He again leant towards her and took her hand. 'If you have him, I'll have both of you. If you don't, then in a way I'll lose both of you, because he'll think we'll hitch up sometime together and he'll go off. And I couldn't stand that, Jinny, not to lose two sons. I've got four girls but quite candidly, lass, they don't mean much to me, never did. It was the lads I was for from the beginning. You see, a son is something different, he's the male part of you. You won't understand that, but a man would because a son's the one that's going to carry your name on down the generations like. Tell me something, lass, if he was to ask you to marry him, would you? Now come on, straight.'

'Yes.'

There it was, she had committed herself. Yes, if he asked her to marry him she would. But would he ask her to marry him? Yes, perhaps sometime. But days or weeks could go by before he would bring himself to it, for he would determine he wasn't going to jump in to do his father one in the eye.

There now arose in her a lightness. It was like slow laughter. It took the stiffness out of her limbs and softened the look on her face; it even brought a little colour back on her cheeks, and he was quick to notice this, and he said, 'Well, well, you're smiling. What's funny?'

'Nothing. Nothing.' Then rising to her feet, she leant towards him. Softly she placed her lips on his, and as she did so she felt his body jerk and she expected his arms to come about her, but he remained still, stiffly still. When she withdrew her face from his she kept it still leaning forward towards him. Their eyes held, each reflecting inner depth, desire and unimaginable imaginings. For a split second the gates of their inner minds were flung back and they stood as it were with arms outstretched holding them wide and viewing each other across a gulf that was too dangerous for them to jump.

When she straightened up and turned away neither of them uttered a word, and a moment later she was in her own room and once again sitting on the side of the bed. And now slow tears were running down her face. The feeling of lightness had vanished; there was on her now, a sadness, and it was a revealing sadness, like a lesson being learnt through pain. It was telling her that there were levels of love that went beyond the body, that transgressed the desire to express yourself through a man, that surmounted the imagined joy of suckling a child. By such love she was learning one desired only to give, in fact, simply to be a handmaiden. That was the feeling the man across the corridor had aroused in her a moment ago . . . a great overwhelming desire to give. And if there hadn't been John, she would have joyfully put it into practice. But there was John and in her need of him there was no vestige of the handmaiden. Her need here, she reckoned, came under the heading of love, but a love that was as yet wholly physical.

She dried her face and rose from the bed and as she did she heard the strident tones of Florence Brook coming from the landing saying, 'Three cars in the garage and I have to take a taxi. Take that case downstairs, Dorry. It'll be the last time you'll do anything for me in this house.'

Her voice was determinedly loud enough to carry to her father's bedroom, but there came no answering shout from that quarter. A moment later the front door was banged, and when there was the distant sound of a car starting up Jinny let out a long slow breath. Then after combing her hair back, and powdering her nose, she went out and down the stairs. In the hall, seeing Willie coming from the dining-room carrying a tray on which there was a decanter and a glass, she asked quietly, 'Where's John?'

And he answered as quietly 'He went out in a tear. He took the Jaguar and the roads are icing.' Then bending towards her, his voice even lower now, he said, 'I'm speaking out of turn, but we've worked together for quite a bit, so perhaps I can say to you, on the one hand you'll be a fool if you don't take the chance that's hovering, but on the other, you want something different out of life. He's a fine man, the boss, nobody better, but he's had his run, so to speak, whereas John . . . well, you could do a lot for him. I should imagine, emotionally, he's been knocked from dog to devil, and not just lately either. Big boy Glen, I understand, was the apple of the old man's eye. You see, Jinny, I understand this situation because I was an also ran, although my case went in the opposite direction: I was the oldest of six brothers and had to leave school to help me mother bring them up, because me father was too busy in the pubs, and then when they were all up, there was nobody like our Harry, Jimmy, Dan, Peter and Mike. Where did Willie come in?' He stretched his long face still further, 'Oh, Willie was the old maid of the family. Oh, Willie didn't want to marry. I was thirty-four, you know Jinny, before I went in for me nurse's training. So in a way I understand John's situation. Do you know what I mean? When you've got to take a back seat, people forget that you're there.'

She put her hand gently on his arm, saying, 'Nobody could forget you're there, Willie, but . . . but I get the gist. Anyway, I might as well tell you, I'm not going to be Mrs Henderson senior, and I might as well also confess to you, Willie, that in a certain kind of way I'm sorry it's to be like that.'

'Aye, I can understand that an' all. But go on now, get yourself a drink and wait for the younger version to come back and see if you can smooth his bristles, because they were standing up like a porcupine's when he left.'

He laughed now as he mounted the stairs, and she went into the dining-room and poured herself out a sherry, then took it into the drawing-room and sat sipping at it.

It wasn't until the glass was empty that she looked at the clock and saw that it said half-past eight. At nine o'clock she began to think of the Jaguar on the slippery roads.

At half-past nine she went upstairs to say good-night to Bob. He was sitting straight up in bed as if waiting for her and he said immediately, 'Not very much movement downstairs. Is our John out?'

'Yes.'

'Since when?'

'Oh, earlier on in the evening. I don't know really what time he left.'

'Bloody fool. If I didn't know I would have said he had gone out to get drunk, but he doesn't drink. . . . It's frosty, isn't it?'

'No' – she shook her head – 'not very. It's cold, but the roads are dry,' she lied convincingly.

He now thumped the eiderdown with the flat of his hands, saying, 'Is anything ever going right again in this bloody house? Which car has he taken?'

'Oh, I don't know.'

'Well, I'm not taking that' – he pointed to a glass and a sleeping pill – 'until I know he's in and in one piece. Talking of peace, you're a disturber of the peace, Jinny. Do you know that? You are, you are. You upset men, You always will.'

'Oh, please, don't start on that line.'

'No, no. I'm sorry, but I'm worried. Look, go on downstairs. Wait for him and . . . and put things right, will you?'

She smiled softly at him now as she said, 'All right, I'll put things right. He'll hardly get in the door before I'll put things right. Satisfied?'

'Aye, go on. Then both of you come up here, no matter what time it is, mind. Come up here, because I'll be awake.'

'All right. But I would doze in the meantime if I were you.'

'Ah, go on with you.'

She continued to smile as she left the room, but once on the landing her expression changed to one of almost annoyance.

She was a disturber of the peace. At bottom, men were all alike. They didn't see themselves as disturbers of the peace. Where had that fool of a fellow got to?

She stood now in the hall looking towards the front door; then she went and opened it. The outside light was on and it showed up the bare drive with the frost glistening on the gravel like sprayed stardust. She looked up into the sky. There was a moon shining somewhere. After a moment she shivered, then came in and closed the door.

Dorry was passing through the hall and she said, 'Is there anything more you want, miss?'

'No thanks, Dorry.'

'I've left a tray ready for Mr John in the dining-room: cold stuff, but there's a flask of soup. He likes soup and he didn't have much dinner. Well, I'll be off to me bed. Will you put the lights off, miss?'

'Yes, I'll see to them, Dorry. Good-night.'

'Good-night, miss.'

Jinny was entering the drawing-room and Dorry was near the kitchen door when she turned and called, 'Miss.'

She looked towards Dorry who said, 'I wouldn't take any notice of Miss Florence, miss. She was always argumentative, spoilt she was, the least likeable of the lot, jealous nature. I wouldn't take any notice.'

'Thank you, Dorry. I won't.'

Dorry was nice, comforting. She had the urgent desire to follow her into the kitchen and talk to her and feel her motherly warmth, feel the comfort of her pat on the arm. She had a habit of doing this: 'You all right, miss?' Pat, pat. 'Come and have your breakfast, miss.' Pat, pat.

She wanted someone to be on her side, not a man, a woman. There were times when you needed a woman, and she had a feeling now that she wanted to fly to Nell. Nell would have been a comfort ... but with qualifications because Nell would have wanted to slaughter Florence and anyone else who had said a wrong word against her.

As she sat down before the fire, annoyance rose in her again as she asked herself why she should be having this worry. What had she ever done to deserve it? All she had ever aimed to do in her life was to please people. Oh, that was a mistake. She had found that out some time ago. Yet she still went on doing it, pleasing people. And now here she was, stuck in this house with two men who waged war on her emotions. She was tired of it all, she was really.

Oh, stop it.

She got to her feet and began to pace the room. That's all she needed now was to cultivate self pity when, before her, whatever road she took, was a life of service. Yes, no matter how she looked at it, it stretched before her, a life of service . . . to father and son. So, before it was too late she'd better ask herself if she was up to it. In a way she knew where she stood with the father: he came out with things, he was straightforward. But the son: torrid silences, black looks, sarcastic remarks, throwing opinions at her that he knew to be in absolute opposition to her principles, and revelling in it. . . . But he had been so gentle as he held her in his arms. She stopped in her pacing. Where was he? Where on earth had he got to? She looked at the clock. It said quarter to eleven.

She was sitting by the fire again when the door opened. She swung round, only to see Willie standing there.

'No sign of him yet?'

She shook her head.

'Oh, he'll turn up, never fear. Look, I'll go up to my room. If you need me, just give me a knock.'

'Thank you, Willie. . . . Good-night.'

'Good-night.'

'Willie.'

'Yes?' He turned from the door.

'What . . . what if he doesn't come home at all?'

'Well' – he nipped at his lower lip – 'give him till twelve o'clock. If he's not in then, come and knock me up. We'll have to do something about it then. He hasn't still got that flat, has he?'

'No, not for a long time.'

'He's driving round somewhere then, I expect, getting the sweat out of him. He'll be cool when he comes in, never fear.' He grinned at her, then nodded and went out.

She built the fire up, pushed the couch nearer to the hearth rug, then propped the cushions in the corner of it and settled herself against them. She was tired. She'd had a long day; and the excitement of the morning had been enough for anyone without the drama of this evening, and it certainly had been drama. Nobody would believe it. She shook her head at herself. If you read it in a book you wouldn't believe it.

She resisted the urge to drop off. She looked at the clock. It was half-past eleven. When she next looked it said a quarter to twelve. She had dropped off, but something had woken her.

She got hastily to her feet and went into the hall. The house was quiet. There was no sound either inside or outside it, but something had disturbed her. She looked apprehensively around, then slowly made her way towards the front door. She turned the key in both locks but left the chain on, and when she pulled the door open for the few inches the chain allowed she could see, through the outside light, the bonnet of the car in the middle of the drive.

Quickly now, she undid the chain and pulled the door open, then stood looking towards the car. The lights were full on. Had he come in the back way and not switched them off? She looked behind her. There was still no sound of anyone moving about. Slowly now she walked out on to the porch, then on to the drive and out of the glare of the lights. Then she could see him, slumped in the passenger seat.

She pulled open the door. 'John! John! What is it?'

There was no answer.

As she climbed into the driving seat the smell of spirits wafted over her: and when his head lolled back and he groaned deeply, she drew away from him and sat back and surveyed him for what might have been a full minute before she said aloud, 'Our John doesn't drink. Come on!' She was yelling at him now. 'Come on! John. Come out of this.'

'Wh . . . at?'

She got out from behind the wheel, went round to the other door and made an effort now to drag him from the seat, but he fell sideways from her. She stood shivering on the drive glaring down at him. Then turning and running into the house, she went up the stairs as quietly as possible. Tapping on Willie's door, she opened it and through the darkness she whispered, 'Willie. Willie.'

'Yes?' His voice came muffled. 'Oh, is that you, Jinny? What is it?'

'He's back.' Her voice was a hiss. 'And he's blind drunk. I can't get him out of the car.'

'John blind drunk?' The bedside light switched on now to show him sitting straight up in bed blinking at her.

'Yes; but don't say he doesn't drink. Come on, help me.' She turned from him, and as she went to run on tiptoe down the corridor there came a bellow from Bob's room: 'You, Jinny!'

She stopped for a moment and closed her eyes while lowering her head. Then running back up the corridor, she pushed open his bedroom door, and as she did so he demanded, 'What is it? Something happened to our John?'

'Yes, something's happened to your John.'

'Well, lass, what is it? For God's sake!'

'Your John doesn't drink, does he? Well, your John is drunk, not only drunk, the word is paralytic.'

'Never! He's never liked the stuff.'

'Well, everybody's got to start sometime. I'll be back shortly.' On this she turned and closed the door none too gently after her.

Willie was already at the bottom of the stairs and, looking at her in her thin wool house dress, he said, 'Get a coat on before you come out there.'

She now ran into the cloakroom and picked up the first overcoat she came to, which was one of Bob's; then dragging it on, she followed Willie out to the car.

'God! He is sozzled. Well I never! Come on, up with you!'

'Lea . . . me.'

'I know, leave you alone. We'll leave you alone when we get you inside. We're freezing. Come on, out!' And putting his arms under John's now, Willie heaved him from the seat and onto his feet, and between them they got him through the front door, through the hall and into the drawing-room, and there they dumped him onto the couch.

'Well, well.' Willie stood panting as he looked down on the almost unrecognizable figure of his boss's son, and slowly he began to chuckle as he again said, 'Well, well. I've seen some sozzled, but he's really pickled. How in the name of God did he get the car home without being stopped by the police?' He looked at Jinny now, but she continued to look down on John. His coat was hunched up above his shoulders, his face looked red and swollen, and his fair hair, pushed up at the back by the cushion, seemed to be standing on end. She bit on her lip to prevent herself from laughing, because really she didn't feel like laughing. She had been worried sick over the past hours thinking he might have done something silly. . . . And he had; he was showing the evidence of it.

Another mumbled word brought Willie bending down and, gripping John's shoulders, he heaved him into a more restful position as he said, 'Aye, lad. you'll get another when the cows come home.' He turned his head towards Jinny again, saying now, 'Did you hear him? That's likely what he's been doing all night, standing leaning against some bar saying, "Another" . . . then, "Another." I wonder how many it took to get him like this. Eeh' – he shook his head – 'but I'm amazed that he could drive that car. It's a miracle he's not in clink with a breathalyser on him.'

'Take . . . take ya . . . hands . . . off . . . me.' As John now muttered the fuddled words he tried to rise from the couch, and Willie, pushing him back, said, 'There's nobody got their hands on you. Lie down and go to sleep.'

'Are you going to leave him here?'

Before Willie could answer John tried to rouse himself again, saying, 'Jinny. Jinny. Where's Jinny?'

She made no reply, but moved behind the head of the couch and watched him flop back onto the cushions again, muttering now, 'He's rotten, rotten. He knew. He knew, Willie. Aye, he knew.'

'What did he know?'

'What . . . did . . . he know? Who? Father . . . he's rotten, rotten. Crafty. Rotten.'

'He knew what?'

'You mind . . . your owns . . . business . . . Willie. You like her an' all. . . . Oh yes. You like her an' all. Bloody . . . bloody male harem, 'swhat she's got. But we're all . . . eunuchs to her.'

At this point the smile slid from Jinny's face and she turned away, only to stop, caught by the drunken muttering of his next sentence. 'He knew I was gona ask her . . . marry me. He . . . he knew it. If I could have   if I could have got her to stop arguin', fightin'.' His voice trailed away and he fell back into the cushions, and Willie said softly, 'He's off for the night, I should say. But I wouldn't like to have his head when he wakes up. I'll get a rug to put over him.'

When he left the room Jinny went and stood by the side of the couch, and, putting her hand out, she lifted the tangled hair from John's brow. It was the first time she had touched his hair, and her action wasn't tender. She had often felt his father's hair, but it had aroused no emotion in her such as she was feeling at this moment, for there wasn't a tinge of compassion in this feeling; its main ingredient was irritation, for she wanted to grip handfuls of his hair and shake him as she cried, 'You're an idiot! That's what you are, a stiff-necked idiot. You could have prevented all this, that scene with your father. I've been torn to shreds between the lot of you. Oh!' She thrust a quiff of his hair impatiently to one side, then turned away.

She was nearing the door when Willie entered, carrying a travelling rug, and she said, 'I'm off to bed, Willie. I feel I've had more than enough for one night.'

'Yes, I think you have, Jinny.'

Her lips pressed together now, she said, 'I hope when he wakes up he feels he's got six heads and they're all aching.'

Willie laughed softly now as his hand flapped towards her. 'You don't mean a word of it. He's a good lad. I've said it before. He may not be as tall or as smooth as your other friend that calls, but he's got more in him of the right stuff. I'd bet on that.'

'Well, he's got a champion in you anyway. Good-night, Willie.' She heard him chuckle as he went up the room.

When she reached the landing, there was the voice waiting for her.

'That you, Jinny? Jinny?'

She pushed open the door but kept her hand on the knob, and before he had a chance to speak she said, 'As I told you, he's drunk, paralytic, mortalious, all the words that you yourself would use to describe his state, and that's all I'm going to say about him. I'm tired and my temper is anything but sweet at this moment. Good-night.'

As she pulled the door closed he yelled, 'Good-night. Good-night, Jinny.' And she detected laughter in his voice.

Although she felt very tired, she didn't expect to sleep, for as soon as she lay down her mind presented her with varying attitudes she should adopt when she next came face to face with that stupid individual downstairs, snorting his drink away.

Which of the attitudes she had decided to adopt she never knew. She was only aware that she had been asleep. When she woke up feeling cold, half the bedclothes were on the floor, which pointed to the fact that she must have tossed and turned.

Tucking the quilt around her and preparing to snuggle down again, her mind suddenly cleared and picked up the train of thought that had been snapped by sleep, and at this she put her hand out and lifted up the illuminated bedside clock and she was surprised to see through her blinking lids that it said twenty minutes to seven.

She lay still for a moment staring into the darkness. Then

throwing the bedclothes off her, she grabbed up her dressing-gown from a chair and very softly she opened her bedroom door and on tiptoe went along the corridor and down the stairs.

When she reached the hall she heard movements coming from the direction of the kitchen. Likely Dorry was up, although seven o'clock was her usual time for rising.

When she gently pushed the drawing-room door ajar, she stood still for a moment, her expression becoming alert. She blinked the last of her sleep from her eyes and went towards the couch. The rug was still there, rumpled at the bottom of it, but there was no body. She looked towards the fire. It had been made up.

Well, well. He had likely woken up during the night and gone upstairs.

She turned quickly as someone pushed the drawing-room door open; then her mouth fell into a slight gape as John entered carrying a tray. He was in his shirt-sleeves and it looked as if he had just had a bath or a shower, for his hair was wet and plastered down. He showed no surprise at seeing her, nor did he speak to her, but placed the tray on the table and poured himself out a cup of black coffee. Then going towards the fireplace, he sat down in the leather chair and took a long drink of the seemingly scalding liquid. And as she stood watching him, she again found irritation rising in her. 'Don't speak,' she prompted herself. 'Just see how long he can keep it up.'

She was on the point of giving in and saying, 'Well!' which single word would express all she felt at this moment, when, looking up at her, he said, 'All right. All right. I was drunk. Haven't you ever seen anyone drunk before?'

'Why? Why did you do it?' Her enquiry was quiet.

'Why?' He raised his eyebrows at her; then quickly put his hand to his head and screwed up his face for a moment before saying, 'I . . . I was celebrating a number of things: a new way of life that begins today, meeting up with my old girl-friend. By the way, what happened to her? I know she drove me back. That's the last thing I can remember. Janice is a good sort at bottom. I was, if I remember rightly, for shacking. . . . Oh.' He screwed up his face again, and now shut his eyes and held his brow as he went on, 'You don't approve of that term. Well, let me say, taking her as my girl-friend. But she had a current one if I remember, a little fellow. I felt big beside him. A good feeling that, to feel bigger than your successor. He must have followed us.' He opened his eyes and looked at her and said, 'You didn't see her?'

When she didn't reply he said, 'Pity; you would have liked her. She's very broad-minded, she would have understood all your actions, all your motives. She always reasons things out. Most of all, she would have understood. Oh, she would have applauded you being my mother, my stepmother, because she says everything that happens to me I've brought on myself. I'm one of those. . . .'

'Stop being sorry for yourself.'

She jumped back a full step as the cup and saucer went flying into the fireplace and splintered into countless pieces, and for a moment she couldn't recognize the man who was confronting her.

'Don't you tell me I'm sorry for myself. You come into this house and you cause havoc. You beguiled my father even before my mother died, because your name was never off his tongue then. You get those other two fellows trailing after you and, not satisfied with egging them on, you become disgusted when one of them prefers an older woman. You're the type that ingratiates yourself into men's lives, then when it comes to the crunch you act the innocent maiden. You want marriage, but will you have anything to offer a man when you get your piece of paper? You know what I could do at this moment? I could throttle you.'

When his hands shot out and gripped her by the shoulders she knew a moment of paralysing fear. Then his arms were about her, and he was holding her to him. His face was pressed painfully hard against hers and his body was shaking as if with ague.

He had insulted her. Yes, she supposed he had insulted her. He had said some terrible things to her. But it didn't matter. It only went to prove one thing; even that moment of fear he had aroused in her was proof of his feeling for her. That's all she wanted to know.

'Jinny . . . Oh Jinny. Jinny. I'm sorry.'

When she put one arm about him and with the other gently stroked his damp hair, he became still. After a moment, when he raised his head and they looked at each other she said softly and hesitantly, 'Do you believe in long engagements?'

When she saw the shadow cross his face she added quickly, 'We could be married by special licence.'

He took his hand from around her shoulders and brought it once again to his head, and his eyes narrowed but he didn't speak. And she went on, 'You . . . you told me last night you were going to ask me to marry you and I accepted.'

'What? You. . . . What do you mean?'

'Just what I said. You said you intended to ask me to marry you. I . . . I have a witness. Willie was there.'

His face was stretching now. He wetted his lips; then, his voice thick, he muttered the word, 'Father.'

'Oh' – she pursed her lips – 'he sort of let me down.' She smiled now. 'He told me he had no intention of ever asking me to marry him. I think he was killing two birds with one stone, letting his daughter see that he was still his own master and trying to bring his son up to scratch with regard to how he felt about . . . the secretary.'

'Oh, Jinny. I can't believe it. . . . He's right, it's true. I've fought you every step of the way and fallen deeper with each step. How . . . how do you feel about me, really?'

'I can't tell you how I feel about you, John. I only know I want you, and want you to want me. Oh yes, I want you to want me.' She now smiled at him wryly as she added, 'At the same time I can tell you that you madden me, and I want to throw things at you. . . .'

He tugged her to him now as he said, 'That's a good sign.' Then, his voice taking on a sober note, he said, 'What do you think the reception will be like upstairs?' He jerked his head backwards.

'Well, we had better go and see, hadn't we? But wait. I want to tell you something. It's just this. He . . . he *would* have asked me to marry him but for one thing, he was afraid of losing you. You see, he weighed up the result and found it wasn't worth it, because no matter what you think, he loves you dearly; in fact, whether you believe it or not, you are his main interest in life. And it isn't only because he's lost Glen. Apparently he's always felt this way about you, but he was jealous of your mother's love for you. He'll never tell you this; that's why I'm doing it now. And it isn't surmise on my part, it's exactly as it came from his mouth. So no matter what his attitude is in the future, just remember that above everything and all, he loves you and . . . needs you.'

She watched him now turn to the side and rub his hand tightly across his mouth. Then his other hand reaching out, he gripped hers. And so he stood for a moment perfectly still and in that time she knew that the bitterness and resentment that had replaced his love for his father had gone from him, and from now on they would come together as never before. At the same time she understood there would be the clash of similar personalities, there would be eruptions from time to time causing minor wars, not only in the business but in the household, and she'd have to cope with them. She might be married, but as she saw it, she would, in this household, have to continue being the handmaiden, and definitely not cultured. No, definitely not, but, nevertheless, the handmaiden running between them both, while at the same time trying to ignore outside comments which she could hear now; 'Well, she was determined to get one of them, wasn't she? An affair with the old 'un, now marrying his son, and all to get a finger into the business. Never trust the quiet ones.'

And then there would be Florence. Oh! Florence. And what would the others say?

But what did it matter? What did anything matter? She had John, and she had never felt like this about anyone before. If this wasn't love, real love, then she would settle for it, because she knew it was all she wanted.

When he suddenly thrust his arm around her waist, they ran from the room like children and up the stairs, and paused only at the main bedroom door, and there, their faces falling together, their lips gently touched before John, thrusting out his hand, opened the door.